THE MOON TURNED TO BLOOD

Ruth J. Tiger

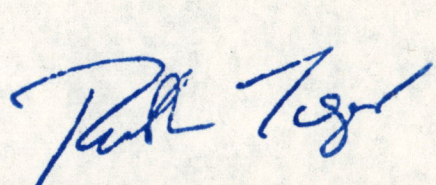

Acknowledgments

I could never have completed this work without the unflagging encouragement of my husband, Alan Tiger. Eternal gratefulness is owed to my friend and author, Connie Connally, whose ongoing support through multiple drafts, and whose literary input were invaluable to me. I am grateful for my readers, Aaron Tiger, Siri Tiger Kaunda, Judi Westberg, Carolyn Westberg-Croessmann, Kurt Schaefer, Sandy Johanson, and Brian Rainforth, as well later readers Machelle Beilke, Jerry Pugnetti, and Rick Trombley for their honest and helpful suggestions. My thanks go to artist Lance Kagey for the striking book cover design, to Aaron Tiger for his patience in taking my author portrait, to Rory Connally for the helpful map, and to Kyle Peirson for technical assistance.

Special thanks to my third cousin, Agnar Eike, who told me two family stories while I visited with him in Norway. The first was passed down through the ages from the time of the first plague that ravaged Norway in 1349. The second was from the 1500's when the king of Norway traveled through our family's village. These stories inspired me to begin my years of research that led to the creation of this novel.

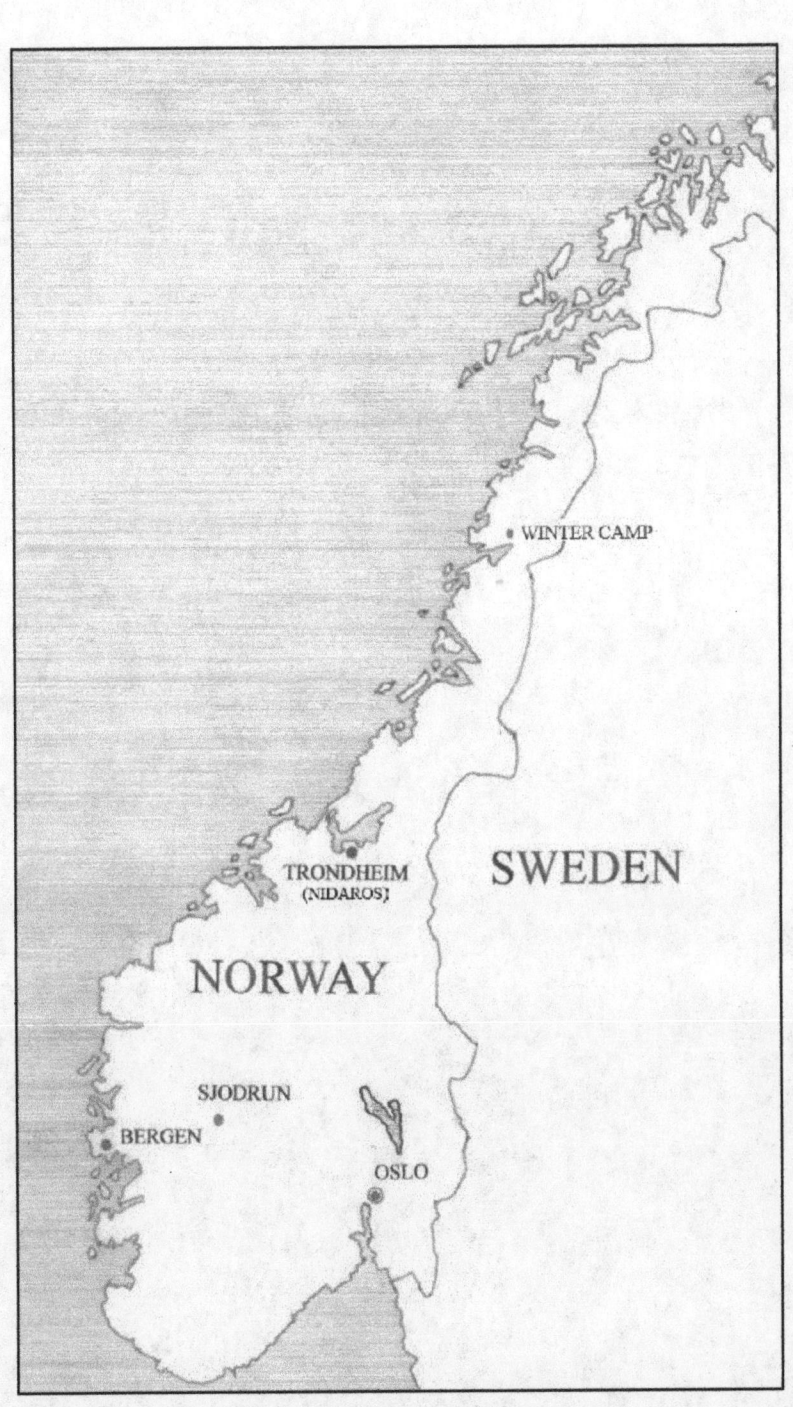

Numedal Valley, Norway, 1349

Chapter 1

At the sudden clatter of hooves behind him, Kjell turned. His dogs raced toward the approaching horses. Riding three abreast on the narrow road, rays of sunlight glinted off weapons and bridles as the soldiers slowed. Kjell noted the lead horse's embroidered caparison fluttering nearly to the ground and displaying the colors of the royal house of King Magnus.

Kjell's throat tightened. "Satan's balls!" he swore under his breath. He wanted nothing to do with king's men. He led Thorden into the stream to let them pass, but his load shifted and the sledge runners slipped down into the water. Kjell cursed once more.

His three *buhunds* circled the riders as they drew close and halted. The dogs growled, hackles raised. Kjell whistled for them and they backed slowly away. He tugged the hood of his cowl low over his eyes and slipped his hand beneath his tunic to grasp the handle of his knife. He had encountered king's men before. He could not afford to be recognized.

From beneath his hood Kjell peered at each face. Luckily, he recognized none. He let out his breath. They looked road-weary. Dust dulled their tunics.

The leader was a knight clad in fine leathers, his helmet strapped atop the steed's rump. The other two were soldiers who held daggers beneath their palms. All had weapons of war fastened to their saddles within easy reach.

Kjell nodded to them deferentially.

The knight said, "A fine morning, pilgrim." His voice was deep, his accent from near Oslo.

"Indeed, friend…sir," Kjell replied, suddenly aware of his unkempt beard and roughly sewn leathers. He hoped he looked older than his twenty-two years. Thorden stepped forward to nibble on nearby grasses, and the load rocked clumsily, nearly tipping over. Kjell reached out to right it.

"If it is a village you seek," he said, "I heard the nearest is Uvdal, some distance down this road yet." Uvdal was a town further along that would lead them past the overgrown trail leading to Sjodrun, where he intended to make his last stop. He had no wish to meet the soldiers again.

"We are on the king's business," the knight said. "We have an urgent errand to complete at villages between here and Bergen, though we will not enter that Hansa rats' nest. Do you know this road?"

Kjell glanced up. "*Nei*, I am afraid I cannot direct you," he lied. "I am going east." He pointed down the road over which he and the soldiers had just ridden.

A rust-haired squire squinted at Kjell. "If you know the nearby villages, you must tell us or you will face my sword."

The knight glanced at the squire and waved him off. He said to Kjell, "We have levies to collect for the king's war. It is no secret."

"Which war is that?" Kjell hoped they would not help themselves to his furs that lay covered by a large brown bear skin. "I have been up north and have had no news for some time."

"Novgorod, you dung heap," snapped the squire, "the trading center the king will win when he arrives there within weeks."

"There are expenses," the knight added, "and the villages must pay their tributes."

Of course there are expenses, Kjell thought in disgust. Who would pay for war but poor villagers? He spat into the dirt.

The squire spurred his horse forward and pointed his sword tip at Kjell's throat.

Thorden reared.

"Something flew in my mouth," Kjell mumbled, quieting his horse.

The knight's eyes narrowed. "What is your name huntsman?"

Kjell swallowed. "Eyvind Baldursson."

The knight's glare persisted. "From where, Eyvind?"

"Hamar," Kjell replied. He had not lived in Hamar for over two years, but he said nothing more.

After a few moments the knight looked away, seemingly satisfied. He turned his horse's head tightly in a circle to control its nervous dancing and said, "You are far from home."

"Indeed. I will stop on the way at any village or farm where I might sell my wares."

The knight straightened in his saddle. "Where? Is there a market or pub hereabouts? I could use some ale."

Kjell shrugged, lying once more. "I could, also, but I know not. I am new to this road."

"Is there a market in Uvdal?" the knight persisted.

"I have only heard of the town but have never been there." Kjell shifted uneasily.

"It is not harvest time yet," said the knight. "I doubt you will find willing buyers for your furs."

"Perhaps not." Kjell summoned his latent manners. "God's speed to you on your journey."

The knight spun his horse around and called over his shoulder, "And to you." His steed jumped forward, the impudent squire at his heels.

The third rider, a bulky soldier with heavy brows, rode up beside Kjell. "You should take care. In these times you could be killed for less than spitting."

"I meant no disrespect," Kjell said.

"In any case, watch yourself. I must also warn you of some disturbing news."

"What news, then?" Kjell asked, scuffing his shoe against the pebbles before glancing up.

The soldier gazed after his retreating comrades and said, "There are strange spirits afoot. We heard that a ghost ship arrived in Bergen a fortnight ago. All on board were dead. That is why we will not go that far. We only seek villages from which to recruit soldiers. You are wise to avoid Bergen...or if you must go, say your prayers." The soldier kicked his horse into a gallop, raising a cloud of dust as he thundered away.

Kjell chided himself for his witlessness. He had been foolishly rude and had called attention to himself. He must avoid soldiers at all costs.

He urged Thorden up the embankment, pushing heavily on the load of furs so it would not tip over. When he had mounted once more, he said to his horse, "What do you make of this news about a ghost ship full of the dead, wise friend? Sounds like a curse on the Hansa, payback for their unfair trading ways."

As they moved forward, Kjell pondered long on what the soldier had said. Old tales rummaged through his memory, tales told of evil spirits roaming about, and of Hel, the old Norse goddess of death. A preternatural tingling crawled up his neck.

Chapter 2

Astra and her father walked beside their *fjording* horse, Farwa, who dragged a large sledge carrying two heavy pine doorposts over the potted road. Their aging *hund*, Ledsager, followed for a time, then jumped onto the posts and fell asleep.

The mid-summer sky was overcast, though small patches of blue and a light wind promised afternoon sunshine. Today was Astra's first foray to the village of Sjodrun alone with her father. This past winter she had reached the marriageable age of fifteen and she was anxious to speak to her father alone.

Just before she left home this morning, Astra had once more told her sister, Karin, that she knew that Einarr, the manor lord's son and the love of her life, intended to talk to her father about a marriage proposal. Karin wished her luck, less enthusiastically than Astra had hoped.

Now walking alongside the sledge, Astra nervously rehearsed the words she meant to say. Her father, however, was the first to break the reverie.

"There is something I need to tell you," he said.

She skipped to catch up with him on the pebbled road. Perhaps from his earnings he was going to give her money so she could buy a new mirror, since hers had cracked, or maybe linen for a new *Jul* skirt.

"What is it, Far?"

"You are past fifteen. Old enough to be a wife."

Her breath caught. "Has someone already asked for me?"

Far squeezed her shoulder, then let go. "Do not rake out the coals before the kiln is cold. Your mother and I have a responsibility to do the best for each of our *datters*. We want only that for you, Little Sparrow."

"But I will have a say, *nei*? I must have a say, Far." She had planned what to say for such a moment, but he had taken her by surprise. She knew Einarr wanted to marry her. Two years ago, he had said they would be together forever, and last *Jul* he had expressed his true love through stolen kisses and caresses. She must tell Einarr what her father had said, lest Far betroth her to someone else.

Her father patted her cheek with his calloused hand. "Do not worry. I should not have spoken of it now. I will tell you more when the time comes."

She kicked apart a clod in the road. "What if I do not like him? What if he is old and ugly? I must…"

Her father pressed his finger to her lips. "If you do not like him, you will learn to respect him…over time. It is the quality of a man that counts. And his money." He turned to smile at her and laughed, patting the old horse's neck.

"Have you talked to someone already?" she asked. "Someone I know? Someone I like?" Perhaps Einarr had already sent word.

He smiled. "When the bargain is struck, then you will know."

They walked on without speaking. Astra became lost in worries, wondering if someone other than Einarr had already asked for her. Their laden sledge scraped past a small field of ripening barley, a large grassy lea surrounded by a birch forest, then a rocky outcropping covered in lichen. Soon they crossed the wooden bridge over Standing Rock Creek as it burbled beneath the timbers. Astra reached into the sledge and took out the picnic basket. She unwrapped cheese and rye *brød* Mar had sent and offered some to her father.

He shook his head. "It is Saint Olav's feast today. Until evening, we drink only." He offered Astra ale from his flask. Her stomach rumbled and she replaced the basket. They spoke no more.

At last, they came to the shaded entrance that led steeply downward toward Sjodrun. Far jerked the reins back severely when the old mare started to trot down the familiar trail. They passed through the glen that hid the village from the road. Four *miil* below at the end of the winding path, they came to a clearing where dozens of log structures, great and small, dotted the secluded valley. The gate to the great manor yard was open, and the guard, sitting on a stump and whittling, waved them through.

The imposing double-storied manor house made of thick oak logs dominated the grassy courtyard. Astra had been inside at Jultides and was always awed by its lofty ceilings and three great fireplaces. This was where Einarr lived with his knighted father, and his mother and sister. Maybe someday she would live there, too.

Astra surveyed the courtyard as they entered, praying to see Einarr strolling by, but only servants and town folk crisscrossed the yard going about their errands. Astra and her father passed by dwellings and shops of many kinds. Down the hill away from the manor and clustered near the fields were the single-room tenant huts with one-cow barns.

Astra gazed past the fields to the small lake shimmering at the far end of a pasture. Beyond this sheltered pond, a brook wound its way toward the river before finding its way to where it eventually plummeted into the fjord. Astra knew the place well. It was the swimming hole where they played as children, and it was where Einarr had first kissed her.

At the far end of the upper compound near the forest stood the *stavkirke,* the place of worship for the village. Astra both loved and feared this imposing structure. Made of black-tarred pine logs, the strikingly severe *kirke* was roofed by multiple, narrowing peaks, each with a ghoul to scare away evil spirits. At the very top, a sturdy birch cross was perched like a beacon of hope, a cross her father had made.

Guest cottages, including the one she and her sister, Karin, had stayed in last summer, were directly across the yard from the *kirke*.

Far handed her the reins. "I need to find Didrik," he said. "Take Farwa to the stable where we will unload."

Astra led the lathered old horse forward. Ledsager jumped off the sledge and followed, his snout sniffing along the well-trodden grounds. They passed the benches where the local council, the *Thing*, met. Empty *gapestockks* stood ominously nearby, the place where petty thieves or trespassers were pilloried. Unfortunately, she had never actually seen anyone punished so.

As she passed the bladesmith's cottage, she saw a man with dirty breeches and leather jerkin speaking to the vendor.

"Indeed," she heard the bladesmith say while displaying an array of blades on a barrelhead. "What did the soldiers seek?"

"Recruits for a war to win back Novgorod, that northernmost Rus trading center," said the man.

"Novgorod? *Nei*, that is useless," scoffed the bladesmith.

The rugged man leaned forward. "But more disturbing was the other news they carried."

Astra pulled the horse to a stop to listen.

"A soldier warned me about a great sickness in Bergen," continued he. "A ship drifted into the harbor and all aboard were dead."

"*Nei!*" cried the bladesmith. "Do they know what happenned?"

The man shrugged. "That is all I know."

"A curse," the bladesmith clucked at the news. Just then he noticed Astra and waved. The woodsman turned to look at her. His hair was shaggy, his beard unkempt, and she thought she could smell his swarthy clothing from where she stood. She waved in a friendly manner at the bladesmith before tugging the old horse forward.

The stable hand seemed surprised when she halted and unhitched the sledge herself. She asked for a curry comb and the lad watched her brush the horse down.

Feeling his eyes tickling her back, Astra snapped, "Have you never seen a girl brushing a horse before?"

"Never," he said. "Indeed, I did not think you were allowed to."

She felt anger rise. "Well, now you know differently. Girls should always be allowed to work with horses."

When the stable boy led old Farwa out to the pasture, Astra sat on a bench in the aisle of the stable waiting for her father. The stable was dim, lit only by the open barn doors at either end. Against the yawning opening to the courtyard, flecks of straw dust floated in the air like gnats. After a short time, she heard hoof treads and a man on a horse appeared in the stable doorway silhouetted against the light. The rider dismounted and lifted three rabbits, their ears tied together, from the back of his saddle. The stable boy took the game and led the man's horse toward a stall.

The rider shook his head. Light curls settled on his shoulders. He brushed off his tunic and adjusted his breeches before looking up.

It was Einarr!

Astra tucked stray hairs under her head linen, smoothed her skirt and stood.

"Hallo?" he called. His voice bounced among the stalls. "Astra, is that you?" He strode toward her.

Her heart sang. "*Ja*, I did not expect to meet you here in the stable." How handsome he had become! As he approached, she saw whispers of stubble on his chin.

She rubbed her own cheek. "You have changed since *Jul*."

Einarr fingered the whiskers and blushed. "More irritating than helpful," he said. His gaze traveled down her frame before returning to catch her eyes. "You have changed, too. You are... very comely these days."

She flushed, thinking of their stolen caresses in the *kirke* last *Jul*.

Einarr smiled broadly and reached for her hands. "You did not come at Easter. I missed you."

"Mar had a baby on Easter eve, a girl."

"Sit with me." Einarr drew her to a bench and wrapped her hands in his. He spoke somberly. "Have you heard the sad news of my father?"

"*Nei*, Far and I just arrived and brought the door posts for the new *stabbur*."

Einarr's brows gathered and he pursed his lips before he spoke. "He fell from his horse three weeks ago. He lay abed with a broken hip, then passed several days later from a fever."

Astra's heart was pierced. She squeezed his hand. "Ah, *nei!*" She realized a time of mourning could delay a decision about a betrothal. On the other hand, a hurried marriage might bring joy to a grieving family.

"Mother is mournful and wonders what will become of us without my father," he said. "She fears we will be put out."

"Out of Sjodrun? Why would you be put out? This is your home."

"We will not know anything for some time, but the king can decide to replace my father with another lord. If we are lucky, I will be brought into the king's service and we can keep the manor."

"I shall pray that you will always stay here," she said quietly. What would happen to her if Einarr's family was put out of the manor? What if he went to serve the king in Oslo? All the more reason to marry quickly.

Einarr stroked her hand. "At least we have Olav's feast day to distract us. Mother says we will celebrate anyway, despite my father's accident."

Astra paused, then decided she should talk to him about her father's intention, even in this time of sadness. If she did not, someone else might speak to her father. That must never be!

Leaning close and gripping his arm she whispered, "I have news you need to know. Far told me on our way here that I am to be betrothed. I fear he may seek a contract soon, even today."

Einarr leaned his head against the log wall. "*Nei!* To whom?"

"I do not know, but it must be you." She leaned against his shoulder. "Speak to him today before someone else does."

Einarr straightened. "Today? I do not think I can. This is a difficult time for Mother."

She sat up. "I am fifteen since I last saw you, and you are sixteen. We are of age."

He said nothing, only staring at their clasped hands.

She whispered, "Remember when we were very young and we made a fort by stamping down grass in the pasture? We rode broken branches as horses."

Einarr nodded. "You made trenchers out of bark and we had pine cones for food."

"You made a Great Hall out of rocks with a fire ring in the middle."

"I tried to start a fire with a stick and a flint."

"Good thing it did not light. We would have burned up the field."

They both laughed, then she said into his ear, "We knew even then we were meant to be together."

They both turned at the sound of voices approaching the barn. Her father and Didrik, the overseer of the manor, stopped next to Far's heavily laden sledge just outside the stable door. Astra was fond of Didrik. He had always been kind to her and fair in his dealings with her father. He sometimes acquiesced to her pleas to help groom the horses and had even once let her ride the English mare.

She gripped Einarr's hand tightly. "Remember our pledge."

"I do," he whispered back, letting go of her hand. "I will speak to Mother…when I can." He strode through the stable, greeted Astra's father, then headed toward the manor house.

An inkling of doubt at his hesitation passed through Astra's thoughts as she rose and walked toward the two men. Einarr was going to ask his mother for permission to marry her…when he could.

Didrik was getting older, his thick beard and black hair streaked with white, but he smiled with his whole face as he watched her come toward them.

He said to her father, "This feast day just improved, now that your horse-loving *datter* is here." He winked at Astra, adding, "You are growing up nicely indeed."

Blushing, Astra looked away.

Didrik laughed, then ran his hand along an intricately carved dragon on one of Far's door posts that were intended for the new guest house.

"You have outdone yourself, Sven Larsson," said Didrik, smiling. "I am sure the lady of the manor will be pleased. In the meantime, I think we have a bargain to seal, do we not?"

For one moment Astra's breathing stopped. What bargain? Was Didrik her suitor? The thought was not impossible. He had long been a bachelor and was head man at the manor, though not a land owner. She nervously squeezed her skirts with both hands and opened her mouth to speak, but Far spoke first.

"I brought the doorposts. Do you have the horse?"

"I do," Didrik replied, winking at Astra.

Astra exhaled, relieved. *Nei*, of course not Didrik. A horse, that was the bargain!

"I may buy a horse today if Didrik will meet my price," said Far.

Astra was pleased. "What kind of horse?" With two horses they could plow, reap and do much more farmwork in less time, and maybe she could even ride for pleasure, when her chores were finished.

"A three-year-old mare," said Didrik, "a *dølahest*, and spirited. She is broken and ready for you to ride, Astra."

She stared at Didrik, then her father. "For me?"

Far raised an eyebrow. "Only if a bargain is struck. The horse is mainly to help with farm work, but you will take full care of her."

She kissed her father's cheek, imagining riding to the bluff above the fjord where she could sit alone on the bank of the rill that spilled over the cliff. Living in their one-room house with six, plus a new baby, she yearned for moments of solitude.

Didrik smiled at her. "She is good with horses, this girl."

Astra tore her eyes from him. Nervously, she dismissed the thought of Didrik as a husband. Surely Far would not betroth her to a servant, no matter his high status.

Far added, "She is better with horses than Gunnar ever was." At the mention of Astra's older brother, Far looked down at the barn floor and kicked away a beetle.

Astra was also saddened. Gunnar had passed away nearly two years ago now. Since then, she had taken Gunnar's place alongside Far to do much of the men's work, including horse care. She was becoming adept at the sickle, the flail, the axe and splitting wedge, and she was improving her skills with the arrow and spear.

Far cleared his throat. "I have other business to take care of. I will meet you at the manor," he said to Astra, walking away.

Didrik turned to Astra. "Do you want to see the horse now?"

"Of course!" She followed him to the pasture gate, and a groom was sent to bring in the mare.

"What is her name?" Astra asked.

"Kvikke," replied Didrik.

"Fast One." She grinned. "I like that."

Soon the groom led an amber-colored *dølahest* through the gate. The horse was stocky with powerful shoulders and flanks. Her black eyes were visible only through the long shaggy forelock.

Astra let the horse sniff her hand before stroking the forehead and neck. She buried her face in the horse's musk-scented cheek.

"You are pleased?" Didrik asked when she moved back to take in the whole body.

"She is perfect," Astra replied.

"Perhaps you can ride after our business is concluded." Didrik waved as he walked away, whistling.

Astra leaned on the fence to watch the stable boy release Kvikke into the pasture. What if it was Didrik who had expressed interest in marrying her after all? At least he was kind, and he would let her ride whenever she wanted. But he was old, older than her father, and she would live at the manor where she would see Einarr every day. Please God, not Didrik, she prayed. She recalled the moment she had fallen in love with Einarr.

Two summers ago, not long before Gunnar died of ague, her family made a special trip to the *kirke* to deliver the newly carved beam for a doorway. While Far worked with the manor's carpenter, Einarr, his sister Hedda, Astra, Gunnar, and a few other youths were allowed to picnic at the eddy in the river. They were chaperoned by Einarr's aged grandfather, who had promptly fallen asleep on the mossy bank.

A large rock, the Devil's Diving Stone, loomed over the deepest part of the pool, and the boys jumped off naked. Two girls, including Hedda, jumped too, their dresses floating around them as they surfaced. Astra could not swim, but Hedda told her it was easy to bounce off the bottom and pop back up. Astra decided to jump.

Once in the air she realized she had made a mistake. She sank deeply, pushing off the bottom with her feet and slowly floating upward. She could see the streaks of sunlight piercing the green water above her and realized she would not reach the surface before needing another breath. Just when she began flailing her arms in panic, Einarr was beside her. He lifted her by the waist and they burst above the surface, both gasping. He helped her to shore, letting go only when he set her on the bank to the laughing shouts of the other youth. She crawled onto the rocks and collapsed, embarrassed and weeping like a child.

Despite her shame, she recalled the relief in Einarr's eyes as they surfaced and the comfort of his arms as they came ashore. She was sure then that he felt affection for her, as she did for him.

That evening at twilight they met by chance as she rounded a corner of the manor house on her way to her family's camp. Unexpectedly standing face to face, their breath mingled; her eyes widened.

He kissed her cheek. "You are my best friend," he whispered. "I love you."

Astra kissed him back and fled. Hiding behind a small bush, she held her hand to the precious spot he had kissed until her flaming cheeks cooled.

Chapter 3

The sun had passed the noon hour by the time Kjell unloaded his furs onto the grass near a storehouse. Sjodrun was smaller than many villages, but he preferred its secluded setting where he was unlikely to meet king's men. Last year he was given a station nearer the main house where his goods had caught the eye of the lady of the manor, but this time, regretfully, he had been directed to this out-of-the-way location. He had come a great distance from the northern mountains and was anxious to sell his furs, buy supplies and return home. Sjodrun was only a few days' ride from his cabin—and dear Oda and the baby.

Carefully he laid out his furs: elk, beaver, reindeer, lynx, wolf, and a large brown bear. The rare white reindeer and snowy fox he left in the sledge, pelts for which he had traded with the Saami people up north. Only for the head servant, or the lady of the manor, would he bring these out.

He sat on a stump and took out his carving while he waited for customers. The yard was alive with people crisscrossing between various buildings on errands. By the time he had carved two figurines of children that he set on the grass by the furs, only two women had paused to inspect his goods, but they did not buy.

From the pigs roasting over the fires in the center of the courtyard drifted the most delectable scent. Though Kjell still had wind-dried venison, his ale flask was long empty and he was anxious to earn coins in order to sample the manor's brew and taste of the roasted pig. Was this a celebration day? He would ask the next villager who stopped.

Kjell gnawed a leathery venison shank wishing he could at least fish in the river that gurgled in the distance. He knew, however, that all the fish and game on the manor's lands belonged to the lord. He tossed a scrap of venison to each of his three dogs, the largest chunk going to Beskytter, his loyal hunter.

After picking a strand of tendon from between his teeth with his knifepoint, Kjell wiped it on his leather breeches noting the streaks of grease from many such meals. Now among villagers, he awakened to his unkempt condition and worked his fingers through his tangled hair, picking out small sticks and bits of moss before tying it back. Oda, his lonely wife, would be displeased if she saw him like this. He must bathe and wash his clothes in a lake or stream before returning home.

Kjell stood up, stretched, and tested the wooden spike that held his horse's rope. Thorden seemed content munching the grass at his hooves, so Kjell ambled toward a man sitting on a stool nearby making rope of gut. The man nodded silently when Kjell asked him to watch over his furs. Kjell strolled casually through the yard of the demesne, several times stepping out of the way of scurrying townswomen. He had not been among so many people since last year, and not in a larger town like his home in Hamar since he and Oda married two years ago. That trip had turned out poorly.

He approached the imposing Great Hall that dominated the courtyard, struck again by its immensity. He wondered at the labor and the cost of such a structure. The building was made of huge pine logs with a pitched wooden roof that rose almost as high as the aspens beside it. Wide steps led up to double doors that were taller than the height of two men. The massive door posts and the lintel were carved with complex figures of snakes, dragons and branches—the best carvings Kjell had ever seen. What would the inside of such a grand structure be like? He would give three hides to peer inside.

Meandering around the courtyard he passed workshops of many sorts, storage houses, and stables for dozens of horses. Situated near the forest at the far side of the clearing was a grand guest house, freshly built. Not far away sat the stave *kirke*, the holy stratified structure that loomed before him like an omen. He had seen the *kirke* last year, but had not entered. He peered up at the carved fiends on the multiple roof points, reminding him that evil beings and spirits of the restless dead lurked about. The *kirke* was surrounded by a *svalgang*, the dark passage that protected the log walls and served for processionals in foul weather.

The door to the dark interior of the *kirke* was ajar. Something compelled him to enter, but he balked. The burnt odor of the recently tarred logs stung his nostrils as he mounted the porch. Silently, he paused on the threshold squinting into the blackness. There was no sound. Good. He dipped under the low lintel. The scent of the morning's incense hung faintly in the air. Thin rays of light from the slotted openings under the roof dimly lit the intertwined log beams of the vaulted ceiling. Several moments passed before his eyes adapted and shapes appeared.

The altar held a carved crucifix that dominated the apse. A wooden baptismal font sat in the center of the room. Four thick supporting staves divided the *kirke* into transepts, the women on the north and the men to the south. The raised pulpit was affixed to a thick stave, gained only by narrow winding steps.

Recessed into the side of the apse was a screened booth, likely for the priest's wife and family to sit unseen, if he had them. Kjell spied the small hole cut into a log at the back of the apse where lepers or outcasts could stand in the outer *svalgang* to make confession and receive Holy Communion.

He well remembered winter masses in the *katedral* in Hamar. As a child, he cowered beneath his father's elbow listening restlessly to the Latin words of which he understood nothing. He could still feel the icy fingers creeping up his legs from the stone floor while he clung to his father's legs for warmth. With dread he had stared up at the ghoulish faces carved into the stone staves of the rafters that disappeared into the void above. He could still hear the chanting of the priest, the gong, the droning of the collective repetition of the *Pater Noster*.

As Kjell stood still in the dimness of the small nave, a heaviness fell over him like chainmail. Unshriven, he could not partake in Holy Communion. If he died before going to confession, his soul would wander in purgatory for untold ages. Yet…how could he voice what lay so heavily on his heart to a holy priest, even here where no one knew him? This *kirke*, like all others, evoked nightmares that plagued Kjell ever since that terrible night. He genuflected, crossed himself, bowed under the lintel and slipped out the door.

Throughout the afternoon Kjell sold only a few small furs. He decided he must wash up, then bribe someone to help him find the head house servant whom he had met last year. If she would only look at his wares she would surely want his finest for the household beds, cloaks, and overcoats.

Kjell had just scrubbed much of the road dirt from his head, arms, and hair from a bucket of water when a shadow passed over him. He swung around and shielded his eyes. Backlit by receding afternoon sunlight stood the figure of a slight woman perusing his stock.

"Which furs do you like best?" he asked, squeezing water from his long tresses and twisting them back with a strap.

She stepped into a patch of light and he saw that she was young, barely more than a girl, and plainly clothed. Indeed, the yellow braid draped long over her shoulder meant she was unmarried. Then he recognized her. She was the one who had stopped her horse and cart near the bladesmith's hut, listening to him tell of the soldier's warning about the death ship. He smiled. She was going to be beautiful when she grew older; *nei*, she was already comely.

"God be with you," the maiden replied.

Kjell grappled for the expected reply for a moment before saying, "And with you."

"I cannot buy much, but perhaps something for my mother, or for my wedding chest." She held out two coins, enough for a weasel pelt.

He paused.

"Probably *nei*," she said, clamping the coins in her fist. Her cheeks colored.

"You are soon to marry then?" he asked, pulling out some of his smallest skins.

"Not yet…"

"But someday you will. Sooner rather than later, I suspect."

She reached out to examine the finer furs on the sledge, touching the edge of the white reindeer pelt just visible under the pile. "What is this one?"

He spread the skin on the ground. "Reindeer from up north, very rare and expensive, I am sorry to say."

"What is the cost?" She fumbled in the small money pouch at her belt.

He was tempted to lower its value for her, but not on this first day. He named his price.

"Ach, *nei*. Too rich for me." She squatted down to run her fingers over the fleece and said, "At least I have touched such a precious skin."

He had to smile at her open innocence and squatted beside her. "It comes from the land of the Saami, a long journey from here."

"I do not doubt it." She stood. "Perhaps the mistress of the manor will buy it. Have you spoken to her?"

"*Nei*, I thought to seek out the head house servant first."

"You can try. She is very busy preparing for Saint Olav's feast."

"Ah, Saint Olav's feast. I have lost track." She must think me a rube, Kjell thought.

She laughed. "Her name is Gudrun, if you want to ask after her."

"*Ja*, I met her last year. Do you live here?" Perhaps she was the *datter* of a servant, or peasant after all. He found his heart quickening.

The girl raked her fingers through the thick brown bear fur. "*Nei*, a half-day's walk from here. My father and I came bringing Far's carved doorposts."

"So that is what was in the cart your horse pulled." Kjell leaned against his load. "I saw you, remember? I was talking to the bladesmith when you passed by."

Her eyes widened and she laughed aloud. "Ah, *ja*! You have bathed! I did not recognize you."

Kjell had to laugh, as well. "My toilet has been lacking, of late."

She grinned. "It is good to laugh." Then her face sobered. "You should know that the manor is in mourning since the manor lord recently died. Did you hear?"

"Ach, bad news. I did not know."

"They will still want some of your lovely skins. Ask for Gudrun at the back door of the manor."

"*Takk*, I will. You say your father is the carver? The carver of the exquisite doorposts of the manor house?"

The maiden smiled broadly. "You saw them? *Ja*, that is my father's work. He has brought the final posts for the new guest house." She pointed to the adorned *stabbur* Kjell had passed on his way to the *kirke*.

"His is the finest work I have ever seen." He studied her youthful features. Her eyes were like the sea and her smile angelic.

The girl's eyes fluttered away.

Kjell forced himself to picture Oda, dimpled and appealing in her own way. He had been too long away from his wife.

The girl said, "Tonight there will be feasting, dancing and an all-night vigil at the *kirke*. You should come."

"Dancing? *Nei*." Kjell shook his head. "Definitely not an all-night vigil."

She smiled again. "You must come, at least for a while. There will be plenty of food, and the Lady's ale is the best."

Kjell wavered. "Perhaps. What are you called, in case I see you there?"

"Astra Svensdatter. And you?"

"Kjell. Just Kjell."

"Kjell, the hunter, then." The maiden turned to go. "If I see Gudrun or Lady Marta, I will send them your way."

"Much obliged." Kjell watched her touch the bearskin once more, digging her fingers into the thick pile and squeezing a handful. She shot him a sidelong glance before walking briskly away.

So, she was an artisan's *datter* and acquainted with the lady of the manor. His thoughts strayed as he watched her walk away. An ache seized his heart and he reminded himself that he loved his wife and would soon see her. Why had he not diverted his path to go home? Indeed, it had been far too long.

Chapter 4

Astra made her way across the courtyard tagged by Ledsager. She thought about the hunter's white reindeer fur, so luxuriant and pure. Her mother would love it and she wished she could buy it as a gift, but her few coins were only enough for a comb and ribbons after all. That hunter, Kjell, was a rough-looking fellow with his unkempt sandy hair and red beard that reached to his breast bone. Even after washing he still smelled of animals—Mar would say his clothing should be burned. There was a wildness in his eyes, too, a way of looking at her that made her feel unsettled. Still, his smile and his laugh were disarming, kind even, despite his disheveled appearance.

Far was not near the sledge but his heavy doorposts had been taken away. In their place were two boxes of salt and a soapstone slab. Astra shouldered her leather satchel and strolled across the yard to the women's cottage where she was to sleep. No one else was inside. She wished Karin had come along. Her sister was only one year younger than Astra and her closest confidante. But Far said Karin was needed at home to help Mar with chores and the new baby.

Inside the women's cottage Astra shook out her Lord's Day frock and hung it over one of the bedposts to straighten. She would wear it this evening to Saint Olav's meal at the manor house. Picking up her spinning basket, she stepped outside to wait for Far and to look for Einarr.

As she hurried down the steps, she noticed the scent of freshly hewn logs just across the way. The nearly finished *stabbur* where Far's carved doorposts would be installed was a combined storehouse and guest lodge. Thick railings surrounded the upper deck's porch that protruded over the lower level. From up there a guest could view the entire manor grounds. A stylized horse's head that Far had carved peaked the roof. Far's doorposts would aptly adorn the large entrance door of this fine structure.

Astra found her father standing on the steps of the massive manor house talking to someone, their heads bent close together. The man, whose back was turned, was tall and wore a black cloak embroidered with many colors. His dark hair, streaked with gray, was tied at the back of his neck with a red ribbon. He and her father seemed engaged in a serious discussion—Far's voice was not quite friendly.

What business was this? She knew of nothing except the sale of the door posts, the purchase of a few supplies, and hopefully a horse. Astra stopped and waited, soon becoming restless for her father to finish his conversation. She inched forward, forming the words she would say to him about Einarr's promise: "Einarr wishes to speak with you." *Nei*: "You must speak to the lord's son right away about an important matter." Maybe. She shook her head, trying to think of the best approach to take with her likely skeptical father.

The man stepped back and turned. In profile Astra recognized him now. She had seen him before at council meetings. He was a wealthy landowner and the *sysselmand* for the whole county. He had come to the Michaelmas fair last year and was known for buying the finest jewelry and furs for his fleshy, childless wife. Indeed, around his neck was a heavy gold chain. Vegar Eriksson was his name. Astra had never spoken to him but disliked him for his vanity…was that not a mortal sin? She glanced about. Where was his wife, the linen-clad woman who perpetually looked down at others over her hooked nose?

Far motioned Astra to him. To Astra's chagrin, the *sysselmand* watched her approach. He was old, certainly past forty, with creases down his jawline alongside his disagreeably pursed mouth.

"*Datter*," Far said as she mounted the steps, "do you remember *Sysselmand* Vegar Eriksson from Kravik?"

She nodded deferentially. "Bless the day, sir."

"And you, as well." The haughty man bowed his head to her. "It is good to see you and your father again."

Again? She curtsied slightly. "Have we met before?"

"Not officially...until now." Vegar reached for her hand and kissed it. His hand was soft, like a gentlewoman's. After an instant of discomfort, she slipped her hand away.

"The *sysselmand* and I have *fylke* business to discuss," Far explained. He fidgeted with his ear, a rare sign of nervousness.

To Vegar he said, "Let me consider, and we can speak again after supper."

"Until then." Vegar backed up and bowed to Astra again, briefly scanning her frame as if appraising a horse. He said to her, "Perhaps we shall meet later tonight."

When he was past earshot Astra asked, "What business have you with him, Far? He is a peacock."

"It is a matter between him and me," was all Far would say.

Fylke business involved matters of governing for which she cared little. Astra shook off the specter of Vegar's presence and followed Far toward the outdoor bonfire in mid-courtyard. There he settled on a bench with other free landowners where they would drink ale and swap stories. Astra moved a stool into a sunny spot where she could see the manor steps and the servant's side door as well. From here she could watch for Einarr, or his younger sister Hedda at least. They had been friends since they were children, playing together every time her family came to Sjodrun for trading and holidays. She took the spindle from her basket and began to spin. Where was Einarr, anyway?

Before long she moved her stool closer to the side door, following the patch of sunlight that had moved. Suddenly, the door slammed open. Astra spun around to see Einarr back out followed by his mother, Lady Marta, dressed in black. Shrubbery partially obscured Astra's view and she scooted over a bit more.

Lady Marta snatched Einarr's arm and pulled him close to her face. "You will listen to me."

"*Nei*, you cannot force me," Einarr said angrily.

His mother shushed him. "Quiet! You do not speak to me that way." She shook her finger in his face and pulled him behind the open door.

Unable to see them now, Astra strained to listen.

"You would never treat your father this way," said Lady Marta. "As lady of the manor I make the decisions now."

Astra looked around but no one else seemed to notice them. Far sat near the fire with his back to her, laughing with other men and draining his ale bowl. She craned her neck, but Einarr and his mother were still hidden from view.

"I must be allowed some say," Einarr grumbled.

"This is what your father wanted and this is what you will do," said Lady Marta.

"But he is gone."

Astra heard a hard slap. "You will do as I say." Lady Marta's voice was fierce.

Einarr grunted, then he sprinted away from the scene toward the stables.

Lady Marta grumbled, "The *djevel* take him. Why did you give me such a stubborn child?" The manor door slammed shut behind her.

Shocked, Astra dropped her spindle. She had never heard Lady Marta swear, nor Einarr speak so insolently. What was she forcing him to do? Einarr should seek to please his mother, especially if he wanted her to accept Astra, a council member's *datter*, as his wife.

She had quickly tucked her spool away rising to find Einarr, when a hooded girl ran toward her across the yard.

"Astra! Cousin!"

It was Nikolina, her aunt Thyra's *datter* whose family lived in Veggli and occasionally met Astra's family in Sjodrun for holy days.

Nikolina threw her arms around Astra tightly. A bundle under her cloak pressed against Astra's chest. "I am so glad I found you," Nikolina laughed into Astra's ear. "I just heard you were here."

Astra peered at the top of a tiny head within Nikolina's sling. "Boy or girl?" she asked, cooing and stroking the fine feathery scalp.

Nikolina teased the swaddling away so Astra could see the angelic face. "Girl, six weeks old."

"So little." Astra smiled and looked about the yard for her aunt. "Where is *Tante* Thyra? I am surprised she would travel so soon after delivering. Mar just had a baby, too. We have twin cousins."

Nikolina tugged Astra by the arm and led her to one side. "Astra, she is *my* baby. We just churched her yesterday. Her name is Amalie, after our grandmother."

Silently Astra calculated the months since she had seen Nikolina at Jultide. Only seven. Nikolina had not been wedded then, nor had there been a betrothal announced.

"I know what you are thinking," Nikolina blurted, "and *ja* I am wed, just before Gregory's mass. Dag and I met last Michaelmas, and now I live here with his family. He is building a house for us. It will be done before summer ends, thanks be to God."

Astra absorbed her cousin's unexpected news with consternation. She wondered that no word had come to her family of this event. At best in these situations, a couple quickly married with a cloud over their heads; at worst the girl was shamed and disinherited, or even sent to a nunnery while her parents took the child as their own.

Astra gently stroked the baby's cheek. At least Nikolina was married. She repeated the words Mar said to all new mothers, "God be praised. Children are always a blessing." Later, Mar would have privately added, "What is hidden in the darkness will be seen in the daylight."

Nikolina exhaled audibly. "Oh, *takk*, Astra. I knew you would understand."

Astra smiled consolingly. "What did *Tante* and *Onkel* say?"

Nikolina's eyes filled with tears. "They were...not pleased, of course, but they attended the wedding. They have not seen the baby yet, but I sent word. Dag says we can travel to Veggli to see them after the harvest. I hope they will receive us."

Astra took her cousin's hand. "What grandparents do not want to see their first grandchild?" Inwardly, she dreaded telling Far. More than once her parents had commented on Nikolina's impetuous nature. Far derided girls who found themselves in this predicament, using each story to warn Astra and Karin of the wiles of young men.

"Are you happy in your new life with Dag?" Astra asked.

"Happy? Dag is a good husband, but..."

"But?"

Nikolina whispered behind her hand. "His mother is cruel. My parents gave them only the smallest dowry, my clothing and a chest of linens, and now I work like a slave for Dag's mother." She raised her sleeve to reveal bruised fingerprints on her forearm. "She beats me. I will be happy when we can at least have our own house."

"I am sorry, Niki." Astra hugged her cousin in sympathy. What a mistake she had made! Now she must reap the consequences, as Mar would say.

"And what about you? Is there a marriage contract yet? You are only six months younger than me—it is time you have good news."

Astra sighed. "I hope so. A boy, well, nearly a man, is going to talk to Far very soon, perhaps tonight."

Nikolina hugged her again. "That is wonderful. I want to hear as soon as it happens."

Astra grinned sheepishly. "I think everyone will know, since he is...important."

"Aha! Someone wealthy then. All the better for you." Nikolina's smile was wan. "Will you join me for Saint Olav's feast in the yard tonight? I hear there will be food for the tenants, and I want you to meet Dag."

Somewhat relieved, Astra said, "I am sorry. We are invited to dine in the manor. Far is a member of the council."

"Do not worry." Nikolina's tone was rather too bright. "I hope I will see you at the dance, then, if Dag's mother lets us stay."

"I will look for you." Astra kissed the infant's head. "She is beautiful, Niki."

"*Takk*, cousin. I must be getting back." Nikolina squeezed Astra's arm and rushed off.

Poor girl, Astra thought. Far would likely say, "Sins may be forgiven, but the price must be paid."

When the horn sounded, calling everyone to dinner, Astra hurried to change into her Lord's Day frock, then joined the stream of guests flowing toward the Great Hall. She had been inside the manor several times before, yet its splendor always awed her. Stepping onto the pine plank flooring, she felt the polished smoothness beneath her deerskin shoes. The hall was big enough for three fires. Smoke drifting slowly upward to the roof vents lent a hazy aura to the room.

On one wall hung a shield with Lord Jonas's coat of arms surrounded by a display of swords and an array of weapons. Down the length of the cavernous room, long boards were set up with at least a hundred pewter plates and ale horns. At the far end of the room, on the raised dais, was perched the grand table where the lord's family and honored guests would be seated.

The head servant, Gudrun, led in a group of well-appointed guests. She seated the visiting nobleman and his wife at the main table abutting the dais. Other local *fylke* members and free land owners, including Far, were seated on the benches near them, followed by merchants, craftsmen, and the single men.

The women sat furthest down the long table in order of rank and age. Children were herded outside to be fed with the tenants.

Unsheathing her knife and spoon from her belt, Astra sat beside two girls she knew to be near her age, *datters* of shopkeepers. Both girls' long hair was tucked into long white wimples as a sign that they were now married. Their frocks were finer than Astra's, and one of the girls glanced askance at Astra's homespun dress. After greeting Astra, these two leaned toward one another sharing rumors of betrothals and pregnancies, while disparaging other girls' clothing as they trailed in.

Astra rolled her eyes and looked away. When she married Einarr they would see the beautiful clothes she wore as the wife of the manor lord and they would ignore her no longer.

When everyone else was seated, the honored guests were led in: Sir Jokkum, the manor's only remaining resident knight, Father Johan and his wife, and…*Sysselmand* Vegar Eriksson. Astra winced. In addition to his heavy golden neck chain, his fingers were adorned with several large rings. What a garish display of wealth, she thought disdainfully.

Lastly, Lady Marta, Einarr, and Hedda climbed the dais steps wearing black. They sat, leaving the largest and most ornate seat vacant between them in memory of the late Lord Jonas.

Servants hurried in with dripping bowls of ale to set along the boards. Everyone dipped their cups into the bowls, leaving sudsy trails across the planks. A few sucked the foam off the top but they did not drink, waiting for the toasts.

A mournful blast on a trumpet sent shivers up Astra's back, then the hall was silent. A village girl known for her lyrical voice sang a tune of sadness that echoed through the rafters.

Lady Marta stood and raised a gold wine goblet. She placed her hand on the empty chair back. Her voice was husky. "*Takk*, honored friends and neighbors, for coming to Saint Olav's feast." She tipped her head to Father Johan. "And you, Father, for your comfort to our family."

Father Johan nodded solemnly and pressed his hands together in a gesture of prayer.

Lady Marta spread her arms out to the guests. "Thank you also for your kind words of condolence. Lord Jonas is sorely missed. Father Johan assures us that my husband has entered God's glory. I have provided for an annual mass to be said in his name."

A low murmur of approval passed over the crowd. Astra's eyes watered. She had feared Lord Jonas because of his severe reputation, but felt sorrow for his family nonetheless.

Lady Marta cleared her throat and continued, "But now, in celebration of our own Saint Olav Haraldsson, let us raise our cups."

Everyone stood. Lady Marta held her goblet high. "To my husband and Saint Olav, together in paradise."

"*Skål!*" shouted all, lifting their ale bowls.

Father Johan raised his and said, "Thanks be to God for the generous feast provided by the Lady Marta. May God bless us all. Let Saint Olav's fast be broken."

Everyone cheered and took a long swill. Astra touched her bowl to her neighbors' and took a sip.

The kitchen door banged open and servants entered carrying platters of goose, ptarmigan, roasted pork, salmon, and brisket. A cheer arose and all proceeded to serve themselves hefty portions.

Shoulder-to-shoulder with her neighbors, Astra cut morsels with her knife, filling her pewter plate. As she ate, she stole glances at the dais. Once, Einarr's eyes met hers and he smiled, filling her with yearning. When Einarr spoke quietly but intently to his mother, Astra wondered if he spoke about her. Or did they talk of the family affairs over which they had argued this afternoon? Most importantly, when would she be able to see him in private?

Reaching for the cheeses, Astra watched Vegar walk down from the dais to sit next to her father. As she chewed, Vegar turned and bent forward to look down the table at her, his lips cracking slightly upward. Was that a smile?

Mortified, blood rushed up Astra's neck and she turned away, hoping the other girls had not noticed. A married man should not look at a maiden thusly. His wife would surely disapprove, if she were present. Looking around, Astra did not see his over-stuffed moose among the guests.

After many portions were eaten, guests began to be satiated and leaned back, patting their rounded stomachs in satisfaction. Someone opened the manor hall door and the sound of musicians tuning up in the yard reached their ears. Several young women, including the two next to Astra, rose. Young men close by noticed and stuffed their mouths as they, too, stood up. All of them quickly bowed to Lady Marta before hurrying out into the yard to dance.

Astra stowed her knife and spoon at her belt and got up slowly, stopping at the threshold of the grand doors to wait for Einarr. From the dais, Einarr's sister, Hedda, waved and hurried toward Astra crying, "Wait for me. I need to change my dress." She swept across the room and up the ladder to the loft, lifting her black dress of mourning above her ornate shoes.

Astra leaned against a pillar to wait for Hedda. How could she bring Einarr and her father together? She determined that whoever came outside first, Far or Einarr, she would seat him by the fire and fetch the other so they would be forced to talk. But turning back to the dais, Astra saw that Einarr was being led down the steps by his mother who pressed him into a vacant seat beside the visiting nobles.

Einarr glanced Astra's way. She smiled and nodded toward the door, but he shook his head slightly. He nodded toward Lady Marta and shrugged, clearly unable to escape his duty. Astra pouted her lower lip.

Perhaps she should get her father outside first, to wait for Einarr. She started toward him but was thwarted when she saw Far stab another piece of ptarmigan and reach for more *brød*. Vegar continued to talk to him intently while Far nodded and chewed. Astra waited beside a nearby post for her chance to get Far's attention. Soon Vegar raised his cup. He and Far tapped their ale horns together and drained them.

Thanks be to God! They had concluded their *syssel* business. Astra strode over to her father and touched his shoulder.

He turned. "*Ja?*" He looked at her, his eyes watery.

Astra blew out an exasperated breath. He was already *drukken,* as he often was when he enjoyed the manor's generous ale bowls.

She started, "I...I thought you might want to..." She stopped short. Vegar was staring at her and the words, talk to Einarr, became lost on her lips.

"To what?" Far sounded mildly annoyed.

"To come outside...to dance." She knew this was ill-timed—he still had food on his plate and he dipped into the ale bowl as she spoke.

"You dance," Far said. "I will be right here all night."

"But Far..."

He held up his hand to stop her. "I failed to tell you that Vegar recently lost his wife."

Astra was taken aback. She stammered, "I, I am sorry for your loss, sir."

The *sysselmand*'s face was stern. She noted the deep creases that lined his mouth and forehead. Was he as old as Far? Older?

"It was sudden," said he, "at Easter. We lost the baby, too."

Astra tried to feel sadness for him, but his wife was snobbish and gluttonous, and Astra had disliked her the only time she had seen her.

"Off with you, Little Sparrow," said Far.

Astra touched his shoulder. "But I need to talk to you about something important..."

Far patted her hand then waved her away. "Later. Go."

She stepped back. She had seen him like this before. He was immovable when he was *drukken*. She backed away, fuming. Stalking sulkily to the bottom of the loft's ladder she leaned against the railing to wait for Hedda to come down. If Far would not go outside, then Einarr must speak with him here in the manor house. But Vegar could not be sitting with Far!

Einarr still sat with his mother and the nobles. He leaned his chin on his entwined fingers, propped up on his elbows. This meeting must be part of his new duties. Astra winced in irritation.

Servants began to clear away empty platters, tossing scraps of food and bones to the dogs that thronged under the tables.

Soon, Vegar stepped over the bench, looking Astra's way.

Perfect, she thought. She would get Vegar away from Far, and when Einarr was finished speaking with the nobles he could talk to her father.

She walked up to the *sysselmand* and asked, "Do you wish to dance?"

"Indeed," he said, a bit too keenly.

The bonfire in the center of the courtyard leapt and crackled, sending sparks high into the slowly darkening midsummer evening. The music had started; the gaiety of lyres, *gigjuns*, lutes, and *saltreriums* swam over the yard like a star shower. Dozens of dancers pranced around the ever-growing circle in pairs.

Though Astra felt no more like dancing with Vegar than cleaning out the pigsty, she let him lead her into the circle. His hand was as smooth as a cow's udder. She could think of nothing else but his flesh on hers. Each time he turned his head toward her she felt his gaze burning her cheek.

When the dance ended Astra saw Hedda flying down the manor steps in a black kirtle of mourning, short enough for dancing.

"Astra!" Hedda called. "I am so glad you came!"

Astra let go of Vegar's hand and ran to Hedda, thankful to be rescued.

Hedda hugged Astra, then curtsied to Vegar, who had stepped back. "Greetings, Vegar Eriksson," she said politely.

He bowed. "Adjoining business with pleasure this visit."

"I heard about your wife," Hedda said, "and I grieve with you. I hope you can enjoy the dance."

"Kind of you, indeed." He bowed and backed away.

Astra whispered into Hedda's ear, "Thank you for getting me away from that man."

Hedda whispered back, "Of course. He has money, but he thinks himself better than he is."

"Why does Einarr not come out to join the dance?" Astra asked, glancing at the open manor door.

Hedda shook her head. "He and Mar are still talking to Sir Aksel and his wife—about what, I do not know. I do know he wants to see you."

Astra hugged her friend and they joyfully swung each other around.

The music started and Hedda pulled Astra in, circling the fire with the others. Astra took the man's part, holding her friend's hand as they stepped on cue. Hedda passed under Astra's twirling arm, then they kicked alternating feet as they promenaded. Hedda giggled when Astra forgot to swing her around, and they burst into laughter. Astra wished again that her sister was with them. How Karin would love to be dancing with them tonight! The three of them had often wished they were all sisters. Maybe they would be soon, when she and Einarr married. Astra grinned at the thought.

When the dance ended, Astra noticed Vegar standing at the edge of the crowd face-to-face with a flinching servant. The serving lass nodded and tried to back away, but Vegar pushed his face close and grumbled something, shaking his finger in the poor girl's face. Astra could not hear what he said, but she saw the crimson maid back up, bow, then turn and run toward the manor.

"Why is he yelling at her?" she asked Hedda.

"Who knows? I hear he is very particular that things are done his way."

Astra grabbed Hedda's hand saying, "Let us go and free your brother," but Hedda jerked Astra toward the shadows.

"There he is!" Hedda cried. Einarr sat alone on a large stone looking forlorn. The two girls ran to him.

"Astra has been looking for you," Hedda said, taking Astra's hand and placing it in Einarr's. The music started and she loped off.

Astra sat down beside him. "What were you talking about with those people?" She wanted to hold onto him but there were others milling about nearby. She let go of his hand.

"About what will happen now that my father is gone," he said. His forehead was creased, his mouth drawn downward.

"Will you become the lord?" She leaned so that their sleeves touched.

He did not meet her eyes. "I must first become a knight. It is complicated."

Astra noticed Vegar heading toward them. "Einarr, dance with me...now." She grabbed his arm and dragged him toward the circle, passing the approaching *sysselmand* without a glance.

Einarr's dancing was lackluster but she prodded him on. She felt Vegar's wraithlike eyes on her from the sidelines. Why was he still watching her? She suddenly remembered what Far had just told her in the Great Hall, that Vegar was now widowed. Was he already looking for another wife? Is that what he and her father had spoken of? God in heaven! She gasped, then stumbled, but Einarr caught her before she fell.

When the dance ended Einarr drew her to the back steps and they sat. She leaned over and whispered, "My father is inside. You should talk to him right now."

Einarr stroked her hand. "I cannot. Not yet. I have duties, Astra. My mother is making demands."

She grabbed his hand tightly. "Whatever they are, they are not more important than securing our betrothal, are they? Einarr, do you still love me?"

"Of course I do, but..."

Her heart raced. "Then you will act quickly before…"

He turned to look at her. "Before what?"

"Vegar Eriksson has been watching me. See?"

She turned and Einarr followed her gaze. Indeed, Vegar was watching them through the foliage, but he quickly turned away and reached for his cup.

Astra whispered, "He lost his wife and he was just talking with my father in a very friendly way. What if they were talking of a betrothal?"

Einarr squinted his eyes. "Vegar?" He paused. "*Nei*. That could never be."

"You do not know that. It could be!"

Einarr gazed at her. "He is the *sysselmand*. He is wealthy and would marry…up." His voice faded as his eyes glanced away.

Marry up. A woman of high status. Of course, Vegar would marry up, considering his position and his first wife's trousseau. Astra was not sure if she should feel relieved or insulted.

"My mother expects me back," Einarr said, rising. "We will have to wait for now. There is much to consider, more than I thought." He plucked her hand from his arm. "I must go."

As she watched him return to the manor, alarm rose in Astra's breast. Einarr must marry up, too!

When the horn blew at midnight for Saint Olav's mass, the music stopped. Several folks lit torches from the fire to guide their way to the *kirke*. Astra and Hedda followed hand in hand. At the entrance, men laid down their weapons and removed their hats. Astra and Hedda crowded in with the women. The only benches lining the wall filled up quickly with the elderly and the very young.

Tapers shed pale circles of light in the darkened apse. Astra peered upward, but the rafters with their grotesquely carved faces were hidden in darkness. She searched for Einarr's head among the men, finally spying him. He had come after all, but his eyes did not search for hers.

Out of habit, the women and girls stood shoulder to shoulder for warmth, even though the oft-frigid cavern was warmer now that it was mid-summer. Astra and Hedda linked arms for the long, incomprehensible service ahead.

Two boys dressed in wadmal tunics proceeded down the center of the short nave and lit the tapers at the altar. Father Johan lifted the thurible and swung the pungent incense back and forth, filling the room with a smoky haze. Astra breathed it in—the scent of holiness, her mother called it.

Father Johan read two psalms in Latin followed by a hymn, which few joined him in singing. He sang the required versicle phrase that was followed by the congregants' echoed response, then he chanted the canticle alone. Astra poked Hedda and the girl pinched her in return. While the priest repeated the litany of saints, Astra's thoughts carried her back to the midnight service last *Jul* eve, just six months ago.

That night was winter-black and bitterly cold. Like this night, she had enjoyed a feast and drunk too much along with everyone else. At the end of the mass while everyone was hurrying out, Einarr had snatched Astra from the crowd and pulled her deep into the lightless *svalgang* that ran around the perimeter of the *kirke*. Einarr covered her mouth with his icy hand. In the darkness, flush against his chest, her heart beat like a blacksmith's hammer. When the priest closed the door and walked away, Einarr removed his hand and kissed her long on the mouth, arousing in her sensations she had never before felt. He kissed her forehead and cheeks, then her neck. She did not resist, holding still as an owl.

Steam from their combined breaths turned into icy crystals around their faces. Einarr parted her heavy cloak and cupped her breast with his hand. Astra gasped but did not push his hand away. He kissed her deeply and pressed her to him. A strange longing crept into her loins. They held each other tightly, wordlessly, desperately. She did not want him to let her go. Raising her heavy skirts, his hand moved up her leg to clutch her buttocks. Astra was startled. Wanting him, but afraid for her purity, she pushed him away. "*Nei*, not yet."

He dropped her skirts and drew back, breathing heavily. Clouds of frozen breath circled their heads. Astra wrapped her coat tightly around herself, her heart hammering. He kissed her once more and whispered, "I love you," then fled. Astra's chest heaved as if she had climbed Gaustatoppen Mountain. The surge of desire turned to shame as she stumbled back to the women's guest house in a fog of tears.

Father Johan finished his midnight litany with a loud "Amen." Several people startled from their late-night repose. Father Johan began to sing and the congregation roused themselves to join him in *Kyrie Eleison*. The Father said prayers for Saint Olav, Saint Michael, his angels, Lord Jonas' family, and the humble village folk. He invited those who would stay for the all-night vigil to do so. After reciting the *Pater Noster* together, and a short pause, everyone silently filed out.

Far caught Astra just outside and slung his arm around her shoulder, leaning on her unsteadily. Next to him walked Vegar. Far tripped on a stone and Vegar caught him, standing him upright again.

"*Takk*," Astra murmured to Vegar. "Far has drunk too much again."

"I am not *drukken*," Far slurred.

"I will get him back to a bench at the manor," Vegar offered.

Astra said, "*Nei*, we will not trouble you. I can do it."

But Vegar tossed her father's arm over his shoulder and hauled him forward. "Where are you sleeping? I will see you safely there, as well."

She pointed to the women's cottage just across the yard and the three stepped carefully through the dark until they arrived. Two other girls were entering the cottage and one held the door open for Astra.

Vegar adjusted Far's arm onto his shoulder as her father's head lolled over to rest on Vegar's neck.

Astra stepped up onto the threshold of the women's house and said, "*Takk* for taking care of my father, sir."

He tipped his head. "It is no trouble in the least. I will see you tomorrow."

Astra ducked inside and shut the door. Tomorrow? Not if she could avoid him. By the light of the single candle, she changed into her night dress, stuffed her hair in her night cap, and slipped into bed beside a snoring woman. The woman turned over, breathing into Astra's face. Astra flipped to her other shoulder and closed her eyes. Vegar's stern, creased face swam before her. "Not him, not him, God," she moaned into her pillow. "I'll do anything…"

Astra woke to the sound of women's voices passing by the cottage. Light shone through cracks around the door and between the rafters. She slid out of bed trying not to wake her bed partner. She threw a cloak over her night clothes, slipped her toes into her shoes, and tiptoed past the other sleeping bodies that were crowded into the four straw-stuffed beds. Drawing up the latch she eased through quietly. She would relieve herself in the woods since the chamber pot in the women's house was brimming.

The morning sun hid behind low-hanging clouds along the northeast tree line. Dew darkened the toes of Astra's shoes as she strode through the grass. She startled a redwing pecking for insects and it flew close over her head, making her jump. In the chilly morning air, the previous night's events struck her like a cold slap. Far was over-friendly with the *sysselmand* and they had talked of her. What else could explain her father's strangeness and the way that old man looked at her? What if Einarr's troubles with his mother indeed kept him from standing up and talking to Far about marriage? If Einarr said nothing, her father might, maybe already had…God help me!

When she had dressed, the aroma from the outdoor cooking fire made Astra's stomach rumble on her way to the yard. She glanced about in case Einarr should be out early, then swerved around the milkmaid and a man carrying firewood on her way to find her father. He was usually an early riser, but the lateness of last night's mass and his drunkenness might make him oversleep. It mattered not. She would wait for him and tell him she would marry no one but Einarr. If he said *nei*, she would tell him she would run away to a nunnery and he would never see her again.

She was surprised to find her father sitting near the manor gate on a log by their sledge. He held a piece of *brød* in his hand and took a bite. Ledsager rose from his place beside Far and wagged his tail as she approached.

"Good *morgen*," she said to her father, patting the dog's head.

Far's face was rumpled, older. "And to you. How did you sleep?"

"I slept quickly," she answered, hoping to lighten the mood with their old joke.

He stuffed *brød* into his mouth but did not look at her.

She sat beside him quietly, forming the words she wanted to say.

"What did you do yesterday?" he asked, breaking off a piece of *brød* and handing it to her.

Astra's mind swirled. Now that she was with him, she hesitated to use the nunnery ploy. Could she really leave home and never return? She would use that as her final threat, only if she needed it.

Instead, she said, "I met up with cousin Nikolina. She is here with her husband and their infant."

"She is married? And an infant already? Hmmm. When?"

She fingered the *brød*. "Before Easter. She married Dag Bjorgulfson."

He grunted.

"She loves Dag, but she is not happy. Her mother-in-law is cruel. Do you know his family?"

"Ach, I do," Far scoffed. "That woman is made of iron. Nikolina has chosen a difficult way. That is the plight of those who stray off the path and do not obey their parents." On these last words he poked his finger into Astra's shoulder like he used to do to make a point. She shrugged him away.

"Whom have you talked to besides Nikolina?" he asked.

"I went to the dance with Hedda. You should have come out." She took a bite of *brød*.

Far asked, "Did you speak with any men?"

"I spoke with friends, of course, like Einarr. He may be the manor lord someday, you know. You should talk with him."

Her father glanced at her sidelong. "What have I to do with him?"

Astra took a tremulous breath, squishing her *brød* tightly in her fingers. "I want you to talk to him, Far. It is about us, the two of us." She paused, cleared her throat. "I love him and he loves me."

Far looked at her aslant. "There is no 'two of you.'"

"*Ja*, there is. We want to marry."

Far showed her his palm to stop her from going on. "*Nei*. There is nothing more to say about this. You will not be marrying him, so throw that thought into the creek."

Seething, she stood. "You want me to be happy, *nei*? This is what will make me happy, to marry Einarr. He feels the same."

He glanced up at her. "There are more important things than being happy."

She raised her voice. "What is more important than a happy life? Nothing!"

"Shh." He gripped her arm and pulled her down to sit. "Have we taught you nothing? Faithfulness to God, hard work, fulfilling responsibility, raising a family. You know this."

Ja, she knew what her parents had preached to her for as long as she could remember. "But I want more in life than that."

They sat still, side-by-side staring at the ground. Finally, Far cleared his throat. "What about Vegar Eriksson? Did you dance with him?"

Satan and his angels! "We danced once, but Far!" Her gut tightened and she wrapped her arms around herself as she began to tremble.

"What did he say?"

"Why are you talking about that haughty man?"

He shrugged. "He has asked about you."

Astra glared at her father. "He is a conceited braggart."

"He has many assets, *datter*. He is an important leader, and very rich." Far reached for her hand.

She snatched it away. "And insufferably arrogant. Far, please understand. Einarr will be rich, too, someday. He and I love each other."

Her father stiffened. "What do you mean by love? Has he touched you?"

"*Nei*, not like that." She knew he would severely chastise her if he knew of their encounter at the *kirke*.

He stared at her, took a few breaths, then said, "Marriage is not about love. It is about alliance, hard work, and faithfulness."

"But that cannot be all." Angry tears dripped onto her cheeks.

He dusted crumbs off his hands and got up. "We will talk later. This morning I need to settle on the price for the horse. Come along."

He walked toward the stable. She waited until he was halfway across the yard before following. Ledsager tagged at her heels.

The stable boy ran to fetch Didrik. Astra stood at the mare's stall smoothing the horse's forelock. She could not look at her father.

Didrik soon joined them, smiling. "What do you think of her?" he asked Astra.

Far cleared his throat loudly, signaling her that she was to let him do the talking.

"She is truly fine. I love her," she said defiantly.

Didrik said, "Walk her down the barn and back so your father can see her stride."

Astra led the mare out of the stall to the gaping barn door then stopped, stroking the mare's neck in the sunlight. She could mount right now and race to find Einarr, take him to a secluded glen where they could seal their love. Then Lady Marta and her father would have no choice but to let them marry quickly.

"She is strong for her size," she heard Didrik say, "and broken for pulling as well as riding. Sometimes she can be headstrong, but she has stamina."

"If she is so good then why sell her?" Far used his stern bartering tone.

"If it were up to me I would not," said Didrik, "but Lady Marta was bitten and insists we sell her. I have never seen the horse bite anyone else. Unlike Astra, the lady is no horsewoman."

"Bring her back," her father called to Astra.

When Astra stopped the horse in front of him, Far palpated the horse's legs, lifted each foot, then opened her mouth to examine her teeth.

"How much?" he barked.

Didrik named the price.

Far groused, "*Nei, nei.* I cannot afford that."

Astra stepped around to the other side of the horse so she would not have to see her father's face. Why did men always have to yell and argue when bargaining?

The two men haggled until finally Far said, "If you include a few lambs and a goat next spring, I can meet your price."

They shook hands.

At last, Far patted the mare's neck, saying to Astra, "A fine horse like this will need extra care, young lady."

She was tight-lipped. "I know." Had it not been for Far's talk about Vegar she would have hugged him in gratitude but she would not.

Didrik slapped Far on the back then took Astra about the waist. "Astra, girl, come with us to the manor to seal our bargain with a horn-full."

She squirmed from his grip and Didrik laughed. He had always been kind to her as a child, but she suddenly did not feel like a child around him anymore.

They entered the hall where remnants of last night's meal were set up on the boards. Astra sat beside Far across the table from Didrik. They all dipped cups into the ale bowl and Didrik raised a toast.

"You have a good horse for a bargain price," he laughed. Then he winked at Astra. "You know, Sven, I only did it for the girl."

Far squeezed Astra's shoulder. "She is a fine one, my *datter*," he replied.

They helped themselves to porridge and hunks of leftover meats. Several other guests, mostly men, were already eating. She felt their eyes on her and focused on her plate.

"The rye is not as tall as it should be," said one man, a manor worker she recognized.

"We need more sun," added another.

They talked of crops and weather until a man Astra did not know said, "Did you hear about the terrible sickness in Bergen? I heard it is an ugly blight. Many have already died there."

"You don't say," remarked Didrik.

Astra recalled overhearing the hunter telling the bladesmith about this sickness, but she said nothing.

"You should pray it does not come to our village," added the man.

"We are far enough from Bergen," Far said, "thanks be to God for that."

The men nodded in agreement. Astra knew that Bergen was overrun with German Hansa, whom the Norse resented greatly.

"I heard that King Magnus is in the country," said a wrinkled old man who brought firewood into the manor house. He swung his stiff leg carefully over the bench. "I heard it from my son-in-law, who just rode back from Veggli last night."

Far smirked, "What? The absent king has left his castle and his foreign wife in Sweden?"

The men chuckled.

"He likely wants more taxes for his wife's dream of uniting *Skandinavia*," Far scoffed.

"We should break from Sweden altogether," said one.

"*Ja, ja,*" agreed the others.

"Let us pray the king stays far away from us," said the old man.

"How old now is that runt of a boy who is supposed to be our Norwegian king?" asked the manor worker.

"Must be ten," Didrik said.

"Will not be long before he is sixteen, *ja?*" noted the worker.

The stranger added, "Since he is being raised in Norway, at least he will understand our country and will be a true Norse king, born here."

The men pounded the table in approval.

Summoning her courage, Astra spoke up. "I heard the king is starting another war. He wants to capture Novgorod trading center."

Everyone turned to stare at her.

"How do you know this?" asked Far.

"I heard the fur trader speak of it," she said. "He heard it from some soldiers on the Ra road."

The old man scowled, "Then he will need money."

"Another war?" Didrik shook his head. "Have we not paid enough for his foolishness?"

Far harrumphed, glancing at Astra skeptically. "Let us pray it is not true."

"Maybe we should close the gate in case he and his knights show up," joked the old man.

They all laughed and someone remarked, "Bar the gates, light the cairns."

Far laughed, too, then nodded Astra toward the door. "This is men's business."

Astra strode across the yard in a dark mood, but was surprised to see her cousin, Nikolina, standing with someone at the boilermaker's hut. The woman, presumably her mother-in-law, was arguing with the seller, quibbling loudly over the cost of a small copper pot. Nikolina noticed Astra and touched her mother-in-law's elbow.

"Mother Thorgerd, this is my cousin…"

The woman brushed Nikolina's hand away, glancing only briefly in Astra's direction. She finished her purchase and headed toward the tenants' huts. Astra noted that the boilermaker's face was scarlet and thin-lipped.

Following them, she called, "Madam, I am Nikolina's kin. May I speak with you?"

"I am no madam, as you can see," the woman said, marching on.

Nikolina beckoned Astra to follow.

When Astra caught up with them she said, "Excuse me, Thorgerd, but I do not get to see my cousin often. May she visit me before I leave today?"

The woman puffed, then glowered over her shoulder. "Only if all her chores are finished." She roughly yanked Niki onward by the arm. If Mar were here she would remark, "All shoes are not made with the same leather."

"I will find you when I finish," Nikolina called back gleefully. Astra waved. Her cousin's plight was unfortunate.

Astra waited by their cart for her father to come out, plotting again how to convince him of her case. After a while he emerged, spied her, and lumbered over.

Far sat down heavily on the cart. "*Datter*, I need to tell you some good news." He reached inside his tunic and started to pull out a velum scroll.

Astra's countenance twisted in pain. "*Nei*, Far, please…"

Just then, the drumming of a horse's hooves made them turn toward the manor entrance. Far stood up.

The lazy gatekeeper jumped to his feet and drew his sword, shouting, "Halt!"

A helmeted rider wearing a vest with a blue lion crest pulled up sharply and his war horse skidded to a stop. The horse, draped with a yellow flag adorned by a red cross, snorted loudly.

Astra ran after her father as he jogged toward the scene.

The guard pointed his sword at the rider. "State your business," he shouted.

"Get out of my way and call the lord of the manor," cried the horseman. "King Magnus is coming to your village and you must prepare the way."

Chapter 5

Kjell had just delivered several deer pelts to the manor's tanner when he heard a ruckus at the main gate. Men from all over the courtyard ran toward the commotion, gripping their knives. Kjell followed. He saw that a rider on a war horse carrying a royal flag had been stopped by the guard at the gate. He recognized the horseman as the impudent red-haired squire Kjell had met on the road. He watched from a distance in the shade of a small shed.

The manor's head man, Didrik, ran toward the rider and his lathered steed. "What is your business here?" Didrik demanded.

The squire's voice boomed loudly enough for all to hear, "I repeat, His Majesty King Magnus is traveling this way and will be here within the hour. He will speak with the manor lord immediately when he arrives. Sixty knights, their squires, and many foot soldiers are with him. All will need food and lodging. The manor must prepare for His Majesty King Magnus."

Kjell's heart raced. A previous encounter with king's men had given him reason to fear them. If he were wise, he would pack up and leave quickly, but he had not yet sold his goods, and there were no other villages on his way home. The *djevels* be damned!

Didrik said to the squire, "You must tell the king that Lord Jonas has recently passed away. I will call Lady Marta to speak with you." With a wave of his hand Didrik motioned a servant away to find her. "How long will the king stay?"

"Only a night or two," replied the squire. "He requires food, supplies, and as many able-bodied men as you have. They must be readied to go to war. In addition, he will require the war levy from the lord's household."

Kjell saw Didrik's back stiffen. "Where is there war?"

"The king goes to Novgorod to retake the trading center," said the squire.

"Novgorod? A very long journey," said Didrik.

Kjell knew that this northern trading center was many weeks' travel into disputed *Russik's* territory. This, in addition to the king's many other wars, was likely to cause further resentment and dissention among the people.

"Indeed," contended the squire, "which is why he needs winter supplies and the war levy."

Gliding through the manor yard, a finely clothed older woman in black, the Lady Marta herself, marched directly toward the messenger. She was accompanied by a young man, likely her son.

Confronting the man, her stately voice sang out. "I am Lady Marta. What is your errand?"

Impatiently he repeated the king's commands for men and supplies.

Lady Marta paused. Then she raised her head high and said, "I assure you that we will do everything we can to prepare. You may give His Majesty my humble welcome."

Bowing to her, the rider twisted his horse's head around and kicked its ribs. The stallion jumped into a gallop and they soon disappeared.

For a moment the crowd of onlookers stared after the soldier in silence. Then Lady Marta began issuing orders to the head man and other servants who had gathered as she marched back toward the manor house. Everyone rushed to comply...everyone except the lady's son, who stood staring after the horseman.

The maiden, Astra, whom Kjell recognized from the day before, ran quickly to the young man's side and spoke into his ear.

The lady's son shook his head. Astra grabbed his arm. The young man's face contorted as he pried her hand away, then ran

The Moon Turned to Blood

toward the Great Hall. The hapless lass bent over her knees and brought her apron to her eyes.

Straight away, an older man, possibly the girl's father, came to her side and tried to get her to stand up. She pushed him away and shouted for him to leave her alone. The old man tried once more, but gave up and ambled away toward the manor.

So, the lady's son was the young man the girl hoped to wed, Kjell thought. She, an odal farmer's *datter*, was in for heartache. Yet, the poor girl's troubles were not his. He must stay out of the fray, finish his sales, and leave quickly. He traipsed back to his camp where he stared at his large pile of furs. A thought struck him. Lush furs would be needed for bedding for a king, and he had just such expensive furs to sell.

He strode into the courtyard and caught the arm of an older woman who rushed by. "Is the lady in need of fine pelts for the king's bed?" he asked. "If so, I have some."

She stopped. "Indeed, she is." She followed Kjell to his camp and examined his furs. "These are very fine," she said. "I am Gudrun, head house servant, and I am authorized to purchase what is needed for the king. I will take your most precious ones." She conscripted several passing servants to lug several fine furs away toward the new *stabbur*.

As Gudrun turned to leave, she said, "You should feel honored that these pelts will adorn the king's chamber."

Kjell did not feel honored, but he was happy that Gudrun did not haggle over price. He had made his year's wages in one sale. As soon as he was paid, hopefully before the king arrived, he would buy the supplies he needed and a special gift for Oda. Then he could leave quickly and hopefully not encounter king's men at all.

By early afternoon the thudding of horses' hooves reverberated down the path that led to the entrance of the manor. Kjell had not yet been paid, and he swore to himself, anxious to leave. He had reason to fear the crown's power. He told himself that in this uproar, there was little chance anyone would recognize him: after all, three years had passed. His long beard and hair disguised him well.

Keeping his distance, he followed behind the throng that surged to meet the king. Clinking of weapons and armor resonated down the tree-lined path. A gasp from the villagers went up when the royal troops came into view. Kjell strained to look over the heads of the crowd. Horses and colorfully clad knights slowed as they approached the gate. Dust from the road rose in a cloud from the thudding hooves.

Two flag bearers led the way. The king's yellow banners flapped aloft like gulls' wings. The troops halted at the gate. Leather creaked; a horse snorted. A veil of silence fell.

Dread swept over Kjell like an evil wind. He had made a mistake. He did not belong here. He must get his money and be gone. He crept up behind the crowd and pulled his hood low.

A trumpeter, his dusty yellow cape flowing over his horse's rump, raised a long horn and blew a fanfare above the heads of the crowd. Children covered their ears. A baby cried.

When the sound died away the trumpeter moved aside. A line of knights rode forward, all wearing chainmail beneath their vestments. Helmets were tucked under their arms or strapped to their saddles. Kjell stared at the array of lances, swords, axes, clubs, and maces. His chest tightened and he instinctively gripped the hilt of his knife.

Lady Marta stood before the throng, clasping her hands tightly before her. Kjell noted that her black mourning dress was adorned by a lynx cape. She liked fine furs.

The leading knight spoke loudly. "God's speed to you, M'Lady, and to the people of Sjodrun. I greet you in the name of His Majesty King Magnus."

Lady Marta spoke out boldly. "His Majesty is welcome to Sjodrun. We have prepared our best lodging. We serve His Majesty, our Lord the King."

The knights parted and King Magnus rode forward on a black war horse. He removed his helmet, handing it to a squire.

The king shook his head, loosening his blonde locks, some of which stuck to his sweating neck. To Kjell, he appeared older than his thirty-three years, haggard and weary. How many battles had he fought? How many opponents had he sent to their deaths?

Lady Marta curtsied deeply and everyone in the courtyard followed her lead. Kjell dropped to one knee.

"Arise, people of Sjodrun," said the king. His voice was sonorous, practiced.

A rustling ensued as everyone stood up. "I greet you," he said, "and bring greetings in the name of my son, Haakon, the crowned and future king of Norway. His mother, Queen Blanca, sends regards as well. God be with you."

Kjell had heard, as had everyone, that queen Blanca of Namur had little interest in Norway, living only in Sweden, her native land. King Magnus had granted her the Norwegian region of Vestfold as a very generous morning gift, yet she had never come to see the land she ruled. There was great resentment among the people over this, and the king's lack of attendance to Norway's many needs. Everyone knew that the king ruled over Norway only until his young son came of age.

"And with you, Your Majesty," said Lady Marta. Kjell saw her force her trembling hands into the folds of her skirts. "You may have been informed that Lord Jonas was recently killed in an accident." Her voice broke and silence reigned for a few painful moments. Shortly, she continued, "But I and all of Sjodrun serve at your pleasure." She curtsied once more.

The king motioned her closer and spoke solemnly. "I was sorry to hear about this tragedy. How did Lord Jonas die?"

"He fell from his favorite horse a fortnight ago, but did not recover from his injuries." Lady Marta stretched her hand out to the two young people beside her. "This is our son Einarr, and *datter* Hedda. We are honored by your presence, Your Majesty. Whatever we have is yours."

Kjell knew this was true. The king could take land and manors from any lord whenever he so desired, as they served at

His Majesty's pleasure. Lord Jonas, if he were alive, would now be called to go to war. The Lady and her son must wonder whether they would be allowed to stay at the estate. Another noble who gained the king's favor could easily be appointed as the next lord, displacing the family.

"A fine lad you are, Einarr Jonasson," said the king, "and a lovely, budding young woman, Hedda."

Each genuflected.

To Lady Marta he said, "We would like to rest, bathe, and eat, then I will call a meeting of your *Thing*."

"Of course, Your Majesty," Lady Marta said, bowing. "I have sent riders out to gather the council members. We have readied lodging for you. My servant will lead you there. We are preparing a bath. Supper will be later this evening."

"Very well," the king said. "We are indeed road-weary."

Kjell stepped behind a heavy-set man as the sovereign shook the reins. King Mangus rode through the courtyard as the crowd parted, his eyes roving over his gawking subjects. Momentarily, the king's gaze fixed on someone in the crowd and he turned to the lead knight beside him, tipping his head slightly in that direction. The knight nodded briefly in return.

The king's reputation with women was well-known. Kjell craned his neck to see who the subject of the king's interest might be. Unable to spot a likely lass though the throng, he turned away. The king's indiscretions were none of Kjell's affair. He had learned through trial that it was safer not to interfere.

A manor servant led the king and his troops toward the new guest house that Kjell had admired. There the king dismounted with the help of a squire and was escorted inside. Soldiers unloaded supplies to make camps surrounding the king's quarters.

Kjell strode along the perimeter of the clearing toward his camp keeping his head down and his hood low. As he passed, he glanced over the soldiers' faces for a familiar one whom he never hoped to see again. Recognizing no one, he hurried toward his camp and moved his wagon of furs further into the forest. Kjell wished he could move even deeper into the trees, yet he must wait for the steward to pay him. He sighed. With the ruckus of the king's arrival the payment from the lady would undoubtedly be delayed.

He sat on a stump and brought out his knife to whittle. The shadow of two ravens passed overhead—a foreboding sign. Nothing good would come from the king's arrival.

Chapter 6

Astra and Hedda lay prone on the floor of the manor loft, peeking through the rails and listening as quiet as voles to the impromptu meeting below. Bowls of ale were splashed onto the table as Far, Lady Marta, Einarr, Sir Jokkum, and *Sysselmand* Vegar discussed the king's possible demands.

At first, Astra had difficulty concentrating on the conversation below, relieved that her father's news of her betrothal had been interrupted by the king's arrival. Was there any chance that Einarr would make an agreement with him after all? It would be difficult with all these goings-on. She prayed it was not the old man with the red ribbon sitting at the table below. Her fate was rolled up inside her father's tunic.

"Mar thinks the king wants a lot of money," Hedda whispered into Astra's ear, "probably more than we have right now. He wants fighting men, too. What if he takes Einarr?" She pinched Astra's arm and they glanced at each other. What if, indeed? Astra clenched her friend's arm against her dread.

Lady Marta's voice drifted up from below. "He will ask for as many men as we can muster. Didrik is gathering a list."

"What about me?" Einarr asked.

"I need you here," Lady Marta said. "I will request the king allow you to stay as a mercy to me because of your father's accident. After the war you will be expected to serve him in order to keep the estate. Otherwise, we could be ousted."

"Oh, Mother," Einarr said rather disrespectfully. "That will never happen."

"It happened to Freya of Ufdal," she said reprovingly.

Vegar broke in. "Let us talk about money. The crops are not in, of course, and the autumn fair is more than two months away. How much are you able to contribute from your estate,

Lady Marta? And how much might you gather from the odal farmers?"

From above, Astra saw Vegar's graying hair more clearly. He could be a grandfather!

Lady Marta hesitated. "My steward is assessing this as we speak."

"Do not be distressed," said Sir Aksel. "You should wait until you know what the king demands. He may have mercy on you under the circumstances."

Far groused, "We odal farmers cannot pay a levy when we have not harvested our fields. And if he takes all our young men, who will bring in the harvest? This is our lean season, all of us. We cannot make *thalers* from a rock."

"You must have a plan," said Vegar. "When the other *Thing* members arrive and your steward has determined what the manor can afford, you will know better what to offer, M'Lady."

Lady Marta said, "I will explain our circumstances to His Majesty and beg him to lessen our share for now, say half. We can offer to send the other half either to his castle in Sweden or to wherever he is up north, after the harvest."

"Take it all the way to Novgorod? Why should he accept an offer like that?" scoffed Far. "For my part, I have money from the door posts you purchased, M'Lady, but much of that is already spent on the bishop's tithe and my own supplies. I could contribute an advance from you, Lady Marta, for the guest house's lintel."

"But the money still comes from me." She pounded the table with her fist. "I, too, have expenses, even more now. I must feed all the king's men and outfit the Sjodrun soldiers!"

Vegar laced his over-sized fingers on the tabletop. "Everyone, assess what you have. We will meet again when the others arrive."

Far half-rose, leaning forward on his fists. "And who will profit from this war, Norway? *Nei!* Sweden and his *Svenska* queen. All this trouble to serve a royal thief."

The table was silent for a moment.

Hedda whispered, "Your father should be more careful."

Astra nodded. Far had said far worse at home.

Lady Marta stood up, marched to the kitchen door, and began to give orders to her servants. Vegar, Far, and Sir Aksel, leaning on his cane, departed the hall speaking earnestly to one another.

The girls scrambled back from the ledge. Hedda sneaked to her bedroom, opening and shutting the door as if she and Astra had been inside. They descended and Hedda hurried after her mother.

Astra ran to catch Far. As she hurried down the steps outside Vegar caught her by the arm. Her skin prickled at his touch. "Your father has much business to attend to," he said. "You can be of help by staying out of his way."

She pulled free and leapt down the last step. Her father was headed to the stables and she ran to catch up.

Without stopping, Far said to her, "Vegar and I must ride out to fetch *Thing* members. Wait for me at the manor. And stay away from the soldiers!"

Vegar caught up and joined her father as they quickened their pace.

Behind her, a door slammed shut and Einarr sprinted out.

"Einarr, wait!" Astra ran after him but he waved her away.

"I must ride to fetch someone," he shouted.

She watched in consternation as he disappeared into the stable. Soon the three galloped away without a word. She stomped her foot and slammed her fist on a fence post. Einarr refused to talk to her, her father had befriended the *sysselmand*, and now war had broken out. Fear gathered over her like thunderclouds and ran down her cheeks.

Late in the afternoon Astra had just finished rebraiding her hair in the women's house when she heard marching feet and the clank of arms outside. She opened the door to see royal troops trample across the yard surrounding the king. She adjusted her head linen, fastened the brooch on her cloak, and followed them at a distance to the Great Hall. There they removed their weapons and entered. A few soldiers gripping pikes remained on the porch to keep watch. In the courtyard, women were making supper and boards were being assembled at the outdoor fire.

She spied her father approaching and ran to him. "Where did you go?"

His face was weary. "We notified two *Thing* members, who will come shortly, then went to find Hoskuld, the last council member. He was away hunting but will come as soon as he returns home. Then the council will meet privately. After supper we will hear what the king demands. Things are never so bad that they cannot be worse."

Astra did not smile at this familiar quip. "Are we invited to the manor for supper?"

"Not you. Just the manor household, *Thing* members, the king, and his men. You are to eat outside." He nodded toward the boards. Soldiers were already gathering there, slinging their legs over the benches and quaffing ale.

Her brows drew down. "But they are soldiers, Far."

"The women are separated from the men, and Didrik is there to keep the soldiers in check. We will go home as soon as this is settled, hopefully tomorrow morning."

Astra reluctantly ambled to the fire. None of her friends were there, only a few visitors and curious villagers. Didrik sat on a bench that separated the soldiers from the women. As they ate the women spoke little, attending to their bowls. Rain drizzled as they ate mutton soup and yesterday's *brød*.

After a while, a soldier with ale foam running down his beard leaned forward and called down the table, "Ladies, who would like to join me in my tent after the meal? I will give you a rocking good fuck."

Women gasped. Astra dropped her head, mortified.

Didrik rose and grabbed the man by the tunic. "None of that! If you do not guard your mouth, you will spend the night with your head locked in the *gapestockk!*"

The soldier glanced at the nearby instrument of punishment and chuckled, turning back to his ale cup. Didrik cuffed the soldier on the head and slowly sat down. The other soldiers lowered their voices, but their comments continued more quietly. They snorted and elbowed one another, clearly sharing foul jokes.

Astra and the other women ate in silence. She glanced frequently toward the massive manor doors hoping for her father or Einarr to emerge and release her from this snakepit.

By the time the meal ended, the rain had stopped. The table boards were quickly disassembled and musicians gathered beneath a tent. A man well known for his powerful voice sang a lively tune, then the musicians played their lyres, lutes, and pipes in traditional dance songs. The men circled up and beckoned the women, but none joined in. Three women grabbed their *datters* and hurried off to their lodgings.

Since the women would not dance, a few men took the women's parts, performing faux curtsies with bent wrists as they twirled one another to the laughter of their fellows and even some bystanders. Astra, however, turned her back, wishing she were far away from here. What was Hedda doing? Eating in the manor kitchen, no doubt. If Karin were here, they would go back to the women's house together and talk about all that was happening. She had so much to tell her sister when she got home.

Lost in thought, she did not notice Nikolina until her cousin tapped her shoulder. She carried the baby in a bundle in her arms.

"I cannot believe Dag's mother let me come," Nikolina said breathlessly. "Dag stood up for me for once, since you are here and your father is important."

"Where is Dag?" Astra asked.

Her cousin shrugged. "He said he does not like dancing."

"Would you like to dance?" Astra asked. "They are soldiers, but Didrik is keeping watch."

"I do not think Dag would approve," she said, though she seemed disappointed.

Astra lifted the infant from her cousin's arms. "I will hold the baby."

Nikolina grinned and bounced into the ring. A handsome young soldier held out his hand to her. Seeing them dance, several other women joined, also.

After a few more dances Amalie began to cry. Nikolina came puffing back, flushed and grinning. "That was grand," she gushed, taking Amalie from Astra's arms. "I had better go and feed her. I am sure she is tired."

"I will meet you in the women's cottage," said Astra. "Pick out a good bed for us."

Nikolina gathered the infant and started across the yard, dancing her *datter* as she went.

Astra glanced at the manor but the door remained closed and guarded. She leaned forward with her elbows on her knees to watch the dancers. Unexpectedly, someone sat down beside her. She sat up straight, realizing he was the knight who had ridden beside the king when they arrived.

"Do you not want to dance?" The knight offered her his hand.

She shook her head, abashed. "*Nei, takk.*"

"Are you waiting for someone?" In the waning sunlight the knight's eyes were aqua like the reflection of clouds on a lake. "Your husband? Your betrothed?"

She squirmed. "My father."

He offered his hand again. "Come and dance. The king is here only once. You should enjoy the celebration." There was an insistence in his voice.

Glancing at the manor door once more, she saw that the armed guards still stood before the entrance, unmoving. She was bored and must wait to find out what happened at the meeting with the king. What was the harm in a dance?

She removed her cloak and stood. "Just one dance." He took her hand and they joined the circle.

The knight's dancing was smooth and skillful. His eyes often rested on her face and Astra felt heat rise up her neck. After the dance ended, she pulled away and started for the benches, but the music started again and the knight cajoled her into the circle once more.

After three more dances Astra sat down on a bench to cool off. The knight brought ale for them both and sat beside her.

"What are you called?" he asked.

"Astra. And you?"

"Sir Henrik," he said, "but just Henrik to you."

She felt emboldened. "Why does the king go to Novgorod? I hear it is very far away."

"Norway once held that trading center and the king wants it back," he said. "It is very lucrative."

She did not know what that meant, but it must be good. "How many will he take from Sjodrun?"

Sir Henrik folded his hands over his knee. "As many as he can muster."

"That will be difficult," Astra said, venturing into deeper water. "Our crops are not ready. Who will bring in our winter supply?"

His eyes narrowed. "The people must always be ready to support the king. He is the sovereign."

"But...Lord Jonas has just died," she said. "Can the king not have mercy on us?"

His back stiffened. "Nevertheless..."

Astra looked down at her cup of ale. "I am certain the Lady will do her best."

"That is good to hear."

She glanced up at him.

Sir Henrik squinted at her, then smiled. He walked over to replenish their ale bowls.

Something caught her eye in the shadows beyond the dance circle. A hooded figure leaned against the side of a shed, his face obscured in shadow. Noting the rough clothing and long beard she recognized him as the hunter. Why did he not join the dancing? She motioned him over, but he quickly turned and disappeared.

Sir Henrik returned, handing her another cup. "I have bored you with men's concerns. Would you like to dance again?"

Before she could say no, a clamor arose behind them. The king stomped out of the great manor door, followed by his entourage. The guards marched behind him across the courtyard toward the *stabbur*. Without another word Sir Henrik sprang up, retrieved his sword, and jogged after them. All the soldiers who had been dancing followed as the music faded away.

Astra paled. The meeting must not have gone well. She grabbed her cloak and ran to the manor door, but a servant closed it as she approached. "No one is allowed," he said.

"Christ and all the saints!" she swore.

Astra and a few others waited by the fire as the long summer evening grew dark. Sighing, she gave up and started toward the women's house where Nikolina awaited. Halfway there she heard the manor door open. Vegar, his black cape swinging behind him, emerged. He sheathed his sword and glanced her way, then strode toward her. She hurried on toward the women's house, looking back when she got to the door. He was still coming toward her. With a gasp, she slipped inside the women's house and closed the door.

The few other visiting women were already abed, some sleeping soundly. Nikolina lay in one of the lower bunks nursing Amalie.

"I warmed up the bed for you," she whispered. "Are you all right? You look upset."

Astra sat on the edge of the bed, breathless. "I just saw someone I did not want to see."

A woman shushed them.

Astra whispered into Nikolina's ear, "I have to relieve myself. If he is gone I will go look for Far to find out what happened. Do not stay awake for me."

"I will be here." Nikolina stroked Amalie's head and smiled.

Astra peeked out the door. Lanterns traveled to and fro across the courtyard as people retired for the night. Vegar was not to be seen, nor, unfortunately, was Far. She crept around the side of the house to the path that led to the trees beyond. The night was faintly lit by the last blood-red glow of the midnight-setting sun. When she reached the trees, however, the darkness was deep. Why had she not brought a lantern? She hesitated, listening for the heavy footsteps of ogres. It was said they would snatch maidens and roll away with them in their rolling-breeches. Worse would be a troll, though they were noisy and she would have time to run. She spied a fallen log and crouched behind it.

When she finished, Astra hurried across the open field, stepping high in the dewy grass. She was startled to see three silhouettes headed her way. Firelight from campfires near the *stabbur* glinted faintly off their sword hilts.

Soldiers! Astra felt for her knife, but she had left it in the house, too.

The king's men marched straight at her. She veered toward the nearest structure, a small storage hut, but the soldiers pivoted toward her.

"Astra!" one of them called. They soon caught up and formed a line across her path. "Astra, it is I, Henrik," said he.

She stopped. Why was he intercepting her? Perhaps he had a message.

"Sir Henrik," she said, feigning bravery. "Have you lost your way?"

He laughed. "*Nei*, I just want to speak with you." He took a step closer and held out his hand.

She did not take it. "Do you have news? If not, I must excuse myself. I am expected back at the women's house."

The soldiers spread out around her. Astra tried to push past Sir Henrik's arm but he snatched up her hand. "I will not hurt you. Indeed, I have a pleasant surprise for you."

Astra's breath was shallow and swift. "I...I am too tired. Maybe tomorrow..." She tried to pull away, but he held her fast.

His voice was deep and buttery. "The king would like to meet you. He noticed you and asked us to bring you. Come with us to the guest loft. It is a rare privilege to meet the king."

Astra shook her head and tugged. "*Nei*, I must get back to my cousin. She is waiting for me." She twisted away and tore out running.

They caught up with her easily and one soldier grabbed her about the waist, lifting her off the ground. "You are a spirited one," he jeered. "No wonder the king wants you."

She cried out but he clamped his hand over her mouth. Astra struck at his muscular arms and kicked against his legs.

"Calm down, Astra," said Sir Henrik. "If you are quiet, he can let go. You have nothing to fear. His Majesty only wants to get to know you. After your visit I will see you safely back to your lodging."

Astra stopped struggling, her mind reeling. What did the king truly want? Why would they treat her like this if his intentions were benign?

The soldier removed his hand and set her down. "Will you walk on your own or do I have to carry you?"

Sir Henrik said, "See? You are well. This is a great honor to be summoned by His Majesty." He laid his hand against her back and pushed her toward the guest loft. "All you must do is be polite and show respect."

Astra stumbled forward. How could she refuse? Did the king only want to meet her, as Sir Henrik said? If so, why did he not approach her father first and in the daylight? He had summoned her by force late at night. She feared this meant only one dreadful thing.

Astra glanced toward the manor hoping someone was nearby, but the courtyard was empty. No one could see her. No one but Nikolina would miss her, and she had told Nikolina she might be late.

As she stumbled nearer to the looming *stabbur*, panic charged through Astra's body and she gulped in air. She tried to run again but the soldier grabbed her around her middle and slung her over his shoulder, stifling her breath. Astra beat against his back and kicked at his legs.

"Be still, you little wench," he laughed, slapping her bottom. "You are more trouble than you are worth." He pinned her legs and trudged forward.

At the *stabbur* entrance, two guards lounged on the steps and the soldier set her on her feet. "Do not try anything," he warned.

Other king's men sat around small fires swigging drink. Some reclined under makeshift tents. All eyes were on her. She saw them nudge one another. Some mumbled coarse words and they all laughed.

Sir Henrik offered Astra his hand again. "Are you going to behave?" His voice was as smooth as ice.

She was surrounded by a nest of spiders. What would her mother say to her right now? She would take Astra by the shoulders and look her in the eyes. "Your ancestors are of Viking stock. You are strong, like them." Astra took a breath, smoothed her dress, and raised her chin. "I am ready," she said.

Sir Henrik smiled. "Everything will be well, you shall see. Always remember what a great honor you have received. Wait here." He stepped up the wide treads and rapped on the oaken door. A soldier inside opened it.

"Tell His Majesty I have his guest," said Sir Henrik.

The guard left the door ajar. Astra could see him clamber up the rungs that led to the guest loft.

As she waited, she saw Far's two carved door posts lying on the ground nearby. The thought of his skilled hands on these

The Moon Turned to Blood

intricate carvings somehow gave her comfort. He was not far away. Be strong, she told herself.

The guard descended and motioned Astra inside.

"Do you want me to go with you?" Sir Henrik asked casually. She realized she was not the first girl he had brought to the king.

She nodded. As she followed him in, the scents of newly hewn wood and drying herbs met her. She lifted her skirt and started up the steep ladder treads.

Before he opened the hatch above them, Sir Henrik said, "Remember...the king is God's vicar on earth." He led her up through the hatch door onto the planked floor above. The spacious room was opulently appointed and lit by dozens of beeswax candles. Embroidered hangings adorned the walls and a large bearskin rug was spread over the floor of the sitting area. The open doors of a shuttered bed revealed linen pillows and a white reindeer pelt...Kjell's costly skin. Mother Mary, she thought, what would he think if he knew where it lay? Her legs started to shiver.

"Your Majesty," announced Sir Henrik, bowing. "Astra Svensdatter."

The king was seated on an elaborately carved *kubestol* chair, dressed in leggings and a richly embroidered tunic. His light hair was tied back. He was not unhandsome with his strong jawbone and fjord-blue eyes that glinted in the candlelight. Fine lines creased his temples, but he appeared younger than he had sitting atop his steed in chainmail.

She curtsied as best she could.

"Very good, Henrik," said the king. His smile welcomed her as if she had come of her own free will. "And her father?"

"Sven Larsson, a *Thing* member, but not a nobleman. He will not object."

"Astra." The king repeated her name. "She is lovely. Well done, Henrik."

Sir Henrik bowed, then backed down the steps, pulling the loft's entrance hatch closed.

King Magnus gazed at Astra. "You are indeed beautiful, my dear girl. You may remove your cloak." When she did, he motioned her to a chair with a brocaded cushion.

"Join me in some wine, young Astra," said the king. He filled two golden goblets with red wine and offered her a heavy chalice. Her hand visibly shook as she accepted it.

"*Skål*," said the king and raised his goblet.

"*Skål*," whispered Astra.

He drank, swished the wine in his cheeks, closed his eyes and swallowed. "This is a special night for you," he said, smiling and looking her over once more. "Tonight, I am just Magnus to you, in case you are wondering how to address me."

She searched for words with which to respond, but none came. Maybe wine would give her courage…or at least dull her fear. She swallowed a mouthful, shuddering from its unaccustomed bite.

"This is a fine wine, *nei*?" the king asked. "It is French. Lady Marta had been saving it."

"I suppose, Your Majesty… Magnus."

"Take my word for it. Lady Marta gave me her best." He poured more for himself.

Astra drank again and felt the warmth spread, slowly quelling her quaking limbs. She studied the chalice in her hands, Lady Marta's goblet.

"Astra?" King Magnus smiled. "You are not yet betrothed, I gather."

"I know not. You should ask my father." She gulped more wine and shivered at the tartness.

"My knight tells me you are not. Soon you will be, I am sure."

Sir Henrik, that snake, had inquired of her. Her anger steadied her voice. "When the time comes, I am sure my father will ask me so I may decide."

The king laughed and downed his wine. "You will decide? You are spirited. I like that."

He refilled his goblet. They sat in silence as he watched her intently and drank. She sipped several times, fingering the bejeweled goblet. The room began to spin.

After he finished the next cup of wine and poured still more, the king's expression changed. One eyebrow raised. A corner of his mouth turned slightly upward in a wry smile.

Astra's face burned. She glanced at the floor hatch where she knew the guard waited just below.

The king scooted his chair close to Astra and leaned forward, taking her free hand between his palms. "Do you know why you are here?"

Her eyes moistened. She looked down to hide her tears and shrugged. "To meet you?"

He kissed her palm. "I have been traveling for many weeks away from my castle in Sweden, and away from my wife. You are young and ripe for marriage. You must already know that you are attractive to men."

"Sire...please, Your Majesty." A tear fell onto the back of his hand.

He touched her mouth. "*Nei*, do not speak. You are innocent, thus all the more appealing. That is why I selected you for this distinction. I desire you tonight. Do not fear. I am gentle."

"Your Majesty." She swiped at her tears. "My family will be shamed…"

"Certainly not!" He waved a hand dismissively. "But no one need know unless you tell them. Even if they knew, it would be an honor, not a disgrace. Besides, I hear women have their ways of hiding such things. I will merely lead the way for your soon-to-be husband."

At this, the king pulled Astra to her feet. He untied her head linen and tugged her braid loose. She felt it spill down her back. Then he guided her quivering body to stand beside the luxurious bed.

"Do not worry," he said, unpinning the brooches at the shoulders of her shift. It slipped to her feet. "If you are indeed unplucked, there will be some pain, but it will quickly pass. It is the way for all maidens. The next time there will be only pleasure." In one smooth motion he lifted her under-dress over her head and pulled her arms free from the sleeves. She clasped her arms over her bared breasts.

Mother Mary help me! she cried inwardly.

The king leaned her backward until she fell naked among the furs. She could not breathe. He kneeled over her on the bed and pulled her arms free, raising them above her head with one ring-studded hand while he caressed her breasts with the other.

"Is this truly your first time?" His gray-stone eyes were almost sympathetic.

She clenched her fists, knowing no one may strike the king, yet itching to do so. Tears traced down her temples.

"Ah, it is. Do not resist and it will go easier for you. There is only one first time." He said this casually, as if giving her advice on falling off a horse. "Some say they even enjoy it."

He kissed her mouth. She pursed her lips tightly but his kiss became insistent as his tongue wormed its way between her teeth.

He pulled back. "Do you not enjoy a kiss? Surely a beauty like you has been kissed before."

Astra turned her head away from him.

"You have. I thought so. Just be still. I will do the work."

She lay frozen, as stiff as a stave.

He let go of her hands and ran his finger down her neck and torso. Astra whimpered. He untied the cord of his leggings and pushed them down. The weight of his body expelled her breath. Astra shut her eyes, hiding the only thing she could from him.

Prying her knees apart with his thighs, he gave a thrust. Pain ripped through her hidden place and she felt she had been stabbed. She cried out and dug her fingers into the flesh of his back.

Heedless and panting, the king assailed against her strongly until he shuddered and groaned, suddenly spent. He fell heavily upon her. His heart pounded against her chest and his wine-

The Moon Turned to Blood

soaked breath smothered her. She turned her head and wept into the embroidered feather pillow.

Soon his breathing slowed into the rhythm of deep sleep. He began to snore. She inched out from beneath him and he shifted slightly, but his snoring continued. Slipping away, she stared briefly at his nearly naked form, his leggings around his ankles.

Astra retrieved her clothing and dressed quickly. Rage blew through her like a northerly wind. She thought of pounding him with her fists, screaming into his ears, striking him with his sword. But of course, in peril of her life, she could not do anything. How many other girls had he used like this? Her fingers shook as she braided her hair and tugged on her boots.

So, this was love-making, what men will do anything to obtain. Did some women truly enjoy it? Her virtue was gone in a few heaving moments of pleasure for him. This sin was visited upon her by a powerful man whom she could not refuse. God's vicar on earth indeed! Astra spat into his wine goblet.

As she skittered down the ladder, she formed curses in her mind that she wished to hurl at the king, but she spewed them at a startled Sir Henrik instead. "You vile son of a wolf! You are Satan in sheep's wool. How could you let this happen to me?" She tore out for the women's house as if chased by a bull.

Sir Henrik ran a few steps after her, calling, "Wait! I have something for you." She stopped and threw a stone at him, though she was too far away now for it to strike him. Sir Henrik halted and tossed up his hands. "You should take this!" he called. "You will regret it if you do not."

Astra stumbled to the well and flushed herself with water again and again until her dress was drenched. Even so, she knew she could never wash away this sin perpetrated on her.

Safe in bed next to Nikolina, Astra clamped her arms tightly over her chest. Again and again the scene replayed itself. She felt hatred as she had never felt before. What would Far say if he knew she was despoiled? What would Einarr say? For now, she must act as if nothing happened… but she would make a plan.

An owl hooted. Tiny feet scurried over the rafter above her head. Buried under the sheepskin, with Nikolina's back to warm her, Astra's quivering slowly abated. She mouthed the *Pater Noster*. As her mind drifted toward sleep, she suddenly knew what she must do. She would have to act quickly.

Chapter 7

The early light of mid-summer and sounds of the village stirred Kjell awake. He rolled over under his deerskin, wishing he could sleep a while longer. The previous night had been long. The music around the outdoor fire had continued late into the night, interspersed by the unruly outbursts of soldiers' laughter. Later still, he was wakened by the hoofbeats of horses arriving, snorting as they headed toward the stable.

A servant boy walked closely past him, nearly tripping over Kjell's bivouac. He grumbled and the boy rushed off. Kjell was anxious to get his money from the lady and be on his way. He rose and relieved himself in a nearby bush. Returning to where he had slept, he pulled venison strips from his pack for his breakfast and fed some to his dogs. He stashed his bedding and his saddlebags in the hollow of an oak.

Kjell ambled toward the courtyard. Something was already roasting over the outdoor fire, a calf from the looks of it. Soon servants appeared and set up boards and benches. Soldiers straggled from their camp toward the tables where large bowls of porridge and *brød* were being set out for them. Kjell recalled the commotion he had heard across the yard at the soldiers' camp, laughing, shouting, and a woman's muffled scream, poor lass. He had been inclined to investigate, but the thick knot of heavily armed soldiers surrounding the entrance to the king's quarters dissuaded him.

Untethering Thorden and whistling for the dogs, he led them away from the hubbub toward the stream he had noticed as he rode in. He passed the horse barns where stablemen were brushing down the royal horses, then headed down a footpath alongside the pasture. He could hear the water tumbling over rocks the closer he got, and he stopped at a large pool to wash himself. The dogs lapped their fill, then Lope, the youngest, nipped Lysglint. These two spun into the stream to chase one another before heading straight toward Kjell.

He cried, "*Nei, nei!*" crab-walking backward up the bank, but he was too slow. The dogs ran to him and shook vigorously, splattering him with icy water. He scrambled to his feet, then chased them along the bank, yelling and laughing, until they jumped into the water again to escape.

Wet already, Kjell waded into the pool, the glacier run-off taking away his breath. He rubbed his face and hair, then stripped and scrubbed his shirt and pantaloons with a stone. He wanted Oda to be pleased when she saw him. Wading in deeper he washed himself before sloshing back onto the bank. There he shook his unkempt mane, shedding droplets in a wide circle about him before squeezing water from his hair and beard.

Glancing up and down the stream and seeing no one, Kjell climbed the embankment and found a sunny spot to dry off. He arranged his clothes in a patch of sunlight, then laid back to stare into the clouds that passed overhead. He thought of Oda, his lovely, lonely wife, and little Egill. Maybe their son was walking by now, even saying a word or two. He longed to hold the child, but he ached to make love to his wife.

Just then the dogs perked up their ears. Kjell then heard voices approaching from upstream and the dogs ran barking toward them. Kjell grabbed his wet clothing but could not climb into his soaking pantaloons before two soldiers came into view. His heart raced. His weapons were strapped to the saddle of his horse that was tied to a tree further up the slope. He whistled the dogs back.

The soldiers approached. "What are you doing here?" one asked. He was tall and thin, and he rested his hand on the hilt of his sword.

"Bathing. And you?" Kjell searched their faces for recognition as he slowly backed uphill toward his weapons.

The soldiers raised buckets. "Water for washing."

The second soldier, burnt-haired and red-of-cheek, peered at Kjell and took a step forward.

Kjell's body tensed. He knew this face. Where had he seen him before? He struggled into his pantaloons, saying, "I am a hunter, just passing through with my goods for sale. The lady purchased my pelts and I am waiting for payment before heading out."

The thin soldier said, "I saw him with a load of furs camped out by the smithy."

The other peered at him once more. "I thought I had seen you somewhere." He shrugged. "Well, I hope you can collect. You better get back to your belongings before they are confiscated."

Kjell breathed again. "*Takk*, I will."

Both soldiers filled their buckets.

Kjell grabbed his shirt and backed up the hill, watching the king's men until they lifted their sloshing pails from the stream and started back up the embankment.

Christ's blood! That red-headed soldier had been in the inn three years prior! Thanks be to God that the man did not place Kjell's heavily-bearded face, at least not yet. With trembling hands, he hurriedly mounted Thorden and galloped back to his camp. He needed to get away from Sjodrun as soon as he could. In the meantime, he would stay out of sight.

Chapter 8

When they awoke, Nikolina quizzed Astra about her crying in the night. Astra brushed off her cousin's questions, lying that she had her monthlies. Nikolina dressed and hurried back to her husband's house to make breakfast for the family. Astra was grateful her cousin had no time for further questions. She could not speak about what happened to her last night. She could tell no one, not ever.

When Astra finally stepped outside, having lain abed until the other women were gone, she was met by a sunlit morning. She blinked at the brightness. A bokfink chirped in a hazel bush as she passed, and she watched it flit to the ground for insects. The sun warmed her head, yet the world seemed darker, forever changed. She strode toward the large crowd that had gathered around the *Thing* meeting circle in the center of the courtyard. All were quiet as everyone awaited the king.

Ringing the perimeter of the gathering, guards held lances at attention. The six council members, including Far and Vegar, sat on benches in the roped-off circle for *Thing* members only. Lady Marta and Einarr sat on chairs just outside the ropes.

How could Astra bear to see the king again? Memories of last night caused her empty belly to writhe. She stood near a broad-shouldered villager, glancing often toward the large guest house in dread. Everyone seemed to be holding their breath.

Finally, after a long delay, a page ran up and whispered something into Far's ear. Her father stood, picked up the carved staff of the elected council leader, and stepped forward. "Let us delay no longer," he said. He beckoned someone seated nearby and the man rose. It was Sir Henrik.

Astra gasped and quickly covered her mouth. Loathing oozed from every pore in her body. She wanted to slay him.

Far said to him, "You are to represent the king."

Sir Henrik stepped over the rope into the circle and faced the council members. Astra seethed, gripping herself about the waist until her fingernails dug into her sides.

"Speak your peace," Far said. "What says the king?"

"There is no need for niceties," Sir Henrik replied curtly. "Have you collected the war levy?"

Far nervously cleared his throat. "Sir Henrik, Sjodrun has collected what we could from all tenants and landowners, each giving sacrificially as we are able. The harvest is not in and many of us have recently paid our tithes to the bishop. Here is what we can spare at this time."

Another council member set a small cask at Sir Henrik's feet. The Sjodrun clerk opened it, and he and a squire squatted down to count the contents. Coins clinked as stacks grew in the dirt beside the cask. No one spoke as the minutes dragged on. The clerk and squire each wrote figures onto a piece of velum. Comparing the numbers, they nodded at one another. The clerk stated the amount.

Sir Henrik took a deep breath. His jaw tensed. "This will not do. No half-payment is allowed. You have supplied only poorly trained farm boys as soldiers, but the war levy is due in full when the king demands it. This war will benefit the whole country and you must do your part."

A bent, aged man beside Astra hissed under his breath, "The whole country, eh? When we are cold in our graves." Someone elbowed him.

Far licked his lips. "We humbly ask that you receive this partial payment with our promise to bring the remainder to Oslo before winter sets in."

At this, Sir Henrik roared, "What good will it do us in Oslo when we need it in Novgorod? *Nei.* The king requires the full amount. Go back to your caches and store houses and gather anything of value. We leave by the hour of *sext* today."

Lady Marta stood up. "Sir Henrik, you must ask the king to have mercy on us. Any more than this will leave his people in hunger."

"You feed them," Sir Henrik said. "You heard the king's demand. He expects the levy in whatever commodity we can carry with us. Horses, weapons, tools...otherwise there will be a doubling of the levy and the king will simply take what he needs. If you do not comply, you risk losing the king's protection."

The wizened man beside Astra mumbled, "What protection has he ever given us?" A neighbor shushed him.

Lady Marta's usually stoic mien was fraught as she nervously smoothed her head linen. She faced Sir Henrik again. "We have other obligations, as you must know. Tithes have already been paid, as required, and rents are due after the harvest. That is when the rest of the king's levy will be available."

Astra could see Sir Henrik's eyes narrow. "I am afraid you are wrong, Lady Marta. It is all due now. Sjodrun clearly needs to learn obedience to the king. I will suggest to him an immediate change of lordship for this backwater village."

He lifted the heavy chest, fitting it beneath his arm, and pushed through the crowd toward the guest loft. Guards followed him, walking backward, spears extended toward the townspeople.

"The king cannot command water from a stone," wheezed the old man beside Astra. He shook his fist at Sir Henrik's back and yelled, "It is cruel!"

Sir Henrik's head swiveled toward the speaker, though the old man was short and hidden by the crowd. Astra watched the faces of the townsfolk grimace in despair.

The *Thing* members appeared dazed, looking about at one another in confusion. Lady Marta motioned for them to follow her to the manor house. On his way, Far caught Astra's eye and she saw the strain on his brow. She was ashamed to hold his gaze. How much worse would he feel if he knew her dreadful secret?

Many in the crowd dissipated, but others followed the knight and his guards at a distance. Astra was drawn after them.

Someone cried out, "We do not see the king until he wants money for a foolish war."

"He asks too much," a woman shouted. "We will all starve."

"Dribblers and thieves, all of you," yelled someone else.

Sir Henrik ignored the protests until he stopped at the *kirke* and turned to address the villagers. Several more soldiers left their places near the guest house to back up the guards. The scraping of steel nailed everyone to their places as the king's men drew swords and spread out.

Was Sir Henrik reconsidering? Astra wondered briefly. She stood behind a tall man so as not to be seen.

"I saw no contribution by the *kirke*," Sir Henrik shouted for all to hear. "I am certain this was an oversight. You have recently paid your bishop's tithes, which is the reason you do not have the king's war levy. That can be rectified."

Momentarily, Father Johan bent his head beneath the lintel as he emerged from the *kirke*. He faced Sir Henrik defiantly. "How dare you come to God's house with weapons drawn? You may enter in peace, however. The confessional is always open to you."

There was a low murmur of laughter among the crowd.

Sir Henrik chuckled, then used the honey-laced voice with which he had enticed Astra. "What gift does the *kirke* bring to support her king?"

Astra was incensed. How dare he?

Father Johan's face twitched. "The *kirke* is not required to give gifts to the king, though the king may always bring his tithes to God's house."

Sir Henrik sneered. "The gift of a loyal priest to his sovereign, the gift for a holy cause. This is a crusade."

"A war to capture a trading center is not a holy war." Father Johan planted his feet in the doorway, blocking it.

"Whatever the king does is a holy cause," replied Sir Henrik.

Silently, Astra raged.

Father Johan's voice wavered. "This may be, but I am the keeper of God's house."

Sir Henrik leaned over and pressed his face close to the father's. "Where is the bishops' tithe? The bishop will not miss it. That would help to settle the debt."

"*Nei, nei...* I cannot, I will not. You must kill me first." Father Johan bared his chest.

"Search the *kirke*," Sir Henrik said. He jerked Father Johan away from the entrance by the arm, and a guard held Father Johan's arms behind him while two others ducked through the door. Benches crashed to the floor and heavy items thudded to the floor. The crowd cried out in horror. Soon the guards emerged with a small locked casket and handed it to Sir Henrik.

Father Johan tried to pull away from the guards. "These tithes are for the archbishop in Trondelag, and for the pope in Avignon," he cried. "It is desecration to steal from God. Those who do, will forever dwell in Hades!"

"Indeed, that may be true," said Sir Henrik, "yet I serve only His Majesty the King." He took the cask, nodded to the soldiers, and headed to the *stabbur*. Guards formed a line, keeping the people at bay.

Abhorrence for Sir Henrik filled Astra's soul. He had orchestrated unholy violations, first of her body and now the *kirke*. If only she had a sword! She gritted her teeth against the angry tears that burned her eyes.

The Moon Turned to Blood

A man in the crowd yelled at the soldiers, "Filthy heathens, the lot of you!"

"Robbers!" someone else shouted. "You will end in hell!"

A large woman, whom Astra had seen working in the kitchen, shook her fist and cursed, "You curs! Suck the teat of your bitch dog mother!"

The crowd slowly dispersed and Astra trudged back to the manor, clenching her fists until her fingernails brought red crescents to her palms. She paced at the bottom of the steps, waiting for her father and plotting impossible revenge on Sir Henrik. Where was Far's sword? She would kill the knight as he mounted his horse. She would call out the king for what he had done to her before the entire village and they would... *nei*, they would do nothing. Astra sat down at the bottom of the manor steps. She buried her face in her lap in unutterable rage.

The sky clouded over, becoming a mottled gray blanket of sadness. When the manor door finally creaked open, Astra looked up. Vegar and her father stopped above her on the porch, engaged in a tense conversation. Their heads were bent close together and they appeared to be arguing. After several exchanges of intense conversation, they stepped back. Far smiled and they grasped one another's hands in apparent agreement. Vegar turned and, not noticing Astra, hurried away.

Her father descended more slowly. Astra stood up and grabbed his arm. "What happened, Far?"

"We have a plan," he said, peeling her hand from his forearm. "I have an errand. We will talk later." He hurried away.

She ran after him. "But did you hear Sir Henrik robbed the *kirke*? He stole from God!"

He kept walking. "*Ja*, we heard. Do not worry. We will get the tithes back."

"Will you have to give the king your earnings from the *stabbur* posts? We can give him Kvikke..."

Far did not turn around. "Go and ask Gudrun how you can help."

"But Far..."

He trotted away.

Astra quietly entered the manor house and scanned the large room for Gudrun. Sitting at a table near the dais sat Lady Marta, once more engaged in a conversation with Sir Aksel, his wife, and Einarr. Ale horns sat on the table. The lady's countenance appeared much relieved. Sir Aksel tapped his cup against Lady Marta's. The visitor must be lending them the money. Astra sighed in relief.

Einarr, however, leaned away from the table, tapping it with his finger. Just then he glanced up and spotted Astra. His eyes widened and he nodded slightly toward the side door. Astra hurried out, feeling hopeful.

She waited there, pacing and chewing on a torn nail. Before long, Einarr burst out and walked past her, motioning for her to follow.

He led her through a field of tall grass to the bathhouse and stopped behind it, out of sight of other structures. There he took her in his arms.

"What happened?" she asked, gripping him tightly. "Far said the levy is being paid, but he did not say how."

"Do not fret about that now," Einarr replied. He kissed her cheeks, then her mouth. His hand moved up to her breast.

The memory of the king's hands on her brought a rush of panic. "*Nei!*" She pushed away. "Not here!"

"What is wrong?" He tried to pull her back.

She backed up. "I just want to know what happened. Are you going to war with the king?"

"*Nei*," he said. "I have received a reprieve for now because of my father's death." He reached for her.

She crossed her arms over her chest and stepped back. "Did you talk to your mother about us?"

He glanced up into the trees. "I did, but she and father had plans for me before he died."

"What plans?" Her heart thrashed like a fish fighting the hook.

He turned away and spat on the ground. "My mother is trying to control my life, but I will not accept her wishes."

Astra moved close and grabbed his face with both hands. Their eyes met. "I think Far has received an offer… from Vegar. You must act quickly, if it is not too late already."

He hugged her tightly to him. "By all the gods and Odin's beard! Tell your father to wait. When the king leaves, I will tell mother I must marry you. I will come and find you. Do not give up."

She pushed away. "We leave for home tomorrow, so you had better hurry." Then she turned and ran away. Her eyes burned and her mind was a tumbling boulder.

Astra and Gudrun stood in the anteroom of the manor house staring at a large pile of furs. Astra was sure they were the hunter's.

"Put me to work," she said. "I need to stay busy."

The head servant smiled at her wearily. "Astra, my girl, we need all the help we can get. Would you take these to our boys? M'Lady is donating them to each Sjodrun soldier."

"Of course." Working would keep her thoughts distracted.

Gudrun squeezed her shoulder.

As Astra loaded her arms with pelts, she asked nonchalantly, "What is Sir Aksel's business here?"

"I do not know for sure, but…" Gudrun hesitated.

Astra shifted the pelts to balance them and whispered, "I will say nothing."

Gudrun whispered, "There is talk of a betrothal, even amidst all this commotion, if you please." She shook her head. "It is too much."

"Who?" Astra's pulse quickened in excitement for her friend, Hedda.

Gudrun shrugged. "I cannot say. Do not repeat this. It is only a rumor." She turned away and yelled orders to several servants.

Astra wove her way around piles of sundry supplies and out the side door, thinking about a possible betrothal for her friend. Though Hedda was younger than Astra, girls of high status were often betrothed early and married when they came of age. Sir Aksel was wealthy and he must have a son. She hoped he was the eldest, and even more so, that he was handsome. Did Hedda know?

As she headed toward the yard to deliver the pelts, she stopped dead, dropping several skins on the ground. What if Sir Aksel had a *datter*?

Astra distributed pelts to the recruits, the young men and boys who would be missing for the harvest and putting their lives at risk. "Courtesy of the Lady. God's speed," she told each one. She returned to the anteroom for more pelts, picturing the mountain man's long beard, shaggy hair, and stained clothing. Was he still at the manor or already on his way home?

Servants rushed back and forth through the yard in a web of activity. They filled ale flasks, mended leathers, fitted boots, and issued cloaks. Each recruit was given a weapon, a long knife or club, and a hastily made wooden shield. Younger lads sparred clumsily in the open grass with sticks. Children scurried through the melee delivering cheeses, cured meats and dried fish that were tucked into satchels and saddlebags. Young pages carried messages between the manor, the workshops, and the *stabbur*. A stream of black smoke lazed over the birch trees where the blacksmith's hammer banged relentlessly.

Astra passed by a mother urging her teenage son not to take chances as she filled his satchel with dried foods. The boy's father sharpened an ax for him, his face grim. Another father admonished his son to be brave, to learn from the other soldiers, and to make God and his family proud. The boy, no taller than Astra, wiped tears with his sleeve.

Near the guest house she heard Sir Henrik's voice giving commands as he oversaw the preparations. She watched him from a distance, wishing she dared spit on him.

Down to her last pelt, Astra noticed a young man loading supplies into a satchel. She was about to offer him the remaining deer skin when Nikolina came running across the grass.

"Dag! Dag!" her cousin cried. "Please do not go! What about me and the baby?" She threw herself into his arms.

"*Nei*, I must go," he said, taking the offered pelt from Astra. Dag was a fine-looking young man, slender and lightly bearded. Together they made a handsome couple and Astra could see why Niki loved him.

"Most soldiers do not have children," Nikolina wailed. "I need you."

Dag caressed her cheek. "You know why I must go. We need the money."

"Not like this, Dag, please." Nikolina looked at Astra and said, "I cannot live with his mother without him."

"You can, and you will, for us," Dag said. "With the king's wages we can buy land away from my parents. How else could I do that?" He took her in his arms and kissed her forehead.

"But she is so cruel," Nikolina moaned. She turned to Astra again and said, "You see what I mean?" She lifted up the wimple that held her hair to show them a welt at the base of her neck. "A stick, for not starting breakfast soon enough."

Astra cringed.

Dag said, "I will speak to her and make her promise not to beat you."

Nikolina looked at Astra and lit up. "You can save me, cousin. I could live with you until Dag comes back."

Astra paused, unsure what to say. She did not think her father would agree.

Dag glanced at Astra. "She must stay with my family." He strapped the pelt onto his pack.

Nikolina threw herself into Dag's arms. "What if you do not return?"

Dag pushed her back gently. "You have to be strong. I will come back. Pray for me."

Astra drifted away to give them privacy. Her mother always said that arguing was a bad omen on the cusp of leave-taking.

Spying her father as he crossed the yard on some errand, Astra ran to him and snatched his sleeve. "Far, Nikolina's new husband is going to fight. She asked if she could live with us while he is gone. Otherwise, she will have to live with her horrid mother-in-law."

"What did her husband say to this?" Far asked without stopping.

"He said *nei*, but…"

"Then *nei* it is. All want to climb the lowest fence, Astra. She must obey her husband."

Astra headed back to the manor house. She did not have the heart to tell Nikolina Far's answer right now.

After midday the troops gathered en masse in the courtyard. A large crowd had formed. The armored knights mounted, assisted by their squires. Much shoving and confusion ensued regarding where each horse and rider should be placed in the lineup. The conscripted farm horses stamped their hooves and side-stepped restlessly, testing the lucky riders' patience and skills. The great majority of the soldiers were on foot bringing up the rear, including Dag.

Pressed close in by the crowd, Astra pondered their fate, grateful that Einarr was not among them. Some might not return home. Some might be maimed. She vowed to offer daily prayers for Dag and the Sjodrun boys… for Sir Henrik, she would pray that he be run through with a lance. For the king... spiteful thoughts welled up inside her.

Dag stood near the center of the group of foot soldiers. Nikolina watched, standing beside her in-laws. Streams ran down her cheeks. Astra was filled with pity. She must soon add to her cousin's grief by telling Nikolina she could not come home with them.

At the front of the line, flags carried by heralds waved in the summer breeze. Lady Marta waited on a wooden platform near the gate, accompanied by Einarr, Sven, Vegar, and Sir Aksel. Father Johan was noticeably absent.

A trumpet blasted. With great pomp, flanked by Sir Henrik and Sjodrun's own Sir Jokkum, the king's grand steed high-stepped across the courtyard. King Magnus was dressed in his colored vestments and wore a helmet with a plume dancing above it. His majestic horse was adorned with ornate trappings and the black mane and tail dazzled with braided ribbons.

The crowd parted.

As the king moved regally through the onlookers, he lifted his visor and swiveled his steel-framed face to survey the crowd and accept their obeisance.

Astra felt ill. She pulled her shawl over her head and looked away.

The king reached the front of the column and stopped beside the platform where Lady Marta awaited. She curtsied deeply before she spoke. Her voice was thin in the tension-charged air, and barely audible over the crowd. Astra strained to listen. "...I wish you success in your quest," she was saying, "... honoring us with your presence... God's speed, Your Majesty."

The king replied, turning his head to address the crowd. "I will not forget the generosity of Sjodrun. By God's grace I will send all your young men home unscathed. Pray for our success."

I will pray, thought Astra, that you receive an injury that renders you impotent so you will never deflower another maiden.

"God's will be done," said the king. Then he spoke to Einarr. "Come forward."

Einarr climbed onto the platform beside his mother.

King Magnus said to him, "When I return to Oslo, I will send for you. Until then, I trust Sjodrun into your care and that of your mother. If you do well, you may become a knight and follow in your father's footsteps."

Einarr bowed. "I am honored, Your Majesty."

The crowd murmured. Astra could not catch her breath. Einarr's fate had been starkly laid out before her by the king. He would go to Oslo, become a knight, then a lord. Lords married ladies, not farmers' *datters*.

Einarr said, "May I speak?"

The king gestured his assent.

"Respectfully, I must speak on behalf of what my father would say, and register my complaint about the treatment of our priest and the desecration of the *kirke*."

The king interrupted him. "You are not your father."

Absolute silence smothered the crowd.

"If you give any thought to your future, young man," said the king, "you will hold your loose tongue until the proper time to raise concerns. These matters are settled elsewhere. But to be clear, the levy has been fully paid and the tithe returned to your priest."

The crowd remained silent. Lady Marta dropped to her knees and pulled Einarr down with her. "Your Majesty, you must forgive my foolish son. The boy is out of his mind with sorrow. I will instruct him on the ways of honor. He is a loyal subject, as are we all." She bowed her forehead down to the boards and forced Einarr to do the same.

"Rise," King Magnus said. "I see you have a handful in this lad. Because of your husband, M'Lady, this indiscretion is forgotten. Discipline is what he needs to comprehend his duties."

She rose with help from Einarr and said, "I am grateful, my king."

"Your Majesty," Einarr said, head bowed.

The king scanned the village folk once more. His gaze seemed to land momentarily on each face, as if memorizing these reluctant subjects. Astra did not turn aside quickly enough and their eyes met for a brief moment. He registered no recognition, but gave a slight nod to Sir Henrik. Astra saw the knight slip something into a boy's hand.

An unbearable flame spread up into Astra's face. She bent over to examine her shoe, fearful that others might have noticed where the king had looked. She slid off the shoe and shook an imaginary stone from it. When she looked up again, however, all eyes were on the departing troops.

The king signaled the heralds to start out, and the horses fell in line as the entourage filed slowly through the gate. Mothers and wives followed, waving and crying. Astra backed up against a stone fence. Her breath was jagged as she watched them go.

While everyone else was attending to the departing men, the boy to whom Sir Henrik had given something appeared at her side.

"Are you Astra?" he asked.

She cocked her head. "How did you know?"

"Here." He drew something from inside his shirt and pushed it toward her with both hands. Instinctively, she reached out and he dropped a velvet bag onto her palm. She quickly clutched it and tucked it into her pouch. Without another word the boy spun and disappeared among the onlookers.

Astra looked to see if anyone had noticed, but only a small girl stared at her, thumb in her mouth. Her mother bent and lifted the tot to her shoulders, pointing to the departing king.

Astra trembled. What had she been given? Had the king paid her for her services like a common whore? She had no time to think further as Nikolina broke through the crowd and ran toward her, the baby wrapped to her chest.

Her cousin fell against Astra's neck. "What did your Far say?" she cried. "Please let me come."

"Oh, cousin," Astra whispered, hugging her. "I wish we could. Far says we have too many mouths to feed now, and no extra bed. I am sorry."

Nikolina began to sob into her hands. Astra led her to a bench where they sat down until Nikolina's ragged breaths calmed. Astra wiped the tears off the baby's head. They sat in silence for a few minutes, then Nikolina stood up to go. "Pray for me," she said, "and for Dag."

Astra squeezed her hand before her cousin shuffled away. She felt sorry for Nikolina's sad situation, but she had chosen her road and must travel it. Astra breathed a sigh of relief.

As the crowd began to disperse, Astra's father approached her. His face revealed nothing of his mood. He led her to a quiet spot outside the manor grounds where they sat on a fallen log. There he drew a scroll from beneath his tunic. "It is time I shared this with you." He unrolled the parchment and laid it on the log between them. "This is the news I was telling you about. I have made a marriage contract for you, Little Sparrow."

She stared at the calfskin parchment. Unable to read it for herself, she must wait for Far to tell her the name of her future husband. Let there be a miracle, Mother Mary. Let it be Einarr.

Far took her hand. "This news might not be what you hoped, but you will learn to care for Vegar..."

She jerked her hand away and shouted, "*Nei, nei*, Far. It should be Einarr! He is going to ask you as soon as he can."

Her father touched her shoulder. "But Einarr did not ask. He said nothing to me at all."

The Moon Turned to Blood

Her eyes burned. "We promised each other. He will talk to you soon, I know he will."

"My *datter*, listen. Einarr has not spoken to me, but Vegar has. He is wealthy. You will have a good life, an easy life. Einarr now has heavy responsibilities and will someday serve the king. He must marry the *datter* of a nobleman, not a farmer. Being childhood friends does not a marriage make."

She could not stem the tears. "But you are not just a farmer, you are a respected *Thing* member."

Her father reached out for her. "Oh, dear *datter*, the bargain is struck. I know you are not pleased now, but it is a good match, the best someone from a family like ours could make. You will want for nothing."

She stood up and backed away. "Vegar is old, Far. He is arrogant and smug, and ugly. I can never be happy with him. Please, Far, you can delay the contract."

Her father got up and took her by the shoulders. "Astra, stop this! You are acting like a child. This is part of growing up. The betrothal will not be announced until *Jul*, and Vegar is willing to postpone the wedding until the next summer."

She twisted away, glaring at him as if he were the Satan himself. "Einarr loves me and we will marry. Somehow we will!"

No one was in the women's house so Astra slammed the door and threw herself onto the bed, sobbing. How much could she endure? First the king— God, Mary, and Saint Olav, damn him! And now Vegar? Where was Einarr? "The *djevel* take you, too!" she screamed into her pillow.

When her rage finally abated, it hardened into resolve. She sat up. She must act quickly. She would tell Einarr what Far had done. He must go to her father immediately and offer a bride price more valuable than Vegar could afford.

She straightened her clothing and fixed her hair. As she marched determinedly toward the manor, head down, she nearly bumped into a man coming straight for her. His black cloak formed a wall.

"Vegar!" she cried.

"My lady," Vegar said, "I did not mean to startle you. I was seeking you."

"Were you?" Her voice was cold.

"Indeed. And here you are." He swept his hand toward the manor house. "Will you come and sit with me for a bit?" His eyes were troubled. Far must have told him of her reaction to the betrothal.

She might as well face him now. "I am going that way anyway," she said and walked ahead of him across the grass.

The hall was nearly empty as servants swept the floor and took down boards. Vegar indicated a bench against the wall in the far corner and they sat.

Astra kept a hand's span between them and pressed her palms together between her knees.

In a hushed tone he asked, "Your father spoke to you?"

"*Ja.*" She stared at the glowing coals of the fire.

He paused, then said, "I know I am older than you, but you will find me a good husband. I have much land, many fields of rye, flax, and oats, even wheat from England, and many horses which I know you love. You can bring your mare with you and ride whenever you like."

She glanced at his dark eyes, then studied her skirt. He had inquired about her, about her new horse, her personal affairs.

When she remained quiet, he continued, "I have servants. I also have a large house, not this large, but more than adequate. I have tenants to work the land and enough property to divide among many children. I will help your family, should they ever need anything. What say you?"

It sounded like he was giving her a choice, which was more than Far had done. She knew he expected her to agree.

It came to her that a wealthy man would want an untouched maiden. If Vegar knew about the king he would break the agreement without delay. She should tell him. But she dared not, not until she had spoken to Einarr.

"I, I just found out about your offer and I am not prepared to answer…" She glanced at the door. She should run.

"There is no rush." Vegar laid his silky hand on hers.

She felt as if a snake had slithered onto it. Only with effort did she resist the urge to shake it off. "Good sir, I need more time."

"I can wait. Take time to speak with your mother. I will come later to confirm our alliance."

She met his dark gaze. Alliance? She was only an item to be traded for the benefit of others after all, like most maidens. "It is so … sudden," she said.

Vegar's lips drew his weathered face into an unaccustomed smile. "Sudden to you, but not to me. I noticed you last *Jul*. You do not know me. Let me tell you what kind of man I am." He leaned back against the wall. "I am generous and I keep my word. I was married but as you know, my wife died in childbirth, as did the baby. I am getting older and I want a family, offspring to inherit what I have worked hard to build—my home, my estate and my land holdings."

Astra felt an inkling of sympathy. He was just a rich man who wanted a child-bearing wife. Surely there were others who would gladly accept his offer. She had no reply.

"More importantly to you," he said, "I am the one who paid Sjodrun's war levy to the king."

Ah, *nei!* Astra's heart was torn. He had rescued the village, including her family. How could she refuse the one who had paid so large a debt? "I … did not know," she whispered. "I cannot think right now. I must go."

She fled the hall, ran through the village and across the broad pasture toward the river. Her thoughts spun wildly as she ran through the thicket that hugged the river's edge. At the stony bank, distraught and bewildered, she discarded her cloak and dunked into the swirling stream until she was thigh deep. The glacial flow quickly numbed her legs. She stepped further in and the current rushed up her skirt into her secret place, the place now torn.

Taking a deep breath, she dipped fully beneath the surface. When she emerged, gasping, a chill overtook her and she stumbled toward shore. Her wet garments weighed heavily on her shoulders and bound her feet, tripping her as she slipped over the smooth stones. "*Jesu Kristus*, be merciful to me, a sinner." She mouthed the words repeatedly as she gained the rocky shore.

Chapter 9

His bulging pouch jingling, Kjell tapped Thorden's flanks as they descended from the pasturelands to the river where he had bathed this morning. He shook his head, remembering the close encounter with the soldier who might have turned him in for murder, had he recognized Kjell. It must have been the angle of the sun that saved him from recognition, and perhaps his stark nakedness. That narrow escape, and the purse full of coin, gave him reason to leave as quickly as he could.

Kjell leaned back to keep his balance as Thorden navigated the slippery river rock. Though the king's troops were now gone, Kjell instinctively glanced up and down the burbling stream to make sure no one was about. In the shifting shadows of the overhanging trees something caught his eye. He drew up on the reins.

Stumbling up the bank was the figure of a woman. Her dress was soaked and dragged against her legs.

He halted.

Her head jerked up, then she reached for her cloak on the bank, grappling in its folds. She was searching for a knife, Kjell guessed. His dogs ran over to sniff her, then jumped into the stream frolicking.

"Can I be of help?" he called, trying to put her at ease. "Looks like you took a dunking." He eased his horse down the embankment toward the water's edge. Sunlight bled through the trees and caught her face in a shaft of light. It was the maiden Astra.

"It is you again," he called. "Going for a swim, are you?"

"*Nei*, Kjell the hunter," she replied, looking relieved that it was he. She stuffed something back into her pocket. "I...I saw something in the water. I fell in." She clambered further up the loose river stones and began squeezing water from her skirt.

Were those tears on her cheeks or just water droplets from her dripping hair? Kjell tugged Thorden's reins and moved closer. "Are you well? Do you need help?"

She wrapped her cloak around herself and started up the bank. "*Nei*, I am fine. So, you sold your furs and are headed home."

"Indeed. Lady Marta bought all of them for the king, his taxes, and such, though I had to wait until he left today to collect." Kjell patted his pouch of coins.

"You do well to leave Sjodrun," she replied. Water dripped down her forehead and she wiped it away.

"Though this time I profited, I try to stay out of king's business," he said.

"I tried, too, but…" She looked away. "Sometimes we cannot."

His horse snorted and pawed at the rocks. Kjell readjusted the reins. "Indeed. Sometimes we cannot." He knew that well.

She picked her way up the bank among the stones. "You have seen them before?" she asked.

Kjell stared across the river, unsure if he should answer. "The king? *Nei*. Let us say I have met some of his men before. That was enough."

"Once is enough for me, too," she replied. She wiped her face with her wet sleeve.

"Miss? Astra?" He paused. "Did something happen?"

At this she covered her face with both hands and began to sob softly. The sound of the river gurgling over smooth stones was interrupted by the call of a hawk. Kjell glanced up. He could guess what happened. One of the king's men…

After a few moments she breathed deeply and wiped her face with her dry cloak. "How foolish of me to fall in. I need to get back and dry these clothes out."

Kjell paused, then said, "We all have regrets in life, whether they are our doing or not. I have many. I am sorry for your troubles."

"Have no worries on my account," she said. "I am…I will be…" Her voice trailed off.

"Fine? Will you now?" His eyes held hers for a moment before she turned away.

"Ills befall us all, as you say." Astra started up the embankment once more.

"That they do. Whatever happened was not deserved." He clicked his tongue and his horse stepped into the stream.

"God's blessings on your journey," she called to him.

"May your trials be few," he called back. He shook the reins. His horse waded deeper into the river and the dogs leaped after him.

Chapter 10

From the top of the bank Astra watched Kjell go. His horse swam and they drifted downstream a little before gaining the far shore and disappearing into the aspens beyond.

When he had gone, she retrieved the velvet bag from her pouch, untying the string and tipping it upside down. A gold wristband with tiny jewels dropped into her hand. She shuddered. This was payment from the king for her unwilling service. Did he think he could erase the wrong he had done with a bracelet? Once more she cursed him and his accomplice, Sir Henrik, calling the wrath of angels down upon them both. She raised the ornament above her head to throw it into the river, then stopped her arm mid-arc. Perhaps she would need it after all. Disdainfully, as if harboring an idolater's amulet, she shoved it into her pouch and sloshed her way back to the village.

It was late afternoon and Astra skirted the courtyard on her way back to the women's house. She changed into her dry dress and hung the wet one over a bedpost. Someone knocked on the door and she peeked out.

Far looked perturbed. "Where have you been? I have been looking everywhere for you."

"I...bathed in the river," she said.

His tone was sharp. "The lady has called another gathering for supper. You are to join us."

"Are we not going home tonight?"

"*Nei.* Your mother will understand. But you and I will sleep by the sledge and leave for home at daybreak. Take your things there and come to supper."

"*Ja*, Far." The ride home would surely be unbearable. Astra gathered her things and trudged across the yard. She spread her wet dress over a branch and tossed her satchel into the sledge. Ledsager jumped in and settled his head on the soft leather surface of Astra's bag. "Good boy," said Astra, laying down and petting the dog's head.

When the dinner horn sounded, Astra did not move. She did not want to speak to anyone, not her father, not Vegar, especially not Einarr. He knew what he must do and he had not done it.

After the second horn, Far came looking for her. "Astra. Come to supper." His breath smelled strongly of ale. "People are asking where you are."

She turned away from him. "Tell them I am not well."

Far sat on the edge of the sledge. "I know you are unhappy, but you must eat. You will feel better."

She spoke into Ledsager's furry back. "But you did not even give Einarr a chance, Far."

"Little Sparrow, perhaps the lord's son said he loved you, but he did nothing to win you."

She twisted her neck to face toward him. "His father died, the king came, everyone was in a rush.... How could he?"

Far placed his hand on her scarved head. "He had opportunity, Astra, but he did not even speak to me. Stop fooling yourself."

"He had no chance."

Far's voice deepened, but she turned away from what she knew would be his scowl. "It is you who must give Vegar a chance. Einarr certainly heard that Vegar approached me—these things are hard to keep secret. The sooner you give up your foolish hope, the sooner you will see the wisdom of my decision...and the sooner you will feel better."

She bit her tongue. It was a sin to disrespect one's parents, so she held back the words that tipped it.

Her father sighed. "Please come, child." After a few silent moments he trudged away.

Astra lay still in the empty sledge, clutching Ledsager and watching the sky grow slowly darker. She relived each moment of the last two days with their sorrow, pain, and outrage. Ledsager crawled close, whining and licking Astra's salty tears. She hugged the dog until at last she lay quiet, spent and alone.

She was awakened by her father's moans as he fumbled in the sledge for his bedding. He reeked of ale. She kept her eyes closed. Clumsily, he rolled into his fur on the ground next to the sledge. Very soon his breathing became heavy.

Astra listened to his familiar snoring. In her dream-soaked stupor she thought, no matter what Far said, it is still not too late. I can slip away now and find Einarr. I can give myself to him and he will take me. Then he will be obliged to marry me. She started to lift the sheepskin cover to rise but she was overcome with the thought of the king's body on hers; his weight, his breath, the ripping, his shuddering...she lay back. She pulled the sheepskin over her head, smothering the cries of despair that rose and curled up like a sow bug in her heart.

The next morning was foggy and cold. Far wakened Astra and told her they were leaving as soon as she could make ready. She shook off sleep, regretfully remembering her choice last night. She should have run to Einarr after all, but now it was too late. Today she must travel home with her father, and soon face her mother. What would her parents say if they knew their *datter* was tainted? They would marry her to Vegar soon, by Michaelmas, that was what.

Not far from their camp was a two-horse sledge, newly arrived and bulging with a load covered by a wadmal sheet.

"Who is that?" she asked Far.

He shrugged. "I do not know. He will sell little, arriving at such a time." He motioned her out so he could arrange their supplies in the sledge box.

They sat on a log and ate cold mutton from Far's dinner last night, watching the vendor of the mystery sledge awaken and begin to cough. He was a shabbily clad man of grizzled face and matted hair. He coughed until his face was red, then turned his back to relieve himself beside his sledge.

Astra looked away. Far grumbled about the driver's rudeness.

The man threw off the covering of his sledge to reveal bundles of bound wool.

"You need some fine Cotswold wool, my friend?" the man grunted. He was sweating. "It is the purest of England. Arrived by ship. This is the last of it."

"Cotswold?" Far replied. "How do I know that is what you have?"

The man coughed, spat, then said, "I will not lie to you. I came by it at the docks in Bergen, not my usual haul. I can let it go for a special price. This is the best you will ever see."

He tugged out a shank and smoothed it between his dirty fingers. "Here, feel it. You, too, young maiden."

Far stroked the fibers but Astra hung back. She did not like the looks of him.

"Perhaps my wife would like some, but I cannot pay much," Far said. "The king robbed us all blind yesterday with his war levy. You will find that true for all those who live here, I fear."

Astra knew Far still had his money from the door posts since Vegar had paid the levy. When it came to bartering, men were shrewd.

The man dickered, "One *thaler*. No less."

"That is robbery." Far turned away.

"This is the finest wool in the world," the merchant said. "Since this is my last stop, I can lower the price for you."

Astra busied herself by braiding her hair while the two men haggled. When they agreed on a much-lowered price, the man lifted one of the three remaining bales into the back of their sledge. Ledsager settled himself beside the soft wool cushion just as the man was seized by a coughing fit, bending over and nearly falling. She wished Far had not dealt with this unwell heister.

Far sent her to fetch the horses, whispering that he did not want to leave their sledge unattended. When she returned, they harnessed the sledge to Farwa, leaving Kvikke for Astra to ride bareback. She resolved to lag far behind her father, for he would inevitably try to talk to her again.

"I must give my farewell to the Lady," Far said. "Meet me at the manor." He handed Astra the reins and ambled away.

Astra led the horses toward the Great Hall. From where she waited, she saw the vendor set the other two bundles of wool in front of his sledge and nearly collapse in a coughing fit. To her disgust, the loathsome man tugged a large dead rat out of one of the bales and flung it into the tall grass beyond.

Chapter 11

Kjell stayed off the roads so as not to be caught in the sovereign's net. Throughout the first miles of his journey, he thought of the young maiden, Astra. He knew she would not get her wish to marry the manor lord's son. He recalled her winsome smile at their first meeting as she doted on his pelts. He pictured her wet clothing clinging to her bosom as she struggled up the bank at the river. She was a true beauty. Sadly, he remembered how she wept on the bank of the stream; not the tears of a dispute or disappointment, *nei*. Hers were tears of great remorse. Something had happened to her in the village, something perhaps beyond her lost love. He knew from painful memory the ways of soldiers. He assumed the worst.

Kjell leaned over Thorden's neck as he labored up a steep incline. He told his horse, "By nightfall we should reach Norefjording, then in two days, if we ride hard, we will be home." Two days. The thought of home was an elixir. He would arrive at their hut, and there sweet Oda would greet him with kisses. He would toss little Egill into the air and the child would giggle joyously. That night he would eat a meal cooked by Oda's fair hands. He would sleep in a real bed and make love to his wife, content at last.

Thorden puffed heavily as they rounded the crest of a steep hill and cleared the trees. A forest of green leaves and white-trunked birch spread below, covering the rolling knolls. Kjell pulled up on the reins. The horse grunted and pawed his left foreleg on the rocks impatiently, making his feelings known.

"You are right, my friend," Kjell said, dismounting. "We will take a break here." A breeze swept up the valley and rustled the black forelock of Kjell's companion. Thorden stretched his neck to nibble the alpine grasses. The dogs spread out, sniffing for easy prey.

Now that the solstice had passed, the long summer days would steadily wane, inevitably trekking toward the winter nadir. Before the season of long darkness, Kjell still had time to hunt for winter food and build his wife a small barn attached to their tiny hut. Oda would be pleased with the cheese, oats, bacon, and salt he had stuffed into his saddlebags, along with the barrel of ale tied to Thorden's rump. In the village he hoped to purchase a milk cow, a pig, and chickens to fill out their larder—he fingered his purse full of coins.

Kjell knew his absence was hard on Oda, especially with the young child. Three months up north, and then the stop at Sjodrun had kept him away longer than planned. Would Egill remember him? Kjell felt a pang of regret.

He swigged a dram of ale from his flask then remounted, clicking his tongue to start them moving. Descending slowly, they wound their way into an aspen forest. Green light filtered through the quivering leaves. The woods were atwitter with nuthatches, hawfinches, and yellow hammers, all flitting beneath the canopy gathering food for their chicks. Thorden's hoofbeats and the jingling of coins in Kjell's pouch created a lilting rhythm that seemed to harmonize with the music of the glen.

Kjell was grateful the Lady Marta had bought his whole stock of furs. On the other hand, it was the king and his men who now benefitted under their warmth. "That scoundrel," he said aloud. At this, Thorden pricked up his ears and started to trot.

The forest path soon gave way to a steep downhill slope. Kjell reined in the horse as they jolted down the incline. Thorden suddenly alerted, his ears pivoting. Kjell pulled up on the reins and they stopped. He took his bow from behind the saddle, sliding an arrow into place. Within a few heartbeats a red deer leapt over the ferns and straight across their trail. Kjell let the arrow fly and it struck the buck through the chest. The deer took one stuttered step and collapsed into the brush with a crash.

Kjell readjusted his supplies to drape the young stag across Thorden's flank, roping everything on tightly. The hide would make good shoes for Oda and Egill, a coat for the boy, and meat to wind-dry as a start on their winter supply.

When evening came, he found a suitable campsite and started a small fire with heather and fallen branches. He let his horse wander free to graze, then hung the deer carcass from a tree limb. There he gutted the stag, throwing the lungs and scraps to the dogs. While he roasted the liver and kidney on a spit, he collected mushrooms, then sat on a rock to drink one long draught of ale.

Sated by his meal, he made a bed of moss under thick branches beneath a spruce. The younger dogs, Lope and Lysglnt, nestled in beside him while Beskytter lay facing away, keeping watch.

Early the next morning Kjell woke to the thrumming of rain on the forest floor. He ate the roasted kidney and broke camp. By mid-morning the path became a soggy, rutted road that led to a small village he had previously passed through. An oversized spire topped the simple log *kirke*. Perhaps before winter set in he should come here with Oda and bring Egill to be churched, but only if she suggested it.

Thorden sloshed through the muddy path as the first ramshackle dwellings appeared. Small farms were scattered on patches cleared from the forest. He expected to hear hammering from the smithy and see farmers tending their fields. Instead, he was surprised that no one was about. Were they at the *kirke*? Was it Lord's Day?

The door of a cabin banged open and two men emerged, carrying a supine figure on a plank directly across Kjell's path. He halted. On the pallet lay an elderly dead man, his face marked by mottled lesions, as if someone had repeatedly struck him. Had there been a fight? Had a robber snuck in at night?

A weeping woman, her gray hair falling loosely over her back, ran after them crying, "To the *kirke*! He needs a proper burial."

"If there is still room," grunted one of the men. "You heard what the priest said."

The pallbearers sloshed through the mud with their burden. The woman stumbled after them, tripping into the muck.

Kjell dismounted and offered her his hand. "My condolences for your loss."

Glancing up, she swatted his hand away. "Do you want to die, too?"

Kjell stepped back. The woman struggled to rise, then hobbled after her husband, her clothing soaked with mud.

Bewildered, Kjell gathered Thorden's trailing reins and led him through the small village that seemed otherwise abandoned. Where was everyone? He passed several smokeless huts before he heard the crying of a baby coming from a shabby house. He stopped, looked about, then took a step toward it. The bawling was desperate and choking. Where was the mother?

He rapped on the door. The baby's wails turned to screams. No one answered. Kjell pushed on the door but it was bolted from within. Calling out and knocking harder, all he could hear were the baby's frantic cries. He slid his knife between the door and the jamb, raising the latch inside. The door swung open.

Immediately, a gust of rancid wind struck him. The smell was more than an infant's mess—it was the scent of death. Kjell gagged and covered his nose with his sleeve. Kicking the door further open to let light in, he called, "Is anyone here?" The wail of the babe overwhelmed his words.

The small hut was in disarray; cooking implements on the floor, a stool lying on its side, an unlit fire. From a cradle hanging by ropes from the rafters, a baby's arms flailed. Kjell stepped in. When the baby saw him, its cry turned to a whimper.

"I have you, young one," he soothed. When he started to lift the infant, he saw that it was writhing in its own filth. He

The Moon Turned to Blood

used a nearby blanket to pick up the child and lay it against his shoulder. The babe gulped in staccato breaths.

Kjell's dogs were immediately drawn to the only bed in the sparse room. Kjell shooed them out. There lay a woman with disheveled tresses covering her face. He shook her skirt-covered leg.

"Madam? Are you not well?" She did not move. He used a comb to tease the hair away from her face. Unblinking eyes stared back. Her skin was darkly splotched, like the dead man he had seen outside.

Kjell jumped back, cracking his head on the arm of the broiling spit. Grimacing, he grasped the baby tightly and hurried out of the cabin, stumbling off the threshold into the road. He spat repeatedly to expunge the foul air from his mouth.

The child's cries eased, broken by ever-slowing small gasps. Its mouth groped Kjell's neck, seeking a nipple, and it whimpered when it found no succor. The poor thing was hungry. Kjell stuck his smallest finger into the baby's mouth as he had done with his own child. The infant clamped on, immediately quieting. Kjell walked through the village looking for someone to take this poor thing.

He approached the *kirke* where a few people were gathered in the cemetery. He stopped at a respectful distance. Many fresh grave mounds were evident. Two men dug furiously to create another. Those who had carried the old woman's husband lowered the litter unceremoniously into the hole. As the body reached the bottom, they tipped the ropes to dump it out, then pulled up the empty litter. Immediately, they shoveled dirt into the open pit as the woman stood by, keening.

A few other villagers gathered around another grave nearby, and a priest droned the prayer for the dead. When he finished, the mourners crossed themselves and quickly fled. The priest moved to the elderly wife, repeating his Latin words and making the sign of the cross. He touched her back and spoke softly to her, then started toward the *kirke*.

Kjell called out and hurried after him. The priest turned. His eyes were ringed in fatigue. "Traveler, you must not stay here," he said, waving Kjell away from the graveyard. "There is a sickness upon us, a curse. Many have died and others are ill. Leave quickly."

"What sickness is this?" Kjell asked, recalling the warning he had received from the soldier on his way to Sjodrun.

"We know not. Some say it comes in a poison cloud. It may also be passed from the gaze of a sick person. Do not look anyone in the eye, I warn you. It has struck Bergen, Oslo, and Hamar, and now it has come to us. We are paying for our sins. You must flee, and quickly. And keep your baby away from this evil."

"But Father, this is not my child. I found it in that hut," Kjell said, pointing. "The mother is dead."

The clergyman sighed. "God save us." He crossed himself and held out his arms for the fussing child. "Be off and do not return. Go!"

Kjell's heart raced as he swung into the saddle. The sickness had struck this small village, and also Hamar. What of his parents and siblings? How far had it traveled? He kicked Thorden's sides hard and they sped away.

Chapter 12

"Mar! Mar! Far is home!" Karin called, running toward the sledge from the barn. Signy ran after her sister as the two *buhunds* circled the horses, yipping joyfully. Ledsager jumped down from his bed on the wool bundle while the other dogs, Haret and Irvig, circled, sniffing the foreign scents the dog carried.

Far pulled the sledge to a stop. Astra dismounted. Four-year-old brother Knut ran at them waving his arms. Mar stepped out of the summer house holding a stirring spoon. Her smile creased her sun-darkened face and she swept back a stray hank of hair. Astra noticed small creases on her mother's forehead, though she was still comely with her heavily lashed eyes and sanguine smile.

"So. The prodigals return," Mar said, setting her hands on her hips "Where have you been? I was worried."

Far dropped the harness reins and stood, stretching his back. "We were held up."

Astra brushed the dust off her skirt. She felt older, as if a year had gone by since she had been home.

"I have missed you," Mar said to Astra. "So much work for us to do without your help." Mar glanced at Kvikke. "I see you got your horse. Your father spoils you."

Astra knew her mother did not approve of girls working with horses, but Mar kissed Astra's forehead nevertheless. Then her mother faced Far and tapped her flour-dusted cheek for her husband's expected kiss.

"A tiresome walk," said he, striding stiffly over to oblige his wife.

"They say the way home is always longest," said Mar. A question wrinkled her brow. "What kept you so long?"

"I will tell you when we are unpacked." Far kissed Mar's mouth, and the younger children, who hung onto Far's legs, groaned.

Karin ran up and hugged Astra tightly. "I was worried about you. What happened?" Karin was fourteen, one year younger than Astra, with dark hair and of a serious-minded temperament like their mother.

"I will explain later," Astra whispered into her sister's ear.

"What did you bring us?" Five-year-old Signy, blonde and freckled, jumped up and down excitedly pulling on her father's sleeve. "Do you have surprises?"

Far shook his head sadly. "*Nei*, I forgot."

Knut, his sandy hair as unruly as ever, stretched his chubby hand up to reach into Far's bulging money pouch, but Far tugged the drawstring tight.

Mar scolded, "Do not tease them so, Sven."

Far stumped back to the sledge and reached for his satchel. He inched his hand inside. Signy and Knut jumped up and down squealing, "Hurry, hurry. What have you got?"

Far plucked out a carved wooden doll for Signy and a small soapstone knight for young Knut. They snatched their gifts and screamed joyfully. Far lifted out a rag doll in a red wedding gown and waved Karin over. Astra could see that her sister was self-conscious about appearing childish as she hid the doll behind her back. Signy and Knut ran around the yard laughing while Karin hurried into the house, returning without her gift. Astra had not seen her father purchase these things and was happily surprised for her siblings.

Far handed Mar a small lace-trimmed pillow for the baby girl. Mar smiled, tucked it under her arm, then tapped her foot. "Have you forgotten your wife?"

Far fished in his satchel. He turned it upside down but nothing else fell out. Mar scowled, crossed her arms. Far shrugged, lifting his empty hands. She huffed and turned to go back into the house but Far caught her arm. Then he fished inside his shirt and seemed surprised when he found a small

The Moon Turned to Blood

leather-wrapped packet. Mar grabbed for it, but Far repeatedly yanked it out of her reach until Mar stomped her foot. This was a game Astra had seen them play several times.

Finally, Far lifted Mar's hand and turned it palm up, dumping the contents onto it and squeezing her fingers shut.

Mar opened her hand and her eyes widened. A pewter cross-shaped locket lay in her palm and she held it up to examine all sides. Then she kissed Far's cheek. He grabbed her in a bear hug until she slapped him away, laughing.

Watching them uncomfortably, Astra realized they did love each other after so many years. She wondered if she would ever find any happiness.

"What else have you brought?" Mar asked, touching the large bale of wool. She ran her fingers through it and teased out a shank, twisting it into a tendril. "Where did you get this? It is so fine, almost like linen."

Far chuckled. "I thought you would like it."

"I will make you a cloak," Mar said. "Yours is worn."

"*Nei*, Jutta. Make something for yourself, a new dress. This Cotswold wool should be shown off."

"Cotswold?" she cried. "From England? But that is too costly."

"A special price, thievery, almost. Do not fret."

Mar swatted her wrist, brushing away a fleck. Was that a flea? Astra had seen Ledsager scratching on the way home. She was disgusted that the filthy, sickly wool vender had done nothing to keep the wool clean.

Knut and Signy climbed atop the bale and tried to push each other off. Their laughter rang across the yard. Mar scolded them to get down.

Far said wearily, "I was not able to purchase some of the supplies you wanted, but I do have the baking slab and salt."

"What happened?" Mar asked. "Did the Lady not pay you well for your door posts?"

"She did. I will explain. A lot happened while we were away and I had little time for shopping."

He lifted the weighty slab and lugged it to the house, calling over his shoulder, "Astra, take the horses to the barn and unhitch the sledge." His stern tone told Astra he was still upset with her. The way home had seemed interminable in their near-silence. She felt sorrow that her father was angry, but she was angry, too: angry that he would not listen to her. Deep shame at the thought of the king reddened her cheeks once more. She had left childhood behind. *Nei*, it had been torn from her.

Mar followed her husband into the house and shut the door. Astra rued that Far would tell her mother about Vegar's proposal, and her refusal, without her being able to explain. When Astra had a chance to tell her mother that she loved Einarr, maybe Mar would understand why she could not marry that puffed-up gander of a *sysselmand*. Only Mar could reason with her stubborn father.

The two youngest children climbed onto the wool again, laying down and rubbing their hands into the soft fibers. "I want this for my bed," said Signy.

"Me, too," said Knut. They rolled back and forth, laughing.

Astra reprimanded them. "I do not think Mar would like you ruining her special wool."

Knut and Signy bounced down and ran off, the young dogs at their heels. Ledsager stopped to scratch before trotting after them.

Karin stroked Kvikke's neck. "You are so lucky to have your own horse. She is beautiful. What do you call her?"

"Kvikke. She is not just for me. She will help with the farmwork."

Karin combed her fingers through the thick mane. "Is she fast, like her name?"

"I hope so, but do not tell Far."

Karin laughed. The two sisters kept many secrets between them; in fact, Karin was Astra's only true confidant.

As they led the horses to the stable, chickens and the nanny goat scurried out of their way. Karin glanced back at the house before asking, "Well? Are you betrothed?"

Astra shook her head. "*Nei*. Well, maybe."

They halted.

"What happened?" Karin asked, turning to Astra.

Astra leaned her head against Kvikke's neck. "I am going to tell you, but do not say anything to anyone."

"I promise."

"Far accepted a betrothal from someone else."

"*Nei!*" Karin grabbed Astra's arm. "Why? Does he know about Einarr?"

"*Ja*, but he said Einarr will marry a noble, not an odal farmer's *datter*."

"Who does Far want you to marry?"

"The *sysselmand*, Vegar Eriksson. I barely met him. Far knows how upset I am but he said he will not change his mind." Astra clenched her teeth against the tears.

Karin asked, "Are you sure? Perhaps he will, if you talk to him again."

"I hope so. What makes me angry is that Far did not even speak to Einarr! He did not give him a chance to make a better offer."

"Oh, Astra, I am so sorry. But if Far thinks so, it may be that the *sysselmand* is the best match for you."

Astra turned away and continued leading Kvikke to the stable. "It is NOT the best match for me! I know Far will not listen to me, but maybe Mar will."

Karin drew Farwa and the sledge along beside her. "I did not mean to make you upset, Astra. I just think that our parents know more than we do about what is good for us."

Astra glanced at her sister, so naïve, so compliant. The good sister. Astra did not reply.

"Tell me what else happened at the village," Karin said.

"First, the feast for Saint Olav, and then...then..." Astra swallowed. She could hardly form the words. "The king arrived."

Karin's mouth gaped open. "The king? Our king Magnus? Truly? Why was he there?"

Astra did not stop. "He wanted money for a war up north."

Karin's voice rose. "I cannot believe you saw King Magnus! What was he like? Was he handsome?"

"*Nei*, he is old, and...demanding." Astra swallowed the bile in her throat. "He made Lady Marta raise a war tax that nearly took all her money, and he took most of the young men to go to war."

"War is bad, but still, it must have been grand to see the king, even if he only wanted money."

Astra gritted her teeth. "I do not want to talk about him." She realized that if Karin had been with her, nothing would have happened between Astra and the king. She softened her tone: "I wish you had come."

"I do, too," her sister replied.

They stopped at the entrance to the stabbur, unbridled the horses and led them to the pasture. The two sisters leaned on the fence watching Kvikke run the perimeter until finally settling down to graze. Astra knew the true reason Far had purchased Kvikke. Last winter their twelve-year-old gelding had fallen through the ice while crossing the frozen marsh with a load of winter wild grass. He had died, unable to gain his footing. Nevertheless, she was thankful to have a riding horse to care for.

As Astra and Karin drew water from the well and filled the trough, Far and Mar came out of the house and walked past them to the sledge. Mar's expression was noticeably somber. She and Far muscled the large bale of wool off the sledge and tumbled it inside the *stabbur*.

Astra snatched her satchel and climbed up the *stabbur* ladder to unpack. She, Karin, and this year, little Signy slept upstairs in the *stabbur*'s storage area for the summer. Mar, Far,

Knut, and the baby slept in the one-room summer house just across the yard. Repairs and cleaning would be completed before the family moved back into the larger main house for winter.

Astra threw her satchel on the straw-stuffed mattress. She quickly sought a hiding place for the velvet pouch, poking it into a chink between two logs behind a heavy storage trunk. She hung her Lord's Day frock, still damp from her dunking the day before, over a rail, then placed her small copper-plated mirror, comb, and the new ribbons she had purchased on a ledge.

Karin called up the ladder, "I have to get some milk for supper." Astra heard her calling to Mar about the king as she hurried away.

Porridge was simmering over the outdoor fire when Astra neared the summer house. The door was open and she stepped inside. She sat on a corner of the only bed.

Mar was alone, slicing barley *brød*. "It is good to have you home," she said.

Astra peeked into the hanging cradle where baby Liv was peacefully sleeping. She touched the baby's tender cheek. "She is so fair, Mar."

"That she is," Mar said. "Your father is hungry so we will eat early today."

Astra's stomach rumbled. She and Far had eaten nothing since their breakfast of *brød* and ale at Sjodrun. She retrieved wooden bowls from a shelf and placed them on the small board. There was not room for the whole family to sit there, so two had to sit on the bed to eat.

Mar placed the *brød* on the table and gripped Astra's shoulder. "It seems we have much to discuss."

Astra reached for the butter. "*Ja.* I need to talk to you."

Mar's hand squeezed, then let go. "The porridge will be ready soon." Her mother set a plate of salted pike on the table.

Fish. Astra sighed. So many non-meat days in a year. Her mother never forgot to keep track on the calendar stick that was propped in the corner of the room.

Soon Mar spooned porridge into bowls, topped it with a thin slice of dried fish, and the family sat down to eat. Knut and Signy groaned.

Mar shushed them, then said cheerily, "Now that your father is home we will have fresh fish soon, and tomorrow is a meat day."

As they ate, the children shared stories of what had transpired while Astra and Far were gone. Knut complained that the baby cried all night, though Mar said that Knut had been far worse when he was small. Signy said she had helped Mar with all the chores, and to this Mar added, "Almost all."

"The pig broke loose again," Karin told Far. "I tried several times but could not catch her."

Far said, "It will not hurt for her to scavenge some. Ledsager will herd her in before dark."

When Astra told of seeing Nikolina and her new baby, Mar's brows raised. "That girl…from the ashes to the fire."

"What does that mean?" Karin asked.

"Ask your sister," Mar said.

Far told of the king's arrival, the grandeur of the horses and knights, and the young men who were recruited as soldiers, including Nikolina's new husband. At the mention of the king Astra bent to her bowl to hide her burning face. Far did not tell of the war levy nor how the debt had been paid. He said nothing about Vegar, either, for which Astra was relieved.

When everyone laid down their spoons, they all bowed their heads and Far said the after-meal prayer. The children quibbled about whose turn it was to wash out the bowls but Astra offered, hoping to talk to Mar alone. The others left to do their afternoon chores.

Astra washed out the bowls slowly, hoping Far would leave, but he stayed, propping his elbows on the table. Mar sat on Far's carved *kubestol*, the chair with a dragon's tail circling the base and fire flaming from the dragon's fearsome mouth.

Mar picked up her sewing and said to Astra, "Start the outdoor fire for the wash pail. I am running out of rags for the baby."

"You heard her," said Far. He nodded Astra toward the door.

Before the door closed behind her Far said, "Keep the children outside until I come out. Your mother and I have something more to discuss. We will talk to you tonight after the children are asleep."

Astra latched the door behind her. She had heard that the archbishop in Nidaros said that girls were supposed to give consent to marry, but here in Numedal, far from the cathedral, Father Johan did not thwart tradition. Still, there might be hope. Her mother might listen to her and try to convince Far, though she knew her father was unlikely to change his mind. If he did not, she could run away to Einarr and beg him to take her to his bed. That way her parents could not refuse. If all this failed, she could run away to a convent, though she might never see her family again. Mar's youngest sister had done this and no one was allowed to visit her there. Astra's choices were stark.

She sent Knut and Signy to pick wild raspberries behind the cow barn, then she and Karin went into the woods behind the house with a bucket of oats to entice the pig. They heard it snorting under the bushes and they chased it, but the pig escaped into thick brambles. They sat together on a partially broken branch and swung slowly back and forth, waiting for the pig to come out.

Karin asked, "What did Mar mean by jumping from ashes into fire?"

Astra sighed. "Niki had to marry Dag because she was with child."

Karin thought for a moment. "You mean they did it before they got married?"

"*Ja*, but at least now they are married, so that is better. The problem is, she lives with his wretched mother, and now Dag is gone to war."

"That is sad. But tell me more about Einarr. Did you talk to him? Did he kiss you again?"

Astra had told her sister about the kiss at *Jul*, omitting the more incriminating details. "We had little chance for kisses. Now I am afraid we cannot marry. That is what Mar and Far are talking about. Mar would have to change Far's mind, and you know how hard that is!"

Karin took Astra's hand. "Is the *sysselmand* nice? Handsome, at least?"

Astra shook her head. "He is old, ugly, and arrogant. I cannot marry him."

Karin scooted closer and slung her arm over Astra's shoulder. "I think they should let you marry Einarr. We should all get to marry someone we love."

Astra squeezed her tightly. "We should. I hope Mar will at least let me talk to her about it. I will do everything I can to convince her."

They tried once more to chase after the pig, but it was quick and dodged into a hollow log out of reach.

As Astra and Karin walked slowly back to the house, a strong wind rushed through the trees. Dark clouds were spreading toward them from over the mountain. Astra shouted at the younger children to hurry back to the house. A flash of lightning and a deep rumble sent them all sprinting. Just as large drops began splashing all around them, Far rushed out of the house and waved Astra and Karin after him to put the horses and cattle inside the barn. By the time they reached the house they were thoroughly soaked. A hefty gust followed them in as Far barred the door.

"Looks like a gale," he said, removing his cloak. Astra and Karin stood in the entry and squeezed water from their hair, using rags to wipe their faces and arms.

Mar, who was breastfeeding the baby, said, "Get into those extra night dresses, girls." She pointed to pegs on the wall.

Astra and Karin changed, holding a blanket up to hide each other. They hung their wet things to dry by the fire, then crowded in next to Mar around the small table. Knut and Signy cuddled under the deerskin on the only bed.

A bright flash through the smoke hole was instantly followed by a crack of thunder. The small children screamed and ducked under the furs. The baby pulled away from Mar's breast and started to cry. Mar gently brought her back to her breast.

Far trimmed the wicks on two tallow candles and lit them, shedding a dancing light into the darkened room. He sat on the bed next to the children and commenced to tell a story, as he often did when it stormed.

"You know of the ash lad, do you not?" he asked. The two younger children nodded, leaning into Far's lap.

"The ash lad lived with his father and mother and two older brothers at the edge of the dark woods. The boy's father asked the older brother to go out and chop some wood, but soon the brother came back saying a troll had scared him away. The next day the father sent his second oldest son to chop wood, but he, too, came running back, saying the troll had threatened to kill him if the boy chopped wood in his forest."

Astra watched the children gazing at their father with cow eyes. She remembered many such evening tales and recalled her father's playfulness when she was young. They played Chase, and Hide and Find, and at night Far would read scripture to them. She sighed. Those simple days of fun with her father were gone forever.

He continued, "Finally, the father sent his youngest son, the ash lad, out to chop wood. His brothers laughed at him, saying he would never be able to chop wood by himself and that the troll would surely eat him up."

Knut made a gulping sound and growled at Signy, who stuck her tongue out at him.

"So," said Far, "the boy's mother filled a knapsack with fresh cheese curds for her son to eat that day and kissed him goodbye. The son found a suitable tree and started to chop it down. Sure enough, a most large and ugly troll appeared. 'Do not chop in my forest or I will eat you!' shouted the troll. The ash lad reached into his backpack, pulled out a large cheese curd and yelled, 'If you do not keep quiet, I will squish you like I can squash this white stone.' He then squeezed the curd until its juice spurted out. The troll stepped back. 'Do not hurt me!' he cried. 'I will help you chop the wood if you will leave me be.' The ash lad accepted the troll's offer and the troll chopped down three trees, cutting them into cordwood. After this hard work the troll insisted the boy come with him to his house for supper, telling him he lived nearby."

Signy's brows twisted in worry. "But he will eat him!" she cried.

Karin shushed her. "Just listen to the story."

Signy plugged her ears with her fingers and closed her eyes.

"So, the boy followed the troll home," continued Far. "The troll said, 'You fetch the water and I will make the fire.' But the troll's water bucket was too heavy to pick up, so the boy said, 'This tiny pot is not big enough. I will just bring the whole well.' The troll said, 'Ah, *nei*. I need my well. I will fetch the water and you make the fire.' The ash boy was good at making fires, of course, so by the time the troll returned, the fire danced merrily.

"When the giant pot of porridge had cooked, the boy said to the troll, 'Let us have an eating match. I can eat more than you.' The troll agreed and they sat down to eat. But the boy had put his knapsack under the front of his shirt, and as he ate, he put more porridge into the knapsack than into his mouth. When the knapsack was full, he took a knife and slit the bottom, letting porridge pour out. The troll was surprised but kept quiet. After a while the troll put down his spoon. 'I cannot eat another bite,' he said. 'But you will lose the contest,' the ash lad said. 'Here, I will show you how you can eat more. See how I cut a hole in my stomach? That way I can eat as much as I like.'

"The troll said, 'But does that not hurt?' 'Not much,' said the boy. So, the troll took his knife and cut open his stomach. And that was the end of the troll."

Knut buried his head under Far's elbow and Signy screamed.

"Sven, that is dreadful," said Mar. "You have scared the children. Now they will not want to go into the woods."

Far ignored her. "So, guess what the ash lad did?"

Signy's eyes widened like a whetstone. No one ventured a guess.

"He stole all the troll's gold and silver from the mountain and took it home to his family."

The children laughed and wound around Far, tickling him. Astra looked away. Far used to tickle her, too, but now everything was spoiled between them.

Mar got up, shaking her head at Far. She changed the baby's wet rags before patting her to sleep in the hanging cradle.

Knut popped out from under the furs and began scratching his leg. "I am itchy," he said. He pulled up his pant leg, revealing red scratch lines running up and down his shin. He had several small raised bites.

"Me, too," said Signy, sitting up and scratching her arm.

Mar retrieved the jar of lard, mixed it with ashes, salt, and sour wine, and rubbed it onto the children's legs and arms.

"That will teach you not to lie all over the flea-bitten dogs," Astra said.

Karin put down her sewing and asked Signy to play a game of *hnefatafl* with her. She was teaching her little sister the game that had been passed down through Mar's family for generations. The checkered board and the black and white stone pieces came from the Viking age, Mar had told them. They represented the Norsemen and the Swedes fighting for the kingdom of Norway. Knut begged to play, so Karin let him move her pieces. He jumped on the bed jubilantly when they won, though Signy cried.

Before long, the thunder had receded to a distant rumble. Slanted rays of the sun glowed orange through the smoke hole above. After evening chores and some *brød* with butter, Mar told the girls it was time for bed. Astra and Karin took Signy to the *stabbur* loft.

"I have to go back and talk to Mar and Far," Astra said.
"When are you coming to bed?" Karin asked.
"Soon, I hope."
"They want to talk about the betrothal?" Karin asked.
"I will tell you all about it tomorrow."

The three of them knelt to say their evening prayers and made the sign of the cross over their chests. Then Astra propped them both up on several feather pillows. "As Mar would say, we only lie flat when we are dead," she said, imitating her mother's nightly warning. She kissed them, and Signy snuggled up to Karin under the furs.

The *stabbur* was dark except for the late evening light that shone through the decorative holes Far had carved under the overhanging roof. Astra lit a candle, then called the dogs to lie at the bottom of the ladder that led to the loft. Where was Ledsager? She had not seen him all day.

As she tip-toed through the damp grass to the small summer house, Astra's mind wrestled with her heart. She imagined her parents' speeches about making a good marriage. Her mother would brag about how her love for Far had grown, saying the same would happen for Astra someday. Mar had assured her that there was nothing to fear of the marriage bed, and Astra had heard their rustling and Far's grunting late at night. Now she knew: there was *much* to fear of the marriage bed unless…unless it was Einarr.

She thought about what her father had said, that Einarr had not come to talk to him. But Einarr had been busy! Lady Marta was making demands on him and he had new duties. She would say how much she detested Vegar, how pompous he was, how far away he lived. She would bring up Einarr's promise to her, and hers to him. If this failed, she could still mention the nunnery where her mother's sister lived in seclusion. This would surely change their minds.

If they still insisted, she would sneak away, ride to Sjodrun, creep into the manor and sleep with Einarr. They would confess to Father Johan and ask him to marry them before anyone had time to object.

In the center of the yard Far had built a sputtering fire in the outdoor pit and he squatted beside it. Astra walked by him without a word. Quietly, she pushed the door to the summer house open. Knut was asleep in her parents' bed. Astra sat and picked up the spindle, but her mother covered Astra's hands to stop her from spinning. She met Astra's eyes and whispered, "Get a stool. We will go outside."

When they were seated, Far took a deep breath as if to speak, but Mar spoke first. Her eyes glinted in the firelight. "When your father told me of the marriage proposal to Vegar Eriksson I was very happy for you, my dear *datter*. I know of him. He is a wealthy man. He will provide well for you."

Mar paused, waiting for a response. Getting none, she continued. "I will miss you when you marry, in fact, I do not know how I will manage without you. But it is true that when we lose something, we gain something else. Blessed be our God above for this gentleman's generous offer."

Her mother reached out and clasped her hand. "Dear one, may God go with you and bless you with many children. From small seeds, large trees grow."

Astra pulled her hand away. "Mar, please do not make me do this. You learned to love Far but I will never learn to love Vegar Eriksson. He is old and ugly, and he boasts of himself shamelessly. I can never love someone like him."

"Shh, shh." Mar touched her finger to Astra's lips. "You think this now, but in time you will learn to understand and respect him. He is an honorable man."

Far peered up at Astra through his eyebrows. "This is a good match, Astra. Your mother and I know better than you. We are looking out for your good only, and for the welfare of your children. You will always be provided for, which is our sincerest wish. You *will* marry Vegar."

Astra swallowed the sinful, rebellious words she wished to utter.

"Sven," Mar said. "I will talk to her alone. Give us time."

Her father rose and shuffled toward the barn. The baby began to cry and Mar brought her outside. Astra watched in silence as her mother suckled the child. With a shiver of revulsion, she tried to imagine suckling Vegar's baby. How could she even love such a child?

Mar looked up. "Your father and I are only doing our best for you, my sweet. Sven loves you, as do I. But you are growing up. It is the way for all women."

Peering at her mother, Astra said quietly, "But Mar, you must understand. I love another."

Mar lowered her voice, glancing toward the barn. "I do understand. Once I felt the same, when I was young. But over time, feelings of love wane. They are like the ripples on a still lake that soon disappear. The one you love has another role to fulfill. He will serve the king and someday rule the manor. You must accept that he cannot be yours."

"But he promised we would marry." Astra's tears flowed unheeded.

Her mother's eyes glistened, too. "Listen. I will tell you this because your father could not. Sven did talk to Einarr. He told the lad you were to be betrothed to Vegar and the boy said nothing. He did not fight for you. Einarr, too, knows he cannot marry you."

"But why did Far not tell me this? My life is ruined!" She fell to her knees and leaned over her mother's lap, weeping despondently. Jutta rubbed her *datter's* back and hummed a song from Astra's infancy. Many long minutes went by until Astra's heaving eased.

Far called from outside, "A section of the north fence blew down. I have to mend it before I let the cattle out in the morning." He disappeared into the darkness.

Mar muttered under her breath, whispering something in Old Norse.

Astra stood and slung on her cloak. "I am going to bed."

"Do you want me to walk you out?" Mar's face was still beautiful, despite her thirty-two years.

"*Nei*, I want to be alone."

"Are you flea bitten, too, Astra?" her mother asked, scratching her arm.

"*Nei*, Mar."

Mar took the baby inside and Astra heard the clink of the ceramic lard jar.

Chapter 13

Kjell rode for three days, stopping only when darkness made the slender deer trail too hard to follow and starting out again at first light. He thought of Oda, how she had pleaded with him to move to a village the last time he was home. She suggested he apprentice as a tanner, but Kjell had balked. For him, the farther out they lived, the better. He knew she was strong and would not admit that she was sometimes frightened living alone in the forest. But now, his conscience was pricked. He must hunt closer to home.

After their hasty marriage they had traveled the hills for weeks, discovering a small group of settlers living illegally on property owned by an absent lord. The half-dozen peasant families pooled their resources and scratched out a living in secret. When he and Oda arrived, they were met with pitchforks and knives. Only after explaining their flight, and a blood promise to keep the secret safe, were they allowed to settle in the nearby forest. He cleared a plot in thick woodland a short ride away from the hamlet. There he built a hut and stable. He had promised to build Oda a proper house and barn, but the year had flown by, and now another was nearly past.

Unmet hunger filled Kjell's thoughts as he rode: porridge, goat cheese, and Oda's fire-roasted bannock. He must build her an oven for baking proper *brød* as soon as he arrived home. More than food, though, he longed for the comfort of Oda's naked flesh beneath the furs, the smoothness of her skin, the curve of her back, her breath on his neck. He ached for her touch.

Suddenly, he slapped his leg, startling the horse. "Cow's balls!" he shouted. "How could I be so stupid?" He had bought no special gift for Oda, no trinket, no length of cloth, nor ribbons for her hair. "What a shortwit I am!"

He jostled his purse full of coins and heard its pleasing jingle. "In autumn I will promise to take her to a village and buy her whatever she wants," he told Thorden. The horse tossed his head and picked up his pace as they wound through the trees that led to the hidden hamlet. Entering the clearing where the few cabins and shared outbuildings were scattered, Thorden sensed something before Kjell did and shied, side-stepping. Kjell pulled up. The village was still. Kjell listened for the sounds of tools or voices, but heard none. Perhaps they were all in the forest. Suddenly, a feral pig ran in front of him, followed by a pack of barking dogs. The pig disappeared behind a hut and a chorus of squeals ensued, then snarls and ripping flesh. No one came out to squelch the killing.

Uneasy, Kjell thought of the village of sickness he had passed through. He clicked his tongue. Thorden proceeded warily, ears twitching from side-to-side.

"Hallo! Gizur? Skeggi? Where is everyone?" Kjell called.

No one answered. He reined Thorden close enough to rap his knife hilt on the door of Skeggi's hut.

Nothing.

Steering toward the only house with smoke rising, he pounded on the door. Something scraped across the floor inside. The latch slid free and the door slivered open. An eye peered out.

"Jens? Is that you? Where is everyone?"

The door opened further and Jens stepped out, leaning on a staff. He was red-faced and beaded with sweat. A fetid smell emanated from him.

"Go away, Kjell," the sick man puffed. "We are all cursed, doomed to Hades. It is our punishment for stealing this land. Get away from here. Have you checked on your wife?"

Kjell tugged firmly on Thorden's bit and the horse backed up. "Not yet. Who else is sick?"

Jens wheezed, "I am the last one alive, I think. I thought I might not get it—I cared for many others and buried them. But alas." He raised his sweat-soaked shirt to reveal a large purple pustule beneath his arm and circles of red across his chest. "I will be dead by tomorrow, the next day at the latest. You must come back and bury me! I beg you—do not leave me to the dogs."

Kjell recoiled. "I saw this sickness elsewhere, on my way here."

Jens grimaced. "An unearthly cloud brought it, they say. My brother Albreckt came from Hamar a week or more ago and he was already sick. The scourge is there as well." Jens took a halting breath. "The pain is...worsening. Have you wine?"

"*Nei*, only ale." From his saddle, Kjell untied his flask and tossed it at the feet of the dying man, thinking with great distress of Oda and Egill.

Jens drank, swallowing with difficulty. "After you bury me, if you can, go to Nidaros and pray for our souls. I have no money for a mass, but please..." He took another long draught. Ale ran from the sides of his mouth.

"God save you, Jens," Kjell said, kicking Thorden and galloping away. He wound through the trees, jumped the creek, and cantered over the hills to the small clearing where he had erected their cabin. He must take Oda and the baby away, as far as he could. They would go north. They would stay away from towns and out of sight from strangers. They could camp in the highlands or perhaps travel as far as the Saami's lands and the wilderness beyond. He knew a cave there. Well hidden, they would wait for this evil to pass.

When Kjell approached his homestead, he pulled hard on the reins and Thorden skidded to a stop. He smelled no smoke. It was a warm day, so Oda needed none, he told himself. Or perhaps she was out gathering. Their hut was surely too far from the village for a poison cloud to reach her...unless she had lately visited the settlement.

Kjell ran to the cabin door and slammed it open. An acrid stench came forth as a swath of light spread across the dim interior. Kjell waited in the doorway to let his eyes adjust to the dimness, too alarmed to speak.

"Kjell? Is that you?" Oda said weakly. Her dark form rose up from the bed on one elbow. "Thank God you are here. I prayed you would come."

He searched for the flint and lit a taper. Cupping the flickering candle, he raised it to reveal his wife's face. Her countenance was stony and pale. Her eyes were blood red. On her neck was a black, seeping canker.

Kjell's dread turned to horror. "You are ill." He stepped forward.

Oda thrust up a feeble hand. "Stay back! You cannot help me now."

Kjell reached his hand toward her. "Get up. I will take you to the witch of Geilo. She will have a potion..."

"Do not touch me! You must not die!" Oda groaned as she sat up, grimacing. She turned to a bundle on the bed beside her. "Here lies our darling Egill, already passed on to heaven. I am going to join him soon." With shaking fingers, she tugged the covering off the child's face. Not yet two years of age and he wore the pall of death.

Lightning rent Kjell's heart. "Egill? My boy?" He snatched up the child and grasped him to his chest. "Not him, God. He is innocent. It is me you want. Take me." He broke into sobs.

Oda reached out and eased the child from her husband's arms. "You should not touch him. This sickness...we do not survive it. Now you must dig his grave, husband."

In anguish, Kjell watched her cover Egill's face.

When he did not move, Oda rasped, "Go get the shovel now. And gather many stones...the wolves..." Her voice choked off.

Thickly, wiping his eyes, Kjell replied, "Then after...you and I will leave this place. We will go north, start a new life..." He stumbled back toward the door, his vision enclosing him in a tunnel. He leaned against the doorframe until his sight returned, then reeled to the shed. Grabbing a shovel, he started to dig beneath a twisted spruce. As his shovel plunged deeper, he felt far away from his own body, as if someone else's hands held the shovel, someone else's arms dug the hole…someone else's child had died.

He muttered promises to God: "I will go to a *kirke*, make my confession, give my tithes willingly…if only you will spare Oda." But the deeper he dug, the angrier he became. What cruel god would let his little children die like this? He cursed, swiping tears with his sleeve.

Kjell carried Oda and sat her against a log by the hole he had dug. She watched him lower Egill into the grave, fill it, and pile rocks on top. They said no words—he could not speak. After a long while, he carried his wife back to the hut.

Kjell gave her water to drink but she refused the dried venison he offered. When it grew dark, he covered her and lay on a fur on the floor beside the bed. He kept a candle burning, checking on her each time she moaned.

In the middle of the night, she started to cough. She buried her face in the pillow as a choking sound rattled in her chest. Kjell scrambled up to help her but she kicked him away. Suddenly, she sat up, gasping. Her next breath was followed by a terrifying strangling noise.

Frantically, Kjell shook her shoulders crying, "Oda, Oda, breathe! Do not leave me… come back!" but she slumped forward heavily in his arms.

Kjell's heart was stabbed. "*Nei*, Oda, *nei*! I need you! Stay, my love, please stay!"

Finally, he laid her limp body on the bed. Oda's head lolled to one side. She wore the mask of death.

Chapter 14

When Astra awoke and slowly opened her eyes, she was alone. Bright sunlight shone through the vent holes under the *stabbur* roof. She sighed. The day ahead promised many chores, and Far's disapproving glares, but at least she would get to work alongside Karin. After relishing these few moments to herself, she dressed and hurried to the small summer house.

Mar smiled when Astra came in. "I am glad you are home, child...*nei*, not child, wife-to-be."

"Where is everyone?" Astra asked, ignoring her mother's comment.

"Doing your chores." Mar winked at her. "You seemed so exhausted that we let you sleep, just this once. Would you draw more water for me? Knut has a fever."

Her little brother lay atop Mar's deerskin bed cover, his reddish mop damp with sweat.

"Are you sick, little man?" Astra smoothed curls from his forehead. "Poor Knut."

He leaned against her arm, his eyes red.

Astra wound her hair into a braid and tied on her head linen before picking up the wooden bucket and heading to the well. She caught up with Karin and Signy carrying pails of milk from the cow barn.

"How was your beauty sleep, princess?" Karin teased.

"Beautifying," Astra replied. She chased after the girls until milk began to slosh out of their buckets. Signy toppled to the ground, giggling, and Astra tickled her so that she begged for mercy. Astra veered toward the well, swinging her bucket, for the moment happy to be home.

When she set the bucket down next to Knut's bed, Mar dampened the wadmal cloth and laid it on the boy's forehead. "Ague," she said. "Hopefully, he will be better in a day or two."

Astra dished herself a bowl of cold, congealed porridge, topping it with a spoonful of honey and a little fresh milk.

"There is much work today," Mar said. "The girls are to gather firewood and search for berries. I need you to crush some salt. Start the cheese and then sprinkle salt…"

"I know, Mar," she said irritably. Her mother did not have to remind her anymore. "Sprinkle salt to ward off bugs."

"Yes. Then your father needs you and Karin to dig sod for the roof on the main house. Tomorrow we will scrub it down and move back in." Mar shook her head. "It is too crowded here in the summer cottage."

Astra had hoped to avoid her father today. She especially did not look forward to the heavy work of cutting sod from the woodlands and hauling it to the yard. But she did not argue.

She heated the morning's milk over the outdoor fire and hefted it to the cheese house, pouring it into the sheep's stomach to begin aging it. All the while she tried to think of how she could find time alone with Mar, and what else she could possibly say to avoid marrying Vegar.

Astra crushed a large bowlful of salt, sprinkled it along the edges inside the *stabbur*, and rehearsed her entreaty to Mar as she walked back to the summer house. Opening the door, she heard Far's voice stop as she entered.

Mar said, "Your father needs you to help him fix the fence before working on the roof."

Astra set the salt bowl on the table. Her mood soured.

"Did you get any more orders from the lady, Sven?" Mar asked, as if that was what they had been discussing.

"*Nei*, but I did from the *sysselmand*. He wants door posts nearly as tall as the manor's. He is improving his house for his future wife."

Far's gaze felt like a hot poker and Astra turned away. Did he expect her to be interested in a fancy house that she hoped would belong to someone else?

"How nice," said Mar, brightly. "A large house will be a blessing, will it not, Astra?"

Astra's ears heated. She straightened the coverings in the sleeping baby's hanging crib.

"He wants dragons, snakes, birds," Far added, "with a horse head on each corner...for you, Astra."

Astra restacked the wooden bowls on the small shelf, rubbing one with her apron to remove a spot.

Mar said, "You always do fine work, Sven. I am sure the posts will be well received." She scooped a spoonful of thinned porridge for Knut. "Here, little one. You need to eat." He whined and turned his head away. Mar's face creased. Everyone, including Astra, knew that children often got sick. It was common knowledge that elves put curses on people, especially children when they were naughty, as Knut often was.

Far loaded fence stakes and slats into the small sledge and dragged it with a rope over his shoulder through the pasture. Astra followed, calling for Ledsager to follow, but the dog still did not appear. She trailed behind her father as they strolled the perimeter looking for downed fencing. They found three rotted slats and one post that leaned precariously.

After the repairs were made Far motioned Astra to sit beside him on a sun-warmed boulder. Sullenly, she complied. He was going to lecture her again about Vegar's assets.

Far took her hand. "You know that your mother and I love you, and we have a duty to give you the best life we can."

Astra said nothing.

"That future life is not with us," he continued. "You are not getting younger, you know..."

"I am just fifteen!" she exclaimed.

"Too young for marriage? Your mother was your age when we married. I am sure you would not object if it were Einarr we were discussing."

Astra pulled her hand away and crossed her arms.

Far sighed. "As your elders, we know what will make a good life. You will have children, hopefully many, and they require money to provide for their future. This is what a good life is about."

She cried, "But I cannot marry Vegar! I detest him!"

Her father placed his hand on her shoulder. "Stop, Astra. You can marry Vegar, and you will. You must accept that there is no Einarr in your future. He will marry a nobleman's *datter*—that is the way of the world. Your mother and I know that the feelings of the young change over time. There will be trials, sadness, even heartbreak…it is commitment that lasts, not childish feelings."

Astra stared out across the field, saying nothing.

"Your mother and I learned to work together," he continued, "and eventually to love one another. Promises kept, hard work, and loyalty are what make a family."

Astra realized nothing she said would change his mind. Only her mother would better understand a young woman's heart. Mar would usually go along with what Far said, though not always. Astra had known her father to change his mind the morning after she overheard their late-night rustlings.

Who knew what Einarr might do now that the crisis with the king had passed? He could make a better offer to Far. It was not impossible. She would not give up hope.

Far stood, kissed her head and walked away. She noticed for the first time how his shoulders slumped. As he picked up the sledge rope, he rubbed his nose with a sleeve. Astra's pity was kindled; yet, if he was troubled, he was not as troubled as she.

Astra and Karin worked until well after the noon hour digging thick chunks of earth from the forest and piling them beside the main house. While they did this, Far shoveled off the old sod on which had grown an abundance of grass and a small tree. He stripped the old bark from the roof logs, then overlaid them with fresh bark. Astra and Karin loaded buckets with the heavy sod and Far hauled them up by rope to arrange on top of the waterproof birch bark. It was late afternoon when the roof was finally finished. All three were exhausted. Astra and Karin washed up at the well, then sat beneath a fir tree to rest.

"I hate that job," said Karin, sighing.

"Me, too," Astra replied. "At least we do not have to do it for a couple of years. I am glad Far did not talk much. I do not need another lesson in obeying my parents."

"You are still mad at him," Karin said.

"*Ja*. I can never get over this."

Karin leaned her head against Astra's shoulder. "Oh, Astra, what can you do if Far and Mar have decided? Maybe you should just accept it. At least you will have a rich husband."

Astra whispered, "Mar told me she once loved someone else before she married Far."

Karin sat up. "She did?"

"*Ja,* but she married Far because her parents made her."

"See? And that has worked out well for all of us."

Astra frowned. "I must keep hoping until there is no hope left."

Karin was quiet for a few moments. "Do you think Mar loves Far now?"

Astra shrugged. "She did not say. I think they are used to each other."

Karin put her arm around Astra's shoulder. "Maybe this is what the Virgin wants for you."

They heard Mar calling their names and scrambled to their feet.

From Knut's bedside, Mar said, "Karin, go find Signy and tell her to gather the eggs. Astra, stay here with me."

Karin touched Astra's shoulder and backed out the door. Astra gathered her arguments. If all else failed, she would tell Mar the abhorrent truth, certain that Vegar would not want a sullied bride.

But Mar motioned her closer to the bed. "Look," she said. She lifted Knut's nightshirt and gently moved his thin arm away from his body. Knut cried out. An angry dark blister protruded from his armpit.

"What is it?" Astra asked, taking a step back.

"A strange pox, unlike any I have ever seen." Mar lowered his arm carefully. "Go to the garden and cut agrimony and celery herb. And bring a cabbage and a turnip for the soup pot. He must have vegetable broth. He needs some of Far's wine for the pain, so run and ask him where he hides it."

Astra hurried to harvest the vegetables and herbs from the garden. When she asked Far about wine, he told her he would fetch it himself. She knew he stashed wineskins about the farm, for she had seen one of them hidden in the rafters of the *stabbur*. She gave her mother the herbs and watched Mar mix a paste with chopped bacon, honey, and barley flour. She placed the poultice under Knut's arm just as Far brought the wine. Mar gave Knut an ample drink.

By this time the baby was crying and Mar picked her up to nurse.

"Be strong, Knut, boy," Far said. "Do what your mother says. I will be in the barn, Jutta, if you need me."

When he left, Astra saw her chance. "Mar, may I speak with you?"

"About what?"

"About marriage."

Her mother shook her head. "*Nei,* no more talking."

"Mar, please listen to me. Einarr and I promised to marry. It is a sin to break a promise."

"It is a sin to disobey your parents," she replied. "Those were words shared between childhood friends only. It is not for you children to decide."

"We are not children. We love each other. That means something, Mar. Please…"

"*Nei*, Astra. Do not speak of it again."

Astra's eyes stung with tears. She must tell Mar the truth. "Mar, you have not heard everything. There is something you need to know that Far does not know."

Mar frowned. "What is there that would make any difference? I hope it was not…"

Heat sprouted in Astra's cheeks. "In Sjodrun…something happened to me."

Mar's brows buckled. "What happened? Did Einarr…?"

"*Nei*, Mar, not Einarr."

"Vegar? Did he touch you? Is that why…"

"*Nei*, not him."

"Who is it? I must tell your father!"

"*Nei*, Mar! You must believe me. I did nothing to bring this on myself and I am deeply ashamed. It was…the king."

Her mother stared at her silently for a moment, breathing heavily. Then she slapped Astra's face hard. "You are not usually one to tell tales. It is a grave sin to tell untruths to your parents, especially lies against the king. I am ashamed of you. You will repent on your knees tonight and to the priest when we go to the *kirke*. Go now. Think about the sin you have committed, and repent."

Mar switched the baby to her other breast and turned away. Her disapproval chased Astra out the door like an evil sprite.

Astra stayed away from her parents for the rest of the waning afternoon. She and Karin washed the baby's clothes and bedding, stitched up holes in shoes, swept the barn, and chopped firewood. They both went to fetch more herbs from the garden, and Astra rekindled the outdoor fire to start soup for supper. Then Karin went to check on Knut and told Astra that his fever had risen.

As Astra lugged a bucket of water to the kettle, she noticed Signy sitting in the shade resting her head in her hands. A basket of blackberries was spilled over beside her.

"What is it?" Astra asked, setting down the bucket.

Signy shrugged. "I do not feel well." Astra touched her sister's forehead. It was fiery hot.

"Mar!" she yelled across the yard. "Signy is sick, too!"

Mar ran out and lifted Signy into her arms. "*Jesu Kristus.* Not you, too." She carried Signy inside.

Astra dumped the water into the soup pot. Karin, her arms full of firewood, said to Astra, "I hope Signy does not have what Knut has. What kind of sickness is it?"

"I do not think anyone knows," she answered. At the sound of a child's shriek, they both ran.

Knut bawled loudly, rolling in pain. Mar lifted his arm to administer salve, but the dark pustules had grown from the size of silver coins to those of hens' eggs. Mar shushed him, "Now, now, be brave. I am trying to help you," but her face was fraught.

Both children lay on the bed without cover, their bodies flushed red with fever. Signy beseeched Astra and Karin with glassy eyes. "Am I going to get better?" she asked.

"We will pray for you," was all Astra could think to say, backing out the door.

Far ran up and pushed Astra and Karin aside to see the children. He gripped Mar's shoulder. His voice was thick. "Girls, get more rags. I will fetch more wine."

Astra sprinted to the *stabbur* where she ripped a tattered linen cloth into strips. She caught up with Far in the yard as they returned.

"What is this sickness, Far?" Astra asked.

"I do not know. We have never seen such a thing. It grows like a mushroom." Far kicked the door open and handed Mar the flask. She laced it with herbs.

"Get supper ready," Mar told Astra and Karin. "It is always best to keep busy when there is nothing else you can do."

Astra woke with a jolt. A hazy dream quickly faded, leaving her with the sense of foreboding. Karin still slept soundly beside her in the loft, so Astra slid quietly out of bed and down the ladder. The deep orange light of early dawn was rising over Skardet Mountain. Astra tip-toed across the wet grass bare-footed in her night dress. She noticed her father curled up in a sheepskin at the threshold of the house. Peeking around the door she saw her mother bending over Knut's fetid body that lay on the bed. Signy lay beside him, uncovered and sweating.

"Shh. They are both hotter than ever," Mar whispered.

"I will get more compresses," Astra offered quietly.

Mar nodded. She covered Signy with a light cloth before scooping Knut into her arms and rocking him like a baby.

Astra dipped a clean cloth in the water bucket and laid it on her brother's steaming forehead. She tried not to let her mother see her fear.

Mar lifted the flask to his lips. The wine only dribbled down his cheek. Her fingers shook as she pulled aside the wadmal cloth. Knut's whole body was blotched with dark spots. Suddenly, Knut began to convulse, his limbs thrashing. Guttural, unearthly sounds and spittle spurted from his mouth.

Mar lifted him and dashed out the door with the boy in her arms, leaping over her husband. Astra sprinted after her, hearing her father call, "Where are you going? Jutta, stop!"

But Mar sprinted across the yard, flung open the gate to the corral, and thrust the boy into the water trough. Astra watched aghast as her mother submerged her brother to his neck. He gasped at the shock.

In his nightshirt, Far pushed past Astra. "What are you doing, Jutta?" he shouted. "You are going to drown him!"

"Leave him be," Mar screamed.

"He will catch a chill!" Far wrestled with Mar to pull Knut out of the water, but Mar kicked her husband away with one foot, screaming, "A chill? He is burning up. Can you not see that he is…?"

Astra shrank back against the fence, her breath coming in shallow gasps.

"Now, Jutta," Far said, restraining his voice. His clenched fists quivered at his sides. "He is not dying. He just needs more medicine."

Mar held Knut in the water. "Get away. If you touch him again, I will kill you."

Far stepped back, silenced.

Immobilized by fear that her mother might drown Knut, Astra clung to the gatepost whispering, "*Jesu Kristus* save us. Mother of God have mercy on us."

At last Mar lifted Knut from the water and Far carried the boy back to the house. As they passed by her, Astra glimpsed Knut's listless body. His eyes lolled upward and he was as white as the trunk of an aspen.

When the door to the house closed, Karin ran up beside Astra in her night dress and gripped her sister's arm. "What is wrong? I heard shouting."

Astra could hardly catch her breath. "Knut was too hot, but Mar nearly drowned him trying to cool him off."

Karin looped her arm through Astra's and clung tightly. "Why did she do that?"

"I do not know. Maybe she is possessed by an evil spirit."

"Or she is losing her mind."

They both crossed themselves.

The summer sun had risen high over the mountains by the time Astra and Karin made their way back to the farm from the creek. Far had sent them to fish and check his traps, saying Mar needed time to care for the children on her own. Hungry, having not eaten yet, they strode together to the house with their buckets of squirming fish.

The door stood open. Mar sat on the *kubestol* inside nursing the baby. Her face was gray and her eyes were swollen slits.

The Moon Turned to Blood

Signy lay in bed alone. Mar said nothing to them when they appeared at the door. They set down their buckets.

"Where is Knut?" Astra asked, startled.

"In the old house," her mother said stiffly, nodding toward the small hut now used only for storage. Being in the old house by himself could only mean one thing. Tears sprang from Astra's eyes. She pushed against Karin and they backed out the door. They grabbed each other's hands and ran across the yard toward the workshop where they heard pounding. Choking sobs escaped Karin's throat as she stumbled after Astra.

Far turned at their approach. Around him were scattered dozens of tools strewn about haphazardly, as if thrown.

Far muttered, "At least he is not suffering anymore." He picked up a shovel, and stomped past them out the door. They followed him to the gnarled oak tree where the stones of old graves were now covered with moss. He began to dig.

The girls clutched each other in silence. Astra's mind reeled. Just two days ago, their little brother was happily jumping on piles of hay and throwing pine cones at squirrels. Now Far was digging his grave. Mother Mary! How could this be?

She croaked, "Should we not take him to the *kirke* yard to be with Gunnar?"

"*Nei*," Far answered gruffly. He kept digging. Sweat glistened on his face and neck.

"But he will not be in consecrated ground," Karin said. "How will he be raised again?"

"I know not, but we cannot go." Far tossed dirt onto a growing pile beside the hole. "There is not time."

Of course. Signy was sick, too. Would she die, as well? The thought sent a jolt through Astra. She tried to remember what she had been taught by Father Johan. Were children taken straight to heaven or did they go into limbo first? If they went to limbo, how could they get into heaven? And what about the baby who had not been churched?

When Far finally finished digging, they all walked silently back to the house.

"How is she?" Far asked Mar as he stood in the doorway. Grave dirt clung to his breeches, shoes, and hands.

Mar's cheeks were lined with salt trails. "Hot." She spooned broth between Signy's cracked lips, wiped her chin, and laid her head back on the pillow. Signy's eyes were red as fireballs. Mar's voice was throaty. "Come, let us do this while the baby is asleep."

Astra's parents held hands as they walked across the yard and stopped at the old house where Far's ancestors had lived for generations. Now it stored skis, snowshoes, and winter supplies. Mar and Far entered alone.

A childhood memory stirred. Astra pulled Karin away from the house by the hand and they stood under the apple tree to watch.

Soon, Mar marched rigidly toward the backside of the old house. She said to them, "We will use the *likglugg*," as if she were talking of tallow candles.

Now Astra remembered. The vision of her grandmother's body slithering like a snake through a hole at the back of the house sent a shudder through her. She had nightmares about it all that summer.

"What is that?" Karin asked, grabbing Astra's arm.

Astra pulled Karin by the hand toward where their mother waited. "Shh! You were too young last time they did this. Just watch."

The heavy pounding of a sledge hammer sounded from inside the old house. Momentarily, a chunk of the log wall popped out onto the ground at their feet. Far called from inside the house, "Are you there, Jutta?"

"Almost," their mother cried. "Astra, I need your help." She motioned Astra to stand beside her.

"You stay here," Astra said to Karin. She hurried to her mother's side, trembling.

Mar kicked aside the log pieces that had fallen out of the wall. She and Astra stood on the grass next to the house, directly below the hole Far had created.

"Ready," Mar called.

Shortly, the head of the linen-wrapped bundle that was Knut appeared, pushing through the hole. Mar and Astra reached up to catch him.

"Have you got him?" Far shouted.

Mar called, "*Ja*," as she and Astra accepted the scant weight of the child's body that glided into their up-stretched arms.

Karin screamed.

Astra's mother held Knut to her chest and kissed his shrouded face repeatedly. Far hurried out the door and around the side of the house. Mar's mouth twisted tightly but Far's face was like granite. Together they gingerly carried Knut's body toward the oak tree, moving as if they could hardly bear the weight of him.

Astra backed away, shaking and queasy, then stumbled to her sister's side.

Karin was as pasty as a lump of dough. "Why did they do that?" she asked.

Astra took her sister around the waist and led her toward the old family cemetery. She said quietly, "They had to so he will not come back to haunt us. That is what they did with Bestamor. That is what they must do with everyone."

Karin gagged and vomited into the grass.

Astra patted her trembling back. "Do not worry. It works because Bestamor's spirit never came back."

Astra led Karin past the outbuildings to the large oak tree that Far said was at least three hundred winters old. They sat with their backs against it, staring at the oblong hole Far had dug next to several other old gravestones. Astra wrapped her arms around Karin as they clung to each other in silence.

Gently, Far and Mar set Knut down beside the grave. A warm breeze rustled the leafy oak branches. A raven called.

Mar glanced up as the bird passed overhead. "It is an omen," she muttered.

They were all silent. Finally, Far took Mar's hand and quietly started to recite the prayer for the dead. Mar joined in, her voice cutting in and out. "Holy God, accept our beloved into your eternal care and bring us all together in paradise with you. In the name of the Father, Son, and Holy Ghost. Amen." Their voices died away and silence smothered Astra. She gulped for air. Karin buried her face in Astra's shoulder.

Far scooted Knut toward the lip of the hole.

"Just another minute," Mar said. She squatted and ran her fingers along the length of his body. Speaking into her son's ear, she whispered, "Wait for me. It will not be long."

The back of Astra's neck prickled.

Far lowered Knut tenderly into the grave. Mar bent and scooped up a handful of dirt, tossing it onto Knut's body and saying, "From dust to dust."

Far lifted Mar to her feet. "Jutta, think of the living now. The girls need you."

Mar bent to scoop another handful of dirt and shoved it into her pouch, then trudged toward the house as if dragging a heavy plow. Far waited until Mar was out of sight before he began to shovel.

Kvikke pulled eagerly against the reins as Astra and Karin rode together up the narrow path leading to the high country. Far told them to stay away from the farm for a while, as their mother needed time to herself. The day was fair and the shadow of sorrow lifted somewhat as the sun warmed their faces. They climbed higher and higher up the rocky trail, Karin's arms around her sister's waist. Trees disappeared behind them as they gained the alpine tundra. Delicate wild flowers like yellow saxifrage, alpine saw wort, and red campion bloomed among the mountain mosses.

Astra's overwhelming feelings of grief and disbelief slowly eased. Halfway up to the summer *seter,* the small cabin where Gunnar used to stay when he tended the sheep, they stopped at a glacier-fed creek and dismounted. They heard, then spied several of their black sheep wandering within earshot, bells about their necks. They also saw a fresh ewe carcass.

After taking a chilly drink from the stream they remounted and rode higher. The horse scrambled up loose rock as they approached the cliff and the overlook. They slid off Kvikke's back and climbed the steps of the stone cairn. Far was one of the cairn caretakers, making sure there was dry wood and flint to light a fire should a warning need to be sent through the valley. The two sisters peered over the rim into the crevasse below. Wind whistled up, sending a chill through their clothing.

The fathomless fjord below cut through the deep valley, its jagged rim running as far as they could see. Far below, the Laagen River poured down the cliff, disappearing into the cerulean waters. In the far distance, snow-capped mountains stood like northern sentinels protecting their homeland.

Chilled and trembling, Astra and Karin descended the rocky stairway and led the horse down toward the alpine grasses to graze. They drank from an icy rill, then sat on a sun-soaked rock.

Karin plucked up wild flowers to carry home. She said to Astra, "You said you would show me how to take care of horses. Can we start this evening?"

"*Ja*, but we will not tell Mar," Astra replied. "You know how she is about horses and girls."

"I want to learn everything, now that you are an expert."

Astra smiled at her. "I am no expert, but I will teach you what I know."

There was a pause, and Astra glanced over at Karin's face. It was contorted with emotion. "Do you think Signy will die?" Karin cried. "And what if the baby gets it?"

Astra paused. She had been mulling over the same fearful thoughts. "Mar is doing her best. All we can do is pray for them and take over the chores."

"I do pray, but...what if Mar gets sick?" Tears streamed down Karin's cheeks.

Astra embraced her sister, rocking her like a beloved child. When they finally drew apart Astra said, "You and I must make a pact. We will stay together no matter what else happens. We will be helpful, but most importantly, we will be careful. Promise me."

"I promise," Karin said.

The afternoon clouded over as they made their way downhill. Black smoke from the smithy hung over the farm and they heard the pings of Far's hammer.

Astra led Kvikke to the stable and let Karin brush the horse's lathered flanks. As Astra dug a stone out of Kvikke's foot, Karin whispered, "What if Far dies?"

Astra dropped the hoof and Kvikke shifted her weight, nearly stepping on Astra's toes. "Do not say that," Astra hissed, looking about the barn. "The *nissen* might hear you and make your words come true." Instinctively they both glanced into the dark corners for the tiny tricksters. "We must set out a special treat for them tonight," she whispered.

After releasing Kvikke into the pasture, they gathered wood to bring to the smithy. On the way Karin asked, "Where is Ledsager? I have not seen him since you came home."

"Neither have I," Astra replied. "I looked for him and called several times, but now I am worried." The old dog never went hunting anymore nor strayed far from the barn. She whistled again but only Haret and Irvig ran over to circle the girls' legs.

Astra and Karin dropped the firewood in the pile outside the forge, then stopped to watch their father work. He lifted the tongs and held up a large hook.

"Far?" Karin called. "Have you seen Ledsager?"

Far stuck the hook back into the coals and straightened, arching his back. "I am afraid I have. I found him behind the cow house and buried him yesterday. I am sorry, girls."

Astra turned and walked out. He was a dog, not a person, not worth crying over, as Far would say. Yet her tears fell repeatedly as she went about her afternoon chores. She could not remember life without Ledsager, nor Knut. And what about Signy, Mar, or even Far? She forced her mind to bury deeply the impossible thought of losing Karin.

Astra had added vegetables and a rabbit from one of Far's traps to the pot boiling over the outdoor fire. Far brought the baby outside and handed her to Karin. "Mar is resting," he said.

"How is she?" Karin patted the baby gently on her shoulder.

"Mar? She is tired."

"*Nei*, Signy."

"Worse." Far's eyes were bloodshot. "Spitting up blood." He scooped a bowl of soup for Mar and took it into the house.

Astra and Karin sat by the outdoor firepit sipping the hot soup as a soft drizzle fell. Astra stared at baby Liv in the crook of Karin's arm. How would Mar bear more loss? How would any of them?

They heard rustling from inside the house. Before long Far walked out, holding the cross that was always affixed to the wall above their parents' bed. He propped it up against a stump. Mar followed and knelt in the grass before the cross. She beckoned them to join her. Far prayed aloud to Saint Olav for a miracle, reminding him that Jesu had healed the sick and even brought Lazarus back from the dead.

It was then Astra knew Signy was dying.

After the prayer Mar prostrated herself flat on the damp ground. She pleaded, "God Almighty, *Jesu Kristus* your son, the angels Saraqae, Michael and Saint Olav, hear our prayers. I beg you to accept our Knut—do not turn him away from heaven—and heal your child, Signy. I will gladly forfeit my life in exchange for my children's. Take me instead."

Astra gripped Karin's forearm tightly.

Then Mar sat up on her haunches, raising her arms. "I appeal to all gods, Odin and Freya, Thor, and Baldur, keep my children alive!"

Astra gasped. It was forbidden to pray to the old gods!

"Jutta!" Far bellowed. "You must not speak this heresy."

But Mar pulled a clutch of herbs from inside her kirtle and shook it toward heaven. "I use these *djevel's* fingers to ward off Satan, elves, and evil of every kind." She threw her head back. "This curse I declare on the spirits that dwell in this land, that they wander astray forever, nevermore to find our home. To whatever god heals my *datter* I give my soul."

Far slapped his hands over his ears and cried, "Be quiet, Jutta, for God's sake!" He closed his eyes and reached heavenward. "*Kristus* forgive her. She does not know what she is saying."

Shaken and trembling, Astra bent over her knees, praying, "Jesu *Kristus* and Saint Olav, forgive my mother. If you answer our prayers, I will obey my parents' wishes. I will even marry…Vegar." She crossed herself three times.

For many long moments Mar prostrated herself on the ground, muttering curses and pleadings. When she finally rose, she tucked the herbs back down her kirtle without looking at any of them and stumbled to the house. Far lifted the cross to follow her in. His face wore distress such as Astra had never seen.

Suddenly, from inside the house, Mar screamed. Far dropped the cross and ran. When Astra heard her father bellow, "*Nei*, God, *nei*!" she knew. Signy had been taken, too.

Poor Signy was passed through the *likglugg* the next morning with difficulty. She slipped out of Far's hands, and Astra and Mar barely caught her as an arm swung free from the wrappings. When they lowered her to the ground together, the linen around her face unraveled. Astra cried out when she saw her sister's death pallor. From under the apple tree Karin shrieked and scrambled back up the hill and out of sight.

Astra clumsily tried to rewrap her sister's face and tuck her wayward arm into the wadmal strips, but her fingers trembled frightfully and she thought she might vomit. She scooted away from the body gasping for breath.

Far sped around the side of the house. When he saw Signy's disarranged body, he cursed, "There better be no more, by *Jesu Kristus* and all the saints."

Astra wondered if his curse was in vain.

After the second cross was erected at the family cemetery, Mar ordered Astra and Karin to help the family move back into the newly cleaned main house. She did not say so, but Astra was sure no one would ever sleep in the summer house again.

Astra and Karin hauled over the cooking utensils and chairs, but Mar waved them away from the feather mattress that was now stained and foul-smelling. Far dragged it to the firepit to be burned. Astra and Karin retrieved an empty tick from the *stabbur* and restuffed it with sweet grasses and wool. They hefted it onto Mar's carved bed frame and spread it over with clean furs. Lastly, Astra hung the baby's cradle on its ropes from the rafter. She hoped Mar would find rest here.

When they came outside to announce that the house was ready, smoke from the old mattress hung over the yard. Mar held the young children's clothes and shoes, ready to add them to the fire, but Far blocked her path.

"We still have Liv, Jutta," he said, plucking a pair of leather boots from her arms. "There will be more babies."

Mar glared at him. "No more babies." She snatched the boots from him and tossed everything into the fire. Reaching into her pouch she tossed the handful of grave dirt into the fire, too.

Liv began to cry but Mar only stared into the flames, swaying and mouthing unintelligible words. Far placed the baby in her mother's arms and helped her to a stool. There Mar pulled down her shift and milk spurted from her nipples. She thrust her breast into the child's mouth, oblivious to her nakedness.

Karin ran weeping to the stable as Far walked away toward the workshop, shaking his head. Astra was shocked at her mother's actions. Then she remembered what Mar said after Gunnar died, that losing a child was the worst thing that could ever happen to a woman. She overheard her say to Far that she would never get over it.

Astra found Karin in one of the stalls rolled into a ball. "You must get up," Astra said, lifting her sister from the straw-strewn floor.

Karin wept into Astra's shoulder saying, "I cannot believe our mother...is she a witch?"

"Mar is not a witch." Astra smoothed Karin's hair away from her face.

"How do you know? Are you sure?"

Astra did not answer. She was not sure at all.

After everyone else had finished supper, Far tried again to get Mar to eat, but she refused. They all sat quietly by the fire as the sky began to darken. When stars appeared between the drifting clouds, Mar lit a lantern and headed toward the graves.

"She cannot be out there alone," Astra said to her father, rising to follow.

"*Ja*, it is too dangerous," Karin said. "There could be goblins about, or even trolls."

Far leaned his elbows on his knees. "She just needs to be with them. I will check on her after a while."

"What about the baby?" Astra asked. The infant was beginning to fuss.

Far knocked the leather lambing flask down from the rafter and filled it with milk. "Here. You feed her."

The three of them sat beside the fire in silence as the baby suckled cow's milk from the lamb's nipple and fell asleep. When the darkness was full, Far retrieved a heavy bearskin and strode out into the night after Mar. He was gone a long time.

The Moon Turned to Blood

Astra and Karin put the baby in the cradle then wrapped themselves in furs, lying on the children's bare bedframe. Karin was soon snoring quietly, but Astra's mind was raw. What would Mar do if she could no longer bear the grief? Astra had once heard of a mother of eight who jumped off a cliff when she lost them in a fire.

When Far finally crept into the house alone, Astra whispered, "Is she coming?"

"*Nei,* but I covered her. The dogs will watch over her."

He sat down on the edge of the bed and Astra nestled her head onto his lap. "Your mother is ill," he said. "She is hot as a forging iron."

Astra clung to his legs and breathed, "The baby is sick, too."

Chapter 15

Kjell travelled north, paralleling the heavily trodden King's Way up the Godbrands Valley. He avoided the pilgrims on their trek to Nidaros and the great *katedral*, both the ragged and the richly clad alike. He eschewed the mountain stations at which many travelers received shelter, marveling that so many traveled away from home at harvest time. The sickness must be spreading widely indeed.

One evening he found a secluded place to rest and roasted a rabbit over a low-burning fire. There he bedded down, curled up with his dogs, lying awake and reliving the deaths of his loved ones. Dreadful memories of his last deeds at their home came flooding back.

The night Oda died, Kjell had burned the cabin in a rage to avenge his sorrow. As flames engulfed the shack, he was startled to realize he had saved no token of his wife, no remembrance of his child. In a panic he threw a deerskin coat over his head and reentered the burning hut, but the heat was too intense and he fell back. The flames danced higher, blackening the low branches of the nearby trees. He pulled half-flaming logs from the inferno, singeing his hands.

Despondent, he ran to the stream and brought buckets of water to throw on the roaring fire, but the splatters merely hissed, sending up small puffs of steam. Frantically, Kjell combed the grounds for a scrap of cloth, a forgotten shoe, a lost ribbon. Alas, he found nothing.

His hands blistered and his beard singed, Kjell sat cross-legged in the grass and watched their life together incinerate. At last, the cabin logs fell in and smoldered under the fallen sod roof. Why did he always act without thinking? He beat the ground with his fists, then buried his face in his blackened hands, wailing.

The next morning, Kjell left his ruined home and rode down the path to the squatters' village to check on Jens. As he walked by the cabin, he heard a faint call. The poor soul lay on his bed, his skin indigo even in the dimness of his hut. Rancid sores leaked vile fluid onto his bedding.

"Please," Jens cried. "If you have pity in you, send me to my fate. Then pray for my soul."

Kjell hesitated at the threshold, greatly disturbed by Jens' plight. "*Nei*, I cannot, but I will wait and bury you as I promised."

"Have mercy, I beg you." The man coughed, then held up a wavering hand. He tried to sit up but fell back, twisting in pain.

Kjell's heart was torn. "You must wait for God's time," he said. "What you ask makes me a murderer."

"*Nei*, an angel of mercy," he rasped. "No one knows how long I will suffer. Others suffered for many days."

Kjell had killed a man before, but not like this, not a friend. He backed away. He could not wait for days.

Jens called more urgently. "Do not leave me here to die alone. I forgive you...God forgives you. You will only be doing God's work for him. The dogs..." His voice strangled and broke off.

Kjell looked about the silent village. A chill ran through him as if the dead were watching. Abandoned dogs circled his barking *buhunds*. Kjell ran at them, chasing them to the perimeter of the hamlet where they peered around corners, panting and waiting. Indeed, these dogs would do the job if Kjell did not. Drawing his knife, he approached the cabin and stopped at the threshold.

Jens cried, "Thanks be to God. May He reward your mercy."

Stricken, Kjell stepped into the reeking cabin, covering his nose and mouth with his cloak.

Jens crossed himself and croaked, "I am ready."

"God have mercy on us both," said Kjell. With a skillful hand he sliced the man's carotid and a river of red pooled onto the bed. Relief swept over the dying man's eyes and he smiled as his life ebbed away. Kjell closed Jens' eyes in peace.

He dragged the body on his bloody bedding to the cemetery and buried him, swallowing his sorrow and telling himself he had committed an act of compassion. When he had packed the dirt down firmly on the grave and topped it with rocks, he felt at peace. What was done, was done.

A few cattle lay dead in the pasture, bloated and partly eaten. He opened all the paddock gates to set the other farm animals free. Thin, sickly horses straggled out, several with the same putrid lesions such as Jens'. Bony cows trotted away, bellowing.

One gelding remained, the only healthy horse alive, though thin. This was Jens' horse, always well cared for. "Calm down," he said, soothing the nervous animal with gentle strokes. The horse was black with white legs. "Sokker will be your new name," he said, roping the horse to Thorden's saddle. He mounted and led his small train out of the accursed village.

Several hungry dogs followed for some distance, all eventually dropping away except a half-grown puppy. Kjell whistled for the puppy and tossed it a piece of jerky. The dog trotted happily behind.

Kjell said, "What is your name, little fellow? No matter. I will call you Navnløs." The nameless one. He kicked Thorden's sides and they travelled north.

Chapter 16

Astra sat on the bank of the streamlet that ran through the edge of their farmland. She watched the ripples tumble over pebbles as Kvikke grazed nearby. Memories swirled around one another like leaves spinning in an eddy. She could picture Gunnar and Karin tip-toeing across the slippery rocks of the creek, gasping at the spring runoff that quickly numbed their toes. Gunnar had excelled at catching frogs and would chase the girls through the glen, trying to slip the creature down their necks. They, in turn, hid among trees and fallen logs, screaming as they jumped out to scare their big brother. A chase always ensued, leaping over ferns and moss-covered branches until they tumbled into a heap, laughing uproariously.

On long winter evenings the family played *hnefatafl*, which Gunnar rarely lost. Sometimes Far and Mar told frightening stories of abductions of children by elves, appearances of *djevels*, and the travels and pillaging of Mar's forebearers. Of the Vikings, Mar always spoke not with shame as many did, but with pride. Far just shook his head. The children nestled together under the furs, filled with terror and intrigue as they listened to these tales.

Astra had not forgotten the baby that was born blue when she was a young child. It was quickly wrapped in a deerskin and taken by Far out to the woods into a snowstorm. He came back without it and no one ever spoke of it.

After Signy, then Knut came along. Astra witnessed their births, but Karin was taken to the barn while her mother labored. Attended by a neighbor woman, Mar pushed and screamed as Astra cowered in the corner. Yet, Mar's face changed to delight when each chalky, bawling baby was placed in her arms.

As they grew, Astra and Karin fed the toddlers with tiny carved spoons and changed their soiled cloths. Astra scolded them, hugged them and laughed with them, singing lullabies when she tucked them under the furs. She recalled their sparkling laughter as they danced around the summer bonfires, waving their arms and shouting at the tops of their lungs to scare away the trolls.

But now? How could they be gone? Where were they? Languishing in limbo? Weeping in purgatory, in darkness alone and afraid? With great horror she visualized them beneath the ground, their hands protruding, begging to be set free. When she had asked Father Johan this, he had once whispered that all children went straight to heaven.

"Astra! Are you well? Where are you?" From across the farmyard her father's voice broke through her reminiscences.

"Here, Far!" Her eyelids felt like oak galls as she wiped the tears away and jumped onto Kvikke's back.

"What are you doing?" There was fright in Far's voice as he approached. "I was worried."

"Sorry, Far. I am coming now." Kvikke climbed the bank until Astra spied her father's lined face. She had not noticed until now how old he looked.

Panic charged through her. "Is something wrong?"

He motioned her to hurry. "Vegar is here."

The *sysselmand* sat on a log by the ashes of the firepit. Vegar rose when he heard the horse's footfalls. He wore linen pantaloons and fine leather boots, and his hair, as always, was held back by the ever-present red ribbon.

Astra's countenance fell. She dismounted.

"Greetings, Astra," he said, bowing. "I have just heard the hard news of the children and I give you my deep condolences."

"*Takk.*" She led the horse toward the stable.

Far took the reins from her grip, muttering, "Go and greet your guest."

She turned and curtsied ever so briefly.

"I share your grief," Vegar said. "I have lost loved ones as well."

"Your words are kind," said Far. "Are they not, Astra?"

"Indeed kind," she managed.

Far pushed her toward Vegar and whispered in her ear, "Karin is taking care of your mother. Show Vegar our hospitality while I stable his horse and bring some ale."

She had no choice. She smoothed her shift and tucked loose hair under her scarf.

"I pray your mother will be well soon," Vegar said. He rolled a stump over for Astra to sit on next to him. "I know you are bereaved. Can we sit for just a bit so I can express my sympathies? Let me start a fire."

Astra sat on her hands while Vegar rose and brought kindling from the nearby woodpile. He stacked small sticks over moss and struck his flint, then blew into the nest until it ignited. Astra was surprised that he knew how to start a fire, and even that he carried a flint.

"I wanted to see how you fared," he said between puffs. He added slivers of wood, then twigs to the small blaze. "I left Sjodrun the day you did, but my bailiff stayed a few days to finish up the business."

The fire flamed and he added branches. "When he came home yesterday, he told me that several at the manor were sick, in fact, two had died and others lay bedridden. I came to make sure you are well. I am saddened to see the sickness is here, too, but thank God you are not ill. You must take every precaution."

Astra was in shock. Who had died? What about Einarr? "Did anyone from the manor house die?" she asked.

"Two villagers, I believe. No one of consequence."

She bristled. He was haughty beyond belief. "My cousin lives in the village," she said sharply.

"Of course, I misspoke. Sad, indeed. I do not know who passed."

The fire crackled and sent sparks flying. "I brought you a gift." Vegar eased a packet from his pouch.

"No need for a gift." She glanced toward the door of the house, searching for a reason to get away and check on Mar. "I do not expect anything."

Vegar placed a suede purse on her palm. The bag was bigger than her hand and heavier than she expected.

"Do me the honor of opening it." Creases spread along Vegar's jawline; his face was unaccustomed to smiling.

Astra untied the packet to reveal a simply carved pine box. Far would have used oak for such a gift, she thought, and the carving would have been delicate and fanciful. A silver latch held the lid in place.

"It is…nice," she said. "*Takk*. Now I must get back to my ailing mother."

He unclasped the latch. "Look inside."

On a bed of satin lay a thick gold chain with a dazzling golden dragon's head hanging from it. Brilliant green gems shone in the dragon's eyes. The necklace was more stunning than anything she had ever seen.

"It is…beautiful," she said, "truly, it is. But I…"

"Please accept it as a token of my affection." He smiled again. "I made the box, but I had the necklace created in Skein, just for you. Here, try it on."

He slid it over her head and she pulled her braid from beneath it. The dragon's weight perched on her breastbone. She fingered the detailed surface and sparkling gems. What one could trade for such jewels she could only imagine. With this she could buy whatever her family needed. She clutched the dragon's head in her palm.

Then she realized this token was a promise, one she did not intend to keep. Carefully, she lifted the necklace over her head and placed it gingerly in the box.

"It is lovely," she said. "More than lovely, exquisite."

Vegar leaned back, his fingers threaded over his knee. His face beamed. "I am glad you like it."

She closed the lid. "But it is too fine for me. I would have nowhere to wear such a wonder."

"Ah, but it is for your wedding frock." Vegar grinned broadly. "I will be proud to stand with you while you wear it as an accent to your scarlet gown."

Astra bit her tongue. How could he expect her to think of a wedding while her mother was suffering and her family grieving? She lowered her head so Vegar would not see her clenched jaw. Even as she hesitated, she thought of the things she could purchase with this treasure—linen dresses for Karin and her mother, a new plow for Far, more cattle, another horse.

Far appeared with the ale cask. "Karin," he called into the house. "Bring my finest horns."

Karin emerged with two drinking horns and a pewter ale bowl. She glanced at Astra, lifting an eyebrow. Astra's eyes begged her sister for help. She hated that Karin must care for Mar while she was trapped entertaining the *sysselmand*.

Far filled the horns for Vegar and Astra and used the ale bowl himself. "I am sorry I have no wine," he said.

Vegar raised his horn. "No matter. *Skål*."

Far lifted his bowl as well. "*Skål*."

Astra barely raised hers, then took a small sip.

Both men drank their ale in one go and Far refilled their vessels. The men drank again.

Astra excused herself. "I need to check on my sick mother."

"Of course," Vegar replied. "I will wait."

She carried the gift box into the house, hearing Far exclaim what a splendid son-in-law he was to have. She had sworn to God to marry Vegar, but God had not answered her prayers. Knut and Signy had died, and now her mother and the baby were ill. If all else failed, she would tell Vegar about her impurity. Surely then, he would not have her.

Mar lay on her bed curled up, her forehead beaded with sweat. Astra started to walk past Karin to sit beside her mother, but Mar stopped her. "You will not get near me. There is a wicked spirit about."

"What about Karin? Then she should not be near you, either."

"For today, let your sister tend to me." Mar turned over and grimaced in pain. "I heard you got a gift from Vegar. Show me quickly, then go attend to your guest."

Astra opened the box and placed the necklace over her head. Her mother touched the stones and lay back. "It is lovely, my sweet."

"May I try it on?" Karin asked.

Astra lifted the necklace over Karin's head and held up the copper mirror. Karin ran her fingers over each stone.

"I will never love him, Mar," Astra said, dropping her head.

Mar sat up carefully, clearly in pain. "That matters not. Do not fight us now."

Astra did not respond. Her mother saw her as a liar, and a tarnished one at that. She said, "Vegar says this terrible sickness is at the manor, too."

"It is a curse brought on by sin," her mother replied.

Astra removed the necklace from Karin's neck and backed toward the door. Did her mother think she had brought this evil to them?

To her surprise, Mar sighed. "All have sinned, including me. You heard me in the yard."

"*Nei*, mother, you were deranged by grief," said Karin.

"I committed blasphemy." Mar gently laid back down and looked at Astra. "Others among us have sinned, too." Mortified, Astra turned and fled the house.

The men had left the fire and she heard clanking coming from the workshop. She wiped her tears and strode toward the sound. Vegar was helping Far rebind the staves of a broken barrel using an iron ring Far had forged. Astra was surprised to see the *sysselmand* working at such a job. Clearly, he was trying to impress her father.

The Moon Turned to Blood

"How is your mother?" Far asked without glancing up. The two men struggled to fasten the final stave into place.

"Feverish. How long will you be, Far? Should I start the porridge?" Certain that porridge was not a desired supper for a rich man, she hoped Vegar would be dissuaded and leave soon.

"Vegar will be staying for supper and spending the night," Far announced to her great disappointment. "Kill one of the chickens. You can roast it over the fire. Barley cakes would also be good."

Astra marched angrily away. She should be caring for Mar rather than waiting on a wealthy man. Helping Far with a broken barrel did not make up for the multitude of farm chores they could not complete because of his presence.

Astra chased chickens about the yard, picking one up by the feet and dispatching its head with one blow of the axe. When it was sizzling on the spit over the fire, she brought out yesterday's barley cakes from a tin.

Soon the three of them ate from plates on their laps accompanied by many draughts of ale. Vegar and Far discussed *Thing* business and Vegar's visits with farmers in the region. Far eventually inquired about the necklace Vegar had brought for her and Astra was obliged to show him. Vegar helped to place it about her neck again.

"It becomes you," said her father. She could not recall him ever commenting on her looks before, and she blushed deeply.

"Indeed," said Vegar. "You have a beautiful *datter*, Sven."

Far stood up and stretched his back. "I must check on Jutta." He walked unsteadily to the doorway and turned. "Astra, when you have put the horses away, make up the guest bed for Vegar in the *stabbur*."

She sputtered, "But Karin and I..."

Far talked over her. "Karin will sleep elsewhere and will do your other chores. I hope you will excuse the dust, Vegar. Astra will find bedding."

161

"But Far!"

"Go. Do what I say."

Fuming, Astra brought the horses to the stable and Vegar followed, leading his steed. He sat on a stool near the stalls and watched her brush them down. "You will no longer have to do any of this labor when we are married," he said. "I have servants and stable hands. You will live the life of a lady."

Astra stroked the curry brush hard on a patch of mud on Kvikke's flanks. "But I like to work with horses," she said. "In fact, I love horses."

"As lady of the house you may do as you like," he replied. "You can bring your own horse and ride whenever you please."

She bent beneath Kvikke and brushed the horse's belly. "I like to ride every day, but I cannot take Kvikke because my father needs her to work the farm."

"I will provide your father with a suitable work horse, then. Let us not quarrel so soon, and about something of little importance."

Astra's face flushed in the dimness of the stable. "Horses are important to me."

Vegar sat quietly while she groomed Farwa, then he rose to groom his steed. Astra offered to do it for him and he assented. She took her time, admiring the fine English horse's silky coat, then led the horses into stalls. Vegar helped carry buckets of water from the well.

When they were finished, Vegar took her by the hand to a bench. "Please sit with me."

Astra sat on her hands.

"Astra." His voice was gentle, even fatherly. "I know you do not love me. I think you see me as too old for you, *nei?*"

She stared at her lap.

"Yet, your father and I have struck a bargain that your parents believe is best for you. It is my sincere wish to make you a happy wife. We can wait to marry until the time of mourning is past, even until summer comes again. When you get to know me, you will find I have much to offer."

Astra breathed a sigh of relief. A year. He was giving her a year. "I know my father and mother only want what is good for me," she said into her skirt. "If you knew me better you would not want me. I am willful and disobedient, and..." Should she tell him about her love for Einarr? About what the king had done? Would he even believe her when her mother did not? Instead, she said, "I am not worthy to marry someone such as you."

Vegar straightened. "I see I have pushed too fast. The timing is poor. Your family is in the midst of sickness and grief. I am a patient man."

Astra stepped quietly into the house. She said to Karin, who sat near Mar spinning, "After I make up the bed for Vegar I will bring our tick back for us to sleep on here."

Karin nodded but did not look up at Astra.

Mar whispered, "Make your future husband a nice bed. You know I only want your happiness."

"*Takk*, Mar," she said. "I hope you feel better tomorrow."

Vegar followed Astra up the ladder to the loft where she and Karin slept. She lit a tallow candle that smoked pungently, then dug a fresh tick from a storage chest. She filled it with straw, and pounded a dusty pillow, sure that he would be uncomfortable here. Perhaps this would prompt him to leave.

She shoved the mattress she and Karin would use down the ladder, then said to Vegar, "Good night. I hope you sleep comfortably. Will you join us to break the fast?"

Vegar touched her shoulder and she froze. He turned her toward him. He was tall, much taller and stronger than she. He took her arms.

She backed up.

He stepped close to her. She could feel his breath. Hers came in rapid spurts.

"Do not be afraid," he said. "Since your family is ill, I have offered your father to take you with me to my manor, away from this sickness. I do not want to lose you. We can seal our love tonight and leave in the morning. The wedding can occur in summer, as I said."

Astra pushed him away hard and backed toward the ladder. "*Nei!* I cannot leave my mother while she is ill."

"Do not be afraid," he said smoothly. "I care for you. I will be gentle." He reached for her but she ducked and slid down the ladder, banging her shins on the rungs.

He called, "Wait! Astra, come back! With me you will be safe."

She ran for the house, his voice echoing in her ears.

When she arrived, the door to the main house was bolted. She banged on it, but no one opened it. Karin's cry was quickly shushed. Astra banged her forehead against the planks. Her father had allowed Vegar to spend the night with her to secure their marriage! Wretchedly, she ran to the empty summer house and bolted the door behind her. In the utter darkness she beat her fists against the log wall. How could her father do this? Did her mother agree? Slumping to the dirt floor she curled up, hugging her knees and weeping. It was some time before her breathing slowed.

Just as she was dropping off to sleep, she jerked upright. The thought was like a lightning bolt. This was her father's way of saving her life.

Astra slept little in the only thin cloak she found in the corner of the summer house. When she awoke, achy from the hard dirt floor, she peeked outside. The sky was overcast and the sun well up. No one was about.

Across the yard the door to the main house stood ajar. When she approached, the stench of Mar's now-putrid pustules made Astra wince. She stood in the doorway. Mar lay abed, her eyes blazing.

"Stay away from me," she croaked.

"Let me help you, Mar," Astra pleaded.

"*Nei*, stay away. Karin will return soon to care for me."

"I am sorry we argued," Astra murmured.

Her mother said, "As for that, it was nothing. Do not think of it again."

Astra turned away, heartsick and remorseful. Far strode toward her with a hare dangling from his hand. His face was drawn. "To add to the pot," he said, laying the hare on the butcher block.

"Will Vegar be joining us to break the fast?" Astra asked without meeting his eyes.

"*Nei.* I am sure you will be sad to hear that he left at first light. You successfully chased him away."

She ignored her father's jab as Karin approached, carrying a bucket of water and a few eggs. Karin looked pale. "Have you seen Mar?" she asked Astra.

"She is worse," Astra murmured.

Far's voice cracked. "*Ja,* that she is."

Astra grabbed her father's arm. "We must take her to the manor. Perhaps someone there can help her, a doctor or healer…"

Far pulled away. "Doctors. They just open a vein then ask for a gold coin."

"A medicine woman, then," said Karin, setting down the bucket.

"What about the witch?" Astra was becoming distraught.

"The witch of Nore cannot help us." Far spat on the ground.

Astra took his arm. "But what we are doing is not working."

"Let us go right away," Karin said. "Doing something is better than doing nothing."

Far's eyes swam as he sat down on a stump and put his head in his hands. "I do not think your mother can travel. She barely eats or drinks, except the pain potion. I am afraid she will not survive the trip."

Astra kneeled at his feet. "Please, Far."

He stared at her, then glanced at Karin. "Ach, perhaps you are right. Very well. The manor then."

Astra and Karin ran to the pasture to saddle the horses. When they led them into the yard they heard Far arguing with Mar. "Jutta, it is the best thing. They may have found a treatment at the manor."

"*Nei*, Sven." Mar's reply was weak. "I cannot make it. Just leave me here. Take the baby—perhaps they can save her."

"We will not leave you, Jutta," Far said sternly. "We are going. No arguments. Let us help you up."

"Someone must feed the baby first," Mar said feebly. "I no longer can."

"Astra! Feed her while I get your mother ready," Far shouted.

"Not Astra…Karin."

Astra looked at Karin's bone-weary face saying, "Why not me? Is she angry with me?"

Karin's face paled. "She does not want you to get sick, because of your Vegar."

Astra inhaled raggedly and reached for her sister. "*Nei*, Karin…"

Just then Far emerged from the house ashen-faced. He said a little too loudly, "Karin, here is the baby. Please feed her so we can go."

"Where is the lamb's flask?" she asked as she accepted the wrapped bundle.

Far hissed, "Say nothing, just take her." He went back inside and they heard him say to Mar, "I will help you change your soiled things."

They heard rustling as he tried to lift her, then Mar's yelp of pain rent the air. "*Nei!* I cannot! Let me die in peace."

In Karin's arms Astra tugged gently on the baby's cloths. The infant's face was gray and lifeless.

Despite the summer sun, Astra shivered as she stood beside Karin under the oak tree where Far dug the last shovelfuls for the small grave. They did not pass the infant through the *likglugg*.

"She was not churched," Karin said to Far. "How will she go to heaven?"

Far propped the shovel against the trunk. "God knows that she has not sinned. We must believe that she will be waiting for us when it is our turn." He picked up the bundled baby and lowered her into her resting place.

"Mar should be here," Astra said. "She should know."

"I told her you girls would care for the baby from now on. She did not object. I think she knew." Far stood up and dusted off his pantaloons. Together they mumbled the prayer for the dead and crossed themselves.

Far tossed a handful of dirt into the grave. "From dust to dust," he said hoarsely. He took the shovel and slunk slowly back to his wife.

By morning Mar was gone, too.

Chapter 17

Higher into the Dovre Mountains Kjell rode, galloping long stretches on the gently rising hills, slowing when he entered a clump of trees or a steep pass. As the next days passed, there were moments, even hours, when he thought only of the journey: he was at home in the wild. But suddenly, a crashing wave of grief would strike, forcing a moan of sorrow into the wind. In the evenings, as darkness grew, he was unable to bury the image of Oda's last moments of suffering.

He slept restlessly and woke often. Sometimes he bolted upright, his heart hammering. The dogs, curled beside him, jerked their heads up, then licked his hands and face. He lay back, realizing there was no danger but his own thoughts. During these days he ate little and rode long, contemplating his empty future. What lay ahead for him now? Would he hunt alone until accident or animal killed him? Was that his penance? And what had happened to his parents in Hamar? He should go to them now, but it was said the sickness raged there. His last memories of their rejection of him and Oda had scarred him. He would hunt first, then go.

Trees gave way to rocky soil that sprouted only grasses, cranberries, and low-lying wild flowers. Craggy plateaus with folded layers of rock dotted the undulating expanse of the high country, providing Kjell with vistas of distant snow-capped mountains and glimpses of the fjord's ultramarine shimmer. The horses' pace slowed as they picked their way among the stones, watchful of hidden holes and slippery moss. Legend said that ogres had molded these boulders, shaping them and smashing them like unbaked clay—for what purpose, no one knew. Indeed, ogres were known to live in the caves among the rocks...few people would dare sleep here, including Kjell.

The Moon Turned to Blood

One morning out of the north, a thundering herd of reindeer poured toward Kjell's small company, passing them like a river. The sleek antlered creatures mounted a knell, then flowed down toward the fjord. Watching them, Kjell's melancholy eased. He thought of the hunt: the stealth of stalking his prey, the bursting chase, the whiz of the arrow that scattered game like fish in a lagoon. Kjell could shoot with accuracy at a full gallop. The sensation of rending a reindeer's hide from its muscle was viscerally satisfying; the task of butchering, a gift of life. But this day he was not collecting hides nor meat. He had far yet to travel. He watched the herd disappear over the hillock.

Passing rocky streams and shallow lakebeds in the high grassland, Kjell spotted a few *seters*, the summer cabins where farmers took their sheep to graze on the rich mountain grasses. Not far away, he spied a shepherd boy and his dogs chasing stragglers down the near side of the slope. These were common Norse sheep, gray- and black-wooled with curled horns, their shaggy bodies blending with the stones like patches of lichen. Kjell had seen these hardy survivors run in packs, the strongest on the perimeter to protect the young. They were even known to ward off young wolves. Yet, occasional piles of sodden wool with bones protruding like grave markers gave evidence of grown wolves' prowess.

By the angular light of each waning evening, he searched his skin for boils, running his hands over all his limbs, probing his neck and armpits. So far, nothing. Tonight, Kjell squatted by the peat fire over which roasted a small hare. In the flames, the faces of his loved ones came unbidden before him—his son's death-tarnished features, the bloody sputum on his wife's ashen cheek. He clenched his teeth against the vice in his chest. How he regretted his long absence. Kjell's eyes burned as he pictured his Oda with her golden hair spread across the pillow. He felt her curves cupped in his hands, smelled the earthy scent of her neck. God had taken her from him as punishment for his many sins. And now? God had naught to do with him anymore.

Kjell had met Oda two summers ago on just such a high plain as this. He was hunting in the high country and she was shepherding, chasing down a lamb with the help of her dogs. Kjell watched from a distance as a wolf jumped from behind a boulder and grabbed the lamb by the neck. The frenzied dogs bayed and lunged at the wolf as it backed away, the lamb dangling from its jaws.

The girl, her hair flying free, ran toward the predator with only her staff, screaming and waving her arms like an angry goose. Kjell kicked his horse and galloped toward the wolf full-speed, raising his bow. The arrow pinned the wolf to the ground by the neck. Oda spun around to see whose aim was so true. Kjell yanked on the reins and the horse skidded to a stop. He would never forget the look of surprise, then relief, on her wind-brushed cheeks. Her smile lit her eyes like a sunrise, and Kjell loved her from that moment on.

He did not ask her father for her hand. Instead, the two lovers sneaked away to a small parish *kirke* where a *drukken* priest married them for a few coins. They gave the pretense that they must marry to prevent the sin they had already committed.

Deliriously enthralled, they collected the sheep and drove them to Oda's family farm with the happy news—for which she was promptly disowned. Rejected by his family as well, Kjell tossed Oda atop Thorden's back and they rode away, determined to make life on their own. They settled in an axe-hewn cabin near the squatters' settlement hidden in the woods, thinking they would be happy there. Little did Oda understand how long a hunter of precious furs would be gone. Kjell rued his long absence now.

The northerly road dipped down to a lake and Kjell spied a village where he thought to spend the night in an inn. He jingled the pouch full of coin from his sales to the lady of Sjodrun manor. A real bed would do his back good. He also needed a new blade, since he had broken his best gutting knife prying up a rock for his firepit.

Stopping at the lake to let the horses drink, he studied the village. There was smoke in three chimneys, but the village was quiet. A small *kirke* was situated nearby and Kjell clearly saw the graveyard dotted with fresh graves. Beside one grave, two men were on their knees, digging. One of them pulled out something shiny and showed it to his companion. Then he shoved it inside his cloak. When they looked around and saw Kjell watching them, they both ran.

Kjell's thoughts turned black. Grave robbers. No one could be viler. He mounted and yanked Sokker behind him up the hillside away from the village. Was there no place in Norway safe from God's rage? Had the demons of death already marked his own path? At least he deserved whatever penalty he received. He would travel further north...much further north.

For several more days Kjell followed the road leading toward Trondheim Fjord, by-passing every village as he descended into the Oppdal Valley. Finally, he came upon the King's Way, the road that led north to the holy city of Nidaros. Paralleling this road at a distance he saw pilgrims traveling by foot and on horseback. He stopped at a creek for water, and several richly dressed magistrates on high-stepping steeds rode up to do the same. They greeted him and he nodded, but said nothing. The *katedral* city must be close now.

Kjell sat on a log, forcing himself to swallow the last of his *brød*, so dry he had to dip it in water. An eagle soared overhead then perched on the top of a dead pine nearby. Silently, the female swooped down, snatched a marten from the brush and flew off. Eagles were a sign of good fortune, perhaps a sign that life could be reignited.

Kjell joined the widening path that was scattered with pilgrims. Bedraggled travelers plodded along, many in tattered clothing that spoke of a long trek. Some were emaciated, some bare-footed and bleeding. How far had they walked?

Well into the afternoon as they neared the holy city, the road split. Most took the downward path that led to the river. A few others, including Kjell, climbed the steep trail up to where the castle sat atop the hill. They walked carefully to the rim of an overlook where they could view the whole town of Nidaros. All eyes were drawn to the colossal cross-shaped structure with its multiple pointed spires pointing heavenward. Behind it was the imposing archbishop's palace with its protruding tower. The River Nid wound around the town, forming a peninsula that was connected to the mainland by a small neck of land. Kjell followed his fellow travelers down the steep hill to cross the stone bridge at the base of the incline.

Kjell strode ahead, passing sod-roofed houses and shops, most with a small plot for a garden and a few animals. He hoped to find a comfortable place to rest and to gather supplies before moving northward. When he came to the wide walkway that led through the middle of the town, he stopped and glanced in both directions. To his left, the spires of the *katedral* dominated the skyline. To his right were shops and houses.

Entering a town always felt risky to Kjell, should he, by chance, encounter a soldier who might recognize him. His close call in Sjodrun had shaken him, but seeing no king's men about, he felt safe.

Kjell peered down at his blood-smeared trousers and filthy shirt. He stroked his beard that now reached mid-chest. He must find an inn and pay for a bath.

He led his horses between the houses and shops along the plank-laden path that led toward the main square. Many people were about today, some plying their trades from their domicile doors, some carrying water, a chicken, a piglet, or bundles of sticks. Many others bent at their daily tasks. A baby played on the step of a house from which the enticing odors of roasting meat emanated. Inside, a woman, sewing, glanced out of a doorway and met his eyes. She quickly looked away. Embarrassed by his appearance, Kjell brushed off his dusty garb and tied his matted hair behind his neck with a leather strip.

Soon the lane enlarged and the line of pilgrims thickened. He was surprised by the number of visitors clogging the streets, but thankfully, he saw no pox of the black sickness. These must be fathers, mothers, daughters, and sons, all beseeching God to let the dreaded curse pass them by. He walked by a woman on bloodied knees, whispering incoherently and shuffling slowly with her hands clasped together. Whose soul was she trying to redeem? Her own? A lost loved one?

Before long, Kjell entered the *katedral* courtyard. He halted. The monolithic *katedral* loomed before him like the Sunnmøre Mountains. The massive yawning doors and slotted windows taunted him disapprovingly; the structure before him filled him with foreboding.

He had visited Nidaros once before. Within the *katedral*'s central octagonal nave sat the high altar and the golden reliquary containing Saint Olav's remains. This was the most holy place in Norway. The miraculous sweet-water well was inside, too, the spring that had bubbled up from the saint's burial plot. Travelers were free to draw holy water and drink thereof, hoping for healing and answers to prayers.

Around the perimeter of the *katedral* plaza, booths were set up: merchants sold beaded necklaces, crosses, amulets, and other holy articles. Vendors hawked bread, cheese, and savory victuals, and the scents stirred Kjell's empty belly. A multitude of mourners crawled, wept, and wailed as they made their way toward the open *katedral* doors. Holy men in cowls carried heavy crosses on their bent backs. One man wore a crown of thorns, blood drizzling down his face.

From around the side of the immense structure Kjell heard slapping sounds and voices of men crying out in pain. He turned as a parade of half-naked penitents came into view. They bore stone-tipped whips that they flung over their shoulders, shredding their backs. Still, they carried on, strike after strike, flicking bits of flesh and evoking their own painful cries. A few women followed these flagellators, hands folded in prayer, beseeching God to forgive their loved ones' sins. One woman had shaved her head.

People have lost their senses, Kjell thought. The idea of going into the *katedral* to say prayers for Jens and the villagers, as he had promised, was muted by this raw suffering.

Bells soon rang out high in the towers above. Kjell flinched. His horses snorted and backstepped. He calmed them with gentle strokes as he watched people stream through the *katedral* doors. When most were inside, chanting drifted out. From deep in his childhood memories Kjell felt a reflexive urge to join them. He had much to confess. Yet, why would he approach a God who had taken so many innocents, a God who had robbed him of his beloved wife and sinless child? Kjell turned his horses around, followed by his dogs, and wound back to a quieter lane.

He stopped a stranger he passed to ask for an inn. The man pointed. "The inn at the end of this road may have a room. Otherwise, you can knock on doors and someone might let you share their bed, for a price."

Kjell found the noisy inn, tethered his horses, and stepped inside. At the boards sat men and a few women quaffing ale. One man, well into his cups, was loudly telling a story.

"I saw the giant late at night, hiding among those boulders." He pointed vaguely toward the hills above the fjord. "He was ugly, like you, Harald."

Harald shouted in objection, swatted his friend's head, then laughed along with everyone at their table. Kjell smiled to himself.

The man continued loudly, "I scared him away with my torch, running at him and screaming. He must have heard of my reputation."

Laughter burst out again.

Right next to the man, a serving woman set down her pitcher, leaned on both hands, and said to him, "That's naught to be proud of. I saw the Fairy Maiden when I was just a girl, and she promised me a long and happy life." She paused, then added, "And her prediction came true. See where I am now?"

The men roared, she grinned, and all shouted, "*Skål!*"

Near the stairs to the loft, Kjell spied a red-faced man sitting at a board across from a buxom woman. He was talking vehemently, several empty ale bowls before him. The man surreptitiously brought coins out from his pocket and fingered them across the table to her. She hid them in her pouch, nodded toward the stairs, then preceded him up.

A petite serving maid watched them from nearby. She was not young, but pretty in her way. When she met Kjell's eyes, she blushed.

Kjell sat down at the next table. He ordered ale and a bowl of stew from the innkeeper. The maid cleared dishes from tables and passed by Kjell, her hands laden with empty plates.

Kjell said to her, "Do you know where a man can get a bath?"

She paused. "There is a bathhouse at the back of the inn. Are you staying here tonight?"

"I think I might, if there is a room for myself only. I need a good rest. I have been traveling far."

"As have all," she replied. "I will ask for you." She swept through the door to the kitchen, coming back with his ale and a bowl of stew. "The innkeeper said there is a small private room if you have the money. Water can be heated for a bath, but that will take some time."

"That is what I need, *takk*." Kjell pulled coins from his purse and she picked out enough for the room and bath. "What is your name, lass?" he asked.

"Ingvil. I live nearby...well, now I do." She nodded vaguely toward the street.

Kjell smiled. "I see you are overrun with travelers." He tasted the lamb stew and nodded in satisfaction.

She leaned forward and said quietly, "The black sickness is a curse from God. I lost my parents and my sisters, too. I came here to escape."

Kjell swallowed. "I lost my loved ones as well."

Tears glistened in her eyes. "My father was a tar maker. We lived outside the town, but the sickness came anyway."

Tar makers were among the poorest, and this maiden was likely left with nothing when they died. She was lucky to have found a job at the inn.

"I am the third son of a farmer, so now I hunt. I have not seen my father for two years."

"Then we both must earn our own ways," she remarked, shifting her gaze away.

"Indeed." Kjell shoved a large spoonful of stew into his mouth.

"I will heat the water for your bath. It should be ready within the hour." She hurried to the kitchen.

After his meal he stowed his gear in a room no larger than a closet, but he was glad to have this to himself. He then wandered through the town as he waited for the water to heat. The sun was lowering toward the horizon when he found himself again staring at the intimidating structure of the mighty *katedral*. Mourners and weepers were fewer now. A priest hurried by, carrying scrolls under his arm. Perhaps Kjell would just stand at the door and peer inside. He strolled toward the arched entrance, walking along the wall and running his hand over the fitted soapstone blocks. The vaulted arches, carved outcroppings, and angled windows made him feel lowly and insignificant.

The huge doors gaped in front of him, tall, oaken, and well-carved. Kjell recalled the best carving he had ever seen at the manor in Sjodrun. Every inch of those had been covered with dragons, vines, snakes, and ghoulish faces. The carver was the father of Astra, so bright and full of life. She had been sorely used. He should pray for her, as well as for Jens and his family.

These thoughts led him through the *katedral* doors into the dim interior.

Kjell stood still, straining to see his surroundings in the vast darkness. Footsteps echoed and receded on the stone floor. He peered down the nave to the distant altar and the recessed quire beyond. He lifted his eyes toward the bluff-high beams of the ceiling. Here at Saint Olav's burial place, many miracles had occurred, so they said. To Kjell, this reverent and fearful place was paralyzing.

Confessional booths lined the wall like silent judges, but no one waited on the benches nearby. Kjell had not gone to confession since.... he knew not.

He sidled toward the benches, his heartbeat reverberating along with his footsteps. He sat on a bench and waited for a confessional door to open. Many minutes passed. No one emerged from any of the booths. Kjell crept over and knocked lightly on a confessional door.

No response.

"Father?"

No reply.

Relief broke over him. He backed away. What would he have said anyway? I killed a knight, stole my wife, ran away to get married, then left my love unprotected so that she sickened and died alone along with our son? Then I slit a dying man's throat in cold blood, not the first time I killed a man. What would be the penance for such sins? Kjell trod quietly toward the main entrance where his eye caught the enormous crucifix hanging above the altar. He crossed himself, uttering a short prayer for Astra, his family, and Jens, then he dropped several coins in the alms box before hurrying out.

The inn was busy now. Many patrons were laughing, well into their cups, but others sat somberly at the tables talking to no one. One raggedly dressed patron stared into his ale bowl without drinking. Two men slouched by the fire, one blubbering and leaning his heavy arm over his victim's shoulder. Three diners were bleary-eyed flagellants, their shirts red-soaked. Kjell heard various Norse accents spoken, and even a young couple speaking Swedish. Apparently, people from far and wide were trying to find solace for the black sickness.

Kjell looked about the room for Ingvil. She was serving *brød* and stew at a table full of *drukken* men. Her face was flushed as she twisted to avoid a pinch. The men chortled at this and toasted her with their ale cups.

Kjell crowded onto a bench next to an old man who was silently watching those at the noisiest table. Standing up and leaning heavily on his arms, the old man suddenly slapped the boards loudly, silencing everyone.

His voice was unexpectedly strong as he shouted, "We should not be celebrating with revelry at this wicked time! Did none of you go to the *kirke* today?"

No one spoke or looked his way. A couple of people nodded.

His nostrils flared. "The priests say that we have all displeased God and must pay the price. We must all confess our sins and beg for mercy." Glaring at the men who had been so rowdy, he slowly sat.

After a few silent moments, quiet conversation resumed.

Without looking at him, the old man muttered to Kjell, "Seers say the stars are aligned for disaster. I heard it said that the moon will turn to blood, just as the scriptures say. The end times are coming."

"What do you say?" Kjell asked him.

"I think we have been cursed by Pesta, that witch of death."

A pall passed over Kjell. The witch of death indeed.

Just then Ingvil signaled him to follow her. Kjell downed his ale and left the old man to his prophecies.

When he caught up with her at the door, she smiled and said, "Your bath is ready. I will show you the way."

Chapter 18

Astra woke when she heard her father stir. She sorely missed the warmth of her siblings' bodies, and she covered her head with the deerskins to squelch her sobs at facing another day without them. She heard Far climb out of the box bed, strap on his shoes, and open the door.

Then she rose, pulling on her over-dress and passing her father on his way back into the house. Her stomach roiled. She hurried behind the house to vomit. What had she eaten last night? Did she have ague? This was the third morning she had felt sick. Astra wiped her mouth and squatted in the grass before trudging to the barn to milk the cows.

The weather had warmed and the fields of grasses were ripening. Now that the season had passed its zenith, the days would shorten and turn cooler. There was much work ahead. Before long they would begin the barley harvest.

While hauling the milk to the cheese house, she saw Far leading the horses out of the stable. Today they were traveling to Sjodrun. Far had finished carving the lintel for the manor's guest loft and he hoped to buy beef with the proceeds, since they had lost two cows to the black sickness. The trip would be short. They must return this evening to care for the animals.

Astra was nervous about seeing Einarr, if he still lived. She wondered how many at the village had died. Hedda? Lady Marta? She and Far had had no contact with anyone in the three Sabbaths since Vegar had left without saying goodbye. Was she still betrothed to him? Her father had said nothing more of it; in fact, he rarely spoke anymore.

Astra hurried to gather eggs, then packed *brød* and dried fish into a satchel. Far slid the longest sledge down the ramp from the barn loft and hitched up Farwa, then led her to the workshop. Astra helped him drag the heavy lintel onto the sledge using ropes, then she settled the food basket in a corner. Far strode to his workshop and returned carrying a heavy wooden cross over his shoulder.

"What will you do with that?" Astra asked. She had heard him working on something late for many nights.

Far spoke, his voice raspy from the disuse, or maybe sorrow, she knew not which. "I will ask Father Johan to hang it in the *kirke*, on the women's side." He flipped it over to reveal the finely carved figures of a woman and six children. Astra blinked away tears that burned her eyes. Water welled in Far's eyes as well.

No more was said.

Far retreated to the house and returned with Mar's heavy keyring. He handed it to Astra. "Lock up," he said hoarsely. Only the lady of the house kept the keys.

Her eyes dripped as she locked the two *stabburs*, the main house, and the other buildings that must be secured when no one was home. She felt as if she had shoveled the last scoop of earth onto her mother's body. Just yesterday she flung Mar's cloak over her shoulders, having retrieved it from the *stabbur*. She had unfolded it reverently, stirring Mar's scent from the storage trunk.

Far slapped the reins and the sledge moved forward. Astra walked beside her father in silence. Thoughts of what they would encounter at the manor filled her with angst. Hopefully, there would not be more bad news.

Astra soon became lost in thought. She and Far had accomplished much these last few weeks. They had labored from first light to last; replacing the sod on the workshop roof, repairing the stable gates and fences, and brining venison. The smoke house smoldered day and night, drying fish and venison for days. Her father repaired and sharpened tools. Astra made cheese, dried herbs, and stitched winter boots.

All this farmwork had put her far behind in cloth-making. She had saved their urine for many days to soften the finer wool.

Not knowing when she might use it, she stored it in the *stabbur*. The coarser worsted wool she had washed with lye and tallow soap. Now it all hung over slats in the wool house, waiting for her to spin...all except the Cotswold wool. She could not bring herself to touch this gift to her mother. Someday she would make something special with its rare silkiness. This thought never failed to bring tears.

At the end of each day, she and Far laid a remembrance at the graves—at first wild flowers and herbs, and lately, asters, stones, and early-changing leaves. They stood side-by-side for a few minutes in silence, each lost in private memories. After supper Astra would spin or weave, but Far would often go to his workshop. He would stay out until late in the evening. Astra hated being alone after dark. Her greatest fear was that wolves would attack her father, though he said the dogs kept them away. Still, she could not sleep until he returned.

Her thoughts often turned to her mother's suffering. That last night, after burying the infant, Mar's cries had rung across the yard to where she and Karin slept in the *stabbur* loft. They had clung to each other and buried their heads under pillows. Astra now felt shame at the relief that came over her when her mother's agonized voice stilled.

Since then, she often imagined how her own death would be, sure she would not live a long life, hoping she would not die in agony as her family had.

And then there was Karin. Her death several days later had gouged a bottomless hole in Astra's soul. Soon after Mar died, Karin and Astra moved back into the main house, but Far began sleeping in the stable. One day after milking, Astra noticed Karin scratching her hands and saw tiny red bites on them. She questioned Karin about them, but her sister did not remember where she got them. By the next day, Karin felt tired, then hot, then ill. Astra cared for her as best she could, but Karin worsened.

Seeking her father for supper that evening, she found him sitting on the thinking rock staring into the sky. He gripped her arm and urged her to go to Vegar to save her life. He pulled her to the stable and tried to saddle Kvikke, but Astra refused. "*Nei!* I will not leave Karin!" She knocked the saddle to the ground and ran away to the woods, where she flung herself on the ground and bawled.

Astra cared for Karin as best she could. She sought out her father to help, but he was always busy. When she found him walking slowly through the barley field running his hands over the ripening grain heads, she begged for his help. He said he would come, but he did not. She carried on by herself, rising repeatedly in the night to administer wine and herbs to Karin and dressing her growing nodules, but nothing helped.

On the fifth day, Karin died. Far buried her, but Astra did not go with him to the grave. She did not say her prayers. She could not.

In the following days, Astra walked about doing her chores benumbed. She focused on the placement of her feet as she walked, often forgetting where she was going or returning to a task she had already completed. Far was no better. She sometimes found him sitting on a log staring ahead without seeing. They barely spoke. Once Astra thought she saw Karin's shadow disappear behind a tree; another time she heard her footsteps in the stable. Each time she turned and found no one, a chill scurried up her back. Far and she had not put Karin through the *likglugg*...would Astra be frightened or happy to see Karin's ghost?

The sledge scraped along the rutted road, creating the only sound in the early autumn stillness as Astra trailed well behind on Kvikke. Most nesting birds had flown south, leaving owls and hawks to hunt the muted forest. She watched her father's back as he led Farwa along. His shoulders slumped and his gait was leaden. Astra often saw sorrow on his face—a long pause, an empty stare, watery eyes. He no longer smiled. He asked her often if she was well. Throughout their restless nights she heard him turning, shifting, and even uttering muffled words. She, too, felt rudderless.

They passed out of the pines and into the aspens. Astra tapped Kvikke's sides to catch up with her father and spoke, only to break the intolerable silence. "What do you think it will be like at the manor, Far?"

He turned and stared at her, as if surprised she was behind him. "Depends on how many are alive, I suppose."

"Do not say that. Maybe they had a doctor…" She trailed off.

He did not respond.

After a few silent moments she said, "I am sorry I said that. I know Mar was too sick to travel. I just wanted to help."

"I know." He glanced up at her. After a few more moments he added, "You have helped much, *datter*. I could not finish the farm work without you."

This was as close to an apology as she had received from him.

"*Takk*, Far," she replied.

He cleared his throat. "There is something I need to tell you."

She braced herself for more bad news.

"Your mother wanted me to tell you something, but I have not been able to until now."

"What is it?"

He paused, cleared his throat. "She said she regretted that she slapped you, though she did not tell me why she did so. Can you tell me?"

She was deeply touched by her mother's regret but could not speak to her father about what happened with the king. "*Nei*, Far. It was between us only."

"I see." He walked several steps, then said, "Now that it is just the two of us, I want you to know that you can tell me anything…if you want to."

Astra's eyes filled with tears and she slowed the horse so that she dropped back. "There's nothing I want to tell you, Far."

He said no more.

The horses labored up a long hill then dipped down, joining the Ra road. Astra became anxious about what she would say to Einarr, if she saw him…if he was alive.

They finally took the path that curved down the hill toward the village. Soon the peaked roof of the *kirke*, then the manor came into view. They stopped in the center of the courtyard and Astra dismounted. The usually lively pace of the manor was entirely muted. Only a few workers hurried about the courtyard. One man loaded bales of hay into a sledge, a woman pulled water from the well, and another man rolled a barrel out of the brew house.

"It is strangely quiet, is it not?" her father asked. "Where is everyone?"

Astra's heart throbbed as she dismounted. Her vision faded and she swooned, leaning against the horse's flank.

Far stared at her. "Astra? Are you ill?"

Sparks still dotted her vision but quickly subsided. "I am just tired," she said.

Far fumbled in the basket and pulled out a hunk of cheese. He handed it to her. "You must eat something and rest when we get inside. You have been working too hard."

She followed him to the manor house where he rapped loudly on the door with the hilt of his knife. Malin, Gudrun's *datter*, opened the heavy door. Her young face was weary, her frock smeared.

"Sven Larsson and Astra Svensdatter," she said, worry lines creasing her brow. "What has brought you here?"

"We wish to give our respects to Lady Marta and to trade with Didrik," Far said.

Malin stepped outside and lugged the heavy door closed behind her. "Things are very difficult here. Many have been

The Moon Turned to Blood

sick, many have died. You would be wise to turn around and go home."

"The sickness has not passed?" Far asked. "It has been weeks since we...were struck."

Malin said, "No one here is sick now, though illness continues nearby. I am afraid many, including Lady Marta, succumbed."

Far shook his head. "Ah *nei*, not her. God rest her soul."

Astra's heart thumped viciously. She leaned against the door jamb. "And Einarr?"

"He is well, as is Hedda," said Malin. "Let me call the young mistress for you." She pushed the door open and motioned them inside, then hurried up the ladder to the loft.

Astra and Far sat on a bench near the fire. Only three others, strangers to Astra, sat in a far corner drinking ale. Several minutes passed. Malin soon returned and brought them cups.

At last, Hedda backed down the rungs, her hair loose on her back. "Thank God," she said, sliding onto the bench next to Astra and hugging her tightly. Astra heard a tiny cry escape Hedda's throat. She accepted an ale cup from Malin. "It is good to see you. How is your family?"

Far shook his head. "Only the two of us now."

Hedda clamped one hand over her mouth, her eyes filling.

Far quaffed his drink then said, "We came to speak to Didrik. Is he...?"

Hedda wiped her eyes. "He is fine. You can see him or Einarr about your business. They are outside somewhere, though Einarr might be gone hawking. He has been doing that a lot, of late."

Astra breathed in relief that Einarr was alive.

"I will find them," said Far. "How many have passed away here?"

"At least half the village. We tried to help them at first, but Father Johan explained that we could catch the curse through gazing into sick people's eyes."

Far shook his head mournfully. "A terrible curse on us all."

"Sven," Hedda said, "when you have finished your business, come back to sup with us. There is no more sickness here in the manor now. As you see, we have three other guests, travelers from Oslo." She nodded her head toward the strangers. "They arrived this morning and will share their news with us at table. They say things in Oslo and elsewhere are very bad. You may already know."

"We have heard naught," said Far. "We will stay to eat, then we must get home before dark."

He turned to Astra. "Stay with Hedda and rest. I will take the cross to the *kirke* and speak to Father Johan about a mass for our loved ones. Then I must find Didrik."

Hedda groaned. "Ah, you have not heard. Father Johan also passed away."

"The *djevel* and all his angels!" Far slapped the table. "He, too?"

The strangers looked over, then returned to their drink.

Hedda said, "The Holy Father prayed for all the sick and dying, and even though Mother told him not to go, he still went. He even stopped saying mass so the evil eye would not spread the curse within the *kirke*. He died two weeks ago. Now his poor wife is alone...with only one son left."

Astra's face drained of blood. With no priest, the community had no mass, no confession, no absolution, no holy Eucharist, not even extreme unction for the dying. And no weddings. "May the good Father rest in peace," she said sadly.

The three crossed themselves.

"You can still take your cross into the *kirke*," said Hedda. "Go to the clergy house. His wife has the key."

"Poor woman," Astra said. "Maybe she will marry the next priest, like she married Father Johan after Father Eirik died."

Hedda shrugged. "I would not think so. Seems like very bad luck."

"We will leave right after the meal, Astra," Far said, finishing his ale. "Be ready to go." He strode away.

Hedda leaned forward on her elbows. "Wait here. I have a surprise for you." She hurried up the ladder.

In a few moments a voice shouted from the stairs, "Astra! You are here!" Nikolina hurried down and sat beside her, embracing Astra like a vice.

Astra peered at the baby in her cousin's lap. "How Amalie has grown!"

"She is a hungry little thing." Nikolina glowed, folding down the blanket so Astra could see her better.

"What are you doing here at the manor?" Astra asked. "Where is Dag's family?"

"Gone," Nikolina replied curtly. "Dag's father got sick with the pox and his mother wanted me to care for him. Can you imagine? But I would not. I begged Hedda and Lady Marta to let me stay here for the sake of my baby, and because of your father's status they let me in. Dag's parents are both dead now."

"You left them?" Astra was stunned. A wife's duty was to her husband and his family.

Nikolina said, "I had to. What if Amalie caught it? Besides, that woman treated me like a slave. I have scars across my back from her birch switches."

"Still..." Astra frowned. Nikolina's life and that of her child had likely been spared by this disobedient act. Her cousin was not one to follow the high road, but Astra would never have left her family to get away to safety.

"Those people would have died no matter what I did," Nikolina said defensively. "Amalie is the only one I care about. I was going to ride to your farm, but Hedda said it was too far to go by myself." Nikolina grabbed Astra's arm. "Can I come live with you? I will sleep in the loft, the barn, anywhere."

Astra said, "Since it is only Far and me now, I am sure Far will say *ja*." Astra could use her help.

"Only you two?" Nikolina gasped. "How terrible. In that case, I will do whatever is needed. You are my family."

They sat together and Nikolina and Hedda did most of the talking. The manor had lost so many to the sickness that there were few workers left, and some fields had gone unharvested. Whole families had died and the graveyard had filled, so they had to bury people on top of one another. Nikolina had not heard anything about her own family. And there was no word of the war nor the soldiers.

Astra half-listened, glancing at the doors anxiously, hoping Einarr would appear. She could not think of a reason to excuse herself, and the longer they talked, the more worried she became that she would have no chance to even see him.

Men's laughter echoed from across the nearly empty hall, and the girls glanced at the three guests. They were rough-looking men, gathered in a tight circle and drinking heavily. Hedda and Nikolina whispered about how dirty the men were. Astra worried about the news they bore.

Before long Far returned and Astra said, "Far, Dag's parents have both died and Hedda has kindly taken her in for now. But she should be with family. I could use her help. May she come to stay with us, at least until Dag returns?"

Far glanced at Nikolina, who was watching from her place next to Hedda. "For your sake, *ja*," he said. "You are in charge of her. Remember that."

Astra motioned for Nikolina to come. Her cousin squealed with joy and hugged Sven gratefully, though Far did not return her warmth.

Soon the dinner horn blew. "Sit where you like," Hedda said to the few who arrived. "There is no need for formality anymore."

Far and Astra sat together across from Hedda and Nikolina. The wives of two neighboring land owners and a few mismatched children—orphans, Astra guessed—joined them. The travelers moved closer.

Gudrun brought out a large steaming bowl of porridge, barley *brød*, and a platter of meat, then she and Malin also sat down. Astra was surprised to have the servants join them, but this shared meal arrangement was more intimate. They were all survivors.

Everyone helped themselves, filling their bowls, ripping hunks of *brød* with their hands, and cutting off slabs of beef. Conversation was sparse.

Momentarily, the main entrance door opened and dry leaves blew in along with Didrik and Einarr. Astra froze. They shed their cloaks and Einarr unceremoniously plopped down beside his sister. His eyes widened at the sight of Astra. Didrik squeezed between Einarr and Hedda, forcing them to scoot over to make room.

"Greetings to you and your father," Einarr said, smiling.

"God be with you," Astra replied. How could she get Einarr alone?

"What brings you to Sjodrun, Sven?" Einarr asked.

"I brought the lintel for the guest house," Far answered.

Didrik joked grimly through a mouthful of porridge, "I hope you do not expect payment, old man."

The corners of Far's mouth lifted slightly. "I can wait, if you need time to pay. But the price will increase."

Didrik chuckled.

Far turned to Einarr. "My condolences for the loss of your beloved mother. She was a true lady."

"Indeed, *takk*." Einarr reached for another bowl of porridge, glancing sidelong at Astra. "And how about your family?"

Astra looked down.

Far answered, "They are under the oak tree."

All grew silent.

Just down the table, the travelers crudely gnawed on bones and talked loudly. They called for more ale, then more *brød*, prompting Malin to leave her meal twice.

When their jokes became bawdy, making crude remarks about the younger women, Far slapped the table top with his open hand. "That is enough!"

The travelers' knives paused in mid-air.

"You are guests here, by the apparently undeserved kindness of your hosts," Far shouted. "There are women and children in the room. We will hear your news but need not hear your coarseness."

Astra held her breath, watching to see what Einarr would do.

The color of Einarr's face deepened. He stood and leaned his hands on the table. "This councilman has spoken rightly. This is my house, mine and my sister's, and we could just as soon have you whipped as listen to one more crass word."

Astra breathed out.

One of the men with a shaggy red beard lifted his ale bowl to Einarr. "Sorry, if we offend," he slurred. "We have been on the road too long and lost our manners...somewhere." His friends snickered.

"We have seen a lot," added another, his bald head reflecting the candlelight, "a lot of bad things. Drink helps." He also raised his bowl, then hiccupped loudly.

The first man started to laugh, then shushed himself.

Far slowly sat down and said to them somberly, "Now tell us what you know. What is happening in Oslo and elsewhere? You say the sickness is widespread?"

The third stranger, less disheveled, even ruggedly handsome, said, "We are traveling to get away from the *djevel*-cursed disease, but we find you have had it here, too. We will move along tomorrow."

"It is ugly, as you know," said the bald one. "Oslo is a death house. People lie rotting in the streets."

Gudrun clamped her hands over the ears of a small child sitting beside her. "Please, sir," she said.

"Take the children out," Einarr said, waving her away, "even though they have seen many things they should not have seen, right here in Sjodrun."

Gudrun hustled the children into the anteroom.

After the door shut, the shabby fellow continued, "There are so many dead that people just toss the corpses into the gutter. They pay poor folk to pick them up and dump them in mass graves with no priests, no holy words at all. Everyone who can leave has gotten out."

The bald man exclaimed, "It is worse than the plague in Egypt. People say it comes on the wind…"

"Or moves on its own power," added the disheveled one.

The handsome fellow added, "I heard someone say there were signs in the stars, that the moon turned to blood, just like the scriptures tell us. They say it is the end of the world…"

"Because of sin," added the bald man, "and corruption of the soul. The rich, the poor, they all die. Some even call on the old gods, Odin, Freya, or Thor himself. They are entreating witches to chant incantations." He dipped another bowl of ale.

Far touched Astra's arm and she flinched. She knew he was reminded of Mar's curses.

"There are monks parading in the streets calling people to repent," the handsome man continued. "They carry a big cross and toss holy water on people, begging them to get down on their knees so God will spare them. Some take pilgrimages to Nidaros *Katedral*, but no one gets healed, as far as I have seen. Some run away. Especially the rich."

He glanced at Einarr. "No offense. They run to their manors and put guards around. Not like here," he added. "You let us in."

"But running does not work, either," said the first. "I heard of a lord who ran to the hills but was found dead and half-eaten on the road."

Astra had taken only a few bites and now she set down her spoon. Why did they go on so? Her stomach lurched.

The bald man lowered his voice. "I heard that Pesta has been using her broom."

Hedda cried, "We will all die, then!"

"That is enough!" said Einarr. "We have heard enough. You are right to continue on your way. Take some food and be gone."

The three travelers downed their ale, stuffed what food was near them into their shirts and left. Didrik followed them out.

Everyone else sat mute. Malin started clearing away the empty dishes. Far mumbled that he would finish his business with Didrik and that Astra and Nikolina should be prepared to leave soon. Nikolina picked up the baby and hurried to the loft to pack her things. Einarr moved to sit by the fire.

Hedda grasped Astra's arm. "I wish you could stay. You are my only friend left."

Astra folded Hedda's hand between her own. She eyed Einarr and said to Hedda, "I feel the same, but I need to give Einarr my condolences before we go."

Hedda cupped her hand around her mouth and whispered, "You must. He has been talking about you. Several times he wanted to go and see if you were well, but Mar said *nei*, and then we were afraid he might spread the sickness to your family. Go. I will help Niki pack." She ran to climb the steps.

Astra's mind sped. How could she say what was on her heart? They had only a few precious moments.

Einarr smiled as Astra sat down beside him. "How fare you?"

"In grief, same as you."

"I am glad you and your father are unscathed."

"We all know this loss," she said. "So many…"

Einarr nodded and took a sip of ale. "I have much more work to do now that so many are gone. We have few servants left, and many of the tenants have run away, or died."

Astra grasped his hand. "I must talk to you, and quickly. My father made a marriage contract with Vegar. He says we are to wed next summer."

"I heard." Einarr's eyes clouded. "Vegar is a good match for you. He is rich and getting richer by the day."

"What are you saying?" She let go of his hand. "He is not a good match for me. It is you I love. Talk to my father today! He may change his mind, if you make a better offer."

Einarr squeezed her hand. "Your father is a strong-willed man."

Tears bit her eyes. "Ever since we were children, since the kiss, I knew we would marry. Do you still care for me as I do you? If not, tell me." She was ashamed of her desperate boldness.

Einarr glanced toward the door. "*Ja*, I care."

She must tell him the truth about the king. If he knew, if he loved her, he would act immediately. "I have something important to tell you."

"What is it?" He leaned in. His breath warmed her cheek.

"I cannot marry Vegar because..." She paused; this was her only chance. "Because I am not pure."

Einarr's mouth gaped open and he sat back. He let go of her hand. "What?"

Astra swallowed. "The king...he, he asked for me. I could not refuse."

"You mean he took you..."

She nodded. "If you love me, you will understand. Now you know why you must speak to my father today."

Einarr's face contorted. "I...I need to tell you something, too. But not here."

"What? We are leaving very soon."

"It is just that something happened with my mother before she died. Something I cannot change."

"What happened?" She was frantic.

Suddenly, the door to the hall opened. They both turned. Astra's father entered. "Astra! Get your cousin and come now."

Einarr leaned close and whispered, "Never forget that I love you," then he rose abruptly and rushed from the hall.

Chapter 19

Kjell spent a week drinking away his sorrow at the inn in Nidaros, but now the first snow of the season had dusted the hills and whitened the mountains beyond. He stuffed his saddlebags with flat *brød*, flasks of ale, and dried cod, and retrieved his weapons from the locked trunk he had secured. He waved a hand in goodbye and received only a nod from the busy innkeeper as he left. Regardless of the gruff man's demeanor, Kjell would miss the inn: the noise and laughter, the lively hearth, the hearty meals.

He would definitely not miss the wailing pilgrims that continued to stream in, plugging the streets and inns with their stories of sickness and horror. Two days ago, when he checked on the horses, he saw a pock-marked body lying in a ditch. Then yesterday, several other bodies wrapped in blankets were carried down the lane past the inn. The black sickness brought by these pilgrims had broken out.

At a time before the sickness, Kjell might have been tempted by Ingvil's kindly ways. She often gave him larger portions at table, and always greeted him in a friendly manner when he entered. He thought of her when he was away from the inn, but when he returned she was always kept busy. For this he was glad. His body ached for comfort, but the memory of Oda and her last moments haunted him. At night his grief and remorse overpowered the sounds of laughter below him.

With his packed saddlebag over his shoulder, Kjell sought Ingvil out to say goodbye. He motioned her outside.

"You are leaving?" she asked. Her eyes watered.

"*Ja*, I must go north."

"Can you not stay here for the winter? There is good hunting in the hills. I am sure the inn can use more fresh meat."

He took her into his arms. "I cannot stay. At another time, if I were not grieving…"

She squeezed him tightly. Her voice was strained. "I understand."

They pulled apart. "Who knows what the future might hold," he said, smoothing strands of hair away from her face.

She wiped her tears. "*Ja,* who knows…"

Kjell rode away from the inn and the swelling town, hoping that Ingvil would survive. The calls to prayer, the clamber of the hawkers, and the swarms of supplicants faded behind him. Soon he found his mind beginning to settle on his trek north and the hunt ahead.

As he rode along the Trondheim Fjord toward Stiklestad, the first blasts of ice-tinged wind stung his face. He was reminded that he must replace the heavy bearskin cloak that he had buried with his son.

The path to Stiklestad was a well-trodden destination of pilgrims. Kjell had visited the holy town of Stiklestad last year to resupply on his way to the Gressamoen Mountains. He would stop again for a few nights—his last chance to sleep on a comfortable bed before wintering in a snowy cave. In Stiklestad he planned to linger over rounds of ale with the jovial innkeeper there, and to savor the innkeeper's wife's mutton stew before beginning the long push north. He hoped the black sickness had not reached that village. If it had, he would continue north.

Following the tracks of horses and sledges that wound along the banks of the fjord, he soon crossed the river Lågen. The horses and dogs swam in the bitterly cold water and Kjell's legs were numb when he came ashore. There he built a bonfire where he and the dogs dried out and ate of his deer jerky. As it darkened, Kjell banked his fire and curled up with his dogs around him.

The next day they crossed the vast field of rounded hillocks on the otherwise flat landscape. The strange, unexplained mounds were said to be haunted. No one knew their origin, or what giant beings might be hiding beneath them. Kjell steered east, avoiding the eerie site. He passed a few stone houses that were all abandoned. At the top of a high cliff, he sat on Thorden's back and surveyed the snow-capped mountains ahead.

Utterly alone, he called into the steep ravine before him. "Oda!" The sound reverberated against the walls of the cliff.

"I love you!" He waited until the last echo faded. Deep emptiness carved a hole in his heart. The wind stirred flurries of tiny snowflakes that drifted around him like dust.

Before long, the steep terrain turned into rolling hills with beech forests, now scattered with ochre leaves that crackled underfoot. After another day of travel, farms, pastureland and harvested fields began dotting the landscape. Finally, a broad valley spread before him along the shore of Trondheim Fjord.

Comforted by the scene's serenity, Kjell pulled Thorden to a stop so suddenly that Sokker bumped into the lead horse's rump. Thorden whinnied in complaint. Kjell stared into the distance at the barely-visible spire of the *kirke* of Saint Olav. Traveling a bit further he was able to view the peninsular town of Stiklestad. Smoke drifting from each cottage beckoned him. All seemed well. Kjell tapped Thorden's sides with his heels and they trotted forward.

Kjell tied the horses to the hitching ring near a stable and strode along the dirt lane. There were no pilgrims, no flagellating mourners, no dead bodies carried on pallets. Kjell breathed a heavy sigh of relief. He passed a trader bargaining with a craftsman at the door of a shop, a two-horse sledge carrying bundles of hay through the village, and a man wearing a sheep carcass over his shoulders.

On his way toward the inn where he had previously stayed, the scent of freshly baked *brød* wafted from the oven in the yard of a nearby house. The thought of a warm brown loaf made Kjell salivate. He must have some. He followed his nose to the hut. The door was slightly ajar and he knocked.

An aproned woman, her arms covered with flour, elbowed the plank door open. "*Ja?*" she said. She was plump and rosy-cheeked, with dancing eyes. She was not beautiful, but not unpleasant, either. She set her fists on her waist—he had clearly interrupted her work.

Kjell glanced down at his trail-worn clothing. He must smell of soot and grease. He took a step back. "Excuse me, good lady. I just arrived and I wonder if I might buy some of your fragrant wares."

Her face broke into a pleasing grin. She tossed her head back and laughed freely, catching Kjell by surprise. When had he last heard such an unfettered and joyous sound?

"I am no lady, but *ja*, I will sell you a loaf. Wait here." She turned, partially shutting the door behind her. He saw an auburn braid flipping against her hips as she walked away. She was unmarried.

When the door reopened, she handed him a warm loaf.

"How much?" Kjell asked.

She shrugged. "What is it worth to you?"

He pondered. It was worth far more than he was inclined to give. He pulled a few small coins from his money pouch and placed them on her open hand. She smiled and dropped the money into a purse at her belt.

Kjell tucked the *brød* under his arm, but not before tearing off a large chunk to stuff into his mouth. "Mm, *takk*," he mumbled, turning to go.

She smiled and started to close the door.

"Miss?" he called back.

"*Ja?*" Dimples notched her cheeks.

"Is the inn full, do you know? I am looking to spend a few nights."

She pointed to Gizur's inn, the guest house that Kjell knew well. "I am sure it is not full. We have few travelers this time of year."

"*Mange takk*," he said, backing away.

She smiled again and curtsied. "God be with you now."

"And with you." Kjell paused, then asked, "What is your name, miss?"

She cocked her head. "Dorte Knutsdatter. And yours?"

"Kjell. *Takk* again, Dorte Knutsdatter." He waved and walked away backward, tearing another hearty mouthful from the loaf. How comfortable it was to be in this workaday village. How cheering to be far away from a large town and the wretched sickness that was sweeping Norway.

Gizur was a large, dark-haired man with a speckled graying beard. He greeted Kjell loudly when he pushed through the heavy door. "Kjell, my hunter friend!" cried Gizur. "You are back for more trouble, I see."

The candlelit room was warm and a large cauldron bubbled tantalizingly over the fire.

"More trouble and more ale," Kjell said, chuckling.

The big man laughed and slapped Kjell's back painfully.

"Do you have a bed for a few nights?" Kjell asked.

Gizur spread his long arms wide. "Do you see anyone else here?"

Kjell smiled. "Then I have the rafters to myself...but only after partaking of whatever is boiling in that pot."

"Right away. Do you want to stable your horses first?"

"They can wait."

After a gut-filling meal and two foaming horns of ale, Kjell took his horses to the stableman not far away. Then he hauled his belongings up to the slant-ceilinged loft. He offered Gizur an extra coin for the privilege of keeping the room to himself, but the man refused the additional payment. "I have had almost no one for a fortnight now. Pilgrimages have dried up for the season. Your secrets are safe here." He laughed loudly once more.

After imbibing with his host until the innkeeper's wife beckoned Gizur to bed, Kjell lit a small candle from the fire and took his last bowl of ale into the rafters. He propped himself up on the downy pillows, luxuriating in the wool-filled mattress, then spread the thick sheepskin over himself. The inn was quiet. He stared at the cobwebbed logs above him as he sipped.

At once his thoughts turned to Oda and how little time he had spent with his young wife and their infant son. He had neglected her, no doubt, as she fended for herself in the remote hut secreted in the woods. Even so, when he returned from the hunt last year she had welcomed him with loving arms, covering him with kisses and telling him how much she missed him. After their sweet love-making, she had wept into his chest. She would not say why, but now he realized how lonely she must have been. His body ached for her.

He watched a late-season spider crawl from a beam onto its web. His thoughts turned to the maid in Nidaros. She might have been a winsome distraction, someone to keep the pain at bay, but he was not ready. It seemed like treason.

The ale thickened his mind—he downed the rest. As he closed his eyes, he also thought of the baker he had just met, Dorte by name. He pictured her flour-dusted hair, her quick smile and ready laughter. Was she alone? Surely not.

Then again, was it a sin against his wife if they were no longer married? Oda would understand his sorrow and his needs, but…she would not approve. Was she watching from above? Just in case, he whispered, "I am sorry for my wayward thoughts," and he blew out the candle.

The next day Kjell bought a new hatchet and spoke to a couple of locals about the hunting in the Gressamoens. They had little advice beyond what he already knew, all insisting he must bring items to trade with the Saami people as he passed through their lands. Kjell searched the village for goods the Saami did not have—glass beads, ground barley, salted pork. Before he left, he would buy a few dozen chicken eggs, as well, cushioning them in soft wool for the journey.

The road through the town was muddied now as the light snow was trampled down by passersby. On his way back to the inn, a matronly woman carrying a wash basket stopped to adjust her load. Kjell offered to carry her bulky burden.

In payment she asked, "Good sir, you know that Saint Olav was killed here in Stiklestad. Perhaps you have a donation for his *kirke*."

"In fact, I have," he said, hoping to avoid a lecture. He drew a small coin from his pouch and gave it to her.

She continued anyway, telling of how King Olav was stabbed three times in battle before he died, and that many miracles had occurred after his death. "A blind man received sight," she said, "and a deaf-mute talked. Many battles were won because of him. He even turned bread into a stone! Perhaps you need a miracle, too."

"Everyone needs a miracle," he murmured.

"Then you should visit the *kirke,* or even go to Nidaros where Saint Olav is buried. There is a well there of miraculous water."

"I have just been to Nidaros," Kjell said, "but no one should go now. A great sickness is upon them—have you not heard?"

The woman made the sign of the cross. "*Nei*. May Saint Olav spare us."

They arrived at the woman's hut and Kjell set down her basket. "That is why I am traveling north, to escape the coming plague."

She gasped. "I must tell the priest!" She left her basket at her doorstep and ran back toward the *kirke*.

That evening at the inn, Kjell ate another sumptuous supper of mutton stew. As he sat at the board alone, a few local patrons came in and the innkeeper poured them foaming horns of ale. Kjell listened as the men chatted amiably.

"From the look of the sky, more snow is on its way," someone said.

"It is bound to come. I hope the winter will not be as harsh as last year," said another. "I spotted a large herd of elk just outside the village. It could be an omen."

"Good or bad?" the first man asked.

"No one knows for sure," said the first. They all laughed.

"There is much to do first. My wife is wearing me out," complained a third, "which is why I am here."

Again, they laughed.

One of the men turned to Kjell. "Where are you from, friend?"

"I traveled up the Numedal Valley, then came through Trondelag," Kjell answered.

"I heard from the laundry woman that there is sickness in Nidaros," said the man. "Was it you who brought this news?"

Gossip spreads like lightning, Kjell realized. "Indeed. You are best off staying here until winter has passed. Some say it is a curse."

"We need not go. We have enough to do right here." The man turned his back to Kjell and called for more ale.

Sitting alone, Kjell stared into his pewter bowl. The voices around him droned on, then faded. He became lost in his own thoughts as memories rushed back.

The Moon Turned to Blood

Ruth Tiger

Payments accepted

Ruth Tiger

Cash
Check
Zelle
Venmo—use QR Code

The Moon Turned to Blood

By Ruth Tiger

Norway 1349: the plague strikes Norway just as Astra hopes to become betrothed. Kjell, a renegade, must hide from the law. Neither foresees their worlds crashing nor how their fates will intersect to save them.

⁕

Three years prior, Kjell had stayed a few nights at an inn near Tønsberg. One evening while he was eating mutton stew, several kings' men clattered in and sat down on the bench next to Kjell. They ordered horns of ale from the innkeeper's *datter*.

When their ale arrived, one of them turned to Kjell and called him to join them. Kjell shook his head, attending to his bowl.

The soldiers quickly downed their hornfuls and ordered two more rounds.

The one nearest Kjell turned and slapped Kjell's back. "Come join us, friend. Tell us a joke. You must have stories to tell, and we need entertaining."

Kjell said, "*Nei*, I am no good at tales." He moved to a table in the corner of the inn.

The soldiers laughed at his departure and threw out mock insults about his manhood, but Kjell did not reply to their taunts.

After a time, the loudest and drunkest of them stumbled over and directly sat across from Kjell, staring at him bleary-eyed.

"What is your trouble, knave? Afraid of a little fun? Think you are better than us?"

"*Nei*, I am only travel-weary." Kjell leaned against the wall, his hand on his knife beneath the table.

The soldier bent forward on his elbows and stared at Kjell. "Next time, then." He smiled wryly. He rose and stumbled back to the others, who laughed at his lack of success.

"Fucking coward, he is," one of them sneered. Then he turned to bedevil the innkeeper's comely *datter* instead.

She rolled her eyes at their lewd talk, slapping the hands that pinched her rump and tugged at her bodice. This sent the soldiers into spouting guffaws and did not dissuade them in the least. One yanked her braid, pulling her head down and kissing her lips. She bit his mouth, drawing blood. The innkeeper brought out a club and threatened to thrash them. At this they quieted and settled into their ale bowls.

Kjell had seen the innkeeper's *datter* each of the two days prior and thought her aloof. Now he knew why. The next morning when he rose early before other guests were awake, he found her alone, breaking her fast at the board. He hesitated to bother her, but she brought him a bowl of porridge and invited him to sit with her.

Kjell asked about the goings-on of Tønsberg and she conversed with him as if nothing untoward had happened last night.

After a pause in their conversation the girl said, "It looks to be a fine morning. I must get to work."

Kjell said impulsively, "That soldier got what he deserved. You are brave."

She smiled. "They deserve more than a bite on the lip."

"That they do, the fish bellies."

"They are horses' cocks, all of them."

Kjell laughed at her boldness. "Indeed, that is a better description."

She gathered the dishes and climbed over the bench.

"How many winters have you?" he asked.

"Seventeen." She looked at him straight on. "Going on twenty-five, my father says."

"And you are not wed?"

"*Nei*, whom would I wed? I will not be a farmer's nor a craftsman's wife. We are the best inn hereabouts. I am well satisfied to stay and run the inn when my father gets old. My mother passed when I was just wee, so it is just the two of us."

"I see." Kjell had rarely heard of a woman innkeeper, except perhaps an old widow. "You are bold for one so young, and skilled at handling travelers—even soldiers—without fear."

She reached into the folds of her apron and pulled out a dagger. "I did not say without fear. But I know how to use this and am ready, if needed."

Kjell grinned. "I do not doubt it."

She smiled coyly and hid the knife away. Heavy footsteps descended the stairs and she quickly took the dishes to the kitchen. Kjell had no other chance to talk with the girl, a fair and able lass.

That evening the soldiers' braying drunkenness drove Kjell up to his room early, a room with one bed he shared with an elderly traveler who was already asleep. The old man was wrapped tightly in the only sheepskin, snoring to wake the dead. Kjell lay down and turned his back. He lay awake long into the night because of the snoring, and the raucous singing from below.

Very late, after Kjell had just drifted off to sleep, he was awakened by heavy shuffling sounds outside his door. The muffled cry of a woman was quickly damped, but the bumping sounds continued. Kjell cracked the door open. In the hallway was the innkeeper's *datter*, her face flattened against the wall by the soldier whose lip she had bitten. A rag was stuffed in her mouth. She struggled against him, twisting and trying to free her hands, but he had trapped her crossed arms behind her with one hand, and pressed her to the wall. With his other hand he lifted her night shift, dropping his trousers and spreading her legs with his knees. He thrust against her as a cry escaped the girl's smothered mouth.

Kjell barely thought about what he did next. He slipped his hunting knife from under the mattress, strode two steps, flung open the door, and lunged at the soldier.

The maiden's eyes wavered with fear as Kjell came at them. The blade drove deep between the soldier's ribs. Kjell shoved it upward, into the heart. The man gurgled and collapsed. The girl fell backward atop the dead soldier, then scrambled quickly to her feet, tugging down her shift. Shooting Kjell a look of frightened gratitude, she ran down the stairs.

A slick puddle formed on the floor at Kjell's feet. After a moment of paralyzed hesitation, he snatched his satchel from under the bed, stepped over the body and raced down the steps. In the darkened, empty barroom, the girl was hiding, plastered to a post. There was blood on her night dress; her eyes were wild like a trapped deer. She held a poker in both hands.

Their eyes met. Kjell opened his mouth to speak but she shook her head and nodded toward the door. Footsteps and then a man's cry from above sent him fleeing into the night.

They had hunted him, he was sure. He rode hard, hiding in caves in the high country and traveling at night. He knew the law required he go to the local overseer and confess, purchasing his peace until a trial was set. He could even negotiate with the victim's family for a settlement, but in the case of a knight, the trial would be before the king at the *Gulag* council in Oslo.

What chance would he have there? Kjell would be banished from Norway for life. Regardless of banishment, he would be hunted as long as he lived.

Kjell continued north, riding on deer trails and traveling at night. At each scamper of a fox or swoosh of an owl he tensed, his knife always at the ready. After several weeks he ended up with the Saami. They took him in without asking questions. He traveled with them on their reindeer hunt, learning their traditions and many of their words. They taught him the ways of the north.

He never regretted what he had done.

Now, well soused and alone in bed in the Stiklestad inn, other memories stirred in Kjell's anxious heart. He recalled the king's entry into Sjodrun and the alarm he felt at the sight of the king's knights. Kjell's sale of furs to the lady of the manor had paid his passage to leave the village. He owed the swift departure to the maiden, Astra, who had spoken to the head servant on his behalf. What was the girl's plight now? She had wanted to marry the manor lord's son, but that was doubtful.

He recalled the night before he left, when he had heard a squelched scream coming from the soldiers' encampment. He surmised it was a village girl taken against her will for men's pleasure, perhaps even the king. Kjell had slunk along the perimeter of the yard to find out if he could help her, but by the time he arrived, all was quiet. Many soldiers gathered around the entrance to the new *stabbur* where the king was staying, lounging in tents and on the ground, drinking and laughing. He had pitied the poor maiden, whoever she was.

Suddenly, he sat up, banging his head on a beam. Was it Astra? Kjell remembered the king's knight sitting by her at the dance, perhaps an emissary. She did not look happy. The next time he saw her was on the bank of the creek the morning he left. She was drenched and sobbing. Ach, now he knew. It was she the Sovereign had taken to his bed, that despot! The despair on her tear-streaked face tugged at him.

Kjell sighed. How sad. The girl's unhappy fate belonged to her alone.

When he woke, Kjell ate a meal of mutton knuckles and porridge cooked by the innkeeper's wife. Then he checked on his horses at the stable, stopping to ask the farrier to trim their hooves. He bought a large saddlebag for Sokker, and another bear trap, and stowed them under his bed. Soon he found himself knocking on the door of the *brød*-maker once more.

Dorte seemed happy to see him. Her face wore a fingerprint of flour dust. "Have you finished your loaf already?" she asked. Behind her he saw her *brød* board lined with loaves ready for the oven outside.

"I will be leaving in a few days, a week perhaps, hunting up north." He handed her a coin.

"Are you staying at the inn, then?" she asked, tucking a loaf under his arm. "Will you not freeze in that loft of Gizur's?" Dorte's cherry cheeks spoke of a warm heart. Her blue eyes caught the morning light.

Kjell laughed. She must have been talking to the innkeeper's wife. "It is cold up there, but I will be wintering in snow, so I best be used to it."

She reached out and touched his sleeve. "When you leave you will need supplies, like fresh *brød*. You know where to find it."

"*Ja*, much fresh *brød*," he laughed. What else was she getting at?

"Are you interested in a more comfortable and less expensive place to stay?" She touched her fingers to the back of his hand.

"Perhaps," he answered. His pulse throbbed. "If the price is right and the food savory."

"I might know of a place. Check back with me later."

Kjell felt her eyes on him as he walked away. When he rounded the corner, he turned to look. Still watching him, she raised a brow.

Chapter 20

Astra was pleased at how quickly things improved, now that Nikolina had come to live with them. The first day, Nikolina took over Mar's chores, freeing Astra to work the farm with her father. In the afternoon, the cousins hiked up to the high country to retrieve the sheep, hoping to find that none had been eaten by predators. But when the dogs rounded them up, two were lost.

The cousins worked well together, teasing and laughing. These moments of cheerfulness, and the warm bodies of Nikolina and Amalie in her bed, made Astra feel like she had a sister again. With a smile, Far noticed their comradery and mentioned it to Astra.

Autumn was waning and an early hand's width of snow fell overnight, just enough to halt the final harvesting of hay grasses. Far worried about feed for the animals through the winter. He talked about cutting fodder from the marsh when the lake iced over, but Astra objected since they had already lost a horse that way. Far begrudgingly agreed. Sadly, the small field of flax Mar had planted for linen now lay buried and ruined. Astra understood why Far had left it until last, and he knew that neither she nor Nikolina had time for the many steps required to turn it into the fine cloth.

So much still needed doing to prepare for winter. Before light each day, Far was often out fishing, slowly adding pike, salmon and mackerel to dry in the rafters. Weary and slump-shouldered, Far worked his long days rarely stopping to rest, as did they all. Far had not yet butchered the pig, nor could he spare any sheep. He grumbled that he had no time to burn tar to protect the lower logs of the house and *stabbur*, and he had shot only two deer so far.

In the ever-diminishing evenings, Astra followed him to make the rounds of his traps. She took her bow for practice, a skill she was honing. Though shooting small game in near darkness was a challenge, Astra's aim was improving, and several times she proudly brought home a rabbit or weasel to add to Nikolina's stew.

One chilly afternoon, Astra and Nikolina carried three over-spilling buckets of water to the house, one in each hand and one shared between them. They walked in step, singing a childhood song, and set the buckets down in the entryway, laughing that they had splashed their frayed shifts. Nikolina rushed to baby Amalie who was crying lustily in the cradle. The child's screams ceased when Nikolina picked her up. Having a baby in the house was a joyful spark for Astra. The cradle once again was filled with life.

Astra brought firewood from the *svalgang* and stoked the fire. She sat down on a stool across from her cousin. "I am glad you are here, Niki," she said. "You are a hard worker and a good cook, and Amalie has cheered us up."

"Thank you for taking me in." Nikolina's face was flushed with exertion and she stared lovingly at her suckling child. "I will always be indebted to you and *Onkel* Sven."

Astra leaned forward to rest her elbows on her knees. The dark question of Nikolina leaving Dag's parents while they sickened and died still irked Astra. She hoped their newfound sisterhood would smooth over the query she had decided to make.

"How did you know when Dag's parents died?" she asked.

Nikolina did not look up. "Didrik told me. Dag's father died first and they buried him in the *kirke* cemetery. I do not think a mass was said since so many others were also dying. Someone found his mother a few days later. She is buried on top of her husband."

Astra stared at the fire, not knowing how to respond.

"Astra, that woman was cruel," Nikolina said. "Dag told me she beat him, too, when he was young. I say, 'Everything has an end, except the sausage—it has two ends.'" She laughed overly much.

The fact that Dag's wife had abandoned his parents in a time of sickness gave Astra consternation. How could she joke about their deaths?

"Even so, your husband's parents are due respect," Astra said, picking up her embroidery.

A fierce glint lit Nikolina's eyes. "I know that. Do you not think I feel guilty? There is nothing I can do now."

"But...what will Dag say when he returns?"

Nikolina's face darkened. She raised her voice. "Dag would be angry if he ever found out, which is why I will never tell him! They died of the black sickness. That is all he needs to know because that is the truth."

Astra frowned. "But how could you keep it from him? He is your husband."

Nikolina glared at her. "He must never know. Promise me you will not tell him. My baby, our baby, is more important than two old people. He will be glad we are alive."

Astra realized Nikolina knew she had done wrong. There were things she could have done, like send the baby to the manor or seek help from others. She could have stayed with them until the end and made sure a mass was said. "I think it is just...not right," Astra said.

Nikolina did not reply.

Astra's fingers worked the colorful threads of the traditional Numedal design on a new bodice. Softening her tone she said, "At least at *Jul* you can go to confession, if we have a new priest."

Nikolina snapped, "When you have children you will understand." She changed the baby to the other breast and turned her back.

Astra sighed, laid down her embroidery, and donned her coat to find her father. Mar was right about Nikolina.

Far was in the *stabbur* counting the dried fish hanging from the rafters. He turned when he heard her footsteps, his face lined with worry.

"Ach, my child. We will have to suck the thumb if we do not get more meat. I can hunt, but there is so much to do here on the farm. I must kill that pig. I thought of keeping it one more year to breed with Orm's boar, but we will need the ham."

Astra did not say what she was thinking—the time they had spent caring for their loved ones, and the sorrowful days that followed when they dragged themselves through their chores in a daze, had put them well behind.

"After I finish laying in firewood, I will butcher and smoke the meat," he said. "Then you and Niki can render tallow for candles and make *blodpølsa*. At least we have your cousin to help."

"*Ja*, at least we have Niki," she said, their recent conversation souring in her mouth.

Far glanced at her. "I thought you two were getting along."

She shrugged.

"I know she is not your mother. No one is as good as..." His voice broke off.

At the sight of her father's pain Astra's eyes burned, too.

He rubbed his nose and turned his face away. "I saw a dead pine along the creek past the far field. It will make an excellent doorpost and also help fill the woodshed."

"Do you need help?"

He smiled faintly. "Just check the traps while I am gone. You already do more than a *datter* should."

She snatched at this chance. "But I cannot do all that Mar did. I am not yet ready to be a wife."

Far shook his head and frowned. "Unless we were talking about Einarr. You do not give up."

"Maybe I am stubborn, like you." Neither smiled. Astra realized they no longer jested like they once did. Times of teasing and ease between them seemed well past.

Far sighed. "I will set the traps on my way out tomorrow, and hopefully we will have a hare or two for supper."

Chapter 21

Kjell gathered his weapons and strode to the pasture where his horses were kept. Anticipating this day of hunting, his mood lifted. The dogs circled excitedly as he mounted and rode past Saint Olav's *kirke* toward the higher hills. With a tap from Kjell's heels Thorden sprang into a canter, flinging up chunks of snow that had fallen overnight.

Entering the forest of now-leafless trees, Kjell slowed to a walk. The stillness was familiar and soul-reviving. Ice-crusted snow crunched deliciously beneath Thorden's hooves. A hare, nearly white now, dove into its burrow at their approach. A raven squawked angrily from the low branch of a tall pine. Kjell breathed deeply. Being in these wild places was the only time he felt there must truly be a good God—not the punitive one that the priests espoused, but a God of wild and reckless temperament, as the Norse legends depicted.

Before long the dogs picked up a scent and frantically sniffed the footprints of what must be a large buck. Navnløs, the young dog from the village, frolicked playfully around the more experienced *buhunds*, nipping at them and receiving snarls in return.

When Beskytter, Kjell's oldest but finest hunting dog, spotted the ten-pointer across a gully, he howled. All the dogs dove down the wooded hill. Thorden leapt headlong in pursuit.

The stag sprang forward over bushes and bounded an ice-laced creek. Kjell followed him up a steep embankment, over several hills, and into a thicket of brambles where the roe finally flagged. Kjell whistled for the dogs to halt and jumped out of the saddle. Bending low he crept forward, his bowstring taut. Through the dense foliage, a shaft of sunlight played on ten-point antlers. Kjell dropped to the ground behind an oak and waited. Sensing a reprieve, the deer raised his snout. Slowly, Kjell nocked the arrow. The stag's ears twitched. Kjell drew back the bowstring and shot.

The twang startled the roebuck and he shifted to face the oncoming shaft. It struck him in the shoulder and he fell. Kjell sprinted forward as the howling dogs ran past him. The roe struggled to rise, but the dogs attacked his legs, forcing him to stumble into the open and fall again. They jumped on the deer's torso, biting at his belly. By the time Kjell caught up with them the deer had ceased struggling. Kjell sliced through the throat in one motion, bringing a flood of red that stained the pristine snow. Life drained from his prey's eyes.

An image of the last time he had slit a throat flashed through Kjell's mind. At least he had kept his promise to poor Jens, burying him where dogs could not reach him. Kjell placed his hand on the now-still head and lifted his face upward to acknowledge this gift, as the Saami had taught him.

Turning the carcass onto its back, he slashed open the buck's belly and loosened the organs from the flesh. The kidneys, liver, and heart he stuffed in his satchel—they would be tasty additions to any cauldron, perhaps Dorte's. He removed the entrails, then flipped the deer onto its belly to bleed out. He whistled for Thorden and the horse came galloping.

Kjell hauled the carcass onto Thorden's flanks and secured it tightly. He would use the pelt for a coat and smoke some of the meat. Dorte could dry the rest for her winter supply. She was a pleasant woman, older than his Oda; maybe older than he. But she was jolly and had returned his coin for the *brød* yesterday.

As he had expected, the baker smiled when she saw him and happily snatched the organs he offered. "Kidney stew tonight," said Dorte. "Will you join me?"

"Perhaps…well, *ja*," he said smiling. "*Mange takk*. May I string the carcass up behind your house?"

"Of course." She grinned. "I will find a way to repay you for a portion of the meat, if you can spare some."

Kjell glanced at her. She winked and turned back inside the house. Did she mean what he thought she meant? Maybe. He was still unsure.

He hung the carcass from a post and deftly skinned it, carving out the meat and throwing the legs to the dogs. Then he dunked the pelt in a barrel of water to preserve it overnight. Tomorrow he would scrape it and stretch it out to dry.

At dinner that evening in Dorte's one-room hut, she chattered happily about extra coins she had earned by providing *brød* for traders who had just come to the inn. Kjell noticed she had changed her dress and beribboned her thick plait that now draped over her shoulder and onto her lap. He was reminded of Oda and stopped chewing. How angry she would be if she knew he was here. But...she was not here. She would never be here. His eyes burned as he guzzled his ale and poured more.

Dorte set aside the dishes and joined him at the hearth. She touched his chin and turned his face to look at her. "What is it? You seem sad."

"It is nothing. Only memories."

She picked up his hand. "Perhaps I can help you forget these memories for tonight."

Kjell squeezed her hand. "If only you could." The urge to throw her onto the bed nearly overwhelmed him.

"I can, at least for a time," she said. "Just stay a little longer and let me pour you some more ale."

They drank by the fire, telling stories from their pasts. They laughed much, and cried a little. She had endured sadness, too. In the firelight, through the blur of ale, Dorte grew ever more beautiful in Kjell's eyes. Her easy smile caused his heart to forget.

When he had emptied his bowl yet again, Dorte took his hand and placed it on her breast. He kissed her mouth. She pulled him to the bed and they lay together eagerly, frantically. Their love filled his senses and smothered his sorrow.

Kjell awakened to the sound of Dorte pounding dough on the baking stone. When she saw that he was awake, she wiped her hands and sat beside him on the bed, kissing him on the mouth.

Kjell gently shoved her back onto the bed, then unpinned the brooch on her shift. She laughed and wriggled free. "I have an order to fill this morning," she said, re-pinning the brooch and standing up. She lifted the dough and slapped it down. "There is always tonight, that is, if you want to stay."

The sadness he had felt last night he set behind him now, soaking in the ease of contentment. Dorte was an ointment for his torn soul.

Kjell stoked the fire in the *brød* oven, then left to check on his horses. What would he say to the innkeeper when he sat to break his fast, having already paid for last night's room and breakfast? Boarding at the inn and stabling his horses was costing Kjell a pretty *ort*. Why should he not save money by boarding with Dorte? In return he would build her a cowshed and fill her eaves with meat before leaving to go north. He thought about the woman's eager face and open-hearted laugh. Perhaps he would even delay his travels a bit longer.

As he passed the inn on the way to the stables, he saw two large sledges parked at the side of the inn. Each was covered with skins and guarded by large dogs. Visitors would bring news. He swung the inn door open.

Five strangers sat at the long table quaffing ale. They looked rough and smelled worse, leaning close and speaking in low tones. They stopped talking when Kjell entered, and turned to stare at him in unison.

From the back of the room the innkeeper greeted Kjell. "Breakfast?"

"Please."

"No *brød*, I suppose?" The innkeeper sniggered.

Kjell felt his face redden, but he replied good-naturedly, "*Nei*, I have enough of that."

"Just so," laughed the innkeeper. He set a large horn of ale on the table before Kjell, then went to the kitchen for porridge.

The visitors turned their backs to Kjell and continued their quiet conversation. In the stillness he could not help but hear their whispered words.

"What should we do with him?" one asked. "We cannot take him back."

"We could ask the innkeeper to send for a wise woman's services," said another.

"You know it is the black sickness," hissed a third. "The innkeeper might have heard of it, and if so, he will not keep him here."

The first man lowered his voice even more. Kjell strained to listen. "We could take him out to the forest. It would be a mercy."

They all fell silent at this.

Startled, Kjell addressed them from across the room. "May I join you? I am a traveler as well, and eager for news."

They eyed him and each other, then the first man nodded toward the bench next to him. Instead, Kjell sat at the end of their table and studied their faces for signs of sickness.

"From where have you come?" he asked.

"Nidaros," said one. "Before that, Hamar."

"I have been in Nidaros recently myself," Kjell said. "I did not stay long due to the pestilence there."

The man nodded. "We found that, too. The market at Hamar was...."

"Chaos," another man finished. "We moved on quickly."

"We have goods to sell," said the third man. "If we do not sell here, we will hire a boat for Tromsø."

Kjell whistled. "A very long trip."

"Safer to be far away, we think," said the first.

Kjell took a long drink then said quietly, "I heard you mention someone of your group is sick."

They were all quiet for a moment then the first man answered, "Just one. He is upstairs. He started ailing yesterday on the road. Ague, I am sure."

"*Nei*, today he is worse," muttered another. "It is more than ague."

"If it is the black pestilence," said Kjell, "anyone here could also get sick. You must take him away. Care for him in the forest, perhaps."

"Or leave him there for God to take," whispered the first under his breath.

The man closest to Kjell said, "When I tried to rouse him for breakfast, he spewed blood like a decapitated rooster."

Kjell scrambled to his feet, backed up and yelled, "Get him out of the inn before it spreads!"

No one had noticed the innkeeper enter, but now the man's voice boomed across the room. "Spreads? What sickness is this?"

Kjell backed up toward the door. "One of theirs has the mortal sickness. It will spread to the whole village. I have seen it myself. No one who gets it survives."

"What?" The innkeeper yelled at the visitors, "Get him out of my inn!"

Kjell stumbled through the exit as the innkeeper called after him, but Kjell did not stop. He ran all the way to Dorte's, slipping in the icy sledge tracks, and threw open the door.

"Did you take *brød* to the inn today?" he said, straddling the open doorway.

She jumped. "Not yet, but I have some to bring over when it is baked." She nestled a barley loaf onto the cooking stone.

"One of the visitors at the inn has the black sickness!" Kjell cried. "The others have been near him and they may soon be sick, too. You must not go near the inn. The whole village will be ill and many will die."

Dorte pushed a stray hair away from her face. "What are you talking about? I have promised the inn more *brød*—it is ready to bake now. Here, take it out to the oven for me."

Kjell took her by the shoulders. The heavy baking stone fell to the floor and the loaves rolled into the dirt. "You must not go to the inn, Dorte."

"Ah *nei*, look what you have done." She pushed him away forcefully. "I must go indeed." She lifted the baking stone and brushed dirt off the fallen loaves.

Kjell began to sweat. "Dorte, you must stay away. In fact, you should leave Stiklestad. That is the best thing. This sickness spreads through the air, through a sick person's gaze, and on the wind. One of the travelers is already coughing up blood. It is the same evil I saw in Nidaros and in the villages I passed by...even in my own house." He had not told her of Oda and little Egill. "Just believe me. You will die if you stay."

Dorte stared at him. "Why do you say such a thing? I do not know of this sickness. I cannot leave. Why should I? This is my home. Besides, where would I go?"

"Come with me," he said. "We will stop in the Saami village, then I will build a shelter where we will be safe for the winter. You can return in the spring when the sickness has passed. I will help you pack your things."

Dorte's face bloomed red. "I am not going to live with the Saami! I have a job to do here, a house, a life." She pushed him away. "You are daft."

"Oda..." Kjell stopped, corrected himself. "I mean Dorte, come with me. You do not know this sickness, but I do."

She backed up to the bedpost and clung to it with her hands behind her back. "Kjell, we barely know each other. You are kind and helpful, but I will not leave my home for your...your crazy thoughts. I am not going to die. I am going to stay here and do what I need to do—bake. This house is all I have left of my parents. It is where I belong." Her face was defiant.

Kjell reached for her hand. "Please, come with me. I will take care of you."

She pulled away and crossed her arms over her chest. "I will not."

The Moon Turned to Blood

He withdrew. "Then I hope I will see you when I return. God help you." He walked away and did not look back.

Chapter 22

The sun had barely lightened the overcast sky when Astra brought Far a satchel of dried fish and barley *brød*. She watched him harness Farwa to the long sledge and place his traps, axe, saw, and maul on the sledge boards. She told him to be careful. After a short distance, he stopped, turned, and called to her. "Have the pot boiling when I return, Little Sparrow."

Astra waved, unable to speak. He had not called her Little Sparrow since before the great sickness, since she told him she would not marry Vegar.

As soon as he rounded the first bend, she dashed behind the barn to retch. Shakily, she checked her armpits yet again, looking for boils. Thankfully, she had none. At first, when this sickness started and she found no pox, she figured she had ague, or was sick with worry and grief. But now that several Lord's Days had passed, doubt had crept in. She pushed another possibility back, drowning it instead in her ocean of sadness.

Astra filled the water trough, milked the cows, fed the chickens, and gathered eggs. Then she trudged to the house for the day of spinning and weaving that she and her cousin had agreed upon. Nikolina needed a new cloak; the one her mother-in-law had given her was tattered and patched.

Astra felt a twinge of guilt. Stored in a trunk in the *stabbur* were Mar's perfectly good clothes that Nikolina might wear, but Astra had not offered them. Each time Astra visited the storage loft, she opened the trunk as if it contained a sacred icon. Mar's scent still lingered, fainter now, and she buried her face in the fabrics. She could not bring herself to give Mar's things to Nikolina.

Nikolina was already spinning when Astra entered the house. "You weave," she said to Astra, teasing the wool from the basket and twirling the spindle deftly.

After last night when they had quarreled and slept in the same bed while trying to avoid touching one another, Astra promised herself not to bring up Nikolina's in-laws again. Out of necessity, she buried her qualms about her cousin's faults. They must live in peace, as Far said.

Astra pulled thread from a spool Nikolina had already filled, and tied the dozens of warp strands to the top of the vertical loom. She cut and weighted each one with a small soapstone, then wound the weft around the shuttle and began tossing it through.

"When do you think you might marry?" Nikolina asked. "And who?"

"Why? What have you heard?" Astra tamped the heddle rod downward.

"I heard you were in love with Einarr, but that your father had other plans."

Astra sighed. Rumors spread quickly. "Far made a contract with Vegar Eriksson, but nothing has been finalized yet."

"Do you still love Einarr?"

"I care for him, *ja*. But Far says he is above us. He did not know of our pledge to each other before he made the other agreement with the *sysselmand*."

"But now your father knows?"

Astra nodded.

"And what did he say?"

"He says he will not change his mind."

"Does Einarr feel the same about you?"

"*Ja*, but he did not get a chance to talk to Far with all the turmoil at the manor."

"Too bad, indeed." Nikolina paused her spinning. "Was not the king handsome, though?"

Astra's face grew hot. She was glad her back was to Nikolina. "I...*nei*, I do not think so. He is old and ugly." Her mind ricocheted as she pictured the king's face, remembered his hands touching her, his mouth pushing…She bent down to adjust the stones at the bottom of the loom.

"Well, I think he is handsome. And, why do you not like Vegar? I hear he is rich."

"He is even older than the king, and overweening."

"And ugly," Nikolina snickered. "But rich is better than fine looks. If you wait too long, he may marry someone else."

"I hope so. I wish them well." Irked, she threw the shuttle too hard and missed catching it. It clattered to the floor.

Nikolina laughed. "If I were unmarried, I would take him myself. I would have servants and live like a lady. That would be grand, *nei?*"

Astra picked up the shuttle and rewound it. "Not if I had to live with him." She changed the subject. "Do you miss Dag badly?"

"During the day? *Nei*. But at night, *ja*. Honestly, he is like his father, silent and brooding. He was usually out working when his mother beat me, but he never defended me against her. You do not truly know someone until you marry him."

"Do you regret getting married?"

"I do not regret this sweet angel I have. But marriage is another thing altogether. It is something to be endured to get children."

Amalie woke, chewed on Signy's wooden doll, and tried to crawl forward with her arms. Both cousins cheered for her. Nikolina picked her up to feed her.

They were quiet for a short time, then Nikolina asked, "Astra, are you ill? I have noticed you are sick to your stomach in the morning."

"I am fine." Astra chided herself. She must be more careful.

"Every morning, *nei?*"

"It is nothing." Astra felt her face flush. "I am going to check on the animals." She needed to get away before Niki asked more questions.

"Here, I fixed your boots," said Nikolina, lifting them from the floor and stuffing them with wool. "Try them on."

Astra tugged on the newly fitted deerskin boots, thanked Nikolina, and tossed on her cloak. She opened the door.

"Snow!" she exclaimed. Heavy flakes had already obscured the grass. "I need to bring the cows in."

She hurried to draw water to fill the troughs in the barn, then tossed dried grasses down from the loft. The dogs drove the animals in and she fastened the door shut. Leaving Kvikke outside for now, she made the stalls ready for the horses in case the weather worsened. She hefted armfuls of hay to the pasture where the sheep gathered around, pushing against her legs and bleating. If the snow became too deep, though unlikely at this time of year, she would have to bring them into the sheep house so they would not suffocate.

With snow tugging at the hem of her cloak, she chased the chickens under the house, tossed in some feed and shut the hatch. When all was secure, Astra tromped a distance down the path listening for the axe and calling her father's name, but the coin-sized flakes smothered her voice. Far was probably loading the sledge now to come home.

Astra knocked a large dried fish down from a rafter in the *stabbur* and brought water in for the cooking pot—she had promised Far to have the stew pot ready. Nikolina added an onion and a bit of cabbage while Astra collapsed by the fire, warming her bloodless toes. Above the vent hole, large flakes danced in the rising smoke.

As they waited for Far to return, Astra finished the cloth she was weaving and measured Nikolina's height to cut the cloak.

When she sat down to stitch, Nikolina said, "Let me do that. I am faster than you."

Astra sighed, remembering her oath to be civil. She handed the fabric to her cousin.

The light through the smoke hole slowly darkened, though white flurries were lit from their cooking fire below. "Should we wait for your Far before we eat?" Nikolina asked, checking the pot.

"A bit longer. He will be home soon." Astra's stomach was churning uneasily—she had not eaten for hours. Suddenly, bile rose up from the belly and she dashed to the door, vomiting off the porch into a snowdrift. The dogs, lying on the stone step outside, jumped away, startled.

Nikolina came up behind her. "Sit down. I will get you some soup."

Astra wiped her mouth and shuddered. "I am just worried. Far should have been back by now. It is almost dark."

They both peered into the yard. The wind had picked up and gusts blew snowflakes sideways.

Nikolina said, "The horse knows the way home. Come in and settle your stomach."

Very worried now, Astra steeled herself. "I am going out to find him. Maybe he is already in the barn skinning a hare for our dinner. Besides, I need to put Kvikke in her stall."

Nikolina frowned, hands on her hips. "You should eat first."

"He will need help unloading the wood. I will eat with him."

Though night had fallen, the sheen from the snow lit the yard. Astra pulled Mar's cloak over all but her eyes, pushing through drifts up to her shins. She shuffled to the woodshed, but Far was not there. He was not in the barn, the stable, nor the workshop. She called and called for him in vain. What had happened? The sled could be stuck in the snow or he could be trying to urge Farwa up the hill. Or he could be injured. She tried not to panic.

She brought Kvikke into the stable and brushed the horse down. Then she saddled and bridled her and set out toward the woods. Snow blew hard across the stubbled fields, gusts of wind carrying swirls in all directions. Astra rode alongside the fence to the far field, then dipped down toward the creek through the aspens and into the thick forest beyond. Beneath the cedars, less snow had fallen, but the light disappeared.

Astra pulled up on the reins. Her heartbeat thrummed in her ears. Where was the dead pine Far had gone after? She could see little under the laden branches. She clicked her tongue, moving forward slowly, almost blindly. Kvikke swerved between tree trunks; limbs clawed at Astra's face. She lay flat over the horse's withers, calling for her father to one side and then the other until her voice became raw.

The deeper she drove into the woods the more she imagined shapes and movements around her. She halted, listening. Creatures of the night were awake, animals she would not see until they leaped at her. Ogres or trolls might be watching even now; wolves could be circling.

She spun her horse around. Far could not have come this way. Kvikke knew the path home and maneuvered between the trees until they broke onto the path. The horse charged through the billows of the storm all the way to the farmyard, skidding to a stop at the stable entrance. Astra stowed her safely in her stall.

With the dogs' help she herded the sheep into the sheep house. The ram jammed his head repeatedly into the rails of his pen to get at the ewes, but settled down when she dropped hay for him from the loft.

Astra had to step high over the growing drifts on her way back to the house. Haret nosed her hand for food when she arrived at the door. "Sorry, you have to wait," she said, patting the dog's head. She unlatched the house door and the wind flung it open. The bang woke the baby.

Nikolina stood up. Her face looked frightened. "Where were you? I thought you would be right back."

"I rode down to the woods, but I did not find him." Just saying these words brought a sob to her lips as she slung off her snowy cape.

Nikolina picked up the screaming child. "You cannot leave me like that. What if you had not come back?"

Astra sat by the fire and laid her head in her hands forlornly. "The snow is blowing so hard I could not see anything," she moaned. "How will Far be able to get home?"

Nikolina shushed the baby and sat down to nurse. "He will find his way, cousin. He has seen this kind of storm before."

Astra glanced at Nikolina, who was looking down at her nursing child. Her cousin's features were lovely in the firelight. Astra said, "He would never stay out past dark in a snowstorm unless something was wrong. Mar made him promise."

Nikolina's voice was kind, sympathetic even. "He will be all right. He is a strong, wise man. He knows how to survive in snow."

Astra wanted to believe Nikolina's words. She pulled off her boots. "You are right," she said. "He has seen other storms."

Nikolina ran her hand over Amalie's feathery hair. "He knows your land from nose to tail. He will be back as soon as he can."

All children's fathers taught them about snow survival. Far had said they should find low-hanging limbs, or the root system of a downed tree, and arrange branches all around to form a shelter. A layer of leaves and debris could keep them warm, even in snowy weather. This is what Far must have done, Astra told herself. She dipped a bowl of soup, but her stomach began to rumble. The urge swelled and she ran to the chamber pot, though there was nothing left to vomit.

"Again?" Nikolina asked. "Do you have a fever?"

Astra sat on her haunches leaning over the bowl, waiting for the tide to ebb. "I am just upset and hungry."

Nikolina asked quietly, "When did this start?"

Astra wiped her mouth and came back to the fire. Nikolina should stop prying. "Not long ago. A few days, or a week or two," she said. "It is nothing."

Nikolina asked, "After you were in Sjodrun? That was six sabbaths ago or more, *nei*?"

Astra's hand shook as she sipped from the spoon. "I suppose."

Nikolina stared at her silently.

Squirming under her cousin's gaze, Astra said, "I think I am sick with worry, is all. Or I must have eaten something bad."

Nikolina raised an eyebrow. "I would say you are with child."

"*Nei*, of course not." Astra trembled at the thought that had plagued her mind, the thought she had repeatedly squelched.

"Astra, how can worry make you sick to your stomach? Besides, we have been eating the same food and I feel fine."

They locked eyes.

"You are with child," Nikolina repeated. "You have the *morgenkvalme*. I had it, so I know."

Astra's cheeks flamed.

Balancing Amalie on her hip, Nikolina reached over and placed her hand on Astra's shoulder. "When is the last time you had your monthlies? You can tell me."

Astra's mind spun. Had her monthlies come since the black sickness? Since their visit to Sjodrun? *Nei*. She had been working so hard she had not counted days. Indeed, it had been too long. She stopped eating and stared into her bowl.

"It is true, then!" Nikolina laughed. "If you tell Einarr right away, he will marry you."

Astra shot, "It could not be him."

"Vegar then." Nikolina smiled broadly. "All the better. Your father will not object and you will still be wealthy."

"*Nei*, never him!" Astra buried her face in her hands. "I was forced. Mother Mary help me."

Nikolina leaned forward. "Who? Who forced you?"

Astra glanced at the door. "You will not believe me if I tell you. Do not tell Far."

Nikolina smiled. "Maybe it was not so forced. A secret lover, then. So, you are not so good after all, are you?"

Seething, Astra cried, "That is not so!" She got up and lit the lantern. "I need to check if I latched the barn door."

"Stay. I am just teasing." Nikolina reached for her arm but Astra donned her boots and cloak and tramped into the storm.

The dogs huddled together in the *svalgang* and did not follow. Astra's previous footsteps were already filled.

Indeed, the barn door was not tightly closed. Astra peered into the cows' pen and they lowed restlessly. She shone the light into Kvikke's stall and the mare whinnied softly.

Suddenly, she heard a rustle at the barn door. She whipped around and held the lantern aloft. "Far? Is that you?"

There was no reply. She gripped her knife and crept forward, slowly pushing the door open. The iron hinge squeaked.

In the snow directly in front of her, two yellow eyes reflected the light of her lantern. A silver tail twisted and darted away.

Astra slept little. She heard the wind's whistle over the top of the vent hole, the crackle of embers in the fire, the hoot of an owl on the roof. Where was Far? She pictured him injured, trying to make his way back through mounting drifts. At times her breath came in jagged gasps. When she could lie still no longer, she stoked the fire and quietly opened the door. The dogs that had curled together in the *svalgang* shook themselves awake, weakly wagging their tails.

"Good boys," she whispered. "Stay right there and keep a lookout for Far." She peered into the night. All she saw was an ever-thickening wall of white.

As she started to close the door, the dogs' ears perked up and they stared into the yard. In a moment she, too, heard the snort of a horse and swoosh of sledge runners.

"Far!" she screamed.

Farwa's golden head covered with snow came into view, surrounded by a cloud of hot breath from the horse's nostrils. The empty sledge slid to a stop. When the horse saw Astra, she whinnied and shook off the snow from her mane and withers.

Astra charged out bare-footed, waving her arms. "Far, over here!" she cried. But when she had circled the horse and sledge and run a way down the path, Far was not there.

"Astra, wake up." Nikolina shook her arm. "Are you well?"

Astra startled. "What? What happened?" Then she remembered her distress that the horse had returned alone and how she pushed through deep drifts to lead Farwa to her stall in the middle of the night.

"Shh." Nikolina pointed to the sleeping baby. "It is light already. Are you all right?"

Astra smelled porridge and saw pure white through the vent hole. She twisted to look at Far's empty bed then sat upright. "Far?"

Nikolina shook her head. "*Nei*, not yet."

Astra climbed out of bed and dressed quickly. "The animals will be starving."

"Eat some porridge first to settle your stomach." Nikolina set a bowl on the board.

Embarrassed by last night's discussion, Astra found little to say while she ate. Nikolina helped Astra into her many layers and Mar's shaggy boots.

"Have you looked outside?" Astra asked.

"*Nei*, not yet." Nikolina settled Mar's cloak over Astra's head and shoulders and pinned it with a brooch. "Bring back milk when you come."

Astra cracked the door open. Snow had drifted waist-high and spilled into the entryway. A howling wind blew the top layer spiraling into the air. The farm buildings across the yard were only shadows in the whipping flurries.

"God in heaven," she breathed.

Nikolina came up behind her. "Satan and all his *djevels*!"

A lump on the stepstones moved and the dogs wiggled free of their snow cave. They shook themselves and nosed Astra's mittened hand.

"Give the dogs some porridge," Astra called as she stepped over the dogs into the *svalgang*. Nikolina swept out the snow and shut the door behind her.

Astra crept along the narrow passageway, finding stacked firewood, an axe, Far's sword, and a shovel.

Digging a trench was tedious and bitterly cold. Astra thrust snow to one side then the other, forming a trail she could navigate. Where is Far? she wondered. Why has he not come home? Is he injured or waiting out the storm in a snow cave? She had to believe that was true.

Thinking of yesterday's conversation with Niki, she repeated to herself, "I am with child, the king's child," wishing it were not true yet knowing it was.

She arrived at the barn panting and was met by the mustiness of manure and loud mooing. The barn was fairly warm from the heat of the animals, and Astra removed her cloak. When the milking was done, she carried the milk back to the house where Nikolina forced her to sit and eat *brød* and porridge.

"What about the chickens?" Nikolina asked. "They are complaining."

Astra showed Nikolina where to lift the loose floorboard and Niki dropped some grain into the hole. Feathers flew as the chickens attacked the food.

Digging her way to the sheep house took Astra late into the morning. As she neared, she heard the ram butting angrily against his railings and she prayed the boards would hold. Finding a sharp spade, she held it in one hand while she checked the ram's pen. If he escaped, she might have to kill him or risk being gored. She climbed into the loft and shoved dried grass, twigs, moss, and leaves down into the sheep's pens before shoveling snow into their troughs to melt.

The wind had died down some as Astra trod back to the house, but thick flakes had heightened the walls of her corridor. If it did not stop, she would soon have to tunnel.

"When you get to the *stabbur*, bring more oats and fish," Nikolina said as she hung Astra's wet clothing in the entry. "We are getting low."

Astra flopped down on the bed, exhausted. Nikolina dished her a bowl of porridge, sticking in a piece of dried trout. She said, "You need to eat, for you and the baby."

Astra did not reply, devouring these and another slice of *brød* before leaning back against the bed post, spent.

"You must rest before you go back out," Niki said.

"I must go after him," Astra said, knowing Nikolina would object.

Nikolina sat down beside her cousin and grasped Astra's forearm. "Do not go. Do not leave me alone. What if you get lost? What would happen to me and Amelie? Your father will find his way back, I am sure of it."

Astra pulled free. "Something is keeping him or he would be home by now." She rose. "I will be home before dark."

Astra could see only a few horse-lengths ahead as she urged Kvikke through the drifts that touched the horse's belly. Kvikke's breaths blew clouds that quickly turned to frost, crusting the horse's lashes with white. She shook her head and snorted disagreeably.

Astra followed the line of trees to where their property met the creek. They reached the *stående stein*, the massive stone that marked the farthest border of their land, and followed the gurgling of the now-buried creek.

Astra could only see the lower branches of the pines; their tops disappeared into the blinding white. After several trips back and forth along the road, she still did not see the dead pine Far had spoken of. She pulled up the reins, exasperated. The tree must be fallen and the trunk would be lying flat, well-covered with snow. Astra screamed for him, but her voice was muted by the squall. She turned back.

Astra could not see a stone's throw away. The horse slipped on icy rocks and jumped over drifts, nearly pitching Astra off. She bent low and clung to Kvikke's mane with all her strength. When they skidded to a stop at the barn, Astra was shaking with cold. She dried Kvikke and forked down hay from the loft. By the time she had fed the cattle, milked, and piled their muck in a corner, the snow's depth reached her chest with no sign of lessening.

Frantically, she dug out the trail to deliver the milk to Niki, then worked her way to the sheep house. Heading back home, she was unable to see through the blizzard and became afraid she would miss the house altogether. She slung the longest rope she could find over her shoulder and tied one end to a post. Then she strung the rope behind her as she pushed along the quickly filling trail. Recalling a story Far had told of a man lost in a blizzard and found frozen just steps from his house, she tried to follow the path back. It had collapsed in places, making her uncertain which way to go. She continued to dig until she was sure she had passed the house altogether. Just as she began to panic, the dark roof of the house appeared through the flurries. Astra cried out in relief.

What if she had veered just a bit further to her right? What if she had run out of rope? She dug gratefully along the log wall, unfurling the rope until she was greeted by yips of joy. Her distant hope that Far had returned while she was gone vanished. He would never find his way home in this tempest.

Astra secured the rope to a peg and tried to push the door open. It was bolted. She pounded. "Nikolina, open the door!"

The bar slid free and Nikolina threw herself into Astra's arms. They held each other tightly.

Her cousin yanked Astra inside. "I was worried when you did not come back. Did you find him?"

Tears stung Astra's eyes. "The snow is too deep. I could see nothing."

Nikolina helped Astra out of her wet clothes, wrapped her in a sheepskin by the fire, and dipped warm broth into a bowl. She rubbed Astra's red toes, then placed her cousin's feet on the foot warming bin.

"He will come back after the blizzard stops," Nikolina said. Her voice was less convincing this time.

"He had better." Astra sipped the soup and the warmth spread through her limbs.

By morning the flurries were so thick, that had it not been for her trenches, Astra would have missed the barn that emerged from the void just ahead. The animals bawled at her, restless and hungry. After feeding and milking, she stretched an aching arm over Kvikke's stall rail and her horse nudged her for a treat. Astra felt tired beyond words. She leaned her head against Kvikke's cheek, too weary to cry.

Stomping back to the house, Astra thought, Why am I doing all the hard work by myself? Her cousin must help with the heavy chores—she should have offered already.

Throwing off her cloak, she pulled up the floorboard that covered the underground coop where the chickens clucked and strutted impatiently. "Get the eggs, cousin," she snapped. Nikolina's mouth gaped, but she lay down and reached into the stinking coop, handing Astra the eggs she could reach. Then Niki snatched a scrawny hen and wrung its neck. Astra smiled. There would be chicken in the soup tonight and bones for the dogs.

The rest of that day the storm raged on. Astra thought of little besides her father. As soon as the snow stopped, she would ski out and find him.

By the morning of the fourth day, when she tugged the door open, she was met with a wall of white as tall as she, but above it, blue sky shone.

"God be praised," she shouted. She climbed onto a stool and peered above the snow. For the first time in days, she could see across the yard. Only the snow-laden roofs of the other farm buildings could be seen. A large pine branch had fallen, leaving a jagged scar on its trunk and a hole in the roof of the old house. She sighed. Maybe today Far would find his way home; she would not lose faith, not until she must.

The cousins ate a meal of eggs and the last of the flat *brød*. Astra insisted Nikolina help her get to the *stabbur* for more food, but Amalie was fussy, pushing in a tooth, and Astra ended up shoveling alone. When she reached the *stabbur* she collapsed onto a bench. Her shoulders burned. Before long Nikolina joined her, the sleeping child on her back. They cut down venison, ground barley into a sack, and dragged a cask of ale along the icy corridor. Astra made Nikolina dig a path to the woodshed to refill the firewood supply. That night both cousins ate their fill and collapsed by the fire.

"That helps," Nikolina said, yawning. "I did not realize how hungry I was. If only we had some ham...That would make a good supper."

Ham! Astra bolted upright. "The *djevel* take me. I have not checked on the pig at all!" The pig house was some distance behind the barn because of the stench, and Far always fed her when she was penned up.

Nikolina's jaw dropped. "You forgot the pig? That could be our winter food!"

Astra bristled. "Far always fed her. As you know, I have been busy with everything else!"

Nikolina threw Astra a disgusted scowl. "It is probably dead by now."

Astra yelled, "I did not forget on purpose! You did not remember, either!" She was angry at Nikolina, but mostly at herself.

Nikolina paused, then breathed out loudly. "If it is frozen, you can still butcher it."

"That is Far's job," Astra snapped. "I have not butchered a pig. Have you?"

Nikolina glowered. "Without the pig, do we have enough food for the winter?"

"Of course, we do." But Astra was worried, since they had lost two cows and had not yet filled their larder. Under her breath she muttered, "Less now that you are here."

Nikolina's face colored. "Are you saying Amalie and I are a burden? You would have had even more mouths to feed if your family was alive."

Astra screeched, "How dare you say that? That is spiteful and wicked!" She threw her bowl across the room, where it shattered.

Nikolina stared at Astra with clenched teeth, but quieted her tone. "I did not mean that. I can earn my keep. I am a hard worker—just ask my slave-driving mother-in-law."

"How can I ask her?" Astra shouted. "You let her die."

Nikolina screamed, "She was dying anyway! I could not have saved her no matter what I did, just like you could not save your family. Amalie is all that matters. You would have done the same."

"I am not like you, Nikolina," Astra snapped. "I did not leave my dying family. You weaseled into that family by sleeping with Dag."

Nikolina laughed aloud. "You think you are more righteous than me? Whose baby do you carry, anyway?"

Astra stood up and slapped Nikolina's face. She snatched her cloak. "I have to check on the pig and muck the stalls, since you are a worthless mule. If only I could muck out your mouth."

"Muck out your own mouth, slut! At least I got married. Who is the real sinner here?"

Astra slammed the door behind her.

Astra worked for hours to dig her way to the pig house. Her thoughts raged against her cousin and her back ached. The dogs crowded behind her legs in the narrow snow trench, bumping against her heels. She poked around with a long stick until she hit the roof of the low hut, completely smothered in snow. Before long she uncovered a patch of snow strewn with blood, then the partially eaten carcass of the sow. The dogs leaped over the drifts and started ripping at the bared flesh, growling.

"*Nei!*" screamed Astra. "Get away!" but the dogs did not look up. She relented. They had eaten only scraps these last four days and pork should not go to waste. Angry at herself for this irreplaceable loss, she turned to go back. As she pushed through the narrow passage she had dug, she stopped. She scanned the woods. The wolf might return, now that the storm had passed. The only weapons she had were the shovel and her short knife, which she yanked from her belt. Wolves did not normally hunt in daylight, but if they were starving, they were known to even attack full-grown men.

She called the dogs. Guttural growls arose as they ate ravenously, and they did not come. Astra hurried back to the farmyard, chased by fear.

When she reached the house, melting snow dripped from the eaves. She must search for Far before the snow became too slushy for skis. She shoveled her way to her grandparents' old house, its roof collapsed from the fallen branch, and retrieved her skis. The idea of going alone through wolf-infested woods was frightening, but a wolf would not likely chase a skier by day. She strapped on her father's long knife and pushed off.

The melting snow formed a slippery crust, and she flew down the road past the fields to the woods, zigzagging through the trees and looking for the downed pine. Halfway up the other side of the hill she spied branches sticking up through the white expanse. Was that it? She had been close before.

Astra tramped her skis all around the tree's length and protruding root system, but everything was buried in the deep drifts. She imagined him lying frozen beneath, or worse. Perhaps he had made it to the neighbor's farm.

When she returned home, Astra brought Nikolina a peace offering from the rafters of the *stabbur*: the last of the bacon. She needed her cousin now more than ever—they needed each other. She regretted what she had said, though she was still piqued by Nikolina's biting words. She and Nikolina were family, after all.

The fire danced, welcoming Astra in. She set the slab of bacon on the hearth and said softly, "The pig is dead, but I thought you would like this."

Nikolina barely glanced up from her sewing. "*Takk.*"

"Let me cook," Astra offered, slinging off her cloak.

"*Nei*, I will do it. I know my place." Nikolina laid down her work and reached for the iron skillet. "Would you watch Amalie? She is trying to crawl but I am afraid she will fall off the bed."

Astra sat and Amalie flopped onto her lap, chortling happily. "She is getting so big," Astra said.

"*Ja*, she is." Nikolina placed the frozen bacon over the fire and before long it sizzled.

Astra gulped down her pride. "I have not told you what a good mother I think you are."

Nikolina swiveled to look at her cousin. "Nice of you to say that. I thought you were beginning to detest me."

"I am sorry for what I said." Astra tickled the baby and she giggled.

"Me, too. We should just forget it."

That night they both drank several bowls of ale. Exhausted beyond words, Astra climbed into Far's box bed instead of Nikolina's and wormed under the heavy furs, falling into the sleep of the dead.

Chapter 23

The trail leaving Stiklestad wound away from the Trondheim Fjord along Lake Snaasavatnet, then many *miil* northeast toward the Saami village of Snaasa. Kjell had found these nomadic peoples to be welcoming of traders, having spent a season with them three years ago. At Snaasa Kjell would purchase a bone knife and perhaps a seal coat. He hoped the Saami were at the village, though they might already have moved on.

If they were there, Kjell would ask their permission to hunt east in the Gressamoen Mountains where he had gone last year. These were prime winter hunting grounds for the precious furs he sought: brown bear, lynx, wolverine, and arctic fox. Wolves competed for this same game and were an ever-present threat. Fortunately, Kjell's *buhunds* had proven vigilant and fearless against wolves.

By the afternoon of his sixth day, traveling through knee-high snow that had been brought by a passing storm, Kjell spied the mounded domes of Saami *goahti*, the turf huts festooned with rocks and antlers, of which there were a dozen or more in the village. Scattered among them were a few *lavvus*, skin-covered tents that were stretched upright on forked poles, easy to disassemble and used as their traveling homes.

Smoke curling from the *goahtis'* vent holes blended with the snow-laden clouds and the whitened ground, causing the village to appear to float on a cloud. A small herd of female reindeer used for milking were tied up to wooden stakes.

Barking dogs raced toward Kjell, prompting his own *hunds* to take a growling stance in front of Kjell and the horses. Several figures appeared through the crystalline mist: men in thick coats, fur-side in, wearing colorful, tight-fitting caps.

The Moon Turned to Blood

They carried no weapons that Kjell could see, but formed a silent line in front of the dwellings. Behind them a few women clad in thick reindeer coats hid wide-eyed children behind their heavy skirts and wool leggings.

Kjell dismounted and raised his hands to show that he meant no harm. One man walked toward him, lifting his reindeer-fur mitten in greeting. Kjell knew him as the chief, Fishhawk. The chief called, "May you have long life," in the Åsele language, and he motioned Kjell forward with a smile of recognition. When they clasped right arms in friendship, the onlookers dispersed. Fishhawk showed Kjell where to make his camp just beyond the reindeer paddock. Kjell staked out his horses before joining the chief's family for a meal of welcome.

Fishhawk, his wife Flatfoot, their four children and two elders sat together cross-legged with Kjell around a small fire in the *goahti*. A reindeer flank roasted on a spit, causing Kjell's mouth to water. Flatfoot honored Kjell with the first strip of venison and a blood sausage. He thanked her with the Åsele words, "You are blessed."

During the meal Fishhawk spoke with Kjell using both words and hand gestures. He wanted to know where Kjell was going to hunt this season. Kjell pointed northeast, saying, "Gressamoen Fell," and the man nodded. This was followed by a river of words between the elders that Kjell could not comprehend. When the talking stopped, Fishhawk smiled and nodded, indicating that they had given their permission for his hunt.

After eating his fill, Kjell searched his satchel and gave Flatfoot the barley, six unbroken eggs, and salted pork as a gift. She grinned and nodded in thanks.

Kjell showed Fishhawk his short carving knife, and through gestures, indicated he wanted a similar gutting knife, which he obliged. The Saami's scrimshaw carvings were the most detailed he had ever seen, and their knives were famously durable.

After the meal, his host led him to the skin tent of a bent old woman named Proud Niila. She laid several knives on a stretch of leather, knives with handles of intricately carved walrus tusk, antler, and bone. With some difficulty Kjell selected the walrus tusk. He weighed it in his hand and ran his fingers over the detailed carvings of bear, whale, and seabirds. In payment he gave her beads and coins, which she pirated away in the folds of her coat.

Kjell indicated to Proud Niila that he, too, needed a heavy coat, so she pointed out another hut and motioned him that way. There he traded more coins and the remaining eggs for a bearskin coat and reindeer gloves.

As Kjell headed to his camp, an orange shaft of light shimmered across the nearby lake, catching his eye. Evening was upon them already. After he unsaddled Thorden and settled his other animals in his camp, Fishhawk beckoned Kjell to join them at the evening fire. The small community gathered on their knees in the snow around a large bonfire in the center of the village. Each was clad head to foot in reindeer-hide clothing. Women's coats were richly embroidered with Saami symbols. Warmly wrapped infants were strapped to cradle-boards and propped in the snow.

Kjell had joined their circle before. The first time, he listened uneasily to the soul-wrenching rhythms and chants. The shaman, a hunched figure wearing a mask, was drummed into a frenzy of dancing. When the drumming stopped suddenly, the holy man fell prostrate onto the snow. The villagers then chanted strange words together in a crescendo that had sent a chill rippling up Kjell's back. But this time, Kjell knew what to expect and knew they honored him by his inclusion. He sat down cross-legged next to Fishhawk.

An elderly man they called Ahcci, meaning father, lifted his *fadnu*, a wooden flute-like instrument, and began to whistle an ethereal tune. Drummers held their skin-covered *gievres* between their knees and beat them with carved hammers. Before long, Kjell's thoughts became lost in the throbbing beat.

The villagers started to chant strange syllables, interrupted by the unearthly wail of the *fadnu*. Faces of the Saami were set aglow by the firelight that cast flickering images across their features. The shaman lit a pipe, sucked a long draw and passed it around the circle. Some smoked, others passed it on. When it came to Kjell he inhaled of it deeply, coughed, and passed the pipe along. It slowly circled the crowd twice more and Kjell partook. A soothing fog soon beset him.

The pulsating drumbeats continued as rising invocations pounded within Kjell's chest. He closed his eyes. Through a mist, Oda's face materialized. Her lips moved. "Where were you when I needed you?" she seemed to whisper. His heart slammed. How he had loved her, and how he had failed her! He reached for her but her face deformed. Putrefying sores marred her features. Her mouth opened in a silent scream of pain that melded with the *fadnu's* droning.

Tears burned Kjell's eyes. She was right. He had not been with her when she needed him, nor rescued her from the deathly blight. He had already betrayed her, sleeping with another to appease his carnal needs while her flesh rotted in unsanctified ground. Kjell raised his face to the stars and his pain-filled wail rose with the smoke.

Before first light he awakened to the tinkling of bells as reindeer passed his skin-covered shelter. He poked his head out and a herdsman called a friendly greeting to him in Åsele. Kjell called back, "Morning to you, friend," trying to remember the Åsele response. By the time he did, the man had passed on his way.

Kjell loaded his gear and weapons onto Sokker's back and saddled Thorden. Leading the horses through the sleeping village, he saw only the old carver, awake and kindling a fire. Kjell flashed his knife at her, waved, and received a toothless smile in reply. He rode away, heading east toward the wilderness.

He drove the horses across the snowy plains, past iced-over bogs, and upward toward the high mountain peaks. The snow grew deeper the higher they climbed, and soon crystalline flakes fell. Small game—hares, stoats, and martens—jumped behind rocks, disappearing into burrows. He noted bear scat partially hidden by snow and the two-toed footprints of a red deer tracing across a steep hillside.

In the afternoon as the muted light was beginning to wane, he recognized the copse of rugged spruce at the base of a rocky cliff. He rode down the long slope and halted in the sheltered vale. There he found the remains of the earthen hut that he had dug into the hillside last year. Part of the sod roof was caved in and the sticks of his makeshift door scattered and splintered. Brown fur hung from the wooden shards. A bear had tried to winter here. Should he stay? What if the bear returned? Chances were slim since the structure had collapsed.

As he unloaded his gear, Kjell let the horses roam to paw the snow for grass and nibble on small branches and needles. He cut spruce limbs to form a shelter for the night, then set traps for small game in a perimeter around his camp. Hurriedly he gathered fuel for a fire, digging in the snow for cones and scraping moss from a tree trunk as fire starters. His fingers were icy as he struck the flint. He fed the fire with small sticks, then the remains of his broken door. Tomorrow he would dig out the shelter and rebuild the roof and door.

The dogs curled together beside him and he shared dried venison with them. He knew they would forewarn him of night prowlers. He placed weapons all around him within easy reach as darkness soon descended. The only sound was the crackling of the fire.

The daylight hours were growing fewer, so Kjell had to make the most of each one. He checked his traps morning and evening. During daylight hours with the help of his dogs, he tracked his larger quarry—deer, elk, wolves and bear. The horses dragged his kills back to camp where he scraped the skins and stretched them to dry. He gleaned meat for himself and his dogs and hid the pelts in a snow cave some distance from his camp, erecting stakes and a trap at its entrance to discourage scavengers.

Some days, Kjell ventured out on the snowshoes he made from branches and gut. He tethered the horses under a cluster of pines where the snow was scanter so they could paw for what vegetation lay beneath the protective branches.

For want of a human voice, Kjell often talked aloud, telling the dogs what he must do, how he would find wealthy buyers for his lush furs, and how rich they all would become.

One morning while riding Thorden to check his traps in the gully below his camp, Kjell spotted the massive tracks of a brown bear leading down the slope and into a thicket of trees. He followed the footprints, his bow on his shoulder and his javelins across his lap. Before long he heard heavy snorting and branches breaking. The bear must be huge but had not smelled him yet.

The sharp clap of one of his traps produced a roar of surprise, and branches thrashed as the bear tried to shake it off. Kjell whistled and the three hunting dogs bounded toward the sound, howling. A monster of a bear crashed into the clearing on its hind feet, and Kjell saw that its rear paw had been snagged by the trap. Thorden sprinted down the hill as Kjell shot two arrows that pierced the bear's shoulder and midsection. The dogs leapt at the monster's back, snarling and biting the thick fur. Navnløs, the village dog, stayed back, barking frantically.

When Kjell drew close enough, he waited for the bear to rise up on its hind legs again, then threw his javelin, striking deep between the bear's ribs. Still the beast fought, batting the dogs away like flies and towering to its full, frightful height. Kjell jumped off his horse and threw his second spear into the bear's belly, then a third into its gaping mouth. The bear gagged, swatting at the spear, then gurgled and toppled forward, snapping the spears like twigs beneath its weight.

Kjell jumped atop the shaggy heap and stabbed the bear's neck, ripping the carotid that spouted jugs of hot blood into the powdery snow. When the animal was finally still, Kjell fell back onto its carpeted torso, staring into the sky to thank the heavens.

Two hunting dogs and the village mutt frisked about, barking excitedly at the demise of the downed prey; but Beskytter, the oldest and keenest, bore a red stripe across his back. He lay in the snow, twisting to lick his gaping wound. Kjell cut a strip from his coat and tied it tightly around the dog's torso. He stroked Beskytter's head, saying through a clenched throat, "You have done well, Protector."

Kjell worked the hide free, breaking into a sweat and removing his heavy overcoat. He saved the kidneys, heart, liver, and strips of belly for his food store, sorry that he must leave most of the meat for the wolves.

After a brief rest, he sawed through the neck vertebrae and wrist bones, releasing them from the skeleton so the head and paws remained attached to the pelt. This rich fur would fetch a fine price. Tying the bear's paws to ropes so the pelt served as a travois, he lifted the injured dog onto the bearskin and stuffed the innards into a satchel. Then he whistled for Sokker. The two horses dragged the heavy hide back to camp.

Kjell blew the banked coals back to life. He cauterized Beskytter's wound, deep and jagged, and slathered it with bear grease. Then he strapped on a clean strip of hide and gently stroked the dog's head. The thought of losing this old friend grieved him.

Before long, the aroma of roasting bear circled the clearing. While dinner cooked, he worked his fleshing knife over the underside of the bearskin to render it clean, and stretched the huge pelt between tree trunks to dry. By the time he was finished, the meat was done. He was famished.

Wiping his hands with snow, he squatted by the fire and knifed the cooked liver onto the swatch of leather he used for a plate. Biting chunks off his knife-tip, he savored the dense sweetness. Kjell tossed the dogs morsels and hand-fed Beskytter, who barely lifted his head off the snow to take each bite.

After supper, Kjell gathered extra wood and built a bonfire. Wrapped in heavy furs, he sat on a rock by the fire to watch the stars march across the sky, the dogs curled at his side.

Oda's face swirled before him once again. How long ago it seemed since they had laughed together, since he had made love to her. He tried to recall Oda's voice but could not quite hear it. And his baby boy, the child he barely knew—he was startled that he could not picture his son's face. When he returned south, he must stop at the remnants of their cabin and visit their graves to renew his memories.

And what about his parents, his brothers? He had not seen them for over two years, ever since they rejected his marriage to Oda. Now he realized his anger at them had finally subsided. He thought of the best times of his childhood, the long seasons of *Jul* celebrations when the family would all gather round the hearth singing and dancing to *Onkel* Halldorr's piping and Tante Kolfinna's lyre. In his memory, everyone was rosy-cheeked and jubilant. In these nights of frivolity, they visited neighbors, played games, and told gruesome tales of ogres and trolls. They ate until they could not sit up. When the Hamar *katedral* bells rang the midnight service, they all bundled up and piled into sleighs to join the crowd standing in the frigid *kirke*. He remembered trying to stay awake but falling against his older brother's shoulder, only to be wakened by an elbow jab to the chest.

With sorrow, he also relived the last time he saw his parents.

※

Blushing with new-found love, Kjell had ridden into his home farmyard with Oda behind his saddle. He assured her that, though her father had chased them off the property, Kjell's family would accept the marriage and embrace her.

When they arrived, he told Oda to wait with the horse until he had spoken to his father, Sverre; but his mother, Runnveig, heard the whinny and came running out of the house. Kjell was encouraged by her teary-eyed embrace of him and friendly greeting to Oda. She invited Oda inside, telling Kjell his father was in the oat field.

Kjell strode confidently toward his father, who leaned on a hitching post watching two of his brothers wrestle a plow that was stuck and broken.

"You are just in time for planting," his father said, grabbing Kjell's arm firmly.

Kjell smiled and said, "Father. I have some good news. Come to the house so I can tell you and Mar together."

As they walked across the farmyard Kjell said, "I need to ask a favor that you may not like."

"What is it, son?" Sverre slowed.

"Break off my betrothal to Jurunn."

Sverre scoffed, "*Nei,* it is all arranged. I cannot let Finnr down. The maid will be of age in another year. You can wait."

When they got to the house, his father halted at the doorway. He glared at Oda sitting at the table. Runnveig nervously fingered a horn of ale.

"Who is this?" Sverre asked.

"Let us sit and have a drink, Far." Kjell pulled up a stool for his father and sat on the bench by Oda. Runnveig poured them each a horn.

"Far, this is Oda Flosisdatter. I met her in the high country on my way back from the hunt."

Sverre crossed his arms. He did not drink. "So? What is she doing here?"

Oda clenched Kjell's hand beneath the table.

"We fell in love, Far. In fact, we are wed. That is why you must cancel the contract with Jurunn's father. Please be happy for us."

Runnveig stared at the table.

Sverre's face became florid. "So. You fell in love, and decided to run off and get married. Did you even have a priest, or did you just marry all by yourselves? We call that fornication."

"*Nei*, a priest married us," said Kjell. "We did not expect this to happen, but we swore to each other we could be with no one else. I am sorry we did not come home first, but…we could not wait."

Sverre sprang up and leaned forward, his hands on the table. "Could not wait? Of course, you could wait."

Kjell clenched Oda's hand. "As I said, we made a vow to one another."

Kjell's mother reached out and pulled her husband onto his stool.

Sverre gripped the edge of the table with white knuckles. "What will you do now that you have shamed our family?"

"We did not intend to shame anyone," Kjell said. "If you do not let us stay, we will go north, near my hunting grounds. That will be my trade."

His father roared, "*Nei!* You are to become a cobbler's apprentice with your *Onkel* Halldorr. A marriage is an agreement between two families, not something you decide to do on your own! I do not even know her father's name, nor where her family lives. How dare you make your own vows while you are betrothed to another?"

Kjell did not know how to answer, but Oda spoke up pluckily. "We have visited my family as well, but, like you, they were upset. I am sure when tempers ease, they can be persuaded to meet with you to offer a dowry." Her eyes flashed from Sverre to Kjell, then settled on the tabletop.

Sverre spat on the dirt floor. "It is too late. The deed is done. You will have no help from this family."

"You reject us, your own kin?" Kjell shoved his ale horn, accidently spilling it onto his father's lap.

His father exploded, "You have lost your inheritance *and* your apprenticeship."

Kjell stood and balled his fists.

Sverre's face purpled and he stepped menacingly toward Kjell. "You will not survive without your family. You will come crawling back, begging our forgiveness."

Kjell grabbed Oda's hand and yanked her toward the door. "We will not. We do not need you. We can make it on our own." Beneath his anger he had not sensed the chasm of loss that he would feel only later.

Runnveig cried out, "*Nei, nei*, wait. Let me talk to your father...please, Sverre, let them stay."

Sverre's anger turned to fury and he moved to strike his son, but Kjell blocked the blow. He jerked Oda out the door.

"Do not go!" his mother screamed, running after them. "Give him time!"

But Kjell mounted and hoisted his breathless bride onto the horse's back. To his later regret, he yelled, "Tell Father he will be dead and cold before we come back here again."

That was how he had left them. How foolish was he. He hoped his terrible threat had not come true. He must go to Hamar and see what became of his family. Rare words traced his lips: "Please, God, let them survive this dark sickness."

As he sat with his musings under the vast swath of stars overhead, the heavens began to shimmer with wavering emerald lights. A color-filled swatch of *Nordlys,* the mysterious lights of the north, swept across the horizon, undulating, spreading, and twisting as the sky turned red then indigo, then green again. Light pulsed, changing color along its length that moved like a flight of swiftly flying swallows.

Nordlys were not uncommon, but tonight they were living things, growing in silent waves, reflecting on the mountain peaks, stretching and shooting up spinning tendrils. To Kjell they seemed like God's fingers writing an unreadable message to him—to him only.

What was God saying? Had he not received enough of God's judgment already? Did he not feel the heavy mantle of guilt every day and the burden of loss each night? Was it an omen? Was he to die?

As the array continued, painting the fields of snow with vivid hues, Kjell sensed something else: not a chastisement, not a warning, but a calling, like the heart-wrenching howl of a wolf. To what was he beckoned?

Darkness finally returned. The *Nordlys* and their stunning disquietude were silenced. Kjell stroked the dogs. They nestled close, their noses on his thighs. He felt released somehow by the fierceness of the wild.

At first light, Kjell left Sokker tethered at camp near Beskytter, still alive near the firepit, and started out on Thorden with the dogs to check his traps. The first trap held a squealing marten, and he used the blunt end of his knife to dispatch it. The next, a shallow pit trap, was empty, so he removed the camouflage and pulled up the branch spikes so no animal would impale itself and be left to die—he had only caught one weasel with it anyway. The arrow-launching trap had been triggered but missed its prey. Lastly, he found a white fox squirming in the rope trap, and likewise, he killed it with a blow to the head.

Before Thorden climbed the last rise on their way back toward camp, Kjell heard Sokker's frightened screams. He tore up the hill. The dogs sprinted over piles of snow and reached the camp before Kjell, barking madly.

Kjell's first glimpse was the horse's bucking rear end, then the streaking gray of a large wolf. Thorden balked and reared up. Kjell grabbed his bow and long knife as he slid off the horse's rump. The horse galloped away down the slope, traps falling off behind him.

As Kjell advanced, weapons drawn, the wolf spun and bared his teeth, gripping Beskytter's nape. The dog's tongue drooped to the side. Kjell nocked an arrow and aimed, but just as he was about to let it fly, Lope, his quickest dog, ran in front of the wolf, blocking Kjell's view.

The wolf shook the injured dog that flopped listlessly in its grip. The other dogs growled and nipped at the wolf's legs as it spun around, growling. Kjell could not get a clear shot. Shouldering his bow, he ran full bore toward the mass of fur and teeth, and thrust his knife into the wolf's back. The predator twisted around, dropping Beskytter and lunging at Kjell, who jammed his knife into the wolf's neck. The wolf keeled over. Blood ran from its mouth and it stilled.

Kjell kicked the carcass, screaming, "You fucking murderer! That is my best *hund!*" He plunged his knife into the fallen foe over and over, ruining the pelt and splattering his clothing with blood. Finally, he chopped at the neck until the wolf's head lopped off.

Reeling, he turned to Beskytter. The dog lay askew, his neck clearly broken. Kjell dropped to his knees, lifted the dog's head onto his lap, but he was gone. He pulled the animal to his chest like a lost child, its warmth next to his heart. The other dogs whined, crawling about the body of their comrade. Kjell had seen many animals die, but this was unspeakable.

Finally laying Beskytter down, Kjell rose to soothe Sokker, still tethered and whinnying, wild-eyed. A thin gash on the horse's rear fetlock would need treatment but was not serious. Kjell then went after Thorden, whistling. The equipment-scattered trail led him over the next hill and down into a valley. There he spied the stallion among the trees, pawing at the snow. The horses had fended for themselves these many days, and from this distance, Kjell grimaced at Thorden's sunken flanks and visible ribs.

He whistled. Thorden's head jerked up and he trotted toward his master. Kjell gathered the trailing reins and they slogged back to camp, picking up fallen traps along the way.

By nightfall Kjell had buried Beskytter beside a tree and carved a cross into its trunk. The wolf provided supper for the remaining dogs while Kjell sat by the fire roasting strips of bear meat and watching the wolf pelt burn.

The loss of Beskytter hit him hard. He had been a strong dog, with him eight years now. More than once he had saved Kjell's life: one time pulling him up through shattered ice, and another, chasing away an angry she-bear when Kjell had gotten between the sow and her cub. Beskytter had been there when Kjell first met Oda in the highlands and through uncounted hunts, over unmeasured *miil*.

Though he had always cherished the quiet of the forest and the thrill of the hunt, Kjell had suddenly become weary of his own company. He missed the sounds of human voices, especially those he had loved and lost. He picked up a stick to whittle, shaping it skillfully and fitting it with four legs that could move. "For you, Egill, my son," he said, setting the toy dog on a log. He imagined the boy as a lad, running up, snatching it and laughing. "I would have traded my life for yours, if I only had the chance," he whispered.

He selected two more wood scraps. One he shaped into the figure of a woman, the other into a small child. These he strung on a leather strap around his neck.

He realized he had no heart for the hunt. Tomorrow he would break camp and would not come back to this lonely place again.

Kjell felled an aspen, honed runners, and made a sledge bed, strapping everything together with gut-rope. He loaded the sledge with pelts and started out. If the Saami were still in the village, he would trade with them for arrow tips, and possibly a narwal tusk or two. Then he would head south to Stiklestad on his way to Hamar, perhaps stopping to see Dorte—she was a winsome one, but stubborn. What if she had agreed to come with him to the high country? She would have been screaming at him in misery. Had the sickness spread in that town? If so, had Dorte survived? He would decide whether to stop when he got there. If not, he would go on to Hamar to see his family.

Would they welcome him back? What if they did not? Then he could go to the market at Oslo, even Tonsberg. *Nei*, the pestilence had surely decimated those towns. Besides, they were crawling with knights.

Now Sjodrun, that small and pleasant village, was off the beaten path. Surely king's men would never return to that insolent village. Who knew how many souls the village had lost to the black sickness? But if it had passed, he could ask to stay a while, hunt...even become a tanner. And whatever happened to Astra? She was comely, but young and naive. His conclusion that the king had taken her maidenhood explained her despair at the creek. Did she marry the manor lord's son after all? It seemed unlikely. Yet, he hoped her fortunes were good.

The trek southward was slow. The skins were heavy and often caught on rocks and branches. Three days passed before he spied the Saami *goahtis,* but no smoke rose from them. They had already moved north for the winter hunt.

Nine more days led him to the ridge overlooking Stiklestad. He stopped his small caravan and sat on a boulder studying the village.

Smoke drifted from several houses below, but not all. From this distance he saw the stable, the inn, and Dorte's small hut. Her *brød* oven was not smoking, nor was her hut's chimney. Two figures walked about, otherwise the village was unduly still. He chewed on a strip of venison jerky. What would he say if he met Dorte? She was friendly with men. Maybe someone else was with her now. Or...she could be dead. He led his small entourage in a wide berth around the town and continued on.

Chapter 24

In the crystal crispness of the dark December morning, Astra tied *Jul* bells onto the horses' harness collars. Even through her thick mittens, the tips of her fingers were numb as she fastened the trace into the girth to hitch up the two-horse sleigh. She and Nikolina were traveling to Sjodrun for *Jul* celebrations. Far should be coming with them but he had never come home after the autumn snowstorm. The hole in her heart was still an open gash.

Though the unseasonable autumn snowfall had receded somewhat, more snow came and the ground was never bare again. In the days following Far's disappearance Astra had searched in widening perimeters for any sign of him—bits of clothing, broken tree limbs, mounds where he might have made a cave. In all her searching she found no trace of him at all.

Astra checked the harnesses once more and shook it to hear the bells jingle. She patted the horses' necks and ran her fingers through their coats of thick winter hair. Under her father's heavy fur, she wore her mother's best frock, the red linen undershift and green woolen kirtle, so beautifully embroidered at the neck and hem. Two woolen skirts were layered beneath for warmth. Mar's cloak was clasped with her pewter brooch. Astra had fastened it with care, realizing that it was her mother who had touched it last.

In her fifth month now, Astra's belly formed a small mound. She had asked Nikolina to make sure nothing showed and her cousin said no one would guess.

"Come on, Niki," Astra called toward the house. If they left before first light, they would arrive in plenty of time for *Julaften*, the festivities of the day before *Jul* and best day of the year. Into the back of the sleigh she had tossed her satchel and gifts of cheese and woven fabric for the manor household. She had also tucked in the scrolled betrothal document and Vegar's necklace. If he came to the celebration, she would return these and break off the agreement. If not, she would pay someone to deliver them to him. Then she could tell Einarr she was free to marry. She was anxious to see Einarr again, praying daily that he had survived. They could marry straight away. The thought of seeing him brought a throb of joy, something that was in short supply.

"Coming!" Nikolina called from the house. She dragged a bag in one hand and carried Amalie on her hip with the other. Astra crunched over the snow to lock up behind her, leaving the bulk of the keys on the table and removing only the single house key which she dropped into her pouch. No one was likely to come while they were gone, but she did it for Mar's sake.

"I wish we had more than two nights," Nikolina grumbled as she climbed on board. Amalie was cocooned in fur and settled herself comfortably into her mother's lap.

Astra's family could never stay in Sjodrun more than two nights because of the farm chores, always returning home to celebrate the rest of the thirteen-day celebration on their own. During this joyful time, no work was allowed aside from caring for the animals.

"Better than not at all," Astra replied, hoisting herself into the sleigh and spreading the bearskin over their laps. Astra had given the animals extra hay and filled the water troughs, though she knew they would be restless and bawling when they returned.

Astra rattled the horses' reins and they jerked into motion. "Stay," she ordered the dogs that leapt beside them, then slunk back, whining. They would have to guard the farm and fend for themselves while she was gone.

The horses seemed happy to be out, and they picked up the pace as the sleigh skated over the shimmering surface. They tossed their heads, spewing clouds of steam that dissipated over their backs. Halfway to Sjodrun the first morning, rays of the winter sun shone obliquely across their path through the trees. Snow-laden pine, cedar, and spruce branches hung low, while stances of bare-limbed birch trunks blended into the shifting morning shadows. The cry of a hawk sent several nuthatches scurrying into the branches. A white fox jumped across an open stretch and dove into a hole beneath a rock.

Both young women were quiet, cuddling together under the bearskin and surveying the awakening landscape. Astra's aggrieved spirit lightened in the frigid air. She reminisced about past *Jul* eves when her family traveled to enjoy the generous table the manor provided. Then the sleigh ride was boisterous with singing. At the manor, feasting, games, music, and dancing entertained the guests.

Each year before the holiday, houses must be thoroughly cleaned, fresh beds made, and meat prepared. Mar always brewed the *Jul* ale during the rising full moon, according to tradition. In the evenings, children were expected to drink beer moderately, but Far drank until his tongue was thick. He told the children terrifying stories of the dark season, tales of people falling through the ice, of babies born without limbs, and of ghouls and witches haunting both the wicked and the righteous. Children were not allowed outside unaccompanied by Mar or Far for fear that the Elf Maiden would carry them away. Mostly, though, the family laughed, played games, and sang, enjoying the season of frivolity.

Nikolina broke the quietude. "What are you looking forward to most?"

"The food, I suppose," Astra replied. "I am ready for something besides porridge and dried fish."

Amalie squirmed and Nikolina tugged the fur down so the child could see better. "For me it is the dancing."

"Dancing, with Dag, perhaps? That would be a wonderful gift for you and Amalie."

"*Ja*, of course, if he is back. I hope he is. I wonder who else will be there."

"Many, I pray," said Astra, but her thoughts were only of Einarr. He had not come to see her, nor had he sent Didrik to check on them at all, but of course they would assume that Far was with them. What must Einarr think of her now? He was the only one who knew about the king. And now that she was with child…would he want her? Would he be willing to claim the king's child as his own? Even though weddings were forbidden at *Jul*, she wore Mar's finest dress in case he should insist they marry right away.

Nikolina chimed to Amalie, "So much snow! Cold?"

Astra smiled and tickled Amalie's chin. The child babbled and tried to tickle her back.

What about Vegar? Astra wondered. He had not come to check on them, either, not since he ran away from the farm the night when Mar was sick…the night he had wanted her to sleep with him with her parents' blessing. Did he wonder if she were alive? Was he alive?

"I am sure Vegar will be there," Nikolina said, as if reading Astra's mind. "He will want to see you."

"I hope not." Astra kept her face a mask.

"But you must speak to him sometime. You are still betrothed."

"The betrothal celebration was never held, so it is not sealed."

Nikolina caught her eye. "You know you must marry soon, very soon."

"I am never going to marry him. He is unbearable."

"But the baby is his, right?"

"*Nei*, I told you." Astra frowned at her cousin.

"Maybe if you marry him right away, tomorrow even, he will not figure out the baby is not his. Men are not good at tracking women's secrets."

"I am already five months along," Astra scoffed. "He would soon know. Besides, it is <u>Einarr</u> I must talk to."

Nikolina nodded knowingly. "So Einarr is the father after all."

"*Nei.* Stop asking me." Astra changed the subject. "If Dag is not back, there might be word of him, at least. Do soldiers keep fighting in winter?"

Nikolina shrugged. "I do not know." Amalie reached for the reins, but Nikolina pulled her back and tore off a bite of *brød* to give her. "I hope..."

"That he is there?"

Nikolina shook her head. "That he is not. I will stay with you in any case. You need me."

Astra focused on the horses' bobbing heads. "I thought you loved him."

"I thought I did, too." Nikolina hesitated, then said, "When I told him how I felt about his mother, he called me ungrateful and said I was lucky he married me. He even asked if the baby was his." She paused and looked away. "There is love, and then there is marriage."

Astra knew her cousin had not been happy living with her husband's family but assumed she would return to her husband when he came home.

They were interrupted by Amalie's crying. Nikolina wrestled the growing child beneath the heavy fur to nurse. In the shimmering silence of the forest, marked only by the swooshing of the sledge runners, Astra listened to the sounds of the suckling child. She wondered again what it was like to breastfeed a baby. Her free hand strayed to her swollen belly. Recently, she had dreamed she could see the baby through her skin, a tiny, perfectly formed infant sucking its thumb. Not long ago, when Nikolina had asked if she felt movement, Astra described a fluttering butterfly sensation, and Nikolina said that was the first sign. She had been right. There was no denying it now.

Gliding over the snow brought them to Sjodrun's courtyard in half the time of that in summer, and soon they were banging on the manor house door. The door creaked open and Gudrun cried, "Astra and Nikolina, I am so glad to see you sweet girls. We have been wondering how you are getting along."

Gudrun craned to look behind them into the snowy yard. "And where is your worthy father, dear?"

Astra hesitated, turned away to hide her sudden tearfulness, but Nikolina answered for her. "He was lost in that snowstorm before Michaelmas and has not returned."

"Poor girl," Gudrun said, drawing them inside. "That storm was indeed cruel. This is a time of great loss, for you, for all of us."

"Have any soldiers returned?" Nikolina asked.

Gudrun closed the door. "I have no word of them. Come. Warm yourselves. I will have someone take care of the horses. You will sleep in the Great Hall. Few are here for *Jul* this year so there is plenty of room here on the benches." She helped them remove their heavy cloaks, admired Amalie, then pointed them to one of the three blazing fires.

Astra gazed about the hall, usually festively arrayed. This year, only the table was adorned with cedar boughs and red-berried holly, but not the walls and doorways. The grand *Julebukk*, the large goat of straw, still stood protectively by the door and the floor was strewn with hay in remembrance of Christ's manger.

"The manor looks welcoming, Gudrun," Astra said, brightening.

"You are kind." Gudrun bowed and rushed away.

As Astra's eyes roamed the Great Hall, she noticed that Gudrun spoke rightly: only a few small groups of guests were gathered at table and on benches. Several figures sat around a duo playing chess. Nearby, men threw dice.

Hedda, dressed in red, rose from a nearby bench and ran toward them. "You came!" She flung herself around Astra's neck. When Astra pushed Hedda to arm's length, she saw that tears rolled down her friend's rouged cheeks.

"What is this?" Astra asked, near tears herself.

"It is just that this *Jul* is so sad. So many are gone."

Astra wiped Hedda's tears.

"Astra's family is gone, too," Nikolina said.

Hedda pursed her lips and hugged Astra tightly, not asking what happened.

Astra asked, "Where is your brother? I must give him my *Jul* greeting."

Hedda pointed to a group of men sitting by the farthest fire. Einarr had turned and was looking directly at Astra. When she met his gaze, he spoke to those at his table, stood up and walked toward her. Her heart skipped. They met midway across the room and he gestured to an empty bench against the wall where they sat down.

Shamelessly, Astra laid her hand on his. "I need to talk to you."

Einarr glanced toward the group he had just left at the fireside. "There is something I must tell you first."

"So you said when we last met. But first I beg you to listen." She whispered, "I am with child by the king. We should marry quickly so others will think it is yours. I will break off the betrothal with Vegar, since my father is…missing. The *sysselmand* will not have me, anyway, once he knows."

Einarr's face turned pale. He squeezed her hand, then let go. "I wish I could, Astra. Believe me, I do…" Then he turned his head to look at something.

Astra followed his gaze and saw a woman approaching. She was several years older than Astra, older than Einarr, and overly tall. She was not handsome, with a hooked nose, but was dressed in silky linen and carried herself with poise. A finely woven wimple hid her hair.

Einarr stood up and said to the woman, "There is someone I must introduce you to."

The woman stopped in front of them and bowed her head. "*God Jul! Velkommen.*" She smiled kindly.

Astra stood and nodded in return. She looked at Einarr questioningly.

His neck flamed. "Steinulv, this is Astra, the friend I told you about. Astra, this is Steinulv Akselsdatter…my wife."

Lightning shot through Astra's veins. She stared at the woman's friendly countenance. "Your…wife? I…did not know you were…"

Einarr took a breath. "That is what I was going to tell you."

Steinulv said smoothly, "It is nice to finally meet you." She spoke easily, as if she had not just torn Astra's heart from her chest. "I have heard good things about your friendship with Einarr's family."

Astra stammered, "I…I am just…surprised." In an instant, her childhood dreams of a life with her beloved were dashed against the great Standing Stone.

"The marriage was a surprise to many," Steinulv said, pulling Einarr to sit down beside her on the bench. She slid her hand through his elbow. "My father and Lady Marta discussed the match last summer, and we were to be married at Easter, but the betrothal and marriage had to be rushed."

"Mother became ill," Einarr said, avoiding Astra's shocked gaze. "She signed the betrothal before she passed and made us promise to marry at Michaelmas."

"Sadly, she passed away before the wedding," added Steinulv.

Astra hid her clenched fingers in the folds of her dress. They married only two weeks after her last visit to Sjodrun. He knew…he tried to tell her. She mumbled, "*Gratulerer.* I wish you…happiness." Then she stood and walked away, trying not to topple over.

Einarr called, "Wait," but she hurried to don her cloak and slipped outside just as a great sob erupted from her throat.

She ran across the icy crust to the *kirke* where she fell against the wall gasping for air. Einarr had not fought for her, had not insisted he must marry for love. It was just as her parents had said—nobles marry nobles. Oh, God in heaven! What was she to do?

Finding the *kirke* door unlocked, she entered. The nave was dark. Father Johan would have provided her comfort, if he were alive. Now there was only silence. Astra knelt before the crucifix. As she began to recite words of petition, a deep geyser of sorrow spewed up through her chest and burst from her lips. She dropped to the floor and curled up around the lump in her belly, crying, "Why did you take everyone I love? Why did you not take me, too? Take me now, I do not want to live!" She wept and beat the plank floor with her fists.

After some time, chilled to the marrow, she clambered unsteadily to her feet. As she shuffled past the Virgin's effigy, the Holy Mother seemed to whisper to her. Astra stopped. *Kristus'* mother understood. She knew what it was to lose a loved one, and she knew what it was to be pregnant and unmarried. Astra kissed the wooden figure's hand. The Blessed Virgin breathed Mar's words into Astra's heart, "The east wind blows where it must, but from small seeds, large trees grow."

Hedda rushed to Astra's side when she reentered the Great Hall. "Where did you go? I did not get to share with you my news." She pulled Astra to a bench near the steps to the loft where Nikolina sat with Amalie.

Hedda whispered, "Firstly, I am sorry I did not warn you about Einarr, Astra. He wanted to tell you himself."

Astra felt empty, smothered. "What is your news?" She gripped her arms around her trembling torso.

Hedda's eyes were sparkling. "I am to be married."

Astra could not even pretend happiness. "Really? You and your brother both."

"Einarr is getting married?" Nikolina asked, jerking her head to look around the room.

Astra said, "He is already married. The Lady arranged it before she passed."

"To her?" Nikolina stared at Einarr and Steinulv as they sat at a table with a few others.

"*Ja*," said Hedda. "Steinulv Akselsdatter."

"Did your mother arrange your marriage then, too?" Nikolina asked.

Hedda shook her head. "*Nei*, but when I was younger, she told me she wished she could have married for love. I think she wanted that for me." Tears spilled from the girl's eyes and she wiped them with her fingertips. "Are you not going to ask me who?"

Astra tore her eyes from Einarr's wife. "Who is the lucky young man?"

Hedda squeezed her friends' hands. "You will be surprised. He is actually not young. He is strong and a hard worker, and very capable of taking care of me. I have fancied him all my life, and he says it is the same for him. He will be a wonderful husband."

Astra could think of no one who fit this description.

"Tell us," Nikolina said.

"Didrik." Hedda glowed, her eyes shimmering.

Astra was stunned. She had never heard of a noblewoman marrying an estate's manager. She struggled to think of what to say.

Nikolina spoke what Astra dared not. "The head man? The servant?"

"He is not a servant," Hedda objected, looking hurt. "He has a very important position. I know he is older, and not a nobleman, but I love him. He comforted me like no other when I lost my mother."

"I am sure he did," Nikolina muttered.

"Please be happy for me," Hedda pleaded.

Astra forced a smile. "*Gratulerer.*"

Hedda quickly glanced around the room, then took Astra's hand and placed it on her belly. "And be happy for our baby," she whispered. Large tears dropped onto her linen skirt.

Astra, dumfounded for a moment, remembered the losses Hedda had faced. Who could blame her for finding comfort where she might? "I am happy for you," she said at last. "Didrik is a man of honor. He has been kind to me and fair to my father. I am sure he will make a good husband."

The Moon Turned to Blood

Nikolina set Amalie on the straw-covered floor and gave her a doll. She said, "In that case, you are doing the right thing. The sooner the better."

Astra hugged Hedda and purred into her friend's ear, "All children are like gold in the mouth. That is what Mother would say." As soon as she spoke them, these words seemed meant for her as well.

"When will you marry?" Nikolina asked.

Hedda bit her thumb. "The wedding is tomorrow, on *Jul*. I know it is not usually permitted because of the priest's holiday, but we have no priest. We are marrying the old way before our Jultide guests."

Marrying the old way was common among peasants and odal families, though not among nobles. A country wedding was often followed by an ecclesiastical ceremony when the family traveled to a town. Astra knew of times when the baby was baptized at the same time.

"Can I count on you to help me?" Hedda asked.

"Of course," said Astra.

Hedda hugged them both and hurried away.

"Babies are going around," remarked Nikolina.

Astra sighed. "I am trying to be happy for her, but she is just fourteen. At least she will have someone to care for her. But I wonder what Lady Marta would have said."

"I am sure she would not be rejoicing," Nikolina nodded to where Einarr and Steinulv sat. "You must be livid. I would be."

"I cannot believe it yet," said Astra. "He does not look happy, does he?"

"*Nei*, and she is old and horse-faced." Nikolina touched Astra's shoulder. "Now that door is closed. Let us hope Vegar comes."

Astra stayed near Nikolina, nursing her sorrows as guests arrived. Some brought a child or two, others came alone: a grandmother, an uncle, an orphan. The priest's wife, looking pale and drawn, arrived with her two surviving children. Astra wondered how she would support them with so few to contribute to the widow's fund.

The door to the kitchen opened and Astra turned, hoping someone was bringing food. She had eaten nothing since they left home and her stomach growled in anticipation. But instead of a server, Astra saw Kjell, the hunter, enter. He strode past without looking her way and sat on a bench against the wall.

Astra stared after him, agape.

"Who is that?" Nikolina asked. "Do you know him?"

"*Ja*, he was here last summer selling his furs to the lady."

"He is handsome, *nei*?"

Astra shrugged. He looked better than when she had met him last summer. At least now his beard was trimmed and he wore clean clothing. What brings him here again? she wondered.

She turned her attention to Einarr, who proved to be a poor substitute for his stately parents. He and Steinulv sat on a bench at the table, and arriving guests had to seek them out to greet them. Lord Jonas and Lady Marta would have stood by the door to welcome all and present them with *Jul* gifts. The peasants looked the most uncomfortable. Without a greeting they shyly gathered in pockets by the fires. Astra saw the stable hand sit down by Kjell. They conversed, laughing at something that was said.

The mood in the Great Hall was at first subdued. Along with the guests came news of sadness and reckonings of those who were lost. Many cried as they learned of a new death, while others remained stoic, now hardened to bad news. Stories were told of those who had fled, abandoning their family farms or deserting the manor. Everyone had losses. At least the ale was plentiful. Large bowls were filled and guests dipped their cups at will.

Astra filled cups for Nikolina and herself and let her eyes wander over the hall. She watched Kjell rise, refill his cup, and lean against a pillar where he surveyed the room, looking ill at ease. For a moment their eyes held. He smiled and raised his cup to her. Astra raised hers in return before looking away.

What was he doing here? He had left to go home to his family. Why was he back now? She glanced around the room but saw no wife with him, no one she did not recognize. Perhaps tragedy had struck for him, too. What else would bring him back to Sjodrun? She had last seen him at the river after her deepest shame. He had said he had regrets in his life. So did she. Astra decided to find out what happened when she got a chance, when Nikolina was not with her.

As the afternoon wore on, those gathered grew louder and more boisterous, laughing, telling jokes, and playing games of chance.

Suddenly, with a gust of cold wind, the large manor doors opened and two tattered young men arrived; one with his upper arm wrapped in a rag, the other limping on a crutch. Beneath their beards and layers of dirt, Astra recognized them as local boys from among King Magnus's recruits. Doffing ragged cloaks, the young men stumbled in and fell onto the hearth by the fire.

They were rushed by survivors. "What is the news? Are you the only ones coming back? Where are the others?" the guests demanded.

"Four others are on their way home," said the young man with the injured arm. "They should be here soon, in the next day or two."

"The war is over—it was a rout," said the other. He used his crutch to scoot the ale bowl closer. "The king abandoned the effort with barely a fight—too cold, not enough men. Many died of the black death."

Nikolina pushed her way through the circle, followed closely by Astra. "Have you seen my husband, Dag?" she asked.

The one with the crutch looked up. His face fell. "I am sorry to tell you that we buried him along the roadside south of Tromsø."

Nikolina slumped onto a bench, her face ashen. "How did he...?"

"He took a spear to the shoulder," said the soldier. "He seemed fairly well, but his wound festered. We carried him for many days but his fever only worsened. He died quietly."

Astra lifted Amalie from her cousin's arms and led Nikolina to the stairway bench. They sat together and Astra took her hand. "I am so sorry, Niki."

Nikolina stared at the closed manor door dry-eyed. She said, "I knew it. Somehow, I knew it."

Astra tried to put an arm around her cousin, but Nikolina shrugged her away. "I need to be alone." She disappeared up into the loft.

Astra sat with Amalie on her lap, brooding, as she waited for the meal to be served. Gudrun and Malin rushed about setting plates of silver on the dais, wooden troughs for the guests, and large mounds of butter and preserved fruits on the table for the sweet *Jul brød*.

Einarr now sat at the far end of the board, drinking with a group of men. Astra stared at him and tried to harden her heart. She must forget him. She should detest him for his betrayal. Now her future loomed ahead like the steep cliff of Preikestolen. She imagined pushing Einarr from that high rock and watching him fall.

Just when she felt she could sit still no longer, Nikolina returned. She lifted her *datter* and retreated to a bench in a dark corner to nurse. Her face was drawn and bloodless, but not tear-stained.

Just then a cold wind rushed through the hall. A tall man in a heavy coat and fur cap stepped through the open doorway. It was Vegar.

Malin hurried to close the door behind him and helped him out of his coat, bowing as if to a master. Vegar spoke to her and she replied at some length. They both scanned the room and Malin pointed Astra out to him. Astra quickly turned away, but she heard his footsteps approaching.

Nikolina nudged her arm. "Here he comes."

Astra felt his presence behind her. She turned.

"Good *Jul*," he said, unsmiling.

She grasped his extended hand tenuously. "Good *Jul*, to you."

"I hoped I might see you here," he said.

Astra tugged her hand free and touched Nikolina's back. "You know my cousin, Nikolina."

He raised his eyebrows and nodded. "There is a family resemblance. Both very comely."

Astra ignored his comment. "How have you fared?" she asked.

"I am well. I heard you lost your family to the sickness," he said, "and the servant just told me your father is missing as well. For this I grieve with you."

"*Takk*," she managed.

He turned and surveyed the room as if it were his fiefdom. "Excuse me," he said. "I must greet the lady's son and his new wife. I am sure you have met her."

"I have," she answered. His snobbish demeanor raised her hackles. She wanted to run.

"I will talk with you later." He bowed and strode away.

Astra watched as Vegar sat down across the table from Einarr. He murmured something to Einarr and they laughed. What was he doing? Ingratiating himself? Joking with Einarr about her? She sat on her hands and mulled over what to do.

Nikolina said, "Go and sit by him. Show him you are interested."

Astra shook her head. "What would I say? I can think of nothing."

"Just sit by him. He will take the lead. Try to smile and be pleasant, as hard as that is for you." Nikolina pushed her to stand up.

Astra glowered back at her cousin. She had been determined to decline Vegar's offer and return the necklace, but now he might be her only hope of marriage and for providing a father for her child. Could she wed such a pedant? If Vegar knew what she nurtured within her belly he would certainly reject her. He could even bring a breach of betrothal agreement before the *Thing*, claiming that she had betrayed him and requiring recompense. She gasped—the farm!

Her heart raced. "I will wait until he is alone," she said.

Nikolina shrugged. "Amalie's rags are wet. Save a place for me at the table."

Shortly, Gudrun called them all to eat. According to *Julaften* tradition everyone, including children, took their desired places at the board, sitting by friends and family. The peasant farmers settled at the far end of the long board conversing among themselves. Astra sat in the middle, saving a space for Nikolina.

Einarr and Steinulv climbed onto the dais, followed by Hedda and the priest's wife. There were two empty chairs beside them. Astra presumed they were in honor of Lord Jonas and Lady Marta, but to her dismay, Vegar joined them. Glancing around, she realized that as the only *Thing* member present, he held the highest status in their shrunken community.

When everyone was seated, Steinulv whispered into Einarr's ear. He nodded and stood up. All eyes turned to him expectantly. It was tradition that the manor lord start the festivities with welcoming words and a toast. Einarr looked nervous. His eyes skirted over the long table without alighting. He tipped to one side clumsily, planting both hands on the table to steady himself. Astra shaded her eyes, embarrassed.

"Good *Jul*," said he.

All responded, "Good *Jul*."

He took a deep breath and slurred, "I...I greet you in remembrance of my beloved mother, Lady Marta, and my...exacting father, Lord Jonas."

Quiet groans traveled through the crowd. Steinulv grimaced, clinging to her chalice with both hands.

"He was the lord, that he was. In these wretched days, I think there is no need for formality. I know Mar would have had fine words for you, but I am not good at speaking to a crowd. Still, I do want to give a toast."

Someone near Astra mumbled, "Amen."

Everyone stood up.

Einarr raised his father's golden goblet and waved it about, splashing the table with wine. "To this year of great mortality, I say good riddance."

"Good riddance," nodded a few. Others glanced around, appearing confused.

"For all of us who have lost family and friends I raise a toast. May the coming year be better than this foul one. *Skål*." Einarr took a drink.

"*Skål*," came the muted reply.

Einarr continued even as Steinulv tugged on his sleeve. "May all the good folks reach heaven before Loki knows they are dead, and may the wicked ones get what they deserve." He drained his goblet.

Only two people said, "*Skål*." Most lowered their cups and all sat.

Einarr remained standing. "As we all know, we do not all get what we want, or what we deserve." He tilted and nearly fell. His eyes wandered the room and alit on Astra.

She ducked her head, her face on fire.

Steinulv grabbed her husband's arm and eased him into his chair. Then she stood, straight and regal.

"This is the celebration of the night of *Kristus'* birth." Her voice was clear and forthright. "We know that this is also the dark season, when spirits of the dead may roam, and the mischief of the elves appears."

Many crossed themselves or nodded knowingly.

"Therefore, if you wish, we invite you all to stay within the Great Hall this night to keep your children safe from the trolls, and goblins that may be wandering about. After the meal the children may accompany Didrik to the barn to set out the porridge for the *nissen,* those little rascals. No spells will be cast by them tonight. Children, after supper you can wear your goat masks and skins to frighten away the evil spirits."

Children tugged on adults' sleeves, whispering excitedly.

Steinulv continued, "Due to the sad event of the passing of Father Johan, we will not have the midnight mass. We welcome you to join in all the other *Jul* activities here at the manor. Good *Jul*." She raised her horn and all followed suit.

When Steinulv sat down, Einarr stood up and leaned on the table unsteadily. "One more thing," he said. "Tomorrow there will be a *Jul* Day celebration unlike previous years: there will also be a wedding." He thrust his wavering finger toward Hedda. "My sister will be wed to our trustworthy head man, Didrik."

The unheard-of betrothal caused a hush throughout the room. All eyes turned to Didrik, who leaned against the wall at the side of the hall, grinning. On this cue, he joined Hedda on the dais and sat in the last empty chair. The two gazed at one another, Hedda's cheeks red as rubies. Didrik grasped Hedda's hand and raised it high.

Without taking time to think, Astra jumped up and lifted her cup. "*Gratulerer*. May God bless your union."

"*Ja, skål!*" cried Steinulv, rising.

Everyone else stood and shouted, "*Gratulerer!*" raising their cups. Hedda shot Astra a pained look of gratitude.

The serving door burst open and large troughs of food were borne in on servants' shoulders. Roasted lamb, a large goose, ham, plates of fish, pickled pigs' feet, and rye and barley *brød* with butter were all set before them. These fragrant aromas filled the hall. Astra was suddenly starving.

No one moved as the crowd awaited the expected surprise centerpiece. After a short delay the doors opened again and two servants carried in a large plank holding a glazed pig on a bed of holly and fir boughs. Everyone cheered.

Einarr shouted, "Let us eat."

Immediately guests used their knives to carve off hunks of meat. Astra did the same for herself, then served Nikolina, who had come back to sit beside her. A contented hum drifted into the rafters as the succulent meal brought long-needed smiles to sallow cheeks, and laughter to sorrowful voices. As she ate, Astra glanced down the table where she spied Kjell sitting at the end next to a servant. He caught her eye, smiled, and raised his glass to her once more.

The woman next to Astra, whom Astra knew to be a basket maker, nudged Astra's shoulder. "How are you faring, you and your cousin? I hear your father..."

"Disappeared." Astra held a large bite of ham on her knife point. "And you?"

"We are getting along," said the woman. She was not yet thirty, but worry lines marred her former beauty. Astra had heard that her husband and five of her seven children had died of the black sickness.

The woman continued, "Now that Vegar Eriksson bought our land with the agreement that we can stay on, and my boys can share a half-portion, we are surviving well. He gave us cows and sheep, and fodder for the winter."

"How generous of him." Astra stuffed the ham into her mouth.

The neighbor cupped her hand so only Astra could hear. "Vegar is taking on many abandoned farms. Did you know?"

Astra shook her head.

The woman lowered her voice even more. "He will be richer than the manor lord, whoever that will be, when all is said and done."

Astra swallowed with difficulty. "But the *Thing* has not met to decide the fate of these lands," she said.

The woman shrugged. "Who is left in the *Thing*? I do not see anyone here at this table except Vegar Eriksson, do you?"

Indeed, who would stop Vegar from acquiring whatever he desired? Astra said, "When the *Gulagthing* meets at Lent, this will all be sorted out. Others who have fled may return. It is too early to decide anything." She spoke as calmly as she could, but inside she burned. How dare that man buy up abandoned lands, taking advantage of the many losses?

"You will be a wealthy woman when you marry him," said the woman, poking a sharp elbow into Astra's ribs.

How did she know? "We shall see," Astra said under her breath.

When the eating frenzy slowed, three musicians reached for their instruments and tuned up. The pipe, cithern and lyre began a lively tune. A father and *datter* ventured out to dance, reaching their hands toward others to join them in the circle. Astra was not intending to dance, but within moments a hand was thrust before her: Vegar's. She had no choice but to take it.

Round and round they pranced, the circle growing bigger until all but the frail and inebriated were dancing. Astra laughed in spite of herself as she stumbled over unpracticed steps. Once she almost smiled at Vegar as he guided her back into rhythm. She was glad that Einarr was not among the dancers so that she did not have to grasp his hand. He was engaged in a betting game, leaving Steinulv to select a dance partner from among the guests.

After several songs the musicians stopped to let the dancers rest. Many rushed for the ale bowls. Vegar bowed and said to Astra, "Come with me to the dice table."

"I must check on my cousin," she said, walking the other way.

Astra could tell by Nikolina's drawn face that she needed rest from her bad news. She said, "Go upstairs for a while. Come back when you feel better." Nikolina's eyes were red-rimmed. She nodded and took Amelie with her.

By this time the children were running around the room, chasing one another and laughing. Gudrun stopped them and gave them treats and milk for the barn *nissen*. Didrik and Hedda offered to take them to the barn, lighting torches to ward off the

Elf Maiden as the children donned coats. When they headed for the door, Vegar rose from the game table to follow them. With a flourish, he threw on his cape and accompanied the squealing children out into the frigid darkness. He glanced back at Astra as he closed the door behind him.

Astra rolled her eyes. Was she supposed to be impressed that he was interested in children? Everything he did was meant to impress someone. She found a recently refreshed ale bowl and filled her cup.

She spied Kjell sitting by himself on a bench at the back wall and she ambled over to sit beside him. "What brings you back to Sjodrun?" she asked.

He leaned his elbows on his knees and smiled up at her. "I am working here for the season."

"Indeed? As a hunter?"

"That, and apprenticing with the tanner. I do whatever else is needed. The manor lost many good workers, as you likely know."

Astra studied the ale cup in her hands. "And where are your wife and child? Did they not come for *Jul*?"

He cleared his throat. "They...they died of the pestilence, like so many."

"Ah, *nei!*" Astra wanted to touch his arm in friendship, but dared not in case others saw her. "I grieve for you."

"I heard you lost your family as well," he said. "And someone else married your beloved after all."

Astra sighed. "I just found out this evening."

"Life does not go as planned," he said.

Astra drank a draught. "His mother betrothed him to Steinulv on her deathbed. Now I must marry Vegar Eriksson."

Kjell sat up. "*Nei*, truly? I know the man. Why him?" He paused. "Ah. He is rich."

Astra grew angry. "My father agreed to it against my will. I wish I could do else."

Kjell looked at her questioningly. "Do else, then."

She whispered, "I must marry him, hopefully tomorrow, because I am…" She leaned close to his ear, "…with child."

Kjell looked down at his threaded fingers. "Who is the father? Vegar?"

She snapped, "*Nei*! He knows nothing. If I tell you, will you promise to say nothing to anyone?" Even as she said this, she wondered why she trusted him to keep her secret.

"I have a guess." He leaned close to whisper into her ear. "The king himself."

"Shhh. How do you know this?"

"I saw it in your eyes at the creek. Vegar will be angry when he finds out you have tricked him into marrying you."

Astra chafed. "When you put it that way…but my father made the contract before he disappeared. Vegar is bound to it. He might be angry, but I am now alone at the farm, with only my cousin to help me. I must marry him to keep my land."

"Must you? You and your cousin have already been running the farm, have you not? You both seem strong and able."

Astra bit her lip against his challenging words. "I may be strong, but my cousin will find someone else to marry. She is beautiful…though difficult."

"Perhaps you can hire help." He drained his cup.

"With what money?" She leaned over and whispered, "Besides, how can I run a farm when I have a baby to care for?"

"You can do it if you choose," he said. "It will not be easy, but you have already lived through much. You are a survivor."

Her eyes watered. "You do not understand. I am not as strong as you think. I cannot run a farm by myself. Even with Niki it is very difficult."

"But if you marry, will he not own the greater portion of the land anyway?"

She paused, caught by his spoken truth. She covered her face.

The hunter was quiet. Astra could hear his uneven breaths, as if he wanted to say more, but he did not.

"I should go," she said, standing.

He stood up, too. His eyes riveted her to the floor. "We all do what we must, it seems." Then he turned and walked away.

With shouts of glee the children burst through the door and ran unhindered throughout the hall in their goat skins and masks, chasing and laughing. Gudrun shushed them and herded them to the fire to warm up, giving them each a honeyed treat. Some flopped onto the straw-strewn floor. Little ones yawned.

Astra was doubly surprised when Vegar came to sit with them on a stool. They gathered at his feet, faces raised expectantly. Vegar commenced to tell the story of "The Seventh Father of the House," his voice resonant, drawing attention from adults, as well. Astra watched from the bench where she had sat with Kjell.

With enthusiastic gestures and a demonstrative voice, Vegar enraptured the children. "A traveler asked a man he met for a place to spend the night. The man told him he must ask his father. When the traveler found the man's father, the traveler was told he must ask HIS father. The traveler went to the grandfather, but the grandfather said the traveler must ask HIS father, and so on. The traveler met older and older grandfathers and great-grandfathers who became increasingly ancient and shriveled." Vegar bent over and raised his hands like claws. The children were rapt.

"Finally, the traveler found the oldest, most wrinkled and smallest man, no bigger than a baby, hanging in a horn on the wall. Though the traveler was not sure this being was alive, he asked if he might stay the night. The seventh grandfather said, 'You may.'" Vegar said this with an astonishingly shriveled voice. "The man was very grateful for a warm bed that night. What is the lesson to be learned?" he asked.

"Take care of strangers?" a child offered.

"Ask your father?" asked another.

"Good," Vegar replied, patting the children on the head. "And also, beware of an old man in a horn!"

The children giggled and rolled in the hay on the floor. Adults chuckled. Astra felt tipsy after her third, *nei* fourth cup of ale. What was she to think of this confusing man? He was greedy, buying vacant land before the victims were cold in their graves. But tonight, he was also entertaining, gracious, and smooth. Could she be beside him? Would she at least learn to respect or even admire him, like her father said? Would she learn to love him, like her mother told her she would? She had to admit he had more charms than she had realized. Regardless, her path was clear. Einarr had betrayed her, her father was not coming home, and she was having a baby. One thought climbed over all the others—she needed Vegar.

Chapter 25

For the remainder of *Jul* night, which could go on until morning, Kjell decided to escape all the intrigue. He snatched a pig's foot from a platter and stomped back to the stable carrying a coal pan for warming his feet. As he trod over the encrusted snow, he tried to set aside all the troubles of others at the manor, though he was especially concerned about those that Astra faced. She was learning that life is hard, short, and often ends in tragedy...he knew that well. That is the way of the world and she might as well accept it.

Mostly, Kjell had enough of that ass, Vegar, putting on a show for the children, but more so, for the adults. Astra was betrothed to him by her father but had resisted because of her love for the manor lord's son. Why would the maiden have wanted Einarr in the first place? From what Kjell had seen, the youth was proud beyond his skills, and relished his privilege. Regardless, Kjell pitied her for her lost love. Even worse, she confirmed his suspicion that she had been despoiled by the king himself, and now she was with child, that villain. The king should be gelded, if there was any justice.

And now...she seemed caught in Vegar's snare. Kjell had watched her talking to him, dancing with him, eying him. Her responses to the man were lackluster. If she agreed to marry that haughty braggart she was indeed desperate, or foolish. But...could she manage a farm and raise a child on her own?

Kjell had heard from Didrik that Einarr had married quickly after the lady died and was now unhappily strapped to another lord's *datter*. Steinulv seemed like a worthy catch to Kjell, refined, elegant, well-spoken. Einarr should learn to be content with his privilege. Instead, the boy was surly and sometimes rude. He treated Kjell like a servant, asking him to do tasks beyond Didrik's expectations, such as cleaning stalls. Not that Kjell minded this task, but that was the stable boy's job. He tried to stay out of Einarr's way, except when he was asked to take him hunting, which the youth was doing more and more often.

Hunting with Einarr was a different tale. The youth was good at shooting and never failed to bring in game. Away from the manor, Einarr treated Kjell more like a teacher than a servant, gleaning from him advice on tracking, trapping, and stealth in pursuit of game. Kjell treated him as a younger brother while they were in the forest, but he was put in his place as soon as they returned.

When Kjell had first arrived in Sjodrun less than two months ago, Didrik had hired him right away. There was plenty of work since so many laborers had died or run away, and Kjell was taken on without question. He was pleased to be allowed to hunt on the manor grounds, finding plenty of deer and smaller critters that came out of their dens to find food. The bears were hibernating, but wolves with their thick winter pelts were plentiful.

Kjell's tasks had grown since then, and he had willingly worked to keep busy helping the aged tanner. His apprenticeship with the old man was less than satisfying, however. The work was tedious and difficult, and the smells of the tannery were hard to stomach. By the end of the day, he stank.

Part of Kjell sorely missed the mountains, the solitude, the *Nordlys,* though they were often visible here in Sjodrun also. Much of his work was in the stable working with horses, maintaining gear and grooming. For now, this work was satisfying. The mountains would have to wait.

Kjell chose to stay away from the manor house whenever he could, getting his meals from the kitchen and eating there with the staff. But yesterday he had been expressly requested by Didrik to come to the *Jul* celebration in the manor house, and to attend Didrik's wedding to Einarr's sister tomorrow.

The Moon Turned to Blood

That scandal was spoken of only in hushed tones between the servants. Even so, Kjell noted the delight in Didrik's eyes whenever he talked of young Hedda. At his age he had been given a fine gift.

Kjell entered the stable and stopped to stroke Thorden and Sokker, giving them each a handful of grain. Eilifr, the stable boy, joined him. He had secured a skin of ale from a kitchen maid and they decided to play *hnefatafl* in the lad's bunk room. Kjell found himself telling the boy about his hunting escapades, about Nideros and the self-flagellating pilgrims, and the strange ways of the Saami people. The boy listened agape, asking many questions and in awe that Kjell had seen these things.

Finally, when the stable was spinning, Kjell stood unsteadily, wished Eilifr a happy *Jul*, and wove his way to his bunk room. At least tonight he had a comfortable bed, food he did not have to cook, and work that gave him coin. Who knew what was to come? No sense in worrying since there was naught he could do about the future.

He crawled under the furs of his closet bed, settled his feet against the still-warm coal pan, shut the door, and went to sleep.

Chapter 26

Lying awake in the manor loft, Astra heard stirrings in the Great Hall below. Several other single girls slept on mats on the floor nearby. Astra crawled gingerly over her cousin and the sleeping baby, stood up and stretched. Her back was sore.

"Where are you going?" Nikolina whispered.

"To the necessary."

"Is it morning?"

"It is early. Go back to sleep if you can."

But Nikolina bestirred herself and sat up, twisting her hair back into her nightcap. "I will go with you."

"Good *Jul*," Astra mouthed.

"Good *Jul* to you," Nikolina replied.

They padded to the far corner of the loft where the night furniture sat, shielding one another with their night dresses in case anyone else was awake.

"How are you feeling today?" Astra whispered.

"Relieved," Nikolina said as she squatted and the stream echoed into the crockery.

Astra smiled, glad to hear Nikolina's silly jest.

Nikolina stood and let her night dress fall into place. She said quietly, "I cannot believe he is gone. I expect him to crawl into my bed right now."

Astra squeezed her cousin tightly, then pulled back to look at her. "At least today is *Jul,* and there is a wedding."

They stopped to peer over the railing into the Great Hall below. They saw Malin lighting candles and creeping quietly among the sleeping bodies that lay on the floor and wall-benches. Rustling from waking guests told them morning had come.

The cousins dressed quietly. Astra donned her mother's fine dress and picked up her purse. Vegar's gift lay heavily inside. The necklace would look splendid on this gown, but she was not yet ready to wear it, this sign of betrothal. She must speak to Vegar first about the conditions of the contract. She shoved it into the bottom of her bag.

The fires on the main floor were rekindled and guests rose. They helped themselves to porridge that was set out on the boards, along with meats and cheeses. Astra took two large slices of Gudrun's fruit *brød*, still warm. Nikolina sat beside her, absently stirring her porridge.

When Gudrun delivered cups of ale, Astra noticed dark circles under her eyes—she and Malin must have slept little last night, if at all.

"Poor Gudrun," she said to Nikolina.

Nikolina grunted in reply.

"I am very sorry about Dag," Astra ventured.

Nikolina's spoon hung in mid-air. "There is naught to be done about it."

"I hope you will be able to enjoy the wedding, anyway," said Astra.

Nikolina leaned over and whispered, "Another wedding with a child soon to follow. I hope Hedda ends up happier than I."

Astra only nodded. She hoped the same for herself. She must look for a time to approach Vegar alone.

The wedding took place in the manor house. Hedda wore her mother's scarlet dress and crown, her head and face veiled by a wedding cloth. The couple stood face to face, one young and privileged, the other a workman old enough to be her father. Yet, their faces glowed. They swore to be faithful and love one another for life. His fingers trembled as he slipped a ring onto her finger.

Oh, to be loved like that! Astra's heart ached. She stood with Nikolina, their arms locked together. When Didrik lifted the wedding cloth and kissed Hedda, everyone cheered. The celebration enlivened the countenances of all, including Astra's. They needed joy in the midst of so much sorrow.

The final moment came, the ancient benediction. An elderly man hobbled forward. He raised his gnarled hands toward them and proclaimed a blessing from the old ways. "I call on the spirits of lost loved ones and friends to watch over this man and this woman in their new life together. I ask Odin to keep away evil from their midst. May the protection of the gods embrace them and the blanket of love warm them. May they have many children safely born and live to see their children's children."

He burned bits of amadon in a crucible, then gave charred morsels to the bride and groom to eat. After passing a lighted stick over their heads three times, he retreated.

While everyone was congratulating them, Didrik's brother, who had traveled far to be here, banged the table with his knife hilt. He said loudly, "Welcome, friends. The bride and groom invite you to share the wedding feast."

"God be praised," grinned Didrik.

His brother added, "Just not quite yet."

"First things first," said his new brother-in-law, Einarr. "To bed with you!"

Didrik and Hedda protested, but allowed themselves to be draped with coats and pushed toward the door where they would go to Didrik's cabin. Astra cringed. She had always dreaded the thought of the public bedding.

While villagers donned their cloaks to follow, a man in the crowd called, "Want me to teach her for you, Didrik?"

"It is just like riding a horse, honey," laughed an older woman.

"The first night is the best," said another woman, "for the man, that is."

Didrik smiled good-naturedly while Hedda's cheeks reddened.

The small crowd pushed them out the door to escort them to Didrik's house.

"A ram must have his ewe," called a man. A few others snickered as the door closed behind them.

Astra felt a hand on her arm and turned. Vegar said, "An endearing wedding."

"I thought it was lovely," Astra answered.

"Ours will be much grander." He peered down at her smugly, then walked away.

Music started. Some danced while others gathered in small groups to wait for the wedded couple to return.

Astra went to check on Nikolina. She found her sitting on a bench by the stairs holding Amelie. Astra sat down, nervously biting a fingernail.

Nikolina said, "What are you waiting for? Go and talk to him."

From across the room, Vegar caught Astra's eye. She forced a smile. She knew what she must do before she lost her nerve. Squeezing Niki's arm for strength, she climbed the ladder and dug Vegar's necklace from her satchel. She slipped it over her neck.

After descending, she sat down again by Nikolina and wrung her hands together on her lap. Nikolina said in hushed tones, "Go talk to him. Go now."

Astra whispered, "I need to think of what to say. Here, give me Amalie, just for a few minutes."

"You are a fool if you do not take his offer as soon as you can...before he changes his mind."

Astra lifted Amalie from Nikolina's lap. "You get some food and then I will go."

Nikolina stood up, shook her head, and strode to the ale table instead. Amalie yawned and rubbed her eyes. Astra cradled her, singing a quiet lullaby, and the child quickly fell asleep.

Glancing up, Astra was startled to see Einarr approach and quickly slide onto the bench beside her. "Did you enjoy the wedding? You are not dancing," he said.

"Nor you." Astra gently rocked the baby, meeting Einarr's eyes fleetingly.

He leaned forward to rest his elbows on his knees and spoke quietly. "I know you were shocked to hear of my marriage. Believe me when I say it was not what I wanted."

She glanced around the room to make sure Steinulv was not nearby. "But here you are, married," she said bitterly. "You just let it happen."

Einarr whispered, "When the sickness started Mar made me promise to honor the betrothal Father had agreed on for Lord Aksel's *datter*. Then when Mother became sick, she said we must marry at Michaelmas, though she did not know she would die before that."

"So, you kept your promise to her, but not to me." Astra boiled.

"I argued with her, pleaded to marry you, but her sickness worsened and I could not press my case further. After she died, it was my duty—only that."

"Do you love Steinulv now?"

He glanced at his wife across the room. She was dancing gaily, paying no attention to Einarr. "I will never care for her as I care for you."

"Care for? Nothing more?"

He tried to object but Astra swatted his words away. "It is best anyway. You must forget about me and be a good husband. And I must marry Vegar."

He leaned close to her. "I wish it had been different. I do love you, Astra. Never forget that."

"Marrying someone else is a strange way to show your love."

Einarr sighed, started to say something, then stalked away. Astra shook off the hot tears that stung her eyes. She would not let herself cry over him anymore. She had no choice but to accept Vegar's offer.

She scanned the room for her cousin. Where was she? She needed to hand Amalie back so she could speak to Vegar before she lost her resolve.

In the shadow of a pillar Astra spotted Nikolina speaking adamantly to Vegar. He scowled. Nikolina grasped his arm, whispering something into his ear. He pulled back. His brow darkened and he glanced toward Astra. Nikolina said something else but Vegar shook his head. He turned and walked stiffly to the wine table where he filled his cup.

Nikolina paled as she watched him go. She took a step toward him, stopped, bit her lip. Then she turned and saw Astra staring at her. She grimaced.

Astra watched her cousin slowly approach. Was Vegar angry at Nikolina, or at her? What had her cousin said?

Nikolina strode over and took Amalie from Astra's arms. She wrapped Amalie in blankets and laid her on a blanket on the floor.

Astra grabbed her cousin's arm. "What were you and Vegar talking about?"

Nikolina pulled away. "He was just asking about you."

"He looked angry. What did he say?"

"Maybe he is giving up on you since you pay him little attention."

Astra pressed her fingernails into Nikolina's arm. "Why? What did you say? By Thor's hammer, tell me!"

"I told him you must, you should marry right away. I was just trying to help."

Astra gasped, "Did you tell him I am…"

Nikolina pulled away. "You need to talk to him yourself."

Just then an older woman with a crying baby approached Nikolina. She was trying to feed the infant with a leather nipple. The baby was red-faced and sweating, refusing the milk and screaming louder. Gently, Nikolina tucked the infant under her shift, silencing the little one immediately. The grandmother dabbed at her eyes gratefully.

Astra stared at her cousin, frozen. Finally, she smoothed the folds of her mother's dress with trembling hands and drew a wavering breath. Then she stood and searched the room for Vegar.

There, leaning against a pillar she spotted him. He, too, was watching Nikolina breastfeed. At that moment Nikolina looked up. Her eyes met his but flickered away. Astra glanced from suckling widow to leering elder.

Incensed, she strode toward him. Vegar watched her approach; his eyes were glassy with drink. The corners of his mouth turned down in something like a satisfied smirk.

As she neared, he lifted his cup and spoke over the music, "A wedding is good, but wine is best."

Astra felt heat rise into her cheeks. "*Jul* and a wedding are a joyful combination. May God bless their union."

"I hear He already has."

Astra paused. Was there nothing he did not know about the goings-on at Sjodrun? She said, "If so, may they have a quiver full."

"I will drink to that." Vegar emptied his goblet. "I see you finally wore the necklace I gave you."

"It is so beautiful. I was saving it…"

"Ah." He rolled his eyes.

Astra fought the urge to flee. "Vegar…"

He glared at her. "You have something to say?"

She took a deep breath, then replied, "I have been thinking…"

He interrupted her. "I am sure you have. Are your supplies running low? I heard you lack enough food for the winter, so now you need help." He glared at her.

"I know I treated you less than cordially when I last saw you, but my mother was dying, as you recall."

His stare was unsympathetic.

She felt her neck grow hot. "So...sometimes I am foolish, and as my father says, I do not know what is best for me."

He tilted his head to the side and watched her squirm.

"What I mean to say is, I realize I may need help with the farm after all."

"What kind of help?"

She glanced at her feet, took another breath, then met his gaze. "By spring I will not be able to manage the farmwork without help."

"Indeed. I am sure that is true."

Astra's lips quivered. "I...thought you would come back to check on us so I could speak to you at home, to finalize the betrothal."

"I have been very busy these last several months helping others, lending supplies, assessing losses. Those people actually appreciate my help. In return they show me gratitude in different ways."

"Land, you mean." Anger strengthened her voice.

Vegar grabbed her by the arm and drew her further away from the dancing to an unoccupied corner of the hall. "*Ja*, land. Some farms are totally abandoned and these I have taken under my care...unless and until a relative comes to claim them."

"But the *Thing* has not met to decide these matters, Vegar. The land is not free for the taking."

"Maybe not yet, but you must realize, right now, I *am* the *Thing*. Who can tell me what I can and cannot acquire, whom I may and may not help?"

Astra stared at him, galled to the bone. Would he simply absorb her farm, too? If they married, would he give her the bride's portion, half of his lands as required by law? How could she ever give herself to this pretentious cock? Yet, who else was there to help her?

Vegar lifted her chin with two fingers. "Did you have something to say to me?"

Desperately, she scrambled for words. "I...I would like to reconsider your offer."

He laughed aloud, then his face hardened. "Would you, now? It appears I must reconsider, too. I just had a very enlightening conversation with your cousin."

Astra's mind whirled. Oh, God! What had Nikolina told him?

He clasped her chin firmly, pinching her jaw. When he spoke, it was a sharp rebuke. "She says she knows you are bearing my child, and she suggested that we, too, marry right away, like Hedda and Didrik."

Astra jerked away.

He grabbed her arm. "So clearly, you are only coming to me now because of your dishonor, not because of our betrothal."

Stunned by her cousin's betrayal, and seeing her future turning to ash, she pleaded, "But I was forced against my wishes. Now I am willing to complete our betrothal and marry you."

"It is not up to you. Listen." He spun her and pressed her back against the wall. "I will take you only on condition. You must say the child is mine, you will tell no one it is not. Then you will give your land to me without dispute."

Her lips trembled. "Except the bridal portion."

"*Nei*, all of it. And you will forever be a grateful wife, keeping your vow of obedience. We must marry straight away, tomorrow. I will make the announcement this night. Those are my terms."

Astra's eyes overflowed. Nikolina. Christ in heaven, what had she done?

"But first you must tell me who the father is." His eyes glinted like ice.

She swallowed, then whispered, "It was the king, King Magnus. He called for me and I could not refuse. He is demanding, like you."

"Liar!" Vegar raised his hand to strike her. At his outcry several turned to look. He clenched his fist and lowered it to his side. He wrestled the necklace over her head shoved it into his jerkin. Grabbing his cloak, he spat, "Offer withdrawn," as he careened out the door.

Tears froze on Astra's cheek as she harnessed the sledge to the horses. Distraught, she had gathered her things and fled to the stable. She must leave right away, unable to endure the shame she felt from her encounter with Vegar. Curses for which her father would have slapped her face filled her mouth. As she tightened a strap, she heard footsteps behind her and turned around. A man walked toward her, stopping a short distance away.

"It looks to me like you do not need help," said Kjell.

"*Nei*, I do not." She sniffed, embarrassed that she had been caught crying. Had he seen her in the manor talking to Vegar? She asked, "Were you at the wedding? I did not see you."

"I was," he replied. "I saw you there."

Astra patted the horse's neck. He had probably seen her altercation, as everyone had. She could think of nothing to say to assuage that shameful scene.

Kjell said, "You are lucky not to marry Vegar, if I may say so."

"Lucky? I am lucky at nothing." She tightened the last strap on the harness.

"You are better off with your cousin than with an arrogant strutter like him."

Astra's mouth pursed. "That he is, and worse. Men are tyrants, thinking of women only as vessels to serve them."

Kjell leaned his arm over a stall gate. "Indeed, you may be right. That is, most men."

Astra pressed her face against Kvikke's shoulder. "But you are not like that, Kjell the hunter."

He smiled. "How will you manage by yourselves, you and your cousin?"

"However we can. Women must be strong."

He smiled again. "I know that to be true."

"Because of your wife."

He looked down at the floor. "She had to do everything since I was seldom there to help her." He kicked at the straw.

She said, "You have always treated me with kindness. I wish you well here at the manor and wherever your travels take you next."

He looked up. "*Takk*. I wish you a good life and a happy baby."

Astra led the horses and sledge toward the manor house where Nikolina and the baby were waiting outside. When she glanced back, Kjell still leaned against the stable door, watching her. She waved.

Chapter 27

The days and weeks after Christmas were bitterly cold and sorrowful. Baby Amalie died of ague on the first day of the Year of Our Lord, 1350. Nikolina and Astra had buried the child in the family cemetery, scraping away the snow from the frozen ground and piling stones upon the shrouded little body to ward off animals. Astra bound two sticks together with rope to form a cross and laid it atop the rocks while Nikolina stood by in her heavy fur coat, ashen-faced. Astra had recited the *Pater Noster* alone.

Nikolina had lain with her face to the wall for two days, silent as death while Astra forced *brød* soaked in broth into her cousin's mouth.

Nikolina's grief was both terrifying and deeply moving. Her pain brought Astra to the shore of her own lake of sorrow, the yawning crevasse that lay just under the surface. Her mother's warning that "Grief is a mantle that soon smothers," was not comforting. Astra had watched her mother mourn her own lost infant secretly and long.

Finally, on the third day after Amalie died, Astra flipped the sheepskins off Nikolina's bed. Grief was smothering her, just as Mar said it would.

"Get up. I need your help." Astra pulled her cousin out of bed and stood her up. "Besides, you will rot away if you stay in bed."

Nikolina groaned, elbowed Astra away. "That wicked woman!" she yelled. "She knew the baby was sick but she let me feed her anyway. I hope the hag dies for poisoning my milk."

Astra stripped off Nikolina's sour night dress. "You must get dressed and earn your keep. I cannot do everything on this farm by myself."

Nikolina pushed her away and tried to sit down. "You know nothing of grief until you have lost a child. Leave me be."

Astra caught her cousin's arm, squeezing her fingernails into Nikolina's wrist. "I *do* know grief. I lost my whole family, yet I am not lying abed with my head buried in a pillow. Get up and get to work."

She handed Nikolina a cold damp cloth with which to scrub herself, then jammed a clean shift over her cousin's head. She combed through her snarled hair, ignoring the yelps of pain. Astra gave her porridge and sat down beside her at the fire.

"I need you, Niki," she said more calmly. "I need help with the animals, meals, the whole farm. The barn door is broken, and now the ewes are lambing. You *must* help me." Her voice cracked.

Nikolina stopped her with a raised hand. "Enough. What do you want me to do?"

Astra handed her the soap and wrapped Nikolina's fingers around the handle of the pail. "Go wash your things." She threw a cloak over her cousin's shoulders and shoved her out the door.

When Astra went to check on her later, she half-expected Nikolina to be curled up on the dirt floor of the *svalgang* with the dogs. But her cousin had hung her wet things over the drying rope and was chopping firewood.

"Work is good for you, Niki," Astra called.

Nikolina set down the axe and her eyes spilled tears. "Astra, I do not think I can do this…go on, that is."

"Of course, you can. Women lose children." Astra's mother's voice whispered in her ears and she said softly, "It is the way of things."

Nikolina studied her icy hands and whispered, "You said babies go straight to heaven. Do you believe that?"

Astra nodded, though she was not sure. "I do."

Nikolina wiped tears from her chin. "But I heard that babies go into limbo to wait to be rescued by the prayers of the holy family. Where is limbo? Are there adults to comfort the babies?"

Astra took Nikolina's arm and led her back inside. "Since Amalie was baptized, she went to heaven straight away. There are saints there to care for them."

"How do you know?"

"Father Johan told us. Priests just know things." Father Johan had never said such a thing, but Astra said what she and Nikolina both needed to believe. "We have to just keep going."

"But why?"

Astra hesitated. "Because we are the ones who did not die."

Nikolina threw herself around Astra, squeezing so hard she took Astra's breath away. They clung together for many minutes, as if standing on the edge of a precipice.

As the weather warmed and the snow began to melt, skylarks and lapwings appeared along with the bright green growth on the tips of the pine tree branches. Spring was biting at the heels of winter darkness.

One morning Astra set her buckets of milk on the ground and leaned on the fence rail, studying the field. She must plow soon. She placed her hand on her bulge and felt a sharp jab. The joy that most women knew when they felt the baby stir eluded her. Could she ever love a child conceived by force? She felt nothing for this creature. Why should she? The child might not even live—most women lost babies. She would heed her mother's advice and hold her feelings at bay.

Striding to the sheep pasture, she saw that one of the ewes had given birth to a stillborn lamb. She tossed its tiny form onto the ever-growing manure pile behind the barn. Despite her best effort, this common loss pricked her heart. She bent over her lap and wept.

Astra's back ached as she shoveled manure and hauled water. Kvikke stepped on her foot accidently, causing her to cry out and punch the horse's neck. The mare threw her head, sending Astra against the rail. She limped back to the house, longing for her father to come and put his arm around her.

The rest of that day Nikolina was quiet, but at least she was upright. She helped Astra fix the barn hinge and did the afternoon milking. They discovered twin lambs had been born, but the ewe refused to feed the smaller of the two. Astra tried to get the lamb to latch on, but each time, the ewe side-stepped, nosing the tiny lamb away.

"Do not let it die," Nikolina said, picking up the small ram.

"Bring it to the house." Astra knew this meant frequent feedings day and night, an exhausting regime, but Mar had nursed many lambs and kept other animals in the house when needed. Far always warned the children not to make a male lamb a pet, though they did anyway. When the young ram was butchered the children always cried, in spite of Far's reprimand.

Astra retrieved the leather pouch with an elongated nipple and carried the lamb to the house in the crook of her arm.

Nikolina made the evening porridge and cleaned the dishes before telling Astra, "I am so tired I could sleep standing up." She changed into her night dress and dropped into bed.

Astra patted her shoulder. "You did well today, cousin. You will feel better soon."

Almost immediately Nikolina began to snore. Astra was tired, too. She filled the pouch with milk and let the lamb sleep with her so she would know when it was hungry. The night was long and wakeful.

Within a week Nikolina had taken over care of the lamb and was working all day, even weaving again, though her face was often tear-stained.

One evening when they sat by the fire and Nikolina was holding the lamb, Astra said, "The baby is moving."

Nikolina brightened. "Can I feel it?" She placed her hand on Astra's belly. The baby kicked and Astra saw her cousin's face light up. Nikolina' excitement made Astra feel a glimmer of hope.

As daylight hours slowly grew longer and spring approached, Nikolina cried less and worked harder. One day Astra noticed that Amalie's few things had been packed away in the extra room.

Chapter 28

Spring approached, and the days grew longer. Swallows swooped through the rafters in one of the manor's barns as Kjell and three other workers followed Didrik to retrieve shovels. The lowest fields of the manor property were clearing of snow and ready for manuring. The men strode to the far end of the cow barn where the roof-high manure pile loomed. Horse-drawn sledges waited close by.

"Kjell, you take the field by the large cedar," Didrik said. "Borg, go down by the grove of ash. Hans and Eirik, work the lowland by the creek."

The men started to shovel manure into the sledges, but Didrik gripped Kjell's shoulder and pulled him aside. "I do not usually use hunters for this, but as you know, we all have to pitch in."

Of course, Kjell knew. Fully half the workers had died. He nodded.

He and the other farmhands filled their sledges and led the horses out into the fields, now a mixture of mud and frozen clods. The field hands yelled and yanked the horses' harnesses as they slopped their way through the sucking mud. Kjell was reminded again why he had left his father's homestead. He was a hunter, not a farmer.

Despite today's work, he had to admit that his services as a hunter and leather-maker had been used well at Sjodrun. Besides his own bunk room, he was given a place in the livery to skin and clean his prey. The pelts and meat from his kills were always welcomed by the household staff, and he was well paid. But the farmwork, like what he was asked to do today, and the task of taking Einarr hunting had become drudgery, too.

Just yesterday, Kjell and Didrik had accompanied the young man on a Lord's Day hunting foray while the villagers gathered to pray in the *kirke*. Though the three had often hunted together, Kjell's relationship with Einarr was tenuous. The young man, unhappily married, was sometimes rude and ill-tempered, other times boorish. Though Kjell said little to him, Einarr loudly spoke of the ills of marriage and the oppressiveness of responsibility. Didrik and Kjell silently glanced at one another when Einarr fumed like this, but they kept their thoughts to themselves. When Einarr's arrows went astray he blamed Kjell for not instructing him well enough. If they could, Kjell and Didrik tried to stay out of the young man's path on his bad days, though these were often the times Einarr wanted to get away and hunt.

That Lord's Day evening all the workers were invited to dine in the Great Hall where Kjell's latest kill was served, as it often was. At table, Einarr, Steinulv, Hedda, and Didrik sat up on the dais. Didrik's young wife no longer attempted to hide her growing belly since everyone knew she had been pregnant when they married. A child would be a gift for an old man like Didrik, Kjell thought. These four seated higher than the others were served wine while laborers and village folk drank ale. Kjell knew this was a symbol of Einarr's presumed future lordship, but he also knew that such an outcome was far from certain.

That night well after dark, Einarr appeared at Kjell's bunk room and knocked. By the light of the boy's lantern Kjell could see that he was upset. His mouth was twisted, his fist was balled.

Kjell propped up on his elbows. "Do you need something?"

Einarr set the lantern on a shelf and slammed his fist on the wall boards. He paced the small space, four steps to one wall, four steps back. "Her! Why did I marry her?" he seethed.

Kjell sat up. He did not know how to safely respond.

"She criticizes me for everything I do," he fumed, "constantly comparing me to her great father. He is the best manager, the best at making deals, knows horses better than anyone, is the most respected in the region. The list is endless. *And* she feels entitled to the most expensive things, jewelry and fine goods that I cannot afford. She says I will never live up to her father's skills and character. She is right! I do not strive to be like her father, filled with snobbery and grandiosity. I wish to God I had refused to honor the contract Mother made. She was already gone by then. Why did I not follow my heart?"

Kjell was taken aback by the boy's honesty. Was he drunk? Einarr leaned against the wall across from Kjell's bunk and slumped to the floor, hugging his knees to his chest. Kjell did not want to guess what the temperamental young man's wife had truly said to him, nor he to her. He did not want to be involved in Einarr's marriage troubles at all. What would Astra think of her true love after such an outburst?

"Fighting is normal for new marriages, I hear," said Kjell finally, trying to calm this young overlord.

"Perhaps, but we fight every day, every hour. Tonight is no exception. She is insufferable." Einarr paused, then said, "She wants a child." He buried his head in his folded arms as if he did not want Kjell to hear what he said next. "But I do not, not with her."

Kjell's discomfort at being witness to this demeaning confession left him speechless. Had the boy not slept with his wife? If not, no wonder they were both quarrelsome. Then with whom did he want to have a child? Kjell could guess. Did he know about Astra's encounter with the king? And what did this boy-man want from Kjell now? Sympathy? He dared offer no advice, and had none to give.

After several long moments, Kjell asked, "Is there something you need from me?"

Einarr shook his head. He looked up at Kjell as if to say more, then clenched his teeth. Finally, he said, "*Nei*, this is my lot and I must suffer it." He stood up, snatched his lantern, and closed the door quietly behind him.

Kjell lay awake a good long while before dropping off into a restless sleep.

He rose early, saddled Thorden, and rode out to hunt alone. Kjell had become more and more restless as the days grew longer. He had grown tired of working under Didrik's command, doing farmwork, and listening to the spoiled manor lord's complaints. He wanted to be free to hunt where he wished and travel where he would. Mostly, he wanted to get away from Sjodrun. He missed the smells of the northern wilderness, the broad skies, the silence. He also wanted, *nei*, must visit his family in Hamar. He had been avoiding it for fear of what he would find, but the time had come.

Deeper still, his body ached for a woman to love. He thought of poor Oda often, *ja,* but he thought of Dorte, too. Why had he not stopped to see her in Stiklestad on his way south? Perhaps he should go there again to see if she had survived the great sickness. For now, he would at least ask Didrik if he could hunt further afield, up into the high country, the barren rocks above the fjord or the wooded plains of the great river basin. If he knew where the young woman, Astra, lived, he might check on her welfare. He hoped all was well with her and her cousin, despite their many troubles. Astra would have the king's child before long. Would she be happy about the baby? He had observed in his own mother that the expectation of yet another child carried a mixture of emotions. Even so, when each baby came she loved it, and was crushed by the ones she lost.

When he returned from today's hunt he would tell Didrik he wanted to go north for better game, reindeer and brown bear. But he would first travel to Hamar to see his family. Then, depending on what he found there, he would decide whether to return to Sjodrun…or not.

Chapter 29

Traveling north after securing permission from Didrik for a trip to Hamar, Kjell skirted the shore of Mjosa Lake until he saw the *Kristus Kirke* spires rising above the town. At the sight of his hometown jutting out on the peninsula, a warm rush of longing poured through Kjell like wine. He was almost home.

The family farm had been inherited by his father, and his father before him, as far back as anyone could recall. It was set in a fertile valley ten *favns* east of town, an easy walk. On his way he passed the apple orchards of Saint Olav's Priory with their verdant, budding leaves, then small farms and fields with patches of melting snow. All belonged to families Kjell knew well. He studied the few faces he passed: an old friend's cousin, the ash lad, and the salt seller. They greeted him with a nod or kind word. He wondered who had survived here and who was lost.

As he drew near, Kjell imagined his father's face when he saw his long absent son. Would he be glad, or was he still angry? The black sickness had been through Hamar, that he knew. Who was alive at the family farm? Perhaps it was better not to know. He pulled up on the reins, tempted to turn back, but *nei*, he must find out. He tapped Thorden's ribs and continued on.

At the gate he halted. The yard was quiet. A rusted plow leaned on the fence. A large pile of manure had not yet been spread on the fields. Kjell tied the horses to a post and the dogs followed him toward the door of the house, licking his hands.

Just then he heard pounding coming from the workshop and he strode across the overgrown grass. "Far? Is that you?" he called. "It is I, Kjell."

A heavy tool dropped at the sound of his voice. A figure emerged, shading his eyes with his hand. "Kjell?"

"*Onkel* Halldorr?" Kjell's father's brother was a cobbler, the one with whom Kjell was to have apprenticed.

"Is it really you, Kjell?" Halldorr ran to Kjell and hugged him tightly, then pulled back to have a look at his nephew. "So good to see you. We thought you were..." His eyes misted. The man had aged. Gray tinged his sideburns.

Kjell gripped his *onkel's* forearms. "What are you doing here, *Onkel*? Where are Far and Mar and the rest of the family?"

Halldorr's eyes reddened. "They are gone, Kjell."

A vice gripped Kjell's chest.

Halldorr pulled Kjell by the arm. "Come. Kolfinna will be so happy to see you. Let us have a bowl of ale and we will tell you all."

He led Kjell toward the house and pushed the door open. "Kolfinna, look who is here."

Kjell's *tante*, Barren Kolfinna as many called her, cried, "Kjell! Praise be to God that you have returned!" She embraced him. "You will be happy to know that the farm is still in the family, as you see."

She pushed him into a chair before hurriedly grabbing ale bowls and pouring generously. "This is a time to celebrate your homecoming," she said, offering one to him.

"*Skål*," his *tante* and *onkel* said, each taking a sip.

But Kjell stared at them blankly and did not drink. "Is my family all dead?"

Kolfinna took a long quaff. "We do not know. Your *onkel* and I are here guarding the farm for any who might...that is, for whoever returns. And now here you are." Kolfinna clung tightly to her bowl with both hands, smiling nervously.

Kjell crossed his arms. "What do you mean, you do not know where they are?"

"I will explain," said Halldorr, his face flushing. "You see, when the black sickness came, so many in Hamar died that your father sent your mother and the girls to the summer *seter* in the high country. Three of your brothers succumbed to the illness,

God rest their souls, but Solvi, as the eldest, was sent away by your father to be kept safe."

Kolfinna reached out and touched Kjell's forearm. "I am sorry for your losses, nephew."

Kjell stiffened, as if struck across the face. Three brothers gone, but the favored brother saved. "And Solvi...where is he?"

A cloud fell over Kolfinna. "We await his return. And you, of course."

Kjell braced himself. "Where is the rest of my family now?"

Onkel Halldorr's tone became defensive. "After losing the boys, your mother was beside herself. Your father asked us to watch the farm until he got back, and he joined your mother in the high country. We thought it would be a couple of days or a week, but they have not returned. You can see we are still guarding the farm, as we promised."

Something was greatly amiss. Kjell glared at them. "A half-year has passed and they never returned? Did they take supplies to winter there?"

"I do not know," said his *onkel*. He avoided Kjell's eyes. Kolfinna wrung her hands and bit her lip.

Kjell pushed back from the table and raised his voice. "If they were well, they would have come home before winter. And by now planting should be underway. Where else would they have gone?"

His *onkel* stammered. "I...we are here to welcome them, but...but alas, they have not come."

Kjell poked his *onkel*'s chest with his finger. "So, you do not know if they are alive or dead, yet you did not think to check on them?"

Halldorr leaned back. "We do not know where the *seter* is. We have been so busy with the animals and my trade—I still have shoes, saddles, and many things to make. Now that the snow is melting, and since you know the way, we should go now. I will go with you."

Kjell and Halldorr rode out and climbed the hills, Kjell leading the way toward the family *seter*. Kjell rode ahead on the familiar rocky path, leaving Halldorr farther and farther behind. Did his *onkel* not think to search the hills? He remembered that Halldorr was wont to express his envy of his oldest brother, and it was clear that he and Kolfinna assumed no one was coming back to claim the farm. They had taken it as their own.

After the steep, rock-strewn climb, Thorden finally leaped over the crest of the summit and they headed toward the summer hut situated alee of a rocky outcropping. This *seter*, where Kjell had spent parts of several summers watching the sheep and goats, was a place wholly unsuited for wintering over.

A few sheep wandered nearby, someone else's, by the sound of the bells. The cabin was deserted with no signs of horses or dogs, though animal footprints had muddied the entrance. The ashes of an outdoor fire pit had been blown clean, leaving a sooty trail across the patchy snow. Behind the hut three crude crosses stood like *drukken* sentinels. Spring run-off had spilled through the camp, sweeping a river of stones down the hill.

Kjell dismounted. The door to the hut was open. A soggy wool blanket had been dragged through the opening and abandoned across the threshold. He approached the hut slowly, bracing himself.

The cabin was dark and the overcast day lent no light to the dim interior. A buzzard flapped out of the hut close over Kjell's head and out the door. He flinched. He felt for the flint on the shelf and tugged tinder from the small jar. Lighting a candle, he shone it about the room. The table and stools were overturned. Ale horns and plates were scattered on the floor, shattered. The only bed, the one he had used when he watched the sheep, held crumpled bedding. Dread wormed down his spine.

Kjell stepped closer. The covers had been chewed away, leaving a hole amidst the wool. He held the candle forward and leaned in, gingerly tugging the blanket down.

Ribs, a spine, and graying hair revealed what was once his father. Something had eaten the soft parts but left the rest. Kjell stumbled backward, gagging.

Onkel Halldorr's horse skidded to a stop outside and he called, "Kjell! What did you find?"

Kjell tripped over the threshold and tumbled out of the hut, falling on his knees and retching.

"*Jesu Kristus* and Saint Olav," breathed Halldorr, "have mercy on their souls."

Wrapping the remains in his reindeer coat, Kjell buried his father next to the three graves of his mother and sisters. He fashioned a fourth cross and strengthened the others so they all stood upright. Halldorr mounded rocks atop each grave. Then Kjell and his *onkel* stood side-by-side, lingering for a time of silence. Kjell recalled happy memories of his early childhood, then with remorse, the final rejection his father had bequeathed on him and Oda. At last, he rose and dusted the grave dirt off his hands. He could not bring himself to pray.

Chapter 30

Crocus shoots sprouted through the quickly melting snow on Astra's farm, and the buds on birch branches were dipped in green. One day a warm wind blew up from the south, and by day's end, the snow in well-trampled paths had melted, leaving debris-strewn splotches on piles left from shoveling. Soon the ice on the creek broke free and water burbled once more. The songs of the bramblings, bokfinks, and linerles filled the morning air with life.

One morning Astra let the horses, cows, and sheep out to graze on the fresh tendrils of grass that poked through the melting snow. Six surviving lambs jumped playfully in the yard, including Astra's favorite, the lamb she and Nikolina had nursed. He ran to meet her and she patted his black wooly head affectionately.

Astra leaned her arms on a fence post. By now she was growing heavy with child. Whenever she needed to bend over, chop a log, or reach something tall, she cursed the king once more for visiting this disgrace upon her. The child would always be someone given against her will, and ridiculed as a bastard by others. She thought of Far with aching loss. Mar said all babies are blessings, but how would he feel about this baby?

Now, dozens, *nei,* hundreds of tasks lay ahead; tools needed sharpening, the stable roof leaked, and shearing, delousing, plowing, harrowing, and planting all lay ahead—just the beginning of the summer's work. Lent and Easter were approaching as well, according to Mar's calendar stick. Astra and Nikolina would not have time for the preparations required: cleaning the house, making new clothes, observing the fast. They had no eggs for Easter Day since they had long since eaten all the chickens. In fact, only dried fish and *blodpølsa* hung from the rafters.

Astra headed toward the ram's pen, holding her belly up with both hands like an over-full udder. She thought about Nikolina's excitement over the baby. Every day she asked Astra how she felt, how she had slept, whether the child was moving. Along with her cousin's help came advice: "Do not think of ogres or trolls lest the baby be born ugly"; "Do not look at the sun or your child will be blind"; "Keep all the knots tied and the doors shut until the birth pangs start lest the birth canal open too soon." Astra did not respond to Nikolina's stories of childbirth woes.

She waddled into the sheep shed, and the ram thrust himself against the rails. She needed to run the ram into the pasture with the ewes, but she felt nervous about releasing him by herself. She stopped to lean against the gate.

Nikolina appeared in the doorway. "There you are," she said spritely. "He is a feisty fellow."

"I know," Astra sighed. "Can you help me shoo him out?"

Nikolina grabbed a pitchfork and stood by the open doorway. Astra opened the gate and the ram shot out, bawling. They stood and watched him leaping after the ewes as they scattered in all directions.

"How are you feeling today?" Nikolina asked. "You look ripe."

"I want to wait until Easter. There is so much to do."

"You will not make it to Easter. I am anxious to meet your little one, but you do not seem excited at all."

"Mar once told me that if you love a newborn too much, it hurts all the more if it does not survive."

Nikolina shook her head. "Do not say that. It is cold-hearted. Being with child was the best thing that ever happened to me." They strolled out into the yard. "You know it could be born anytime, by the looks of you."

Astra sighed. "I know. You will have to take over my chores for a few days."

"I can help with everything. I will care for the baby, be the *tante*. You will see how well I will do." Nikolina propped her hands on her hips. "I wish you were as excited as I am about the baby."

Astra's voice rose. "How can I be excited? This is a child that belongs to someone else."

Nikolina gaped. "Not you? Please, please tell me who the father is."

Astra glanced at her cousin. "Someone you do not know."

Nikolina's eyes glinted. "Do you even want the baby?"

Astra paused. "Wanting has nothing to do with it."

As Astra toddled away, she turned back and said, "It is my duty, Niki. What choice do I have?"

Nikolina called after her, "I want the baby. Let me take care of it then!"

Astra passed the weed-filled garden on her way to the cheese house with the milk buckets and sighed. What loomed ahead of her like Mount Galdhøpiggen was plowing the grain fields and planting. The fallow field would be oats, since it was well manured from the cattle, but dung must be spread by hand for the barley and rye fields.

Astra stopped to rest at the well, setting the buckets down. If only Far were here. He loved spring after the long winter indoors. On brisk spring mornings like this he often gazed at his fields, standing with his hands on his hips, and breathed deeply of the earthy scents. He would pick up a clod of earth, crumble the soil between his fingers, then bring it to his nose. Then he would say, "It is a gift to work the fields God has given us. We must be grateful for the fruits of our labors."

For the hundredth time she tried to imagine delivering a child. What if she died, as so many women did? At least Nikolina would gladly take the baby. And what if the infant was deformed or died? Nikolina must take it to the woods so no one would ever know. She prayed for forgiveness for these thoughts, and for all her sins, in case she died in childbirth.

Lifting the pails, her back ached frightfully. Suddenly her belly tightened. She drew a sharp breath. The spasm slowly eased. "Not now, God," she whispered. "I have too much to do."

That night she woke to a binding cramp. The pain swelled, then gradually released. She exhaled audibly.

Nikolina's voice was sleep-soaked. "What is it?"

"Maybe nothing."

Astra heard the rustling of Nikolina's bed covers. "Tell me if you have another."

Just as Astra drifted off to sleep, another pang gripped her. "Ugh!" she cried.

In the blackness she heard Nikolina fumble from her covers. She lit a candle, and stirred the embers to life. "How long have you been having pains?" she asked, coiling her tresses into a braid.

"Not long."

Nikolina poured water into the kettle on its hook above the fire. Soon another cramp came, more painful this time. Astra tried to hold in a groan but it escaped.

"Worse?"

"*Ja*. Niki, I am not ready to have a baby. I need to make more soiling cloths, and I have not finished the lambswool blanket. There is so much farmwork to do." Astra began to weep.

"No one is ready," her cousin said. "Babies come when they want to. I am here to take care of you. I will open everything now to make the birth easier." She unbolted the door, untied all knotted cords, and loosened the ties on their clothing. Then she poured a bowl of ale, sprinkling it with herbs, and tipped it to Astra's lips. "Here. This will help." She placed a birthing amulet into Astra's palm for her to squeeze tightly during each pain.

Over the hours toward dawn the pains increased. Nikolina sat at her side wiping her brow and giving her encouraging words.

When the birth waters suddenly broke, Nikolina shouted. "Good! The baby will be here soon."

Astra moaned, "I cannot bear it any longer. I am dying."

"*Nei, nei.* You are doing fine. Let me look to see where the baby is now. Get on your knees."

Nikolina peered inside the birth canal. "I see the baby's head. You are nearly there."

When Niki finally told her to push, Astra bore down, holding her breath until pricks of light sparkled beneath her eyelids. "Mother Mary and Joseph!" she screamed. After several more pushes the mass slid away into Nikolina's hands and Astra collapsed over the mattress.

"Is it alive?" she cried, fearful that her terrible thoughts had caused the baby to die.

"Look here." Nikolina held the baby up and smiled. "A boy."

The wriggling, waxy infant opened his tiny mouth and breathed his first. A lusty cry followed, his lips quavering.

Nikolina rubbed away the gauzy caul and wrapped him in a soft blanket, then helped Astra prop up on pillows as she placed the infant in her arms.

Astra gazed at his perfect features and breathed in the scent of him. Unexpectedly, a compelling feeling of completeness overbore her. It was impossible for her to look away from his face. She barely noticed Nikolina busily tying the braided red yarn around the cord and cutting it through with a knife. When the blood mass came forth minutes later, Nikolina quickly wrapped it in a cloth.

Astra's voice was thick with emotion. "Bury it under the oak, in the dirt over Mar's grave. Somehow, she will know."

Nikolina helped Astra nestle the child to her breast and he latched on. Astra stared in wonder at the downy head, the tiny arms and slender fingers. She felt his quick soft breaths against her skin, the gentle tug of his lips.

"What will his name be?" Nikolina asked.

"I do not know yet." Astra had considered many names but none seemed quite right, surely not his father's.

"I hope you will decide soon," her cousin replied. "I have been waiting to hear."

Astra cooed to the infant and ignored Nikolina. She would have to tell her cousin the truth about his father soon, just not now, not yet.

Nikolina made Astra stay in bed that day. When the baby cried, Nikolina helped prop him up on pillows, giving Astra tips on how to hold him, how to nurse, and how to position him when he slept so he could breathe. Nikolina changed the baby's first cloths and cuddled him in her practiced arms, swaying rhythmically. Her face shone like the manor's brass bell in sunlight.

"I need to milk the cows," Nikolina said finally. "I will be back soon." She hurried out, tucking the bundled placenta under her arm.

When the door closed, Astra gazed at the infant. She had tried to hold back her love. He was the king's son, given against her will, yet here he was, Mar and Far's grandchild. How Mar would have loved to see her first grandbaby. "You are my kin," Astra whispered, "bone of my bone, heart of my heart." Love poured through her. Her unchecked tears baptized him.

While Nikolina was out, Astra tenderly rose. She laid the blanket she had woven in the cradle and placed the sleeping child inside. She combed and braided her hair, washed, and changed into a fresh night dress. At last, she lay down, weariness overtaking her.

She woke when Nikolina entered with a bucket of milk. Her cousin glanced at the neatened bed and the child in the cradle and scolded, "You should not be working. I said I would take care of everything."

"I did little," Astra said. "I need to get up as soon as I can. There is so much work to do."

"Do not worry about the farm right now. I am taking care of everything." Nikolina peered at the baby. "He is comely. He must have a handsome father. Are you going to tell me who it is now?"

Astra sat up. What would her cousin say? Now that Einarr was married and Vegar had rejected her, what did it matter if her cousin knew? "You may not believe me, but I will tell you the truth," she said.

Nikolina sat eagerly on the bed.

Astra took a breath, then forced the words out. "It was…King Magnus."

Nikolina's eyes widened. "How? When?"

"When the king was there, remember how I came back to the women's house very late?"

Nikolina nodded.

"Sir Henrik, the knight, and two soldiers grabbed me on my way back from the woods. They took me to the king. I had no choice."

Nikolina gazed from the baby to Astra before speaking. "So, he is royal."

Astra had not thought of him that way until now.

"May I ask what it was like? Was the king…gentle? Kind, at least?"

Astra brushed the question away. She could not speak.

Nikolina said, more to herself than to Astra, "So that is why you did not like to talk about it. I heard this happened to a girl in another village. There are probably many king's children in our country. But now look…we have a prince!" She hugged Astra tightly.

The third morning after the baby was born, Astra wobbled out to check on the horses while Nikolina happily watched the baby. Wildflowers bloomed along the fences and in the fields. Insects buzzed about. The garden had sprouted last year's weeds and grasses sprang up everywhere in brilliant chartreuse. The bright sun and wooly clouds revived Astra's senses as she breathed in the spring freshness. She was relieved to be outside.

The horses came to the fence to greet her and she stroked their forelocks. They had been rolling in the field to shed their winter coats and needed a good brushing. She checked the sheep pasture where they all grazed serenely. The ram had settled down.

Hauling a bucket of water back to the house, she found Nikolina cuddling the infant and singing to him. He was mewling and rooting against her neck.

"I will take him," she said. "He must be hungry."

Nikolina kissed the baby's forehead, then placed him into Astra's arms. Astra fumbled with her shift and the baby began to wail. When he latched on, the sharp pain of his suckle made Astra wince.

Nikolina leaned against the bedpost, watching. "It hurts, does it not?"

"They say it gets better," Astra replied.

"I wish I could feed him for you." Nikolina turned away quickly, but Astra saw her cousin wipe a tear with her sleeve.

When the baby fell asleep, Astra laid him down carefully on the bed and stroked his tiny head.

"Have you thought of his name yet?" Nikolina asked. She had asked every day, threatening to name him herself.

"I have," Astra replied, not looking up.

Nikolina touched the infant's pate. "The baby is definitely princely. Call him Magnus, after his father."

"*Nei*, never!" Astra snapped.

Nikolina poked sticks into the coals.

Astra glared at her cousin. "Hold your tongue. Sometimes you are a vexation."

They were both quiet, then Astra said, "I will name him Gunnar Astrasson, after my brother and me."

"After you?" Nikolina stared at her. "You cannot name a boy after his mother."

"I can do as I please." Astra smiled.

Nikolina sat on the bed beside Astra and was quiet for a few moments. She took a breath. "Gunnar is a good name...I like that. But I am going to call him the Little King."

Only the sounds of the baby's gentle breaths could be heard. Astra's heart softened with pity for her cousin. After all, Nikolina had lost both her husband and her child.

"I do need your help with him, Niki," Astra said. "I am grateful for all you do. You can call him what you like."

Nikolina's face alit. "I will be so good to him. You will not regret this."

But before long, Astra did.

Each day Astra took on more chores. At first, she tried to work with the infant tied to her back, frustrated at how often she had to pause to attend to him. Nikolina suggested she leave the baby with her and that she would bring him out when he was hungry. Each time, as soon as the baby had finished eating Niki whisked him away so Astra could get back to work.

Truth be told, Astra discovered that she must redo Nikolina's slapdash farm work. She found it most productive to let Nikolina care for the baby, the food, and the household while she resumed the farm work.

One late afternoon, exhausted, Astra lay down on her bed to rest and feed the baby. Soon she fell asleep. When she woke from her nap Gunnar was gone. The door stood ajar.

Astra spied her cousin standing at the pasture fence holding the bundled infant to her cheek. Walking quietly up behind them she heard her cousin simper, "Do not forget. I am your *tante* and I love you even more than...."

"What are you doing?" Astra asked, piqued.

Nikolina whipped around. "Nothing. We are just visiting the cows, right, my Little King?"

Astra took the child from Nikolina's hands. "What were you saying to him?"

Nikolina sighed. "Nothing important. Just think. If he lived with the king, he would have a wet nurse. Why not think of me that way."

Astra paused, then walked away. She knew that Nikolina had loved her own child more than her life, and Astra needed her. She was kin, after all.

Caring for the farm took all of Astra's energy in the lengthening daylight hours. There was more and more to do, leaving Astra's head swirling with tasks yet to be completed. Throughout the day, Nikolina brought Gunnar out to Astra for nursing, immediately taking him away to the house when he finished.

Astra tilled and planted, set traps for game, nailed fences into place, and often fished in the evening. At the end of each day she collapsed, sometimes realizing she had barely held little Gunnar all day.

As the days passed, Astra became certain that they would not be able to lay in enough food, and especially fuel for the winter by themselves. If that time came, she must forego her pride and travel to the manor. Her illegitimate child would be made known but that was better than starving. She would use Far's coins or sell the king's gold bracelet to buy supplies…perhaps Einarr would buy it for that mule-jawed wife of his.

That evening Nikolina said, "You look tired. Shall I sleep with the baby tonight?"

Astra cradled the child in her arm and unfastened her night dress. "*Nei*, he suckles throughout the night."

"I would be glad to, when you are ready," her cousin said, eying the nursing baby. "Then you could get a good night's sleep."

"Maybe when he is weaned."

Nikolina leaned over and stroked his head. "I love the Little King like you do," she added quietly. "Maybe more."

"*Nei, nei*," Astra said. But she was too tired to argue.

Late in the night, Astra heard the dogs barking. She opened the door and peered into the moonlit night. The dogs took stuttering steps toward the pasture. Something was out there. She took a knife and walked behind them, her heart galloping.

The dogs ran ahead toward the far end of the fence and stopped, growling. She whistled softly and they ran back to her, hackles up. They nosed her hand and she patted their heads. Whatever they had heard seemed to be gone. Back in bed, she lay awake a long time, listening.

In the morning, she found a disemboweled ewe pulled partway through broken fence slats. Only a wolf could do this. If her father were here, he would hang the remains of the sheep from the fence, then set traps around. He might hide in a tree to wait for the wolf's return. If this failed, he would take the dogs and hunt the creature down. She could do none of these, so she burned the sheep carcass so there would be no remains. She knew, however, that the wolf had discovered easy prey.

The next day as Astra toiled in Far's workshop, she swore and threw down the axe she had been trying to sharpen. The blade was uneven and jagged. She wished she had paid more attention to her father's work. Her breasts were as full as wine bladders and leaking badly, so she hurried back to the house.

When she entered, Nikolina lay on the bed and jerked her head up, her face coloring. She was holding something to the baby's mouth and quickly covered the child with a blanket. "You are back so soon? I was just going to bring him to you," she said.

Astra reached for Gunnar. "I need to feed him."

Nikolina clasped him tighter. "The Little King was hungry and...you were so busy."

Astra flung the covering off and saw what Nikolina was hiding—the lamb's flask lay beside her cousin's bared nipple, as if she were feeding him from her own breast.

"What are you doing?" Astra wrested the baby from Nikolina's arms.

"I had to do something. He was crying," Nikolina said.

"You should have just called me." Angry and troubled, Astra caried the baby to the front step where she sat down to nurse.

Nikolina followed her out. "I am sorry. I thought you wanted to keep working."

Astra glared at her. "I am full to bursting and you were using the lamb's nipple in my place. I am his mother."

"I said I am sorry. I was just trying to help." Nikolina hurried back into the house and busied herself, clanking pots loudly.

Astra steamed. Her cousin was taking over the baby and she was letting it happen. Gunnar was hers alone.

When the baby fell asleep, Astra laid him in his cradle. "I need to repair some fence slats. Call me when he gets hungry!"

Nikolina replied sullenly, as if hurt, "Of course. No need to nag."

Astra carried twine and slats from the workshop to the end of the sheep paddock. A large wolf could jump the high fence, but she hoped her repairs would discourage him. As she worked, she watched the woods, keeping her knife and the dogs close at hand.

On her way back to the workshop she stopped at the house and asked, "Has he wakened?"

"*Nei*, he is still sleeping." Nikolina was repairing leather shoes.

"Then I will be in the workshop. Just call for me if he wakes up."

She worked the axe blade against the whetstone again until the edge was smooth and sharp, pleased when she ran her finger along it and drew a bead of blood. Far would be proud. She sharpened another knife and a few tools.

Ready to feed the baby again, she strode, smiling, to the house. As she approached, she heard the baby cry. Her milk began to flow. She clutched her arms to her chest to staunch the drenching. Just as she got to the threshold, Nikolina's lilting voice drifted out. Astra stopped at the door.

"You are hungry, my little love? Here, take your Mar's milk." Nikolina was lying on the bed trying to feed Gunnar from her own flaccid breast. The child was frustrated and tossed his head back and forth, unable to bring milk. Nikolina then squirted milk into his mouth from a lamb's bladder.

Astra dashed to the bed, outraged. "What in God's name?" She ripped the bladder from Nikolina's hands and flung it across the room, bursting it against the logs. She snatched Gunnar and backed away. The baby began to scream.

She yelled, "I told you not to do this. Only I will feed him. You have lost your mind!"

"Please, Astra," Nikolina cried. "I heard that sometimes milk will come back to a mother who has lost a child. I am just trying to help, to be a wet nurse like we talked about."

"You are not a wet nurse. Your milk will not come back—that is only wishful thinking. If I catch you again…you will…sleep in the barn." Astra pointed outside. "Get out and find something useful to do."

Nikolina slunk past her.

"He is not your baby!" Astra yelled after her. She fed the infant but could not still her heart. Nikolina seemed desperate to replace little Amalie with Gunnar.

"God take you, cousin," she shouted. The baby startled and pulled hard on her nipple, bringing tears of pain and exasperation to her eyes.

The next morning when Astra rose, Nikolina was leading Farwa from the pasture hitched to a sledge.

"Where are you going?" Astra called.

"To find supplies. We are starving." Nikolina swung onto the horse's back.

"What supplies? When will you be back?" Astra shielded her eyes against the morning sun.

"I do not know." She slapped the reins and the horse jerked forward.

"Do not tell anyone about the baby!" Astra yelled at her cousin's retreating back.

Nikolina disappeared around the bend and a wave of concern washed over Astra. Where was her cousin going? Was she just angry and trying to punish Astra for thwarting her attempt to make the baby hers? Would she be back? Dealing with her cousin was like dragging a stone around by her waist. Astra yelled up into the heavens, "What am I supposed to do with her? God, you take her!"

As the afternoon progressed, and Nikolina did not return, Astra kept the baby on her back and moved among the silent buildings uneasily, knowing for the first time she was truly alone. She carried her father's large hunting knife on her belt and kept the dogs close.

Nikolina had not returned by nightfall and Astra slept little, waking at every creature sound. The following afternoon as she was drawing water, she heard the thudding of hooves. The sledge rattled around the bend and drew to a stop by the house. Astra hurried to meet her cousin.

Nikolina jumped off and blurted, "Look what I have. Ale, barley, salt, tallow, and baby chicks. And I brought you something special." She threw off a covering to reveal a calf's carcass, skinned and ready to roast. "This calf fell and broke its leg, so now we have veal." Astra's eyes widened. They had not had beef since last year.

She grinned. "How excellent. We will celebrate tonight. What is the news from Sjodrun?"

Nikolina lifted the heavy salt box to the ground. "I did not have to go to Sjodrun. I got it from a…neighbor," she said.

"What neighbor?"

Nikolina pointed vaguely to the east, away from Sjodrun. "Just a kind soul I met on the road. He lives some distance past those hills. I came at the right time, though. The calf fell the day before."

"How generous. What was the neighbor's name?" Astra tried to picture someone who lived over the hill who could spare such supplies at this time of year, but she could think of no one. And if this were so, what took her cousin so long to get home?

Nikolina avoided Astra's eyes. "I have forgotten his name already. Very nice, though."

Astra petted the sweating horse. "How much do we owe him?"

"It was a gift, for now. We can pay it back as we are able. Just be glad, Astra. I could use some ale. Could you?" Nikolina rolled the barrel off the sledge.

"Definitely." Astra was pleased, but wondered about the cost of these mysterious gifts. Her cousin was hiding something.

Nikolina smiled. "No more worries for a while."

But Astra's doubts about Nikolina lingered.

All the next morning as she worked, Nikolina sought Astra out at intervals to feed the baby. They spoke little. Astra was relieved her cousin was finally behaving as she should. Nikolina worked hard all day, and even helped Astra chop down branches for firewood.

After they finished, Nikolina said, "You go and rest. I will take them to the woodshed and chop them up."

Grateful for a break from heavy work, Astra took the unexpected chance to rest. She lay down with the baby for a short spell. She must have fallen asleep, for when she woke, Nikolina had changed into a clean day shift and sat on a stool watching her.

"I am glad you could rest," Nikolina said. "By the way, I saw a broken fence post in the far field. I am worried the sheep will get out. Do you want me to go and fix it?"

"*Nei*, I will go." Astra crawled over Gunnar, who slept peacefully. "I will be back soon. Yell for me if he wakes up."

Nikolina nodded. "Of course."

Astra grabbed a fence post, nails, and the maul from the workshop. The dogs bounded beside her along the fence line. She walked the perimeter but saw no break. Had she missed it? She retraced her steps.

After another pass, Astra still had seen no damage. Had her cousin been mistaken? Was it a different fence? She circled the horses' pasture, as well.

As she returned to the farmyard, peeved at her wasted time, she heard a horse's whinny. Nikolina sat astride Farwa and was riding toward the road with a bundle tied to her chest.

"Where are you going?" Astra yelled.

Nikolina glanced at her briefly, then kicked Farwa hard. The horse trotted, then loped, rounding the corner and soon out of sight.

Astra dropped her tools and screamed, "Where is the baby?" She sprinted to the house. The cradle was empty.

For a moment Astra was paralyzed, disbelieving her own eyes. She shot out of the house and ran screaming after Nikolina, but the hoofbeats had faded and Nikolina was gone. Astra's breathing was jagged as she gulped for air. Niki had stolen Gunnar!

Astra ran to the pasture and whistled for Kvikke. Her fingers fumbled as she strapped on the bridle. Arming herself with a long knife, bow, and quiver, she jumped onto her horse's back and leaped into a gallop.

At the main road, fresh hoofprints turned east. Nikolina was not going to the manor. Astra cursed loudly for having ever trusted her cousin. Within a short distance the prints veered off the side of the road and disappeared into thick vegetation. She reined Kvikke into the underbrush, searching madly for clues.

Aha! A broken twig with horse hair attached, then a single hoofprint in a patch of mud. Astra urged Kvikke slowly forward. Nikolina could not be too far ahead. Working through the thicket would be difficult for Farwa, too.

Soon she jolted down a steep embankment. Branches broke against her legs as she leaned back for balance. Kvikke's precarious footfalls among the tangled roots caused the horse to trip, slide, then catch her footing again. Astra righted her seat and clung tightly with her legs to the horse's bare back.

The trail soon followed a rushing stream. Scratched and bleeding, Astra listened, but the roar of the tumbling water masked all sounds. She reached the rocky creek bed where the runoff spilled into a turbulent current that gushed past her. Astra knew that downstream the watercourse leveled off and there was a pool where she and Far had fished for trout. Perhaps Nikolina would cross there.

The crashing water fell behind as Kvikke stumbled over the pebbly shore. An eagle swooped overhead, followed by a squawking crow chasing the predator away from its nest. Astra flinched. When she neared the huge boulder beyond which lay the pool, she dismounted and crept forward. A low hum of voices reached her.

She peered around the rock. What she saw panicked her. "God in heaven and Mother Mary save us," she murmured. Just downstream Farwa waded across the creek flank-deep with Nikolina sitting astride, the baby still tied to her chest.

Astra gasped. The pond was too deep. What if Nikolina and the baby fell into the water? She opened her mouth to cry out but the water shallowed and Farwa gained the other shore. There Nikolina dismounted.

Someone else stood on the bank, a man in a black cloak. A sword glinted at his hip. Vegar! That despicable, conniving, ruthless, barn rat was helping Nikolina steal her baby.

Astra realized how ridiculous her show of force would now seem, but she remounted, pulled the long knife from its sheath, and urged Kvikke forward. They plunged into the water.

Nikolina turned to look, then screamed.

Astra held her weapons aloft. "Stop!" she yelled. "Give me my baby this instant!"

Nikolina slithered behind Vegar, pressing the baby to her chest.

Kvikke strode through the deepest part of the pool then into the shallows, where Astra pulled back on the reins. She pointed the long knife at her cousin. "I said give him to me."

"What have we here?" laughed Vegar. "A mother warrior?" He held one arm in front of Nikolina and backed her up a step, unsheathing his sword slowly with the other hand.

Astra ignored Vegar and screamed at Nikolina, "If you do not give Gunnar back right now, I will kill you, cousin, I swear I will."

Vegar stepped to the shoreline, sword pointing down at his side. "Calm down now, Astra. Nikolina said you do not want the baby."

"He is my child!" she bellowed. "Of course, I want him! You cannot get away with this. Give him to me, now!" Her hand wavered from the weight of the knife. "If you protect her, Vegar, neither of you will sleep without fearing for your life. If I must, I will appeal to the *Gulagthing* in Oslo. I will tell the king what you have done to his…son."

Vegar held up his hand. "So, you will appeal to the king, the boy's own father, you say? If that is true, he will not believe you, or even remember you. Put the knife down and let us be reasonable. Nikolina says she is doing you a favor. She said you gave her the baby."

Nikolina peered at Astra from behind Vegar.

Astra placed the knife on her lap and pulled the bow off her shoulder. She nocked an arrow, pointing it at Nikolina's head. "My cousin is a liar."

Nikolina grabbed Vegar's sleeve. "See what I mean? She threatens her own cousin. She is not fit to have a child."

Astra aimed. She pulled the string back. Before she could react, Vegar jumped forward into the water and flipped her arrow away with the tip of his sword. It flew up, landed in the water and began floating downstream.

Startled, Kvikke reared. Astra fell splashing into the creek. She scrambled to her feet, frantically searching for her knife.

Nikolina called, "You know you do not really want him. Let me take him. I love him like my own son. More than you do."

Astra snatched her bow but watched the arrows disappear in the ripples. Vegar stepped into the water and offered her his hand. She slapped it away.

"It seems your cousin is trying to help you," he said. "She and I are going to marry. Did she tell you that she visited me and was given a calf and other supplies?"

Nikolina said, "He already helped us, you see."

Astra gaped at her cousin. So that is where Nikolina had gone for supplies. She had likely promised Vegar anything. They must have lain together already.

"She is willing to care for your child," Vegar continued smoothly, "and we will say that it is hers, by Dag. The lad will have all that he needs: land, servants, wealth. We will treat him as our first born, as a son, a king's son should be treated, if he is one. We will provide for you, too, if you agree to let him go. If you do not accept our offer, we will never help you again."

Nikolina added, "He will be happier and richer with us. This is best for everyone."

Astra spat. "*Nei*, Niki, he is mine."

Nikolina's tone hardened. "You will never make it through the winter without help. Do you want Gunnar to die?"

Astra glared at her cousin. "My son and I will find a way."

"But he is a king's son and he deserves better…better than you."

Astra was stung by this. "You whore! What makes you think you are any better than me? You sleep with men at the call of a lark."

Nikolina started backing up the hill.

Astra stopped, took a breath. "Cousin, you of all people know what it is like to lose a child. You would have done anything… anything…to get Amalie back, would you not? I am no different. You will have a husband, if Vegar indeed marries you, and you will have other children. But Gunnar is my only family."

Nikolina's mouth twitched. She drew back into the trees. "*Nei*, I love him. I deserve him."

Astra waded to the shore. Her soaking dress tugged at her legs as she pressed toward Nikolina. "Give him to me."

Vegar stepped in her way and said, "I did not think you would reject my offer of help. I am surprised you wanted the bastard."

"You were wrong."

He stepped aside.

Nikolina screamed and charged up the hill. Astra climbed after her, hampered by her sodden garments. Nikolina was gaining ground, so Astra tore off her over-dress, then loped up the steep grade yelling, "Stop! You will fall and hurt the baby."

But Nikolina continued on, stumbling over broken limbs and dodging trees. Astra grasped at roots and clambered after her. Then she heard a thud followed by a cry of pain. Nikolina had fallen hard. She grabbed her ankle and wailed. "Vegar, get the baby!"

Astra caught up, searching the ground frantically. She found the bundle resting against a fallen log just out of her cousin's reach. She plucked Gunnar up and unraveled the swaddling cloths. The baby's eyes were open and he gurgled.

"Give him back, damn you," Nikolina sobbed. "He should be mine!"

Astra clung to him as she would a buoy in a storm. She held the baby tightly to her chest and lit down the hill, passing Vegar by as he labored up the slope. She heard Vegar say, "Stop shouting, woman. Calm yourself."

Nikolina sobbed louder, "It is broken. I heard it snap."

Astra swung herself and the baby onto Kvikke's back, securing the baby inside her under-dress. She grabbed Farwa's reins, spun the horses around and kicked Kvikke forward.

Nikolina cried, "Catch her, Vegar, she is taking my baby!"

"*Nei*, you know we cannot," he said, hoisting Nikolina onto his shoulder.

"I hate you, Astra," Nikolina bawled. "I will hate you until the day I die."

Astra finished the evening chores with Gunnar tied to her back and Far's long knife on her hip. She gathered all the weapons she could find and locked every door on the farm. Once inside the house she pulled the latch shut and lugged a heavy trunk against the door, placing weapons within easy reach. Only then did she eat a crust of *brød*, down two bowls of ale, and crawl into Far and Mar's box bed with the baby.

In the dark days after the pestilence when Astra had pined for her lost loved ones, she thought often of her own death. She was sure that some illness, accident, or even childbirth would snuff out her life. After Far disappeared, she had even welcomed the thought of rejoining her family in heaven, wondering why she alone had been spared.

Now she knew. She had survived for this child. A fierce loyalty had sprung up within her. He was her family, her only family.

The dogs barking woke Astra. Their sharp yelps were calls of fright—she had heard this before. The fire had died to embers. Carefully she checked on the sleeping baby, rose, and threw on her cloak. Snatching Far's dagger and bow, she slid open the bolt on the door.

The night was moonlit. Both dogs stared out at the pasture, growling low. They walked beside her as she tip-toed toward the fence in her bare feet. A sheep's bleating at the far side of the field was suddenly choked off. The rest of the flock cowered in a clump by the gate, milling among the legs of the fidgeting cows. The animals turned to look at her in unison, their eyes glinting like coals in the moonlight. Astra was glad she had put the horses in the stable tonight.

She squinted into the eerie gloom. Sounds of scratching and tearing drifted faintly across the grass. She inched along the fence line, her heart beating like a threshing flail.

The sound suddenly stilled. Just when she thought the creature in the darkness had fled, her dogs broke into frantic barking and lunged forward, ducking under the rail and dashing across the field. A silver gleam leapt over the fence and disappeared.

"Mother of God and all the saints," Astra swore.

The dogs sniffed frantically around the silent heap on the ground. Astra whistled and they loped back, hackles bristling.

She dared not go to look until first light. The wolf could be watching from the forest. On her way back she counted the sheep. Seven ewes, the ram, and five lambs; one more was missing.

Back in bed, holding Gunnar close, images of gnashing teeth, torn throats, and dismembered limbs churned through Astra's brain. She said her prayers again, recited the *Pater Noster* and *Ave Maria*. She finally drifted off in the wee hours.

After breakfast, Astra went about the grisly business of gleaning what meat she could from the dead lamb. She wept as she did so, as it turned out to be the lamb she had hand-fed. She clipped the wool, then burned the rest of the carcass in the firepit.

Two nights passed without incident. The third night she was awakened again by the dogs' high-pitched yowls that faded quickly away as they ran into the pasture. Ready this time, Astra shot out of bed and armed herself, speeding after the dogs as she gulped back her fear.

Her dogs' barks turned to howls. Astra crept toward them, nocking an arrow. "Saint George, help me slay this dragon," she prayed silently.

As she approached, her dogs backed up. Inside the fence the wolf's eyes glinted like dagger points, then disappeared. Bones crunched and the animal shuffled backward in the grass, dragging the sheep by the neck. A deep growl warned her away. Her dogs rumbled in return.

Astra waited for the eyes to reappear. She aimed, steadied her grip. When the yellow orbs popped up she released the arrow. A yelp pierced the night and the beast jumped back against the fence. The arrow had struck the wolf's shoulder and the animal fought it. The dogs jumped onto the wolf's back, bellowing. The animal twisted, nipping and yelping to shake the dogs free.

In a rage, Astra raced forward. She jammed her father's knife into its uplifted neck and blood splattered her face and night dress. The wolf collapsed and lay still. Astra screamed, stabbing the wolf again and again. Trembling, she sat back on her haunches. The dogs circled her, whining and licking the blood on her face.

At sunrise, though she had slept only briefly, Astra rose and ate of last night's cold porridge. She had run out of firewood. Slinging Gunnar onto her back, she hitched Kvikke to the sledge and headed out to dispose of the wolf and gather wood.

Spring sun filtered through the leaves. The forest was alive with birds and small animals that scurried out of the way of the horse's hooves. On the path toward the stream, Astra stopped and rolled the wolf's body down a steep embankment. As she watched it go, she knew her father would be proud of what she had done.

She rode through the woodlands, stopping to fill the sledge with broken branches. Luckily, the pickings were abundant. Further downstream she spied a fallen pine, its trunk lying across the forest floor surrounded by a mass of dead branches and dried needles. She had been down this path before on her skis and had circled the tree looking for Far, though the snow was too deep for her to see its trunk.

A hawk screeched overhead. She jumped. Was this the tree Far had cut down after all? She pulled up the reins. She picked her way through the dry branches that clawed at her arms and snagged her clothing. As she approached a thick broken limb, she noticed a jumble of debris protruding from beneath the large splintered branch. Far's fur coat lay flat and matted beneath it. His trousers had rotted to shreds and his boots were chewed away.

    Astra tore at the brittle twigs to get closer until she spotted the ragged remains of his decomposed face and rounded bits of skull. She stumbled back, hungry for air, tripping over broken limbs. When she got to the sledge she collapsed. A scream escaped her lungs and echoed down the gully.

Chapter 31

Kjell spent the spring days revisiting the hills of his childhood, climbing to the tops of ridges, perching on rocks beside gushing streams and pondering all he had lost—parents, siblings, wife and son: everyone he loved. His heart was sometimes numb, and other times pierced through with a saber. Each night he drank himself to sleep from the barrel of ale his *tante* had sent with him.

He hunted, as always, and the game was plentiful. Scraping clean the hides did not bring the visceral pleasure it once had, but he collected the skins of animals that crossed his path. At last, when Sokker and Thorden could carry no more, he headed down to the valley in the direction of Sjodrun. He stopped at two small villages on his way to try to sell the pelts, but no one was willing to part with their coins. Every day he contemplated whether to stop at his old homestead and visit the graves of his wife and son.

When he came to the overgrown path that led to the squatter's village, Kjell halted. What did he hope to see? The wrecked remains of the village? His family's cabin in ashes? The two rough graves he had dug in haste were the only testimony to his brief life with Oda. What if they had been dug up by animals? Had he not suffered enough sorrow? Perhaps he would travel on and return later before the snows came. After pausing a long time in indecision, Kjell clicked his tongue and passed on by.

Several more days brought him to the crossroad that led toward Sjodrun. He was certain Didrik would take him back, and he had a good number of skins to show for his time away.

The day was warm and the road serene. The air was filled with the musical chatter of nesting birds. Kjell strapped his coat onto the back of the saddle. At a rounded bend in the road, he heard rustling in the brush. He reached behind him for his bow, expecting a deer to leap from the forest.

Instead, three men on horseback sprang onto the roadway and quickly surrounded him, swords drawn. Thorden snorted and pawed the dusty road as Kjell pulled up on the reins. His dogs barked madly, circling the men's horses. The village mutt nipped at a horse's legs and was kicked and sent flying.

Kjell aimed his arrow directly at the closest figure, unsure who the leader might be.

"Ill advised, my friend," said the man. He was dressed in a frayed gentlemen's surcoat, too tight and clearly not his own. The three moved closer, forming a tight circle. Kjell lowered the bow to his lap.

"We do not want to harm you," the leader said, "but we will take your horses and goods." The man's voice was smooth, calm, and practiced.

"*Nei*, I think not." Kjell moved to raise his bow.

An accomplice jolted forward and pressed his sword against Kjell's throat. "Drop it or I will cut off your head."

Kjell held still.

"Your money," said the leader. He nodded at Kjell's pouch. "Drop it."

Kjell felt drips of blood trickling down his neck. He loosened his money pouch, which fell into the dust with a clink. The third thief retrieved the coin purse and dropped it into a saddlebag.

Kjell stared at the leader, who motioned for him to dismount. He had no choice but to swing off. When he did so, one thief snatched Thorden's reins. The horse balked, backing up until the thief whipped him and brought him around behind.

"Do not follow us or we will kill you," the leader said, sheathing his sword and turning his horse around.

"I will split the furs with you." Kjell pointed to the many furs strapped onto Sokker's rump. "And give you the horse. He is very strong. But I have had trouble selling furs and so will you. Do me justice and leave me my hunting horse."

The thief holding Thorden led him in a U-turn, while another grabbed Sokker's halter.

"Not this time," said the leader. "But you are brave to ask." His two companions laughed and charged off with all of Kjell's possessions.

The leader called back, "Do not follow us. If I ever see you again, I will show no mercy." With that he broke into a gallop behind the other villains. Kjell watched helplessly, seething as the thieves rounded a bend and quickly disappeared. Kjell picked up his bow and shot his only arrow after them uselessly. He stood agog, staring after them until he could no longer hear hoofbeats.

Those filthy bandits were the worst of all scoundrels! Kjell wanted to kill them slowly. He envisioned slitting the leader's throat, as he had Jens', while the thief begged for mercy.

Kjell stomped up and down the road, cursing until he grew hoarse. The dogs whined and tangled around his legs. Finally, he plopped down onto the dirt road cross-legged, bowing his head into his hands in disbelief. The dogs licked him and pawed his lap. Kjell examined Navnløs for injury. A muddy hoof print was visible on the dog's ribs and tender to touch, but he would live.

Finally, Kjell stood up and started walking, trying to think of what to do. With no food, no money, no horse, and no goods to sell, he could do nothing but trudge onward toward Sjodrun, arriving empty-handed. Depriving a man of his horse and livelihood should be avenged. Perhaps he could convince Didrik to help him chase down the robbers, though he was hours from Sjodrun by foot. The further he walked, the more futile it seemed to try to capture and punish the villains. They were far away by now, hidden and perhaps waiting for their next victim.

Kjell's thoughts turned inward. He pondered his life. He knew his sins. Perhaps he deserved what he got. Perhaps this was his penance.

Ruth Tiger

By mid-afternoon he reached the top of a steep stretch of road and stopped to catch his breath. A lesser-worn path led off through the forest of birch and pines. He was thirsty and growing hungry. Maybe there was a creek or even a lake where he could refresh himself…or a cliff from which to jump.

Just then the scintillating aroma of wood smoke reached his nostrils. Glancing over the trees he saw tell-tale smoky wisps drifting lazily upward: a sign of life. Kjell took the path.

Chapter 32

The morning sky was clear and the air balmy. Astra balanced the milking bucket in one hand and the baby basket in the other on her way to the pasture. She sat down on a three-legged milking stool as the cows crowded near. Her back ached as she straddled the low perch. It seemed that all she did was lift and carry heavy objects. When she finished the milking, she tramped across the pasture with her burdens to the *stabbur*. There she poured the contents into the earthen jar to make cheese, keeping a bit for her porridge at dinner. She headed back to the house to feed and change the baby. Another long day of work awaited.

Today she needed to move the cattle from the small pasture near the barn to the fallow field, where they would find fresh grass and fertilize the next crop, if she had the time to plant one. This meant she would have to make the trek to the far field twice a day, walking them out in the morning and bringing them home each evening for milking.

Before she had stolen baby Gunnar, Nikolina had helped her shear the ewes, but their uneven clippings, some nearly to the roots, made the animals look like they had been flailed rather than shorn. She let them free to roam and sent Irvig out each evening to bring them home. Throughout each day she thought of one, then another of her family members, remembering happy times and sad. She found herself talking aloud to them, just to hear her own voice. These thoughts kept her company on her lonely rounds of chores.

Just as Astra set the porridge over the fire to boil, Irvig and Haret sent up warning barks. She poked her head out of the house and saw them speeding toward the path that led to the main road. The dogs stopped at the turn and growled.

Affrighted, Astra hid the sleeping baby's basket under a blanket in the extra room and grabbed her bow and quiver. Had Vegar and Nikolina returned to fight for her child? When she caught up with the dogs, she saw the silhouette of a man walking down the path toward the farm. He had no horse but was trailed by three dogs.

Astra tensed. She steadied her arms to lift the bow and pointed an arrow at the shaded figure. "Stop where you are," she shouted.

The man halted and thrust his hands straight out to his sides, looking strangely like a cross. "I come in peace," he called. He let his bow slide off his shoulder to the ground.

"Who are you?" Her frightened voice held firm.

"Just a traveler in need of help. I saw your smoke." He knelt on one knee, arms still outstretched. "I mean no harm."

"Are you alone?" She inched forward, glancing to either side of the path.

"I am. Thieves took my horses, my pelts, and most of my weapons." He unsheathed his knife and tossed it out of his reach. "And my money," he added.

She peered at him closely, recognizing his voice. She lowered the bow. "Kjell, the hunter? Is that you?"

"The same!" His beard was unkempt and swept his chest, and his sandy hair curled down his shoulders. He looked worse for his travels.

She slung her bow over her shoulder. "It is I, Astra. How did you find my farm?"

He rose and shaded his eyes. "Astra? God be praised! I only happened upon your farm by a turn of good fortune, it seems."

She motioned him to come. "You must be hungry, Kjell the hunter. All I have is porridge, but enough to share. Then you can tell me what happened and what brought you here."

"Ah, it is a long story." He smiled, and picked up his bow. "For porridge I will tell you everything."

It had been so long since Astra had smiled that her face felt strange doing so. He followed her into the farmyard.

"Wait outside and I will bring you a bowl." She pointed to a log by the cold firepit.

Just then the baby screeched. She ran into the house and lifted the infant from his basket. Soothing him against her shoulder, she walked out and stirred the pot, then scooped a bowl of porridge for Kjell. He took it and began to eat hungrily.

Astra sat on a log stool to feed the crying child. She recalled his parting words to her at the creek, "Whatever happened to you was not deserved." These words had meant something to her then, a small comfort. Then at *Jul* he had guessed rightly that she was pregnant with the king's child. He had advised her against marrying Vegar because of his haughtiness, but also because she intended to deceive Vegar about her pregnancy. She had been angry at Kjell for these biting words of truth.

Kjell finished the bowl as if famished, then ran his dirty finger around the inside of the dish for the last morsels. Astra laid the baby in a basket and brought Kjell another bowl, the last of her pot.

"I am glad the king's child was safely born," Kjell said as she handed him the porridge. She detected no judgment in his voice.

She picked up the squalling baby, switching him to the other breast. "A boy. Gunnar, after my brother."

Kjell ate ravenously, then smiled and set the empty bowl on the ground. He folded his hands over his knee. "At least you have a new life in your home. A child is a blessing, no matter the circumstances."

Astra smoothed the baby's soft head. "Indeed, he is."

Kjell sighed. "I am sorry you could not marry the manor lord's son. He was your true love, *nei*?"

She grimaced. "At one time, but that has passed. I hope he has found happiness."

Kjell leaned forward. "Indeed not. At least she brought a handsome dowry, so that is something."

Astra laughed aloud. "*Ja,* that is something."

Kjell smiled, too. He glanced around the farmyard then he asked, "So, you are working your farm all alone?"

Astra balked. He knew much of her life, including the most intimate event. He had worked for the manor and must be trustworthy. Still, she was alone. "I am getting by," she said.

Kjell cleared his throat. "I do not mean to pry. You have nothing to fear from me. I will soon be on my way. Before I go, perhaps there is work I can do to repay you for the meal? For a night's lodging in the barn, and a sausage or two, I will work hard and help you with any chores you have."

Astra's heart raced. She was falling further behind on the work day by day. How badly she needed help! Could she trust him when she could not even trust her own cousin?

She said, "I could use some help with a few things, but I am afraid I am low on food myself."

He smiled. "Then we are two of a kind. I can hunt and do any chores in exchange for porridge and a bed. Then I must figure out where to go next. As you see, I have nothing."

Astra smoothed the downy whisps on the baby's head. Was the hunter a gift from the Blessed Virgin, to whom she prayed for help every day? If so, he would still have to prove himself. Setting her jumble of feelings aside, she said, "How about three days?"

He stood up and bowed to her. "I am grateful. Put me to work."

Astra led him to the stable and pointed to an empty stall. "You can sleep here. There is a little straw in the loft. I will bring you a sheepskin."

Kjell seemed pleased. "This will do well. What is the first job?"

Dozens of undone tasks came to her mind—which was most pressing? "I have used up my firewood and have to gather sticks, for which I search farther afield every day. If you are willing to cut down a tree and chop rounds, that would be a great help. I find I am not as good with the broad axe as I thought."

She pointed out the woodshed, then led him to the workshop. He picked out the tools he needed and swung the axe over his shoulder.

"Kjell?" Astra's mouth went dry. The most grueling unfinished task ate at her every day.

He turned. "Something else?"

"While you are here, I need help with a task, a most gruesome task."

"Oh? And what might that be? A dead animal caught in the fence?"

She swallowed and held back tears. When she was able to speak she said, "It is my father. He disappeared in a snowstorm and I finally found him…in the forest..." The last words trailed off.

Kjell blew a sympathetic breath. "Of course. Not something anyone should do alone."

She turned and hurried back to the house.

At midday Astra carried Gunnar and a lunch basket to where she had heard the sharp cracks of the axe all morning. She stopped at the top of the slope watching Kjell chop a fallen trunk. Many log rounds were already scattered about. His shirtless chest and arms glistened with sweat. Inexplicably, a rush of heat bloomed in her cheeks.

He looked up, smiled, and wiped his brow.

She lifted the lunch basket high. "Are you hungry?"

Kjell drove the axe into a log and stretched backward. "Indeed."

She set the basket down and swung the baby off her back. "It is not much—flat *brød* and dried lamb."

"Sounds like a feast to me. I could eat an elk." Kjell's grin made her feel at ease. He turned two log rounds upright and sat on one, patting the other. "Join me."

She watched him gobble the meal, regretting her meager offering. She had forgotten how much a man could eat.

Kjell wiped his hands on his grimy trousers. "*Takk*," he said. Again, he smiled at her.

Chagrined that she had not offered him a wash bucket when he arrived, she determined to do so when he returned to the house. "I will bring more food," she said, standing.

"*Nei*, this is enough. I should be finished before supper. Do you have a sledge to haul the wood to the woodshed?"

"I will hitch up my horse when you are ready."

He stood up and nodded to the bundle she held. "May I see the baby?"

She hesitated, thinking of Nikolina's grasping hands. But Kjell was a farm hand, a hunter, not a kidnapper. She tugged back the cloth.

"He is so little," Kjell said. "How old is he?"

"Three months, maybe more. I burned my calendar stick one night by mistake."

Kjell chuckled. "I lost mine years ago."

Astra laughed with him. It felt good.

"I hope you were not alone when the baby was born," he said.

"My cousin was here for a time, but she left suddenly."

Kjell touched the child's soft pate. The look of tenderness in his eyes moved her. He had lost his own son. She longed to trust him, yet she had promised herself never to trust anyone. She swaddled the baby in the cloths and slung him onto her back.

Kjell picked up the axe. "If you will allow me to borrow a horse tomorrow morning, I will go hunting. How does fresh venison sound?"

Her mouth watered at the thought. Only one dried leg of the lamb that the wolf killed remained in the *stabbur*, and it was nearly unchewable. This and squirrels she caught in her traps were her only meats. But could she trust this man with one of her horses? What if he just left and did not return?

She hedged. "I do not know..."

Kjell smiled. "Let me clip the horses' hooves for you, even if I do not go hunting. They are quite overgrown and starting to crack. You do not want a lame horse."

He was observant and helpful. She decided to risk lending him Farwa. "Take the old *fjording*." If by chance he ran, she would still have Kvikke.

Kjell dusted crumbs from his beard. "I will walk back with you. This axe is as dull as a fence post." Astra smiled. She had done her best with the whetstone.

By suppertime, a neat pile of split firewood was stacked handily in the *svalgang*, and the woodshed was partly filled. Gunnar was asleep in his basket next to Astra as she harvested a few small vegetables to add to a soup pot.

Kjell approached, holding up a skinned rabbit. She smiled and gladly accepted it. Soon it boiled over the indoor hearth. The savory aroma seemed sent from heaven.

When she stepped outside to call Kjell to supper, she saw that he had washed himself—his hair was still wet. He had built a fire in the pit that crackled merrily. Two stools were nearby, one adorned with wild flowers. Kjell smiled when he saw her and shoved chunks of pitchy pine into the growing flames so that it crackled.

Astra looked aside to hide her smile. While they sat and ate by the fire, light rain sprinkles fell, dotting her kirtle. She retrieved her cloak and slung it over her shoulders. "If rain today, good harvest tomorrow," she said, quoting Far. Then she added, "Let us wait until tomorrow after your hunt to go for my father. I can face it better in the morning."

Kjell slurped the last of the rabbit stew from his bowl, leaned back and grinned at Astra. "Ah, now that was delicious. Your mother must have taught you well."

"*Nei*, it was only your rabbit that made the meal." She blushed. "Speaking of rabbits, I need some tips on setting traps. I have tried the larger ones several times, but nearly took my hand off."

"My wife had the same trouble," he said. "I will show you a trick tomorrow."

They sat quietly by the fire as the light of the overcast evening slowly waned. Kjell glanced up from whittling a stick. "Do you intend to stay here for the winter alone?"

She bristled. "This is my family farm."

"It is difficult for a woman by herself. Winter is long, even perilous. Perhaps you should go to Sjodrun." He blew the chaff from his carving.

"*Nei*, I have to stay here to keep my land. This is the Little King's…" She corrected herself. "Gunnar's farm."

Kjell glanced up and smiled. "The Little King. I like that."

"That is what Nikolina called him. She thought he would have a more honorable life if he went with her and…Vegar."

Kjell frowned. "Is she with Vegar?"

Astra told him of Nikolina's deception, and how she tried to steal the baby with the help of the *sysselmand*.

Kjell whistled low. "So, your cousin ran to that serpent's tongue. That is despicable, but believable."

"I never want to see either of them again."

"Your cousin is heartless. That was a beastly betrayal."

"And Vegar is a cowardly carrion-eater and a fish-bellied liar."

He laughed. "Also, apt words."

Somewhat chagrined by her outburst, Astra stood up. "I must say good night." She grabbed the basket and disappeared into the house. Outside she heard her guest kick the fire apart and walk away.

Lying in the darkness, she thought about what Kjell had said. Her cousin was beastly. Astra may have been hard on Nikolina, but her doubts were proved right by her cousin's back-stabbing. That girl was nothing but a laggardly baby thief.

Feeling vindicated, her thoughts turned to what else Kjell had said. Even if she somehow gathered enough food and fuel, how would she feed the animals and survive the winter alone? More wolves might come, deep snow, bitter cold. The thought of the long season of lonely nights sent dread burrowing into her marrow.

When Astra got up early the next morning, she saw that Farwa was gone from the pasture. She called for Kjell in the stable but he did not answer. Then she noticed that her father's spear and bow were missing, too. Would the hunter come back with food? Would he come back at all? She prayed to Mother Mary. She must wait.

Kvikke trotted to greet her as she poured water into the trough. She stroked the horse's forehead and smoothed the black and white forelock. Then she noted that Kvikke's hooves were neatly trimmed. She smiled to herself. One less task for her to attempt, and possibly fail.

Astra went about her morning work. She milked and hauled the bucket to the cheese house. With no sheep gut in which to age the milk, she stirred thistles into the bucket. She started a smoky fire in the pit with the green wood Kjell had chopped. Steam was just rising from a pot of water when she heard hoof beats.

"Good morning," Kjell called. He pulled Farwa to a stop. A deer was flung over the horse's croup.

Astra's heart jumped. She stirred the porridge. "You are back."

"Did you have doubts?" His eyes glinted playfully.

She set the spoon on a rock and walked over to examine the stag. "A fine buck you have," she said.

He swung off. "He gave me a good chase and this nag could barely keep up. Your father's spear is true, though. We can be grateful to him for that." He slapped the buck's flank. "We will feast tonight."

In late afternoon, Astra found Kjell working in the pasture. He had built a small booth to trap the sheep and was clipping their feet, as well as finishing the ragged shearing job she and Nikolina had attempted. He had even shorn the ram, which she would never have dared to do.

Stopping at the gate, she waited until he let the last ewe go.

"Kjell?"

He turned, his bare back slick from his work. "*Ja?*"

"We should go to the grove soon, before dark. I would like to get it over with." Ever since she found Far's remains she had wondered if she would ever be able to move him to the family cemetery—she had not the strength to move the fallen branch, nor the fortitude to handle his broken body. She had only once returned to his resting place to lay flowers and cover him with rocks. Kjell's help would bring him home.

"You are right," he said. "Daylight is best for such a task. If you point the way I can do it myself."

Astra shook her head. "*Nei*, I must go with you."

Together they hitched Kvikke to the sledge. Kjell grabbed a few tools and Astra tossed in a large sheepskin blanket. She led the way to the downed pine. When they arrived, she set the baby's basket nearby and stepped carefully among the broken branches until she spied the pile of rocks. Grasses had sprouted from where her father lay. She stepped back, smothering a sob with her elbow.

"Let me," Kjell said, tugging her away by the arm. Astra sat on a nearby rock to wait. Kjell grabbed the axe and began to chop away the branches. Each sharp strike pounded a nail through her.

When he had cut through the fallen log and shoved it away with his foot, he cleared the grave of rocks.

"Ready," he said, turning to catch Astra's eyes.

She stepped forward and peered down at the ravaged body. A cry of sorrow, regret, and horror escaped her mouth. Kjell loosened the soil with a shovel, then nodded for Astra to back away. She brought the sheepskin from the sledge and watched as Kjell spread it over her father's cadaverous remains. He carried the skin-wrapped bundle in his arms to the sledge.

"You go ahead," he said. "I will carry him home."

"*Nei*, put him in the sledge," she insisted.

He said reverently, "Please allow me. It is my honor."

Astra mounted and flicked Kvikke's reins. The horse trudged back up the hill pulling the empty sledge while Kjell followed, carrying his grisly burden. Astra was touched that Kjell would walk her father all the way home, and relieved that he could not see her face slick with tears.

Astra sat on the ground by the oak tree feeding the baby while Kjell dug the grave. Suddenly, she remembered the *likglugg*. Most other family members had been passed through the hole in the old house so their spirits would not haunt the farm.

"Kjell?" she queried.

He stopped shoveling and looked up. "*Ja?*"

"We should pass him through the *likglugg*."

"The what?"

"The hole in the house wall. You know, to prevent his soul from wandering." How could he not know this?

Kjell straightened up and stared at her. "I have never heard of such a thing. And I have never seen a soul wandering after they died. That must just be your family's tradition."

"*Nei*, they do it in Sjodrun, too," she argued.

Kjell rested his crossed arms on the shovel. "He has been gone a long time now and you have not seen his ghost, have you?"

She shook her head.

"Then he must be at rest. Besides, I do not see how you and I could pass him through a hole in the wall, not in his condition..."

Astra understood. The body was crushed. She nodded and motioned for him to dig on.

When the hole was deep enough, Kjell lowered her father gently down. He crawled out of the grave and started to fill the hole.

"Wait," she cried. "We must say something."

"*Ja*, of course." He put the shovel down and offered her his hand.

Silently at first, then with wracking sobs, she wept. Kjell wrapped her in his arms and held her tightly. At last, her heaving eased into staccato-laden breaths and she pushed away.

When she could speak, she recited holy words that came to her mind, knowing they were not the correct burial words. "Into your hands I commend his spirit. From dust we were made and to dust we shall return. Amen."

"Amen," Kjell said, "He was a good man, Astra. I did not know him well, but he raised you and cared for his ailing family. He must have been strong and godly. I will make a cross for him tomorrow."

Astra picked up the fussing baby and held him to her shoulder. She whispered into Gunnar's ear, "That is your *bestefar*. He would have loved you so."

She bent down for a fistful of dirt and tossed it into the pit. Kjell did the same, then filled the hole. They sat down side-by-side before the grave until the crickets began to chirp.

The three days of Astra's agreement with Kjell turned into weeks as they worked ceaselessly. Together they plowed the rye field and planted seeds. No matter how early Astra rose, she found Kjell already toiling. He fired up the forge and repaired hinges and tools. He replaced the birch bark on the *stabbur* and re-sodded it. He buried the rotted pig carcass and rebuilt the bath house that had fallen in from the heavy snow. He cut the broken branch away from the summer house and repaired the roof.

As more and more tasks were completed, and more game meat was smoked, Astra started to think that she would not have to go to the manor for help after all. With no talk of when Kjell might leave, she secretly began to hope she would not have to winter alone.

On Lord's Days, or what they guessed to be the Lord's Days, Kjell struck off into the forest alone, saying only that he needed to tame his thoughts. She remembered her own solitary rides, though she no longer needed time to herself. In fact, she felt lonely when Kjell was gone. As she went about her chores, she pictured Kjell's powerful arms pounding on the anvil, his muscles tensing beneath his wadmal shirt, his naked back when he washed himself at the well. She had noticed his gray-blue eyes peering at her when he thought she was not looking. Feelings welled up inside her, feelings she once had for Einarr. When Kjell returned from his Lord's Day rides, his mood was lifted and he always brought a stoat or a fowl as an offering. Each time he returned, her fears that he would not come back at all were allayed.

One sunny morning, Kjell helped Astra move the furniture out of the winter house so she could thoroughly clean—she had not done so at *Jul*, nor at Easter, as tradition prescribed. She scrubbed the sooty walls as high as she could reach, beat and aired the skins, washed the linens, and restuffed both mattresses with dried grasses and wild flowers. As she was stuffing the second tick, she asked herself why she needed two beds. She realized she was doing this in case Kjell stayed until the weather turned. He could not spend the winter in the stable, and having him in the house would be a great comfort. She felt ashamed when she imagined him coming to her bed, both desiring and fearing such intimacy. Would she turn him away?

Late in the afternoon when she emerged from the freshened house, soot-smudged and exhausted, she found Kjell roasting a ptarmigan on a spit over the fire. She plucked Gunnar out of his basket and bounced the restless baby on her hip.

"Oh, bless you," she puffed. "I am famished. Let me wash up."

"I will hold Gunnar for you," he offered.

She hesitated. In the weeks since he arrived, she had never let him hold the child.

Kjell held his arms out. "I know how to hold a baby. I will not take him away from you. You can trust me."

She paused, stroked the Little King's feathery head, then set the baby in his arms. When she had washed and rejoined him at the fire, Kjell was singing a soft lullaby and suckling the baby with his smallest finger. Gunnar's eyes blinked slowly, about to fall asleep. She waited until the child was still, then laid him in his basket.

Kjell speared a hindquarter of the savory bird for her.

She rolled her eyes. "Delicious. All the more so because I did not cook it."

He laughed. "This is how I cook every night when I am on my own."

"You have seen how I cook every night," she laughed. "You can be the cook from now on."

Kjell gazed at her so that she blushed. "Meals are made better by sharing," he said softly.

Astra devoured everything including the gristle, and sucked the marrow before tossing the scraps to the dogs.

She poured ale, dribbling the last drops into his horn. "I am afraid this is the end of the barrel. No more until the barley ripens."

"Ah, a shame." He seemed truly regretful. They drained the horns in silence.

The fire sizzled from the sappy wood, popping loudly and sending sparks swirling into the sky like fireflies. Kjell set about whittling. A small pile of shavings grew at his feet. Astra watched, reminded of her father's fine skill with wood.

Without looking up Kjell said, "Tell me what happened to your family."

Astra took a deep breath. Stopping occasionally when her words refused to come, she recounted each soul-piercing loss. After telling of Mar's passing, and that they had never made amends, she stopped and covered her face with her apron. Kjell set his whittling down and took her hand. She squeezed it hard.

"What about your family?" she asked, wiping her face. "You must tell me, too."

He was silent at first, then spoke only briefly. "My son was already gone when I arrived home. Oda passed very soon after."

"Where did you bury them?"

"Near our cabin, in the woods."

"Have you gone back to visit their graves?"

"*Nei.*" He picked up his whittling.

"Not yet," she said. It seemed he did not want to talk more, so she changed the subject. "Where did you go after that? Tell me about your travels."

His answer was likewise curt. "To Nidaros, then Stiklestad, then north. There is not much to tell besides hunting." His face sobered.

She asked no more.

From a distance a wolf howled, then another.

"Wolves! I despise wolves," Astra said. "One took three of my sheep last year."

He glanced up. "Did you see it?"

"*Ja*, I saw it near the barn one night, then found it taking a lamb."

"Did your father kill it?"

"Far was gone by then. I killed it myself."

"You what?" The wooden figurine he was carving dropped, and he bent to pick it up.

"He killed my sheep right in my pasture!" Her voice rose. "I had to stop him or he would have eaten them all one by one."

Kjell stared at her. "How did you kill it?"

"With Far's bow, then I stabbed him."

Kjell whistled low. "That is impressive. Especially for a woman."

Astra kicked at his leg. "Women are brave when they need to be."

He laughed. "I would say you are right." Kjell paused, caught her eyes, then said, "I have never before met anyone like you."

Her neck grew red in the dark. "Well, now you have."

"Now I have." He chuckled again. "You are...remarkable." He held the wood carving up and blew the sawdust away, revealing a small Norse horse. "For the Little King," he said, handing it to her.

"He will love it." She grinned broadly at such an unexpected gift.

Their labors continued through the warmest part of summer and into early autumn. Astra wove and sewed winter clothing, including a new tunic and a cloak for Kjell. She planted crops, made cheese, dried meats, and hung herbs in the rafters. When Kjell shot a wild boar, she rendered tallow for candles and soap. The smokehouse smoldered for days. Kjell made deer-hide boots for them both. Enough wood was stacked in the woodshed to last a year, even more.

One day Astra remarked that Gunnar was getting heavy, so Kjell strapped the baby on his own back while they cut field grasses, reaped rye, and gathered foliage for winter feed. She acquiesced to his request to call Gunnar the Little King. From his lips, she grew to like it, mostly because he used it so lovingly.

At the end of each diminishing day Astra and Kjell ate together. If the sky was clear they dined in the yard by the pit fire and Kjell cooked. If it rained, they ate Astra's stew in the house. Often, they talked long after the Little King was asleep and the sky had grown dark. Before he left for the stable, Kjell kissed her good night—first on the forehead, then the cheek, until once, she turned her mouth to meet his. He stroked her cheek and smiled.

She held onto his hand. "Sleep in the other bed, if you like."

"*Nei*, I am comfortable in the stable." Kjell stumbled over the doorstep and left hurriedly that night.

In the morning Astra was glad he refused her offer, for she knew she could not long resist inviting him to her bed. Each night she thought about him until she fell asleep. At times she hugged one of the pillows, pretending it was he. She longed to hold him, but she also feared the act of love. She would not want another child, not alone. He had not said when he might leave, but she thought perhaps when the harvest was finished.

Frustrated, she decided not to reach out to him anymore. That was the way to stay unscathed.

The days and nights were growing colder. Leaves on the birch and aspen yellowed. Kjell came back from the field one day and announced that the oats were ready for harvest. For two days he swept the sickle while Astra followed behind, tying up bundles with twine. At the end of each day, she could hardly stand up straight. Then, finally, they harvested the barley.

More days were spent slapping the sheaves against the threshing stone, the chaff covering them both and setting them to coughing. They filled all the grain bins in the *stabbur*, setting aside a good amount of barley for brewing.

Astra was finally able to try her hand at ale-making. She had helped her mother thrice before, but she worried that her ale would be weak or bitter. When Kjell tried the first of the barrel, he grinned broadly and downed the drink.

He crowed, "Nothing like fresh ale to get the heart pumping."

The next day Astra invited him for a harvest feast. She stewed a rabbit with an eel from the stream, adding garden herbs, a cabbage, and wild mushrooms. She baked fresh *brød* in the earthen oven to be slathered with freshly churned butter. She asked Kjell to roast a trout, but he caught a salmon instead. He claimed it was the best meal he had ever tasted.

After supper, Kjell was unusually talkative. Astra filled and refilled their horns. He spoke of the *katedral* in Nidaros with its great towers and flagellating pilgrims. He told her about his visit to his home, taken over by his *onkel* and *tante*, and the family graves up in the high country. Growing more animated, he talked of the Saami people and their unusual ways, speaking the few words he knew in their language, to her amazement. He stood up and spread his arms to show her the size of his small snow cave, and described the luminous northern aurora and its ethereal impact on him. Excitedly, he described shooting the brown bear, and killing the wolf that killed his best dog.

Astra listened, worrying. She saw excitement in his eyes, and realized how much he loved the wild. Would he ever give up the hunt to settle down on a farm? From the animation in his voice, she doubted it. She should bury the expectations that had taken seed in her heart.

In return, she told Kjell about how her Far had taken her under his wing after her brother died and taught her much of the men's work.

"That is why you are so capable, and so cheeky," Kjell said, lightly slapping her knee.

"And that is why I learned to love horses." She laughed over-much and realized, with dismay, that she was quite tipsy.

"I need to…go," said she, standing up and squirming. Kjell followed her into the dark as she hurried around behind the house. When she tripped over a stone, he caught her.

She giggled, leaning her head against his chest. A warm rush of ardor swept over her.

Kjell turned his back as she squatted, then held her elbow until they got to the door.

"I will see you in the morning," he said thickly.

Astra clasped his arm. "*Nei*, do not leave me here alone. Come in. I have had too much ale."

He smiled. "Indeed, you have. And I." He helped her into the house where she sat down heavily on the bed. She struggled to take off her shift discreetly, finally just lifting it over her head, baring her breasts. Kjell did not turn away.

She pointed to her night dress hanging on the bed post. Kjell handed it to her and she slipped it on, then flopped down on the bed. The room spun. She wanted more than anything for him to lie beside her, to feel his warmth and his touch, to have him hold her, to love her.

Kjell lifted the Little King out of the cradle and laid him next to her on the bed. She opened her night dress to nurse, unabashed that Kjell watched. If Mar knew what she was doing she would be mortified. But Mar was not here; Kjell was.

He sat on a stool next to the bed and smoothed her hair back from her face.

"I am a bit dizzy," she said. "Are you going to sleep here?"

He stroked her cheek. "You are very beautiful. And very *drukken*."

She smiled slyly and pointed. "In Nikolina's bed, I mean. Over there." The memory of the king's body atop her own flashed through her thoughts. But this man was different. He cared for her. He would never hurt her. Did he love her? She reached out and grasped his shirt, pulling him close. He kissed her lips. She felt his hot breath on her neck.

"Sleep with me," she whispered.

Breathing heavily, he kissed her once more, then pushed away. "Strong ale makes brave words. I want to, you must know it. But not like this." Before she could say more, he was gone.

The next evening, sated with the remains of stew and roasted salmon, Astra stood at the loom while Kjell whittled by the fire. She wrestled with what to say, embarrassed about her wantonness the previous night, and chagrined by his rejection. Thoughts tumbled over one another like stones in a waterfall. How long would he stay? Would he be here through the winter? Longer? She wanted to ask him to stay forever but was afraid he would say *nei*.

"Kjell?" she said.

"Hm?" He did not look up.

The shuttle flew back and forth in her hands. "I need some supplies—salt, beeswax, honey, a few new barrels."

"A new plow blade, whetstone, and bellows," he added.

She grinned.

"We should go to Sjodrun," said he. "It would be good for you to get away for a day."

She shook her head. "I do not want to go there…no one there knows about the Little King, unless Vegar has told them."

"I will go then. It is no one else's business about the baby. I have eleven pelts prepared and I can trade those. I will get what I can with them."

"I have coins. Let me get them."

"Keep your coins. You will need them later."

"How will you explain that you are here with me?"

"I will say you hired me for the harvest."

"There is something else I need to ask you." Astra's stomach churned. She stopped the shuttle and turned to look at him. "What will you do when the harvest is finished? I must know."

He bent to stir the fire. "I do not know yet."

She felt heartsick. She had hoped he would ask to stay. "Are you going north? If so, you deserve pay for your work. Take Kvikke."

"*Nei*, I would not take your prized horse."

"You can take Far's weapons and traps, whatever you need...if you are going."

"I had thought of hiring on at the manor like I did last year. If you think I should, I can ask when I go."

She felt desperate. "That would be good—for you and the manor, but not me and the Little King. Is that what you want?"

"Astra." He took her hand and she sat beside him. "I want to stay here. I care greatly for you, but there are things about me you do not know. If you knew, you would not want me to stay."

"What things? Your past does not matter to me."

He squeezed her hand. "I will go to the manor first thing tomorrow. No need to make porridge for me."

Astra woke early enough to watch Kjell lead Kvikke and the sledge into the yard. It was loaded with a pile of deerskins.

"When will you be back?" she called.

"Tonight." He waved.

"Wait." She ran to the *stabbur* and dug out the king's bracelet she had hidden there. She did not look at it. Just the thought of it brought feelings of loathing. She ran to where Kjell waited atop Kvikke.

"Use this to buy what you need for yourself. Consider it the wages I owe you." She handed him the bag.

He peered in at the gold bracelet. "Ah *nei*, I will not take a family heirloom." He tried to hand it back to her.

She clasped her hands behind her back. "It is not an heirloom. I cannot stand the sight of it."

He gazed at her questioningly. "Where did it come from?"

Astra's face reddened. "You can guess."

"Ah, I can. But you may need it in the future. Besides, you owe me no wages. Room and board, remember?"

She stepped further away so he could not hand her the bag. "Use this to buy your own supplies. Then I will give you Farwa for your hunt." She could not keep a smile from her face at the thought of this hunter riding an old sway-backed mare into the snowy north.

He laughed. "I do not believe you, you know that." He stuck the bag into his pouch. "I will be back soon."

"If you see Einarr, tell him…" She stopped. What could she possibly tell Einarr now? "Tell him nothing." She whacked Kvikke's rump and the horse jumped forward.

Chapter 33

All the way to Sjodrun, Kjell pondered whether to buy a horse with the king's bracelet and the skins—Astra had offered, after all. With a horse he could travel again, go north, hunt, spend another season gathering pelts that would bring in money for…for what? He would not return to Hamar, having forfeited his inheritance. Where else did he wish to go? He knew the answer: only back to Astra. She had become dear to him, she and the Little King. They both seemed like family now. Yet, if Astra truly knew him, the things he had done, she would rebuff him. How could he tell her? How could he not? He decided he would not buy a horse, at least not now.

When he arrived at the manor, he found that Didrik was out hunting with Einarr for the day. He must wait to conduct his business. He worried about returning late—Astra might think he was not coming back. He spent the afternoon helping the stable hand.

Einarr and Didrik did not return until dusk. Einarr paid no heed to Kjell as he handed his horse over to the stable boy along with a string of grouse.

But Didrik greeted Kjell with a handshake and asked, "Here you are, my friend. How is it you have Astra Svensdatter's horse and sledge?"

"In my travels I came upon her farm. She hired me to help with the harvest and she needs a few supplies."

Didrik slapped him on the back. "It is good that you are helping Astra, since her cousin left her alone, I hear."

Kjell looked around to make sure no one was in earshot. "Her cousin was deceitful, I understand, so she must work the farm alone, except for me. I am just a hired hand."

By the time Kjell and Didrik completed the trade, it had grown dark. The skins were worth only enough for some of Astra's supplies. The plow blade would have to wait.

"You must stay for supper," Didrik said.

Kjell tried to refuse but the head man insisted, pulling him by the arm to his own small cottage. There Kjell saw Einarr's sister, Hedda. She and Didrik had a baby girl a little younger than Astra's son. The men ate, told tales, and drank ale.

Shortly after supper, Hedda excused herself, saying she needed something from the manor. She returned, bringing her brother with her. Einarr invited Kjell for another drink in the Great Hall, telling Kjell he had something to discuss. There was no way to refuse.

The two sat by a fire in the empty hall. Einarr poured horns of ale. The young man wasted no time on niceties. "I hear you are working at the Sven Larsson farm," he said.

"For the harvest," Kjell replied.

Einarr leaned toward him on his elbows. "And Astra has a child, a boy?"

Kjell absently rubbed the smooth planks of the table. What did Einarr want?

The lord's son waited for a response. Getting none, he said, "Vegar Eriksson told me she lives alone now with the baby. I need you to take a message to her."

"What message?" Kjell swigged his ale.

"You are there through the harvest, but after that she will be by herself. I have been waiting for her to come here for help, and now I know why she has not. Did she tell you Nikolina married Vegar?"

Kjell shook his head. "Only that her cousin left after a falling-out."

"Maybe she does not know. Nevertheless, you will make her an offer from me." This was an order given to an inferior. Kjell bristled.

"Tell her she is to come and live here at the manor. We will bring her cattle to our barns and next year her farm will be leased. She will retain ownership of the land, and it will be passed on to her son. In addition, I will give her and the baby a home here at no cost."

Kjell frowned. There must be something in it for Einarr. "This seems over-generous. How shall I explain your offer?"

Einarr sat back and clasped his hands on the table. "I want to see her live as a lady, to have an easier life than that of a farmer. We were close as children and now she is alone and needs me. She should be here." Einarr clapped his hands together and smiled as if the deal were settled.

Kjell crossed his arms and leaned back. "And leave her family farm? Why would she come when she is doing fine on her own? You are already married."

Einarr glanced around the empty room. He lowered his voice. "My wife has turned out to be...difficult. As they say, 'Everyone knows what to do with a bad wife but he who has her.'"

Kjell understood clearly enough. "So then, am I to tell Astra there would be obligations?"

Einarr blanched. "When you put it that way it seems untoward. But this is not your affair, hunter. I have found a solution for both of us."

Kjell downed his ale and started to rise.

Einarr grabbed his arm. "Listen. Astra and I wanted to wed, but you likely know that Mother made me promise to marry Steinulv. How could I refuse?"

Kjell jerked his arm away. "Do you truly believe she will agree to be your mistress?"

Einarr leaned forward and whispered, "I do. I just need you to fertilize the soil before I come and talk to her myself. I will reward you." He pulled out a gold coin and pushed it across the table toward Kjell. "There is more for you if she agrees."

Kjell stiffened, incensed. "She will not do it."

Einarr stood as well, his jaw clenching and unclenching. "Different times make different people. Say you will at least ask her."

"You will have to make that offer yourself," said Kjell. He shoved the coin away and marched out, disgusted by the fish-bellied prick. Even if his life were threatened, Kjell would never make Einarr's proposal to Astra.

When he reached the darkened bunk house where he was to sleep, he slammed his fist against the boards, causing the slumbering livery boy to grumble.

Astra flew out of the house when Kjell drove the sledge into the yard the next morning. "Welcome back." She grinned and looked relieved.

Kjell smiled and swung off. "I had to wait all day for Didrik, so it was too late to come last night."

"But where is your new horse?"

He pouted falsely. "Sadly, they had none to sell."

She set her hands on her hips. "I doubt that. You are very untrustworthy."

Kjell reached beneath his shirt. "Here is what is left of your treasure." He tossed the empty velvet bag to her.

"So, you spent it on ale, then?"

Kjell laughed. "I was able to get some supplies with the hides alone. You may need it someday." He handed her the bracelet.

"Perhaps at Michaelmas we will have more to offer and they will have a horse for sale, for you," she said.

"Perhaps." But what about after that? He must make a decision about whether he would ask to stay on, and soon.

While she helped him unload the sledge she asked, "Did anyone ask about the Little King?"

"Only Einarr. Apparently Vegar told him."

She was chagrined. "What did he say?"

Kjell did not want to talk about Einarr. "Nothing much, just that he knew."

"Nothing?" Her face fell.

"He asked if you were well." Kjell's heart palpitated at his untruth. She still had feelings for the scoundrel.

"Did he send me a greeting, at least?"

"*Nei*, but Hedda did. She has a fine *datter* now. She sends you a kiss."

Astra thrust her cheek forward and tapped her cheek, just as her mother had done to her father. "Then give it."

Kjell kissed her cheek lightly, feeling heat rise. She smelled of fire and fresh *brød*.

Two days later Kjell was replacing a sledge runner while Astra held the rail in place when they heard hooves thundering up the path. They both turned. Kjell dropped his adze and ran out of the workshop, knife in hand.

"Stay back," he commanded her, but she did not heed his words and ran quickly to his side.

Two riders galloped into the yard. Einarr and Vegar pulled up hard and their horses skidded to a halt.

Astra whispered, "What do they want?"

"Nothing good, I wager." Kjell started forward but Astra held his arm back. "Let me go first," she said.

Einarr bounced off his steed's back, glanced at Kjell, and bowed to Astra. "We come for a visit. It has been too long."

Vegar dismounted and dipped his head to her. "Greetings."

Astra ignored Vegar and reached her hand out to Einarr, smiling. He embraced her instead.

The hug was too long, Kjell thought. The young master had come to convince Astra to accept his improper proposal, and she was glad to see him. Would she accept? Kjell had made no commitment to help her, nor had she asked for any. He backed up a step, wondering if he was mistaken about her.

When Astra drew back from Einarr, red-faced, she said, "Kjell told me all was well at the manor. I assume you have no bad news?"

"We have good news," said Einarr. "The good news first, as you may have already heard." He glanced at Kjell.

Kjell had not "fertilized the soil" as Einarr demanded. He said nothing, kicking at the dirt.

Einarr nodded Kjell toward the barn, saying, "You may go back to your work, huntsman. This visit has naught to do with you."

Kjell balled his fists, perturbed by Einarr's haughtiness and worried about what might transpire. "This is a free-owned farm. I work for the landowner, not you."

Astra looked at them both quizzically and picked up the baby's basket. "No need to quarrel. Let us have some ale."

Vegar followed them, and as he passed Kjell he sneered, "You heard him. This is not your business."

Kjell remained planted, unsure whether he should follow. Was he indeed just a hired hand, now that Einarr was here?

As if in answer to his thoughts, Astra called over her shoulder, "You, too, Kjell."

She led them to the outdoor firepit. She asked Kjell to start a fire, then took the sleeping baby inside. Einarr and Vegar sat on upturned log rounds while Kjell knelt to strike the spark. He felt Einarr's eyes on him. Soon Astra emerged with the ale jug and horns for all four.

"Why is this man here, Astra?" Einarr asked, nodding toward Kjell. "He should be working to earn his keep."

"He works hard every day and deserves ale, just like you," she replied.

"It is not proper that he is here with you alone on the farm," Einarr said. "You should know that."

Kjell glanced up. Einarr dared speak of what was proper when he was about to ask her to become his lover?

"What business is this of yours?" Astra said to Einarr. She heard the baby cry and hurried back to the house to retrieve his basket. She sat it down and plucked up the fussing infant.

Kjell bent to his task and selected sticks to poke into the growing flame.

Einarr said to Astra, "The hunter did not tell you my proposal, did he?"

Astra patted the Little King against her shoulder and asked, "Proposal? What was it, Kjell?"

Kjell sat on his haunches and blew on the fire. "He must tell you himself."

Einarr straightened. "I thought not. I will be forthright, Astra. You cannot work a farm on your own. This hired hand will soon be gone. You will not survive the winter by yourself."

She said curtly, "In fact, I did survive the winter, with no help from you."

"Not by yourself, though," said Vegar. "You had Nikolina."

Kjell glanced up. Astra's eyes narrowed. "My cousin was more work than help," she said. "You need not worry about me. I can take care of myself."

"Can you?" Einarr asked.

"That is not what Nikolina told me," Vegar said. "She said you were both starving. She was very worried about the baby."

Astra raised her voice and began to swing her foot in agitation. "You mean *my* baby, Vegar? Niki is a thief, a liar, and a lazy cow. You deserve each other. Did you bother to marry her or just sleep with her like you tried to do with me?"

Vegar stood and raised his hand as if to strike her, but Kjell jumped up and drew his knife.

Einarr stepped between them. "Be calm, all of you. We are here to talk." Turning to Vegar he said, "I did not bring you along to make things worse."

Vegar's nostrils flared, but he sat.

Astra moved to the other side of the firepit, out of Vegar's reach, but closer to Einarr, who sat down. Kjell slid his knife into its sheath.

"I must speak to you alone, in the house," Einarr said, offering Astra his hand.

"*Nei*, we will speak here." She did not rise, pressing the baby to her neck.

"Very well," said Einarr. "This conversation goes no further than the four of us." He leaned close to Astra. "Look, you wanted me to speak to your father about your hand and I intended to, but fate interfered. As I told you, my marriage was not my choice. Now that I have seen my wife's true character, I find Steinulv conniving, derisive, and cold-hearted...not what I want from a wife. In all honesty, I will never love her. She makes me realize how much I miss you."

Through the smoke Kjell saw Astra's expression darken. Was she torn? Kjell wished he could reach out for her.

She sighed. "You and your wife are none of my affair. You must live the life given you, as must I."

Einarr leaned forward. "I wish to God she were not my wife, and that you were."

Astra's expression hardened. "At one time I wished this, too. But Einarr, it is too late for us. We cannot change our fate."

He reached for her hand. "I think we can. My offer is simple, and I am sure it will make you happy."

Astra did not take his hand. She kicked an ember into the fire. "Say it."

"I want you to come to live at the manor. You will have your own house and a servant, and you may retain your land. I will find a tenant to farm it. We can be together as we promised each other, as we always wanted to be."

Her brows knitted. "Since you already have a wife, what would be my position? A friend? What are you asking?"

"He wants you for his lover," Kjell interjected.

Einarr first glared at Kjell, then turned to Astra. "That way we will both be happy. Please come with me. Come now. I will send others to bring your cattle."

Astra rocked the baby in her lap, her face unreadable. "I did love you, Einarr. Once I hoped I would be your wife, but my parents would be ashamed and broken-hearted if I did what you propose. How can you ask it of me?"

Einarr said quickly, "Do not think of it like that. I ask because I love you. I will provide you with everything you need, a house of your own, goods, food, and a future for your son. What more could I give you?"

Her voice sounded doubtful. "I would get all this in return for being your mistress?"

Kjell tensed. What if she accepted his offer? Indeed, why would she not?

"*Nei,* my second wife. I will adopt your son, raise him as an heir, and give you more children."

She tensed, staring at Einarr. "There is no such thing as a second wife, Einarr. You already have a wife."

"I know of other lords who do this," he said. "It is common."

"I have never heard of this." She shook her head.

"In this time of pestilence and loss, who will forbid us?" Einarr reached toward her again, pleadingly.

Astra patted the now crying baby. "Even if true, it is not proper. It is sinful. This is too much to ask. It is beyond..." She handed the baby to Kjell. "I need time to think." She ran away and disappeared into the barn.

Kjell started after her but Einarr barked, "Stop, huntsman, let her think. She will change her mind and come with me when she realizes it is her only true choice."

"It is not her only choice," Kjell muttered. He rocked the baby and gave him his finger to suck on, clucking softly. The child soon quieted.

Watching him, Einarr scoffed, "Perhaps you have your own designs on her. You must know she could never love you as she loves me. I have everything to offer her, while you have nothing."

Kjell muttered, "At least I have no other wife."

Einarr clenched his fist, but Vegar interrupted them. "This is not helpful, Einarr. She wants you. She always has, as I well know. Just give her time. She will weigh the alternatives and come to you, just as you wish. Perhaps we should leave and return in a few days for her answer."

"*Nei*, I will not leave her here with him." Einarr eyed Kjell, who now paced the baby back and forth before the fire.

The men were silent for some time. Einarr threw sticks into the coals. Vegar spat on his hand and smoothed a loose strand of hair with his spittle.

Kjell walked about the yard until the child fell asleep, then set him in his basket. He feared that Einarr was right. What chance had he with such a beauty, even if she rejected Einarr's offer?

At last Astra walked back from the barn. Her eyes were swollen but she looked resolute. She took a deep breath.

"What say you?" Einarr asked, rising. "Come with me now, today. Let us seal the bargain." He held out his hand to her once more.

Astra did not take it. "Einarr," she said, "What you ask is very tempting, almost an answer to my prayers."

Kjell realized he was about to lose her.

"I would want for nothing and my son would have great advantage," she continued, "but I cannot be a second wife. I have a farm to run."

Einarr took her by the shoulders. "You have not lost me. I am willing to have you, Astra, even though you are sullied, even though you have a bastard son. Who else will take you in?"

Astra slapped him. "Get away from me! How could I be with someone like you who sees me as defiled and my son as unworthy?"

A red handprint marked Einarr's cheek. "I only speak the truth. I mean no offense. If you do not come now, you will come crawling to the manor in winter when you are starving. Even then I will take you in. I offer you your only chance to be happy."

Vegar added, "Though the terms will have changed, I am certain."

"Stay out of this, Vegar," Einarr snapped.

Astra said, "Just go."

Kjell drew his knife. "You heard what she said."

Einarr's face purpled. "You, hunter, do not order me." He backed up and unsheathed his sword. "I should cut you down. This is your fault. You have turned her against me."

Kjell flipped the knife into his palm, ready to throw. "You will be dead before I am," he said.

"*Nei*, please!" Astra cried. "Einarr, you have driven me away on your own. You married another and I have had to release you from my heart."

Einarr looked from Kjell to Astra and back. "Ah, now I see. I saw you with the baby, a ready hand. You have already bedded her and that is why she does not come with me."

Vegar laughed, throwing his head back. "Of course, that is it, the bitch."

"Rogue!" Kjell charged Einarr, his knife flashing.

Einarr thrust his sword but Kjell jumped aside and slashed Einarr's right arm, drawing a streak of blood down his sleeve. Einar tossed his sword to his left hand, cursing.

Vegar stepped in, backing Kjell away from Einarr with the tip of his blade. "You are nothing but a useless fool, a horse's ass. This is not your fight, hunter."

Astra screamed, "Stop, all of you!" She rushed between Kjell and Vegar, sweeping Vegar's sword aside. Red traced down her forearm. She clamped her hand over the wound as blood oozed between her fingers.

"Astra!" Kjell rushed toward her.

Einarr ran toward Kjell. "Get away from her!"

Kjell dove for Einarr's legs, sending him sprawling into the dirt. Einarr scrambled to his feet and brought the sword point to Kjell's neck.

Kjell froze. Astra screamed.

Vegar slowly lifted the weapon from Einarr's fist. "This is not the way, boy. She does not want you. She is a slut…she wants him."

Einarr lowered his weapon.

Kjell scrambled to Astra's side and bound her wound with his tunic.

Einarr dusted off his pantaloons, blood dripping from his arm. His face contorted and he screamed curses into the trees.

After Einarr and Vegar mounted their horses, Einarr spun around and halted. He hollered over his shoulder, "You will come to me eventually, Astra."

She shook her head and turned away as Einarr's horse jumped into a gallop.

Kjell held back a smile. Einarr's unseemly plan had failed. "I pity him, truly," he said. "He is a raven starver."

She murmured, "A lost soul."

They both stepped back when Vegar brought his steed about and came near. He said, "Though you did not ask after your cousin, I will tell you anyway. My wife is content in our home. We will have a child in the spring."

Astra sighed. "I am happy for her, then. Give her my congratulations."

Vegar twisted his horse's neck around and soon disappeared down the path.

Three quiet days passed wherein Astra and Kjell spoke of little but the farm chores. Then one afternoon, while Kjell was in the workshop, he heard the baby's babbling voice approaching the door. Astra stepped inside, shushing the Little King. She was dressed in a new frock and head linen. She looked contented. And beautiful.

"The Little King wants to know what you are doing," she said.

Kjell smiled. "Tell him I am fitting a new handle on this hammer." He held it up for the baby to see.

The Little King quieted and reached for him. Kjell gently took the baby from Astra's arms and tossed him in the air. He giggled, so Kjell did it again, and yet again.

"I want to invite you to sup with me," Astra said. "I lack company."

"Company, am I? I thought we were friends by now."

One side of her mouth smiled. "You are right. We are friends. I invite you because you are my only friend, in fact. Will you be ready to eat soon?"

He handed the baby back to Astra, noticing his blackened hands. Instinctively he rubbed them on the thighs of his breeches, making them more besmirched. "Let me wash up. I will be there shortly."

Astra smiled. "Good." She turned and marched away, flipping her braid behind her.

Kjell strode to the well where he washed his face, arms, and hands. What a fool I am, he thought. She called me her only friend but she does not know who I truly am. I should have told her about myself by now. When she knows, she will likely throw me out and run to that imperious boy-man. Einarr. If she rejects me, at least I will know that I need to move on.

Kjell changed into the clean shirt Astra had made for him and strode from the stable to the house. The scent of roasting meat and herbs drifted through the partially open doorway. He knocked.

"Come," she replied.

Astra had set up the board with a linen cloth, pewter plates and ale horns that he had never seen before. Bowls of nuts and roasted mushrooms, and a small vase of asters lent elegance to the table. Tapers of beeswax, a surprise Kjell had brought from Sjodrun, produced a comforting glow.

A shank of his latest kill, a red deer, now roasted on a spit over the fire. Kjell's stomach grumbled. Astra slathered brown *brød* with butter and placed it on a plate for him.

"What is the occasion?" he asked. "Is it your saint's day?"

"*Nei*, I was born after Epiphany, Saint Julian of Anazarbus's holy day." She nodded to the bench and he sat.

"Then to what do I owe this feast?"

She smiled. "It is not a feast, just a simple meal. It is I who owe you my gratitude. The harvest is in and there is plenty of food for winter. Together we have accomplished much. Are you hungry?"

"*Nei*, not really."

She kicked at him, but he moved his leg and she tripped on the chair leg. He caught her around the waist, gently pushing her upright again. She blushed and set the meat on a platter. Kjell savored the venison, thinking only of the curve of her waist. Astra refilled his horn as soon as he tipped the last drops into his mouth.

He gazed at her between bites. His oft-stolen glances while they worked together proved insufficient for him to appreciate her truly graceful comeliness, fully revealed in this candle-lit setting. At the same time, doubt drifted over his head like smoke. He must speak with her about his past so she would know…so he would know.

"Michaelmas is a couple of weeks away," he said. "Is there something you need in the village? I have several more pelts, and you have an excess of oats to trade."

"I do not want to go," she said. "You go. You can get the things you need for your trip north."

"My trip north, you say." Kjell's eyes clouded.

"If that is still your plan." Astra took a long swig of ale. "Kjell, I must know so I can prepare for winter on my own, if that is to be."

Kjell had been thinking continually about the long trek, the deep snow, the makeshift shelters, the dark nights alone. He no longer wanted that life. He yearned for a family. He yearned mostly for Astra. Now was the time to confess to her. Once she knew, he would beg for absolution and tell her of his love for her, a love that had sent roots deep into his soul. She would either accept or reject him, but at least he would know.

The fire popped and sent a spark flying. The baby gurgled on Astra's lap, and she fed him a morsel of *brød*.

Before he could speak, she said, "I have something to say."

Kjell felt a wave of panic. She was going to accept Einarr's offer after all. He had waited too long, the *djevel* take him!

Astra gave the baby a toy. Without looking up she said, "After Nikolina left I was unsure if I could stay on the farm. I thought of going to the manor, begging to become a servant."

"*Nei*, you must not." Kjell's brows furrowed.

She held up her hand. "If it were not for you I might be at the manor now and Einarr would be compelling me to be his mistress. He may have succeeded." She stopped, seeming to search for words, then continued, "I would be living a shameful life, at his mercy."

"You are stronger than he knows," Kjell said. His stomach knotted.

"I wonder," she continued, "if you would consider staying, at least for the winter...or even longer. You have been a godsend to me."

He lowered his head. "I am no godsend. Before I answer, I too have something to say. It is far worse than your confession." He swallowed, then forced out the words. "The law is after me." Immediately he regretted the manner of his disclosure, so blunt, so stark.

Astra's ale horn dropped and she scrambled to sop up the spill.

"I should have told you before," Kjell said, "but I have felt useful here, welcome and needed. Most of all I have enjoyed your companionship. I did not want to spoil our friendship."

She poured more ale for herself without looking at him. "What is it you have done?"

He paused, wondering how to soften the blow. She will likely throw him out. "I killed a knight," he said.

Her face paled. "What knight? I have no love for knights."

He reached for her hand but she did not take it. "I have never told this to another person, not even Oda." Then he told her of the night at the tavern, the attack on the innkeeper's *datter*, his unplanned act of vengeance against the soldier, and his continuing flight.

Astra listened silently. When he finished, she gave the baby another tidbit to gnaw on.

Kjell's soul was crushed. He said, "You see, that is why I hunted up north...to escape the law and any chance of being caught."

She looked up. Her eyes were watery. "Did you not go to the local authorities or try to make amends to the family? Were you not brought to trial?"

He shook his head. "*Nei*. I am truly outside the law. If I were caught, I would be banished, or worse. Nevertheless, I do not regret it. I would do it again if needed."

Astra studied the surface of the table for several moments. Finally, she looked up and said, "Saving a woman from ruin should not be a crime. In my eyes it is not."

Kjell bent to shove another log into the fire. "There is more."

Astra sat the Little King on the bed and gave him Kjell's carved horse to chew on. She turned back to the table, entwining her fingers tightly in front of her. "Tell me everything."

Kjell's confession spilled forth. "During the great sickness, I rode through the small hamlet near our cabin. The plague had struck hard there, and all were dead except one man. He was sick and begged me to come back and bury him after he died. I went on to our hut and found little Egill dead in my wife's arms. My Oda died soon after." He paused as his throat caught.

Astra said softly, "Oh, Kjell, how terrible..."

He cleared his throat, then continued. "I was out of my right mind and I burned our cabin down, keeping nothing to remind me of my family."

"Ah *nei*..."

He shook his head to stop her expression of sympathy. "On my way back through the village I stopped to fulfill my promise, but the man was still alive, barely. He pleaded with me to kill him and not leave him to the dogs. So, I did. I killed him like an animal."

Astra covered her face with both hands for several long moments. He heard her sniffling. When she finally looked up, she offered him her tear-dampened hands.

He nabbed them like a lifeline. They were warm and he longed to smother them with kisses.

She whispered, "You did rightly. Each was a mercy. I will never fault you for these acts of bravery."

"You may say that now, but you could be blamed for hiding a fugitive. You could be pilloried, or your land confiscated."

"You will never be caught," she said. "Who is looking for you now? So many have died. I say you are running from a phantom."

Kjell stared at their entwined hands. He had relied on his long beard and hood as a disguise, kept his distance from lawmen, avoided well-traveled roads, stayed on the fringes of every crowd. Even when he worked at Sjodrun his identity had never been questioned. "You speak truly," he said quietly.

She leaned toward him and caught his eyes. "Besides, what has the law to do with us? Think what God's vicar did to me."

Kjell squeezed her hands. "I must tell you one more thing. That night at Sjodrun, I heard a young woman scream. I thought to go to her aid but soldiers were everywhere and I was afraid of being recognized. The next day when I saw you so forlorn at the river, I did not know it was you who screamed, but it was, *nei*?"

She sighed. "You could have done nothing. You would have been killed if you tried. And look here." She lifted the sleeping child into the hanging crib, then turned to take Kjell's face in her hands. "God gave me the Little King and now He has given you to me; two people to love."

Kjell pulled her to him. They kissed and absolution seeped into Kjell's bones. When they drew apart, he whispered, "There is one thing I must do. Come with me." He took her hand and led her across the yard through the crackling autumn leaves to the stable where his bed of straw lay. He reached beneath the boards and found the two wooden figurines he had carved, the woman and the child. He held them out on his palm for her to see.

"Dolls? For the Little King?" she asked.

"They are likenesses of Oda and Egill. I have kept them near me during my travels."

As Astra turned them over in her hand, Kjell was suddenly afraid she might tell him to burn them. Instead, she said, "We will bring them to the house. They belong with us."

Her words warmed him, but he had something else in mind. He led her by the hand to the workshop, grabbed a small shovel, and together they strode to the sprawling oak and the family cemetery. He dug out a few shovelfuls of soil.

She grabbed his arm. "Do not bury them because of me."

Kjell lifted her hand off his arm. "*Nei*, I am ready to let their spirits rest." He placed the figures into the shallow hole, refilled it with dirt and tamped it down with his foot. She helped him gather small stones to place on top of the small mound in the shape of a cross.

Astra leaned against his shoulder. "Now they are at peace."

"I never said the words…" His voice broke.

She slipped her arm around his waist. "Our Father who art in heaven…"

It had been a very long time since Kjell had said these words, but when she started, the prayer flowed out of him. "Blessed be thy name…"

Chapter 34

Astra rose early on this crisp spring day, slipping out of bed quietly so that she did not wake Kjell or the Little King. She could see by the clear blue sky showing through the vent hole that the day would be fine. After stoking the coals with neatly split kindling, she snuck out the door for her morning need. On her way back she was greeted with whinnies from the paddock, and strode over to nuzzle Kvikke's soft nose.

"Good morning," she said to her horse. "A fine day this is." She drew three buckets of water from the well and dumped them into the trough before returning to the house. Gently pushing open the door, she heard Gunnar's tender voice saying, "Far. Nose."

"Ouch," Kjell teased. "No pinch." He was still abed with the Little King sitting on his chest and pulling on his nose. They both turned at the sound of the creaking door.

"There you are," Kjell said. "The Little King was just telling me you should have breakfast ready for us by now."

"He did, did he?" Astra came and sat on the bedside. The child reached out to her, saying, "Mama. Up." She picked him up, then poked her finger into Kjell's chest. "His breakfast is free, but if you want to eat, you must earn it."

Kjell grabbed her by the waist and pulled her onto the bed, tickling her sides until she screamed for mercy. Lying next to Kjell, with the Little King crawling over both of them, she settled her head on Kjell's shoulder. He kissed her mouth, then her forehead.

"Sometimes I still cannot believe I am here with you," he said.

She stroked his smooth chin. "I too. It is like a dream. I fear I will wake up and you will be gone."

"I am not going anywhere…unless I get a better offer."

"Ach!" She sat up and punched his arm playfully. "You will never have a better offer than this—two for the price of one."

The child squirmed to get between them but Astra rolled over with him so her back was to Kjell.

"I see that I am not wanted." Kjell wrangled his way off the bed and stepped into his pantaloons.

"*Nei*, you are not. It is your turn to make the porridge while I lie in bed to be served." She tried to coddle her growing child, but he twisted away and slid off the bed. He walked unsteadily to Kjell and reached up. Kjell lifted the toddler into the special seat he had made for the boy.

"If I am not wanted, then I am leaving," he said. "Do not expect me home before dark."

She hid her smile. "Fine with me. Do not expect to find the door unlocked."

Kjell pulled on his shirt. "If you are going to be so cruel, I will not bring any bacon back, which I was going to do."

She laughed, "Well, then. I will let you in."

He pecked her cheek before heading to the *stabbur*.

Astra added water to the pot and handed the Little King a carved dog Kjell had made. She hummed. These last seven months had been a delicious blessing. The mild winter passed uneventfully, her child was healthy and delightful, and Kjell was by her side. She was still in awe of all that had happened. She said thanks to the Blessed Virgin, as she did every day.

These last many months, she and Kjell had heard no more from Einarr or anyone else. They had not gone to the manor at *Jul* nor Easter. Kjell suggested they go for the summer fair, since he had accumulated many fine pelts, but Astra was dubious. The only person she wanted to see there was Hedda. At times she still thought of Einarr, though her feelings had changed from infatuation to disdain. Did he now have a child with his unloved wife?

But most of her thoughts were about her new life with Kjell. She no longer blushed when she thought of their love-filled nights.

※

The evening last autumn after Kjell had buried the effigies of his wife and child, Astra and he had stood at the threshold of her house. She reached out for him and he kissed her cheek. She kissed him back, deeply and with passion. Kjell suddenly pushed back, breathing heavily.

"I must go," he said, trembling slightly. He turned and sprinted to the barn. Astra called to him to come back, but he did not stop.

In the morning, after breaking their fast, Kjell lingered at the table playing with his spoon. He took a deep breath and said to Astra, "I want you. Do you wish to wed?"

Joy swept through her. "In fact, I do."

He bent on one knee and reached for her hand. "Then I ask, will you have me for your husband?"

Tears sprang to her eyes. "I will, I will, of course I will! But how? There is no priest in Sjodrun and I do not want a village wedding. I do not want to see, well, anyone there."

Kjell sat down beside her. "We could travel to another village, search for a priest, if you like. But I cannot wait long."

Astra thought for a moment. "I say we marry ourselves the old way, just you and I."

Kjell ran her long braid through his hand. "This is a good answer. We do not need any of them. You are beautiful; did I ever tell you this?"

"Nei, I think not."

"Well, you are. Very beautiful. If we marry, will you lay with me tonight?"

Her heart jumped. "*Ja,* I will."

Just then the baby fussed and Astra picked him up.

Kjell stood up. "I will be back soon. There is something I must do." He grabbed his knife and the tin mirror from the shelf and left.

By the time the porridge was ready Kjell returned, clean-shaven. Astra stared at his startlingly shortened chin. The Little King cried at the sight of him.

Astra clucked at the child, then examined Kjell's unfamiliar face. His features were firmer than she had imagined. He had strong cheekbones, though a scar marred his chin. He was handsome in his own way.

"I thought you would like to see my face so you will know who it is you marry." He grinned sheepishly. "What do you think?"

She stroked his smooth face and smiled. "I love you no matter what, and as luck would have it, you are pleasant to look upon, Kjell the hunter."

He grinned. "Let us marry today, soon."

She laughed. "We will. But let us enjoy this day together first. This will be our Lord's Day."

He smiled and nodded. "Indeed, a day of rest."

They saddled the horses and rode together for a Lord's Day outing. Kjell held the Little King before him in the saddle. The air was fresh from last night's rain and the day was clear.

Leaves of gold, rust, and crimson crunched beneath the horses' feet. They rode past the harvested fields and the downed pine tree where her father had lain, then up the trail to the high plateau. At the top they could see that the distant mountains were already snow-laden.

"We can bring the sheep up next summer," Astra said. "They will be happy here."

"How can you tell if sheep are happy?" he laughed.

"They smile," she said. "I thought you knew."

Their ride took them further up to the cairn overlook above the fjord. There they stopped and gazed down at the deep ribbon of blue below. They dismounted. While Kjell held the baby,

Astra crawled on her belly to peer over the edge of the steep cliff, remembering when she had looked for her father on the rocks below. What if she had seen him? How could she ever have retrieved him? She closed her eyes and crawled backward to safety.

They made their way home slowly, visiting the farm of her neighbor, Orms. He had lost three children and asked about her family, saddened to hear of Astra's losses. Astra introduced Kjell as her husband, and the neighbor was pleased to see that she was married. If he wondered about the age of the child he did not ask.

After supper, Kjell followed Astra up to the *stabbur* loft with the Little King on his shoulders. She opened a trunk and took out Far's best shirt and cloak, the ones he had worn to Jultide celebrations and his own wedding. She made Kjell try them on.

"I feel like a townsman," he said, peering down at himself and frowning. They were tight, but she said he looked fine. He agreed to wear them this once. She sent him and the Little King back to the house.

From another trunk she carefully unfolded her mother's scarlet wedding dress and the crown of bronze that was laced with ribbons and dried flowers. Tucked in a cloth bag at the bottom of the trunk was a packet that she had never seen. Inside was a tarnished silver necklace adorned with glass beads and shiny stones. Far must have given it to Mar for the morning gift. It was plain compared to others Astra had seen. Had Mar been embarrassed to show it to her *datters*? Astra donned it proudly.

She brought these items down the ladder and changed into them there in the *stabbur* among the barrels of ale and stores of grain. She loosened her hair and spread it around her shoulders as best she could, then set the crown upon her head and marched across the yard to the house. The door stood ajar.

"Are you ready?" she called from outside.

"Am I not the one who should come to fetch you?" Kjell responded.

She slowly pushed the door open. "Too late."

When he saw her, Kjell's eyes widened. He set the baby on the bed. "You...you are stunning." He led her inside by the hand, then stood back, staring as if she were a heavenly angel come to life.

"We are supposed to announce our intention to marry," he said, "but there is no one to receive our pronouncement."

"Only the Little King." She smiled.

Hand in hand they approached the bed where the child sat staring at them with his thumb in his mouth. She elbowed Kjell.

"Good sir," he said, bowing.

Astra stifled her giggle.

Kjell continued. "I wish to marry your mother. Do you have any objections?"

The Little King smacked loudly on his thumb.

"I take that as a *nei*," said Kjell. Astra laughed out loud.

"Get the cross down," she said.

Kjell lifted it from its place over the bed and laid it on the floor. They knelt together to kiss it, then stood. Facing one another Astra said solemnly, "Of my own free will I wed thee, Kjell Sverreson. I will be faithful to you always and love you all my days."

Kjell's voice was husky with emotion. "Of my own free will I wed thee, Astra Svensdatter. I also promise to be faithful and love you as long as I live."

After the Little King was sleeping in his new cradle, and evening had gathered outside, Astra went into the extra room with a candle and removed her mother's wedding dress. She changed into her best night shift, nervously combing her hair. She had worried all day how it would be with Kjell, and knew she had become quieter as dusk grew. Would it hurt? The king had told her the first time is the worst. This time would be different, though...her body longed for Kjell. She took a deep breath. She was coming to the marriage bed willingly. She clasped her hands together before her to stem their tremor and reentered the room where Kjell awaited by the fire.

He watched her come, firelight reflecting in his widening eyes. Astra stopped beside the bed, breathing heavily. Kjell stood and approached her quietly, spreading her hair over her shoulders. He ran his hands down her arms to her hands, turning them over to kiss each palm. Gently, he lifted her shift over her head.

She slipped under the furs, shyly. Kjell undressed and joined her. Lying beside her, he touched her face, kissed her shoulders, her arms, her neck.

"Do not be afraid," he whispered. "I will not hurt you."

"I am not afraid." She pulled him close. "I want you."

Their love-making was slow and tender, softened by his smooth caresses and gentle words. Astra had never felt this way before, so desired, so loved. She let herself fall into him.

After, when they lay entwined in the dwindling firelight, Kjell whispered, "You were meant for me."

She buried her face in his shoulder and her tears traced down his arm.

"Are you upset?" he asked, dabbing at her cheeks.

"*Nei*, just happy."

That first night had been followed by many nights of pressing joy and winter days of shared work. Kjell was there to dig the heavy snow and help care for the animals. He was there to bind wounds and teach the Little King new skills. They had food and firewood aplenty, and on bitterly cold nights they played chess and told stories. She discovered that given enough ale, Kjell could tell a frightful story indeed. She made him promise never to tell these tales to the Little King.

And now spring had come again. Astra walked to the workshop to call Kjell to break his fast. New leaves tipped the tree limbs. Remaining patches of snow were littered with pine needles. Golden plovers, robins, and a ring ouzel had returned, bringing with them a chorus of cheer. A flock of swallows swooped over her head, the first she had seen.

Stopping at the pasture fence, she gazed out over the newly sprouting fields where they would plant their life's sustenance. She recalled standing beside her father at this same place as he surveyed his fields in early spring. He always breathed deeply, taking in the scents of awakening life. She spoke his words of gratitude. "It is a gift to work the fields God has given us. We must be grateful for the fruits of our labors." Finally, she understood what her father meant. He was right. She whispered, "It is a gift, Far. It is worth fighting for."

She noticed a new fancifully carved horsehead on the workshop door as she approached. She stopped suddenly, placing her hand on her belly. The slightest flutter tickled within her. There it was again. New life.

Author Bio

Ruth Tiger has been a life-long traveler and writer, publishing the book The Away Place in 2009 based on her work with individuals with severe disabilities. The idea for The Moon Turned to Blood came from a visit with a relative in Norway who told her two compelling family stories that had been passed down from medieval times. Years of research led her to create a fictionalized story of plague, death, loss, and finally, love. Ruth is a retired speech-language pathologist and school administrator. She lives and writes in Tacoma, Washington.

Printed in the USA
CPSIA information can be obtained
at www.ICGtesting.com
CBHW011950141124
17383CB00001B/1